A
HERITAGE
NOT
Forgotten

Drawing by Charles E. Whitman

A HERITAGE NOT *Forgotten*

The Stories of Four Courageous
Pioneers and Their Journeys to
Minnesota Territory

MARVIN B. EPPARD

Order this book online at www.trafford.com
or email orders@trafford.com

Most Trafford titles are also available at major online book retailers.

All Scripture quotations are taken from the King James Version of the Bible

Printed in the United States of America.

ISBN: 978-1-4669-9514-7 (sc)
ISBN: 978-1-4669-9516-1 (hc)
ISBN: 978-1-4669-9515-4 (e)

Library of Congress Control Number: 2013909811

Trafford rev. 06/14/2013

 www.trafford.com

North America & international
toll-free: 1 888 232 4444 (USA & Canada)
phone: 250 383 6864 ♦ fax: 812 355 4082

For

Janice, my wife of sixty-one years
our children, Janette, Ruth, Paul, and Bob
our grandchildren
our great-grandchildren

Contents

Preface

I T IS AMAZING WHAT CAN come out of a box full of old papers, photographs, and family memories. Just such a box was handed to me following my father's death on April 11, 1993. Like many old things, I stashed it away on a closet shelf. Gradually, I was drawn to the box and began to find records of exciting stories. A visit with my sisters, Carol and Marlys, in which we shared memories from our earliest years, spurred me on. Both of them shared items and memories from their collections. I broadened my search over dinner with Pauline Utzinger, an older distant relative, whom I knew to be a genealogy whiz. She fanned the flame that kept me going. Then I started to think someone ought to record these stories of courage and steadfast faith.

The years passed, and my dear wife, Janice, and I decided to sell our house and move to a less-demanding lifestyle. In the downsizing process, I opened the box once again. This time, I dug deeper than before. Accounts of the lives of my four great-grandparents on my father's side of the family caught my attention. Ancestery.com helped me find still more information. I began to journey back with these great-grandparents to their roots in Germany and Pennsylvania. I found that the commitment to vital evangelical faith runs deep in my roots. I cannot be certain that they were influenced by Pietism in Germany, but I do know they all became members of the Evangelical Association after they arrived in America and were charter members of the Evangelical Church in my hometown of Racine, Minnesota.

I truly believe that Adam and Matilda and Phillip and Lucinda, through their prayers, were a major influence in my life, though they all died before I was born. For half of my life, I had a fire burning within searching for something more. Midway through my years, I came to a heartwarming personal faith in Jesus Christ. I transitioned into a church fellowship that had its beginnings in Pietism in Europe. I can only wonder how much influence these courageous pioneers had in bringing me to this life of abiding in our Savior, Jesus Christ. In writing these stories, I have come to the deepest admiration for those who have gone before me. I desire that this will be a heritage not forgotten for the generations coming after me.

This is a historical novel based on information found in the box and many other places, recounting the life stories of these four pioneers, how they migrated, met, married, and multiplied. The dates are 95 percent accurate, though sources did vary a few years one way or another. The authentic names of family members, townspeople, and church leaders have been used to maintain historical accuracy. (Readers are invited to refer to the family tree and lists of travel groups, since names were repeated from generation to generation.) Fictitious characters have been added to help make the stories come alive. I ask forgiveness for things unavoidably omitted and request responses from readers regarding corrections or additions that could have been included.

The stories are woven with two strands. One is what we know about the lives of these four people who are my great-grandparents. Granted, I have painted these four people in glowing terms. They are my *great-grandparents*, and I want to remember the things that made them *great*. The other strand is the strong evangelical Christian faith of these people. Being of German background, my ancestors did not talk much about this part of their lives. From the information we have, there is no doubt that they were influenced by the pietistic evangelical movement in Pennsylvania, Ohio, and Wisconsin, finding a home in my hometown of Racine, Minnesota. It is "A Heritage Not Forgotten."

Phillip and Lucinda Eppard

Adam and Matilda Utzinger

Acknowledgments

FIRST AND FOREMOST IS MY gratitude to God for his grace and mercy toward me. He is the source of the persistence and endurance that kept me going to complete this work. Time and again, when the goal seemed unreachable, he gave me the determination to press on.

My wife, Janice, a woman of honor and deep faith, has been my encouragement throughout the sixty-one years of our marriage. She has believed in me when I lost confidence in myself. She is a gem well polished by the years of growing faithfulness to God. Without her support, this book would not be.

I am greatly indebted to our daughter, Ruth Anderson. As my editor, she made her way through each chapter three times, giving invaluable suggestions and numerous corrections. All of this while carrying on her demanding career and family responsibilities. Thank you also to her husband, David, for the support he gave her during this endeavor.

My two sisters, Carol Joyner and Marlys Glover, most likely are unaware of how many times I asked them questions to get choice bits of information about our early years. I appreciate the ways they supported this effort.

Charles and Geraldine Whitman, friends with whom we have journeyed for thirty years, read early portions of the manuscript and shared encouragement. I offer special appreciation to Charles Whitman for the frontispiece drawing of a pioneer homesite. Also, with gratitude, I give credit to Darwin Nelson, a friend of our family, for the very professional photo of Janice and me on the cover.

My dear friends Mike and Char Hayes read the manuscript and gave suggestions, corrections, and encouragement. Mike helped put the history of Pietism in proper perspective. Early on, Tim Droogsma read some of the first chapters and offered encouragement as well.

When I needed someone to put my early vision of the cover design into sketch form, Lori Johnson was there with her artistic eye. Thank you, Lori, for the pencil drawings that were used to convey our vision to the Trafford staff.

I am greatly indebted to all of the people on the Trafford Publishing staff for their professional service as we moved through the steps from copyediting to final printing, bringing the book to completion.

The McQuillan Group

THE McQUILLAN GROUP OF FIFTEEN people left Delta, Ohio, in the spring of 1852 and traveled in covered wagons to what would become Mower County, Minnesota. *Lucinda McQuillan* was nine years old.

1. Jacob McQuillan Sr. (His first wife, Elizabeth Cripliver, died in Ohio.)
2. Maria "Polly" McQuillan, Jacob's wife (Her first husband, Harvey Allen, died in Ohio.)

3. Jacob McQuillan Jr., son of Jacob Sr. and his first wife
4. Mary Magdalena McQuillan (Mary M.), Jacob Jr.'s wife
5. Hester, their toddler son

6. Adam Zedeker, Jacob Sr.'s son-in-law
7. Catharine McQuillan Zedeker, Adam's wife and daughter of Jacob Sr. and his first wife
8. John Zedeker, Adam and Catharine's twelve-year-old son
9. Israel Zedeker, Adam and Catharine's eleven-year-old son

Jacob Sr. and Polly's children:

10. *Lucinda Ann McQuillan,* nine-year-old daughter
11. George McQuillan, eight-year-old son
12. Melissa McQuillan, seven-year-old daughter
13. Ezra McQuillan, six-year-old son

14. Harvey McQuillan, four-year-old son
15. Matilda McQuillan, two-year-old daughter

Franklin and Walter were born later in Minnesota.

Joe and Sid are two fictitious characters who traveled with the group as hired drovers.

The Wisconsin Group

FIVE FAMILIES, INCLUDING *ADAM AND Matilda Utzinger*, left Brandon, Wisconsin, in early June of 1862 and traveled by covered wagons to Mower County, Minnesota.

1. *Adam and Matilda Utzinger*
   Albert Utzinger, nine-month-old son

2. Peter and Carolina Utzinger
   Jane Utzinger, three-year-old daughter
   Silas Utzinger, two-month-old son

3. Jacob and Louisa Burkhart
   Louisa Burkhart, three-year-old daughter
   Charles Burkhart, one-year-old son
   Caroline Burkhart, infant daughter

4. Michael and Mary Gahringer
   Eliza Gahringer, eight-year-old daughter
   Mary Gahringer, five-year-old daughter
   Edward Gahringer, three-year-old son
   Emily Gahringer, infant daughter

5. Fredrick and Pauline Schroeder
   Fredrick Schroeder, seven-year-old son
   Henry Schroeder, five-year-old son
   Albert Schroeder, two-year-old son
   Pauline Schroeder, infant daughter

The Eppard/Felch Group

PHILLIP EPPARD TRAVELED TO MOWER County, Minnesota, by covered wagon with the Felch family, leaving Racine, Wisconsin, in the spring of 1856.

1. Judge Charles J. Felch
2. Hannah Felch, his wife
3. David Felch, their thirteen-year-old son
4. *Phillip Eppard*

A fictitious wagon boss, Johnny, is included to enhance the story.

Phillip, Lucinda, Adam, and Matilda are the author's great-grandparents and the primary characters in the story

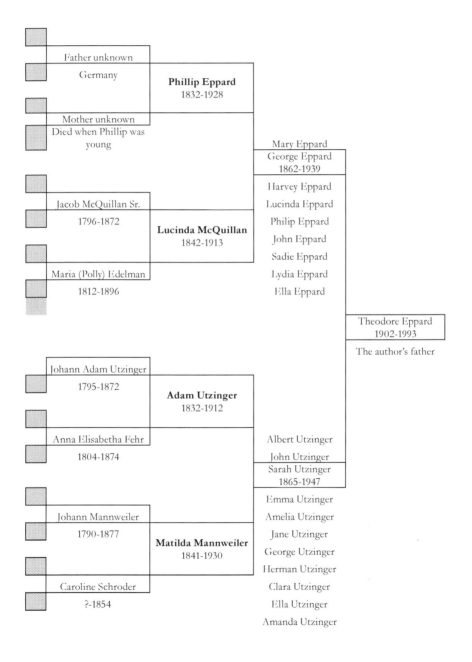

Father unknown
Germany

Phillip Eppard
1832-1928

Mother unknown
Died when Phillip was
young

Jacob McQuillan Sr.
1796-1872

Lucinda McQuillan
1842-1913

Maria (Polly) Edelman
1812-1896

Mary Eppard
George Eppard
1862-1939
Harvey Eppard
Lucinda Eppard
Philip Eppard
John Eppard
Sadie Eppard
Lydia Eppard
Ella Eppard

Theodore Eppard
1902-1993

The author's father

Johann Adam Utzinger
1795-1872

Adam Utzinger
1832-1912

Anna Elisabetha Fehr
1804-1874

Johann Mannweiler
1790-1877

Matilda Mannweiler
1841-1930

Caroline Schroder
?-1854

Albert Utzinger
John Utzinger
Sarah Utzinger
1865-1947
Emma Utzinger
Amelia Utzinger
Jane Utzinger
George Utzinger
Herman Utzinger
Clara Utzinger
Ella Utzinger
Amanda Utzinger

1

Adam Utzinger
Germany
1832-1852

WITH GOOD NEWS IN HIS heart, Adam Utzinger's feet quickly covered the familiar route between school and home. Determined to get an education, he had walked the six-mile round trip to the public school every school day for six years. The smell of his mother's fresh-baked bread drew him into the kitchen. He knew a thick slice with chokecherry jam would be waiting for him. Downing the last crust, he announced, "The Volksschule headmaster informed me today that I'm ready to graduate. I'll graduate second in my class."

"Ja, my son!" Anne exclaimed. "I know you are a good student, but second in your class, how wonderful! We'll have to celebrate. All the family will come." Anne hesitated as a tear formed in her eye. She lamented, "Jacob will not be here. He would be so proud of his brother."

Jacob, the oldest son in the family, had been drafted into the German army and assigned to the cavalry division. His letters told of dreadful living conditions and mean treatment. His mother, living in constant fear for her oldest, vowed, *No more of my sons will ever serve in the German military.*

Adam, born December 12, 1832, was third of the five Utzinger brothers. Jacob and Peter were older than Adam. Valentine and Ludwig were younger, and they had five sisters.

1

The Scharrhof was a cluster of four farms near Regierungsbezirk, Rheinpfalz, Germany. The land was parceled out in small pieces to various members of the four families. The Utzinger's eighty acres was the home of Johann Adam Utzinger and his wife, Anne Elisabetha Fehr. Johann and Anne's children grew up roaming the hilly slopes of the Scharrhof. It was a good life, but Johann often pondered, *How will this small farm provide enough land for my sons to raise their families?*

Keenly aware of Jacob's absence, the Utzinger family gathered on Saturday evening to celebrate Adam's graduation. His mother and sisters had worked diligently to prepare a festive meal. After supper, Johann stood at the head of the table to deliver the speech he had rehearsed all day. "Adam, my son, your accomplishments in school have made me proud. You have graduated in only six years, second in your class." Johann paused and caught his breath. "Today, we honor you in this family. You have become a man. I have a gift for you that you can use all your life. May this gift always remind you that you have a heritage not forgotten." His hand shook as he handed Adam a small black box.

A tear slipped down his father's cheek as Adam received the box. Lifting the cover slowly, his heart raced as he drew out a gold watch on a gold fob.

Twelve-year-old Adam suddenly realized he was expected to take the responsibility of a man in the family. He took a deep breath and spoke. "Thank you, Vater, I will try to honor you as I accept this gift."

With this, Anne stood up and threw her arms around her son. "Oh, Adam, you make me proud!" Others in the family congratulated Adam with handshakes and hugs.

The coming months found Adam working long days alongside his father planting potatoes, wheat, oats, rye, and barley. Summer days were spent trimming fruit trees and harvesting apples, grapes, and walnuts. He loved the farm, but he also longed for more education. One hot summer day, Adam and his father were harvesting wheat. They cut the ripened grain with a hand sickle, tied it in bundles, and set up shocks to dry in the summer sun. Adam could taste the salty sweat as it ran down his face. His throat was parched when his mother arrived with a basket in hand.

Anne spread a cloth on the grass under the canopy of an old oak tree. A small whirlwind caught the corner of the cloth as it picked up dust and leaves and spun out across the field. Refreshing homemade ginger ale and fresh bread with jam went down easily. Anne sat with her back against the tree as the men rested. Adam took advantage of the setting to raise a question that had been on his mind for days. "Vater," he ventured, "I want to honor you by doing my part on the Scharrhof, but there is so much I want to learn. I'm reading everything I can find, but still, I want more. I've been wondering if you would allow me to enroll in the pastor's class at our church."

Johann was stunned by the request. "Why, son, this is a sudden surprise to me. We have worked together, and I have depended on you to increase our crops . . ." His voice drifted off.

Anne's heart raced in her breast at her son's request. She had often wondered if one of her sons might become a pastor. Knowing it was not the time to speak her mind, she resolved to discuss Adam's request with her husband in private.

Summer heat gave way to the cool breezes of fall. The leaves of the hardwoods painted their brilliant autumn colors. Gathering wood and food for winter filled Adam's days as he waited patiently for his father's decision. He knew the pastor's classes would soon begin.

It was an October Sunday. Adam had helped his father feed and water the team after returning from worship. He felt the strong arm of his father on his shoulder as they walked toward the house. "Son," his father said, "I talked to Pastor today. His classes start this Wednesday. He has a place for you. Your mutti and I want you to attend, but I will still need your help on the Scharrhof."

Adam caught his breath and looked up into his father's deep blue eyes. "Thank you, Vati! I will work hard. I will make you proud." The two men entered the kitchen smiling, and Anne knew the decision had been made.

The following year, having mastered everything his pastor had to offer, Adam was confirmed in the Lutheran church. During this time, he began to question the effectiveness of the church in Germany.

Intellectualism overshadowed the true biblical teachings of the apostles. Adam had read about something called Pietism, and his spirit longed for the things of God.

Anne kept her vow that no more of her sons would become soldiers. Peter was five years older than Adam. When Peter's time to be drafted arrived, Johann and Anne supplied him with some clothes, a bedroll, and enough money to get to America, and they sent him quietly out of the country.

With Jacob in the cavalry and Peter in America, Adam was the eldest son left at home. He grew to be a strong, well-proportioned young man. With the draft closing in, Johann and Anne drew Adam aside one evening after supper a few weeks before his nineteenth birthday. His mother spoke with determination. "Adam, I don't want you to get drafted into the army. Jacob has suffered ill-treatment for years, and it breaks my heart. You have a good mind and you fear God. You are not going to waste your life as a German soldier."

Adam remembered the sadness in his heart when his brother Peter left for America. Occasional letters from Peter would tell of his work in the lumber camps in New York. He told of long days in the woods in the cold of winter. In one letter, he lamented, "It's lonely here. There's drinking and fighting all the time. I never get a chance to go to church. Last week, an evangelist came and held revival meetings. Some men were saved, and I'm going to see if their lives change."

"Adam," Johann hesitated, "as much as we hate to see you go, we want you to go to America. You can find Peter and work with him. He says he isn't getting ahead, but you know how to work hard. Maybe the two of you can do better together. God will go with you."

Adam had known the day was coming, but it still seemed abrupt. A huge lump formed in his throat when he realized that once he left, he would never see his father and mother again. A tear slipped down his cheek as he looked into his mother's eyes. "Mutti"—he choked— "I'll go, but you must pray for me. I'm afraid I'll never see you again." His voice cracked, and he could say no more.

"Yes, my son, I pray for you every day. I'll never stop praying for you, no matter how far away you may be. We will wait longingly for your letters."

On a Sunday evening in February 1852, the Utzingers gathered at the family home. Anne prepared many of Adam's favorite foods for a special supper. It was festive and sad at the same time. Everyone knew Adam would leave the family permanently the next morning. His brothers and sisters were silently anticipating the loss. Finally, Johann spoke. "Let's have a prayer for Adam." He chose a familiar prayer.

> God of our fathers, you are a Holy God. You go before us and know our every need. Holy God, you have loved us with an everlasting love. We entrust our son, Adam, to you and ask you to go ahead of him to America.

Johann's voice began to crack, so he hurriedly said, "Through Christ our Lord. Amen!"

Adam didn't sleep much that night. He wondered where Peter was and what it would be like to work in a lumber camp. He thought of Aubrey, the neighbor girl with long brown hair that swirled around her shoulders. He liked the warm feeling he had when he was near her. Even though he was nineteen, his pillow was damp with tears the next morning.

At dawn, Adam packed a bag with several changes of clothing, a quilt, his Bible, and a few personal items. His mother handed him a cloth bag with enough food for the train ride across France. Her eyes filled as she hugged her son and said, "Auf Wiedersehen, my son, if not before, in heaven." Other family members spoke their *tschuss*.

Johann was waiting by the stable with the buggy. Deep in thought, little was spoken between father and son on the way to the train station. Adam was experiencing a certain measure of fear, and Johann was grieving the loss of another son.

At the train station, Johann tied the team at the hitching rail. Adam, possessions in hand, waited. They entered the station together.

A strange thought occurred to Johann: *I wonder what Abraham was thinking when he was taking Isaac to be sacrificed.* He shook his head to clear his mind. *That's a foolish thought.* Then he almost spoke out loud, *God will provide the lamb.* He resolved, *yes, God will provide!*

Father and son approached the wicket where Johann purchased a ticket to Le Havre, France. Across the station, they found the desk of the *Du Vale Maritime Shipping Company.* Beneath the nameplate it said, "Passengers and cargo to America." A reservation was made for Adam on the sailing ship the *Robert Harding* to leave Le Havre in four days. With the train and ship passage paid, Johann took out a leather pouch with strings attached. "Here, son," he said, "keep this tied around your waist and under your belt. This is all the money I could spare. You've read Peter's stories about pickpockets in New York, ja?" Adam nodded.

The train was scheduled to leave in about two hours. The men had little to talk about. Johann suggested lunch at the Gasthaus across the street. This passed some of the time. Finally, the announcement came. "Train now boarding on track 2 for Le Havre . . . Leee Havre, now boarding on track 2."

Father and son faced each other. Adam dropped his bag, stood a moment, and lunged into his father's arms. They hugged and patted one another on the back. They held each other for a few seconds. Adam spoke. "*Tschuss*, Vati, *tschuss!*" Adam reached for his bag.

Johann stammered, "G . . . God go with you, son." They walked in opposite directions without looking back.

A man of even temperament under most circumstances, Adam usually wore a smile on his face. But at this moment, though he knew he could trust God, all he could do was find a seat on the train and put his head down. His mind went blank. He hardly noticed the whistle blast and the jerk of the seat beneath him as his lonely journey to a faraway land began.

The night passed slowly as Adam dozed between stops in well-known cities and nameless towns. Next morning, the sun blazed brightly in the eastern sky. Aware of crossing the Rhine and entering into France, Adam slid across the seat to look out the soot-covered window. Memories of the hills on the Scharrhof clung to his mind. Adam shook his head and mused, *I have to do something about this loneliness.*

Pushing himself away from the window, Adam stood up. It took a moment to adjust to the sway of the moving train before he walked forward through the next car. He found a door marked Die Toilette, where he freshened for the day. Back at his seat, he lifted the cloth bag to his lap. Slices of buttered bread and sharp cheese reminded him of his mother. A lump formed just above his Adam's apple. He saw her in his mind's eye: short in stature, strong in will, beautiful with an impish smile, and firm in the discipline of her children. He was certain of her love for his father, but their affection was never demonstrated among family or in public circles. Adam could almost hear her prayers quoted from the prayer book morning and night. Her faith seemed stronger than that of the village church they frequented. Adam recalled his studies with his pastor. He wondered why the old cleric spoke more of the German theologians than the Bible, and the oft-experienced feeling of emptiness returned. He wondered, *What will fill this emptiness of my soul?*

Having successfully made the transfer in Paris onto the train to Le Havre, Adam settled in for the next leg of his journey. He decided to take inventory of the food his mother had sent with him. There, between the small bag of apples and a wrapped date cake, was a page from a writing tablet. Unfolding the fragile leaf, he found a note scrawled in his mother's shaky hand:

My dear Adam,

Nineteen years you are our son, and you always will be. Proud we are of the man you have become. We brought you this far, now you walk alone, 'cept you put your hand in the hand of God. He will keep you in ways that are not your own. Put your face to the wind and don't look back.

"The Lord watch between me and thee, when we are absent one from another."

Your Vater und Mutter

Adam folded the paper and carefully tucked it into his breast pocket. He swallowed deeply, sat up straighter, and savored his mother's date cake.

Following the conductor's directions, Adam stepped off the train into a foggy morning in the city of Le Havre. He looked for some direction, but every sign was in a language he couldn't read. He inquired from a uniformed man by the station door, "How do I get to *Du Vale Maritime Shipping Company*? I am on my way to New York."

The gentleman shrugged and pointed at a long line of people. The man behind the wicket was shuffling papers and sending people in various directions. Adam got in line.

A family of four—father and mother, a daughter about ten, and a younger boy—were just ahead of him. The boy was restless and ill-tempered. The daughter was bored. The parents were obviously out of sorts. Adam approached the boy and said, "Look . . . look what came out of your ear." Opening his hand, he held a silver coin. The boy responded with wonder. "Is that your coin?" Adam asked. The boy shrugged, and Adam put his hand to the boy's other ear, and the coin was gone. By now, a small crowd of children had gathered. Adam entertained them with his tricks.

"May I help you, young man?" came the stern voice of the man behind the counter. Adam handed over his passage papers with the *Du Vale Maritime Shipping Company*. The official scowled and called for a porter. After the two men talked in whispers, the porter said, "You are in the wrong place, follow me." The little crowd of admirers clapped and shouted, "Thank you!" as Adam was ushered out of the station.

Lucinda McQuillan
Delta, Ohio
1852

"**M**OM, I NEED YOUR HELP," Lucinda McQuillan cried. "I'll never get this spinning done before we leave. I still have to knit two more sweaters for Ezra and Harvey. Pa says we're leavin' as soon as spring thaw."

* * *

Lucinda's mother, Maria Christina Edelman, whom everyone called "Polly," had grown up in Pennsylvania where she married Harvey Allen. When their daughters Jane and Mary were toddlers, the family moved to Ohio. Not long after arriving, Harvey died, leaving Polly alone with two small children. She worked hard from dawn to dark to keep the land and care for her family. They attended worship and Bible study at the Evangelical Association with other families who had come from Pennsylvania. One summer day, Polly prepared a picnic lunch, hitched the team to the buggy, and set out to attend the Evangelical Association camp meeting. She found inspiration from the preaching of the Word of God. At lunchtime, she spread a blanket on the ground by her buggy for a picnic with Jane and Mary.

Suddenly, she heard a soft male voice. "Mrs. Allen, no need for you to eat alone. Would you like to bring your lunch and join Jake, Catharine, and me at our table by the river?"

Startled, she turned and looked into the face of a tall man with bright blue eyes and a well-trimmed beard. About six feet two, Jacob McQuillan Sr. had broad shoulders that tapered to a slim waist. In his forties, he was a man of confidence and determination. He held a gray Stetson hat in his left hand. His smile reflected kindness, and his outstretched hand was inviting. Polly looked down realizing her face had flushed.

"I'm sorry." His steady voice spoke. "I didn't mean to startle you. My name is Jacob McQuillan. My friends told me your name. I just thought you may like to join us for lunch."

Aware of his smile and the flutter in her stomach, she breathed, "Ya, sure, we could do that. Ah, ya, thank you Mr. McQ . . ."

"McQuillan is the name," he said as he reached to carry the lunch basket.

Polly took Mary's hand and glanced at Jane with eyes that said *follow along*. She wondered if her friends were watching her as she walked beside this gentleman.

That was the beginning of a short courtship. Polly grew to love this unpredictable man some fifteen years her senior. A man of faith and courage, Jacob demonstrated kindness toward others while maintaining high expectations of himself. He too had moved to Ohio to conscript land after his area of Pennsylvania had become too crowded. Polly identified with his pain at the death of his wife, as she well knew from her own loss. She felt safe in his strong arms and secure in his self-assured stature.

They married on November 25, 1839. John, Jacob's oldest son, at twenty-one started out on his own. Jacob Jr., now thirteen, and his sister Catharine, eleven, became big brother and sister to Polly's two girls, Jane and Mary.

In February of 1842, Polly realized she was with child. Jacob was excited by Polly's news, and they made plans for the new arrival. On

September 7, 1842, Polly sent Jacob Jr. to get the midwife and told Catharine to let her pa know the time had come. That day, Lucinda McQuillan joined the family.

*   *   *

Back in the McQuillan kitchen, nine-year-old Lucinda was calling for her mother's help. By now, she had five younger siblings, George, Melissa, Ezra, Harvey, and Matilda.

Hearing her daughter's distress, Polly realized she was expecting Lucinda to grow up far too fast. She quickly helped George get busy with his reading and encouraged the younger children to find a game before sitting down with Lucinda to card some wool.

"Mom," Lucinda asked, "are you afraid of what might happen on our trip to Minnesota Territory? It seems so far away. Pa says it'll take us two or three months. Where will we sleep? What about little Matilda, she seems so young to go so far. Pa said we'll need warm clothes for the cold winters. And, Mom, what about the Indians? I heard John and Jake talking about how the Indians sometimes raid wagon trains. I couldn't sleep last night wonderin' what's gonna happen to us."

Polly put her hand on her daughter's arm and said, "Lucy, we don't need to worry. Every day, Papa prays for our trip, asking God to go with us. Remember the story Papa read from the Bible about how God was with Moses when he led the people out of Egypt? We can trust God to be with us too."

"I want to believe that, but I still get scared."

"Lucinda, you have a wonderful father. He always has an adventure in his heart, and he desires to follow God. A hundred years ago, many people came to Pennsylvania from the Palatinate in Germany. People like your father's ancestors from Scotland and Ireland also came to find land and a new life in America. Many of them were godly men and women who knew and loved Jesus as their Savior. Some of them had been influenced by Pietism, a movement resulting from the leadership of Philipp Jakob Spener in Germany. About the time your father was born in 1796 in Pennsylvania, Jacob Albright, a traveling preacher, started going from town to town preaching about Jesus. Neighbors would come together to hear his teaching and worship together. Jacob Albright stayed at your grandpa McQuillan's home when he held meetings in their town. Is it any wonder that your father's name is Jacob?

"Out of the teaching and leadership of Jacob Albright, a group called the Evangelical Association was started. Camp meetings were held near a river or at a farmer's place, and people would come from miles around to hear Jacob preach. Classes were held in the villages and settlements across southern Pennsylvania. Your father grew up learning about Jesus.

"When the land was all taken up in Pennsylvania, many people moved on west. My first husband, Harvey Allen, and I left Allentown, Pennsylvania, when Jane and Mary were only four and two years old. God was with us all the way. The little ones will be just fine on our journey. We can trust God and we can trust your pa."

The afternoon had passed quickly as the mother and daughter talked. Polly had carded most of the wool, and Lucinda had done well on the spinning wheel. Lucinda reached an arm around her mother's neck. "Thank you, Momma, I feel much better, and I have enough yarn to start knitting sweaters for Ezra and George."

Polly, with a tear running down her cheek, put her arms around her daughter and said, "Lucinda, I love you. You are such a momma's helper. Mary and Jane were my helpers for a long time, but now they're grown up. Oh, look! It's five o'clock. We better get started with supper. Pa will be in soon. He's been workin' on those wagons all day."

Lucy peeled potatoes, and Polly fried some venison steaks. Matilda tottered across the room rubbing a fist in her eye. She whined, "Hungry, Mommy." Polly swung her youngest up to her hip and kept working.

Lucinda's half brother, Jacob McQuillan Jr., stuck his head in the door and said, "Pa's still workin' on the wagons. I'll do the milkin'.

Pa said he'd be in for supper about six. Mary M and I'll have supper at our cabin." He grabbed the milk bucket and closed the door. Polly turned to Lucinda and smiled. "We'll be ready."

Lucy set the table. Places for the six children lined both sides. Pa sat at the end by the door, and Ma sat by the stove.

At 6:15, Jacob swung the door open, allowing a blast of late winter air to fill the room. He stomped the snow off his feet, hung his coat on a hook, and washed at the washstand.

When Jacob sat down at the table, the children climbed over the benches and sat ready for the meal. This action was a demonstration of the firm but loving discipline of the head of the family. Eight heads bowed as he prayed:

> Bless, O God these gifts you have given. We are thankful to you for plenty. May they strengthen us for today and prepare us for our journey. God, we thank you for good health. By your blessings, we look to the day we will arrive at our new home in Minnesota. Amen.

After plates were filled, Polly spoke. "Papa, Lucy and I had a talk today. She's wondering where we'll sleep at night on our trip to Minnesota."

Jacob put his hand on Lucinda's arm and said, "That's what I've been workin' on all day. Adam, Catharine, and their boys will sleep in their wagon. Jake, Mary M, and Hester will have their wagon. We'll all sleep in my old Schooner that we used when we came here from Pennsylvania. We'll build bunks for all six of you, and Mom and I will be there too. We'll put new canvas on all three wagons. Today, we were steaming and bending the hoops for the wagons to hold the canvas. Jake, Adam, and I will take turns on watch every night."

"Why do you have to be on watch, Papa? Will the Indians come to raid our wagons?" Lucinda questioned.

"We gonna see Indians," Matilda mimicked.

13

"No," Jacob assured, "we'll be on the territorial tails. Now that these parts are states, it has become safe to travel and camp along the way."

George asked, "Can I stay up on watch with you? I'm big now."

"Maybe some nights you older ones can stay awake for a while." Jacob knew they took that to be a promise.

The smell of spring was in the air. Excitement was building in the McQuillan family. Every morning, Harvey and Matilda would ask, "Is today the day, Mommy?" The children would each have a small drawer under their bunk in the wagon to store their things. Every day, they would decide what to take only to change their minds the next day.

One evening, while washing the supper dishes, Lucinda heard her father talking with his son Jake and son-in-law Adam Zedeker, making plans for their trip to Minnesota.

"The wagons are all ready," Adam assured. "My blacksmith tools are in the box on the side of my wagon. We have some spare parts, and we can get other things that we need at towns along the way."

Jacob added, "I've hired two drovers to help with the stock. You know Joe, the big guy who helped with the cows last fall? And I met Sid in town last week lookin' for work. He seemed like a good guy, kind of quiet. They both have horses and will bring their own bedrolls."

Jacob continued, "We'll need a couple spare horses, and an ox or two in case one goes down. We're takin' the milk cows and the calf. We'll have our riding horses and the ponies for the boys. One of us will scout ahead on a saddle horse every day."

"Tomorrow, we'll load the freight wagons," Jake said. "I've got the water kegs soakin' so they'll swell tight to hold water."

"Ma has the straw mattresses ready." Adam chuckled. "John and Israel can hardly wait to get goin'. They want to sleep in the wagon tonight." The three men agreed they would start out the following Thursday.

Jacob put a hand on each of the younger men's shoulders. "I'm so glad the two of you have decided to travel to Minnesota. Ever since they put in that plank road from here to Toledo, I've been anxious to move on west. It's gettin' too crowded around here for me."

After Jake and Adam left, Jacob sat down in his favorite chair. The house was quiet. Polly came and stood behind him with her hands on his shoulders. "Got a lot on your mind getting ready for our trip?"

"I sure do, Polly. I was just thinkin' about the family and friends we're leavin' behind here in Fulton County. I wish things were better between John and me." Jacob paused, thinking of his oldest son. "Polly, I'm thankful the Lord brought us together." He reached for her hand and brought her to sit on his lap. He said, "I love you, Pol, I love you a lot. We'll miss our church here, but God will be with us, and we'll start over with new friends in Minnesota."

Jacob's three brothers—David, George, and James—had come with him to Ohio in the early 1830s. James built the first cabin in Delta, Ohio, in 1834. Both George and David had farms nearby. When Jacob heard that the Treaty of Mendota had been signed with the Indians in Minnesota Territory, he was ready to make another move.

Jacob and Polly were up before dawn on Thursday. Hearing the activity, Lucinda got dressed and took her things to the wagon. "Lucy, please make a pot of oatmeal so the children have a good breakfast," Polly requested. Soon George and Melissa came to lend a hand. Ezra and Harvey were arguing about who would ride the pony first. Matilda had her doll in her arms and her thumb in her mouth.

Jacob hurried through the door and urged the family to the table. With heads bowed, he prayed for his family, safe travel, and a good place to camp that night. Polly reminded the children to be prepared for a long, hard day. Jacob stood up, saying, "I want you children to be good travelers. Remember, we'll be livin' in the wagons until winter sets in. Let's get started."

George and Melissa carried the last boxes to the wagon. With a lump in her throat, Polly closed the door for the last time. She put her arm around Lucy as they walked toward the wagon train.

Adam Zedeker, with Catharine at his side, was ready to take the lead with his big team of mules. Though Adam was twenty years older than Catharine, he was a good husband and father to their two sons, John and Israel. At ages twelve and eleven, the boys were experienced enough to hitch and drive the teams and to ride their ponies tending the stock.

The drovers Joe and Sid had the oxen yoked and the other stock ready to go. Jake and Mary Magdalena were on the seat of their wagon with Jake's team of bays. Their son, Hester, just under a year old, was jumping up and down on his mother's lap anxious for the horses to get going.

Jacob and his family climbed into the Schooner. His four-horse team of blacks stood ready, each one weighing more than 1,600 pounds, with muscular backs and powerful hindquarters. Over the years, Jacob had bred his mares to produce colts of increased weight and strength for the hard work on his farm. The four blacks were Jacob's favorite draft horses.

Relatives and neighbors gathered near the barn for last hugs and good-byes. A tear rolled down Lucinda's cheek as she waved farewell to her two best friends.

Jacob, Stetson in hand, made a circular motion to signal the start. The drivers urged the draft animals forward. Joe and Sid shouted, "Get up!" as they cracked their whips above the ox teams. Wagons creaked under heavy loads. Barny, the family collie, herded the stock alongside the wagons. Everyone waved good-bye, and the crowd began to sing, "God be with you till we meet again . . ."

At nearly ten years old, on April 15, 1852, Lucinda left everything familiar to start down the road that would end at a new home for her family in Minnesota. Soon after departure, her father handed her the reins of the four-horse team of blacks and jumped down from the wagon. Lucinda admired her father as she watched him ride off on Jenny, his rangy sorrel mare with golden mane and tail. She thought, *I feel safe with Papa riding shotgun, watching over our family.*

Ohio had been a state since 1803. The territorial trails were in good condition making for good traveling as they moved toward the Indiana border. The rocking of the wagon and the morning sun caused Lucinda to feel drowsy as she kept the team in pace with the others. She was glad when her father came by and said, "We found a nice pond near the trail ahead. We'll stop there to water the animals and have lunch."

Back on the trail, the oxen set the pace. They were slower and stronger than the horses. The slow pace made it possible to jump on and off the wagons without the need to stop. Even Matilda learned to get off the wagon to run awhile and climb back on when she got tired.

As Jacob had planned, they camped at the Tiffin River that night. After crossing the river, they put the wagons in a half circle for protection from the wind. Once the harnesses were off, the horses rolled in the dust to rub and scratch their backs.

John and Israel went exploring and came back with a hat full of something that looked like beans. Israel said with excitement, "Look, Grandma, we found these down by the river."

Polly took a handful and thought for a moment. "Ah, that's why some people call this Bean Creek. I've heard tell that beans grow naturally along the banks. I'll boil these up for supper."

George gathered wood and started a fire. Polly took a ham from the box on the side of the Schooner and used the wagon tailgate for a worktable. Soon the hungry family gathered around the fire with their tinplates and cups. Jacob motioned to Joe and Sid to join them as he bowed his head to give thanks to God their provider. He prayed for the family members they left behind in Delta and asked God to lead them to a good place in Minnesota Territory.

While Jacob was eating his supper, he noticed Sid's eyes scan Mary M's figure as she bent over to serve the boys. He vowed to keep an eye on this stranger.

Barny, with a growl, chased a big jackrabbit that outran him with ease. John and Israel looked at each other with a telling grin that said,

We'll get that big guy for supper tomorrow night. Later, Israel got a good shot, and rabbit was on the menu for the next day.

That evening, God blessed the McQuillans with a beautiful sunset as the sun slipped behind the clouds in the western sky. Catharine helped Polly get the children to bed. Lucinda went to the river to wash and prepare for the night. Sitting on a rock, she looked up to the heavens. Sadness came over her as she remembered her friends. Quickly, she promised herself she would look ahead, trusting God to guide her family. John and Israel startled her with a challenge, "We can beat you to your wagon." Lucy set out at top speed, leaving the boys behind. John and Israel decided to get even with her at another time.

Jacob took the first watch of the night. He made the rounds of the wagons on Jenny. He never carried a gun, but hanging from his saddle horn was a long blacksnake whip with a sharp leather tip. He could snuff out a candle with that whip without upsetting the candle stand.

The livestock were settled for the night. Jacob noted that Sid was in his bedroll under the freight wagon. A low whinny from one of the horses signaled that all was well. In the Schooner, he found the children in bed, but not able to sleep after an exciting day. Polly was helping Matilda settle for the night. Jacob put his arm around his wife's shoulders and thanked her for her support through the first day. Matilda quieted, and the other children pulled the wool blankets up against the chill. The call of coyotes in the distance was nothing new to this family. All was quiet in the wagon. Some of the children had drifted off to sleep. Five-year-old Harvey said softly, "Ma, do you like coffee?" Jacob chuckled at his son's voice. Then it came again, "Papa, do you like coffee?"

"Ya, son," Jacob whispered, "I like coffee. You better get some sleep. We have a long day tomorrow." Quietness was interrupted by the deep breathing of sleeping children. Softly came, "Ma, do you like . . ."

Jacob bent down and whispered in Polly's ear, "Good night, and may God bless you with sleep." He slipped out through the canvas, mounted his horse, and spent the next three hours watching over his family. When all was quiet, he sat by the fire, giving thanks to a mighty God for his saving grace and praying that each member of his family would know Jesus as their Savior. Memories from his childhood swept through his head. He thought of his pa back in Pennsylvania and how Jacob Albright would come to their home. He remembered the camp meeting of the Evangelical Association when he asked Jesus to be his Lord.

Rusty the rooster stuck his head out between the slats of the chicken coop and announced the new morning with a mighty crow. Bacon and eggs along with thick slices of bread stood ready for breakfast. Jacob nodded at Jake. After a long silence, Jake gave thanks to God for the food.

Adam and Catharine climbed over the wagon wheel and settled on the seat. The big mules, Ben and Birdie, lowered their heads and started the train on the second day of the long journey.

The McQuillan family fell into a routine. Each day seemed much like the one before. Sunday was a day of rest. With the draft animals grazing nearby, the family gathered for worship. Jacob read from God's Word and shared how God had brought him from Pennsylvania to Ohio twenty years earlier. He assured, "God already has a home for us, and we'll know it when we see it."

"Indiana," Lucinda pondered as they crossed the border, "I remember that Indiana became a state in 1816." Slowly, the caravan moved on toward their destination.

Scouting ahead one day, Jacob checked out a river crossing. The steep, muddy slope on the far side worried him. The sky was threatening. Rain would add to the difficulty of the crossing. Jacob hurried back to the wagon train. "There's a river ahead and rain on the way. We need to get across before it rains."

Adam's mules pulled his wagon across the river without incident. The supply wagon was next, pulled by the four oxen. As they reached the far slope, one of the lead oxen slipped and went down on his knees. The other three oxen stopped, and the wagon settled in the mud. Adam got the fallen ox out of the yoke, and big Joe pulled the animal up on shore. Sid helped get a replacement ox in the yoke. When the team was ready to pull, Jacob came alongside with his blacksnake whip in hand, giving the command, "Get up!" The snap of the whip sounded above the backs of the oxen. Jacob sounded cruel, and the whip cracked sharply, but never was he mean to his livestock. The four oxen leaned into the yokes with all their might. Their feet slipped on the slope, and the wagon would not budge.

The big Schooner, with Polly and the children, was still on the other side of the river. Jacob wondered if his four big blacks could make it up the slope. They were running out of time.

Adam brought Ben and Birdie around, and Jacob helped hitch them ahead of the lead oxen. With the mules on dry ground, Jacob went to the left side of the four oxen, and Adam took the reins of the mule team. Adam urged the mules by slapping the reins to their backs, and Jacob commanded the oxen and cracked his whip an inch above them. All six animals put their weight to the load. Jake, Joe, Sid, and John each took hold of the spokes of a wagon wheel and turned with all their might. The wagon would not move. Joe moved to the rear of the wagon, turned his back to the tailgate, set his feet against a rock and gave a mighty push. Jacob cracked his whip. The wagon moved slowly and then forged ahead as Joe gave a second powerful push. Water drained off the bottom of the wagon as it moved up onto level ground.

Rain was rapidly approaching. Jacob climbed onto the Schooner seat and took the reins of his four blacks. He talked to the horses in a low voice. All four heads came up, knowing the challenge ahead. The blacks leaned into the collars and steadily moved forward. Jacob knew he had to keep the wagon moving or it would settle in the mud. When the lead team reached the far shore, Jacob yelled, "Jack! Jill! Get up there!" When the leaders were on solid ground, the wheel team was on the slope. Jacob knew Mit and Missy, being the strongest of the four, would bring the wagon up out of the water. He called, "Okay, Mit! Missy! Get Up! That's it, here we go."

Just as the wagon came out of the water and Jacob breathed a sigh of relief, Missy's two-month-old stallion colt came romping toward his mother. When he tried to stop, he slid under the front wheel of the Schooner. With a mournful cry, the colt rolled on the ground. The children watched as Adam and Jake picked up the suffering animal and carried him into a grove of willows. The children broke into tears, and Jacob winced when they heard the crack of Adam's revolver.

The rain began to fall, and the wind swept through the trees as they dug a grave for the colt that Jacob was counting on for breeding a new line of horses for his farm in Minnesota Territory.

*　　*　　*

Jacob McQuillan Jr., or Jake as the family called him, resembled his father in stature and character. He and his wife, Mary Magdalena, or "Mary M" for short, were married three years before they left Ohio. Their son Hester was nine months old. Jake had carefully saved his money so he would be able to take a homestead when they arrived in Minnesota. Mary M was a strong, attractive woman. Though somewhat stout, she possessed a beautiful smile. Her naturally curly red hair framed her face under her denim bonnet. Lucinda loved to ride with her sister-in-law for some "woman talk" as they made their way across Indiana. She felt especially proud when she was allowed to drive her half brother's spirited bays, Daisy and Dolly, while Mary M took care of Hester.

One sunny morning, with Lucinda at the reins, Mary M was telling Lucinda a story about her days back in Pennsylvania. Suddenly, the wagon jerked to one side, nearly tipped over to the left, and then settled back to the right. The startled horses lunged forward as the right front wheel collapsed and the axel dug into the ground. Lucinda struggled to stop the team. Jake rode up on his saddle horse to see if Mary M, Hester, and Lucinda were safe. Dismounting, he found the right front wheel broken away from the hub. The iron tire was badly bent. Nearly all of the spokes were broken. The wheel had hit a huge rock on a curve in the trail and wedged behind it, causing the damage.

Repairing the damaged wheel proved impossible. Even with Joe's strength, they could not raise the wagon enough to put on a spare wheel.

Jacob arrived with good news. "The town of South Bend is about a mile up the trail. There's a good place to camp by the St. Joseph River," he said.

With a heavy heart, Jake left his damaged wagon behind and moved on to South Bend with the rest of the family.

3

Phillip Eppard
Germany
1852

Phillip Eppard quietly let himself into the house, hung his coat on a hook in the hall, and turned to go down the steps to his quarters. Squeezed between the fruit cellar and the coal bin, a cot, a small chest, and some hooks on the wall were all he had to call his own. He chose this arrangement when his father remarried after his mother's death, and one after another, six half sisters had been born, crowding Phillip out. His father worked hard to support his new family, but Phillip, born on October 26, 1832, now nearly twenty years old, had to fend for himself. The country was unsettled and jobs hard to come by. Seeing no future for a young man in Hessen Darmstadt, Wallersheim, Germany, Phillip was becoming shiftless.

As Phillip turned the latch on the cellar door, he heard his father's voice from the parlor. "Son, is it rainin' out tonight?"

Phillip was not in the mood for small talk with his father. "Ja, Vati, it's rainin' a little." He started down the steps.

"Phillip, did you have a good evening?"

Still not wanting to linger, Phillip answered, "Ja, I was down at the Gasthaus." He was hoping to let it pass at that, but he heard a chair creak and footsteps coming from the parlor.

"Coffee's hot in the kitchen, let's have a cup."

Knowing he could not refuse, Phillip stepped toward the kitchen. "Ja, Vati that would be good."

The kitchen was a medium-sized room with an iron cookstove on one wall, a pump and sink in the corner, and a cabinet with work space to one side. The table with benches and two chairs was in the middle of the room. His father slid the coffeepot to the hot part of the stove and pulled out one of the chairs. Phillip took the other chair and sat with his elbows on the table feeling like a little boy waiting for his dinner.

An awkward moment followed. His father ventured, "How are you doing, son? Have you found work?"

"Naw, nothin' available here in Wallersheim," Phillip decided to go on. "Vati, the men down at the Gasthaus are talkin' about unrest in our country and the possibility of men my age getting called into the army. I don't know what to think."

"I wish we had work for you at our shop." His father poured two cups of coffee. "My superior says they may be terminating some of the regulars. I'm concerned about Irmgard and the girls." Phillip felt the familiar twinge of jealousy toward his father's new family. It had been thirteen years since his mother died, but he still missed her terribly.

"Ja, I know you have mouths to feed. I need to get out on my own and not add to your burden." He took a sip of coffee and continued, "I talked to a man at the Gasthaus tonight. He said he could get me on a boat to Amsterdam and a job on the docks loading steamers bound for America."

Their eyes met. His father swallowed deeply to hold back the lump in his throat. "Oh, son, I hate to see you leave Germany." He stopped, obviously trying to control his emotions. He held his cup to his lips but didn't drink.

"I've got to do somethin'," Phillip mumbled. "What choice do I have in these hard times?"

His father regained his composure. "I guess you have to find your way, son. Amsterdam Shipping is a rough place. Some have gone there and never returned."

"Alban said he could get me passage on a steamer to America. He has connections with the lumber mills in New York. He said the pay is good and I could earn enough to move west and have land of my own. In less than a year on the docks, I could save enough for the fare to America. Lots of men my age are doin' it."

"Who's Alban? Where's he employed?"

"I don't know. He just came up the Rhine today. He offered me free passage to Amsterdam on Saturday. Alban said I could be a landowner in as little as five years. Sounds better than anything I can do here in Hessen."

The older man's shoulders slumped at Phillip's words. He took another sip of coffee and slowly lowered the cup to the table. "I wonder who this Alban is. Men at work talk about 'Neulanders' who get paid by steamship companies to get fares on their ships. Son, are you sure you can trust him?"

"I don't know, Vati, but I can't live down in that cellar forever. Alban said in five years I could own land, have a wife, and start a family with income to spare."

"It sounds like your mind's made up, son." He pushed the coffeepot back on the stove and moved toward the door.

Phillip knew the conversation was over. "Vati, you said I needed to find my own way. I guess I'll be headin' down to Amsterdam come Saturday. I'd like your blessing, Vati." Tears welled up in his eyes, but he was able to hold them back. "Vati," he croaked, "your blessing . . ."

"Yuppp, son," his father said as he went down the hall toward his bedroom.

Thoughts of his mother filled Phillip's mind as he lay sleepless on his cot. He remembered her prayers for him at bedtime and the smell of fresh-baked bread in the kitchen. He tried to hold back his resentment of Irmgard and the little girls. He longed for his father's approval. Fear overwhelmed him. He could hear his mother saying, "Phillip, you're a good boy, you have a good mind, you can do anything you decide to do. Remember, son, God will always be with you." He recalled how his father would read from the Bible and pray after supper. Now since Irmgard came, he never heard those prayers.

Phillip was awakened by voices from the kitchen. The little girls were fussing at one another. He decided to endure the commotion to satisfy his hunger.

"Good morning, Phillip," Irmgard said without looking up from the pancakes she was turning. "Got some cakes for you, grab a plate."

Phillip grunted, "Gutten morgen," and held out his plate.

She filled his plate without lifting her eyes. "Syrup's on the table," she said. Two of the little girls snickered as he took his place.

I don't have to endure this much longer, Phillip thought. *Saturday, I'll be bound for Amsterdam and places beyond.* He straightened his shoulders and resolved, *My mind's made up!*

His father shuffled into the room dressed for work. Irmgard poured him a cup of coffee. He ate his breakfast the same as he had every day as long as Phillip could remember. The little girls were quiet.

Phillip cleared his throat, hoping his father would look his way. Silence screamed in Phillip's mind. *Please give me your blessing, Vati.* No acknowledgment came. Phillip took his plate to the sink in the corner of the room. He turned to leave, longing for a word from his father. From the doorway, he heard his father's stern voice. *"Tschuss,* son."

Phillip knew his stay in his father's house was over. With a heavy heart, he carefully gathered three changes of clothes, his boots, a heavy quilt, the knife his father gave him when he was fifteen years old, and his mother's Bible and packed them into his bag. Tucking a picture of his mother and father and all the money he had into his pants pocket, Phillip slipped through the cellar door at the back of the house.

His meeting with Alban at the boat dock at 5:00 Saturday morning was almost forty-eight hours away. With very little money and two days to kill, Phillip spent the day wandering the streets and sitting on a bench in the park. *Humm, it's October,* he mused. *On the twenty-sixth of this month, I'll be twenty years old, a good time to start a new life.*

Toward evening, he purchased some bread, cheese, and two apples at a small market. He ate some bread and cheese and found shelter from the cool fall breeze under a bridge by a gristmill. As darkness fell, he opened his mother's Bible and read about the shepherd and the lost sheep. He went down on one knee. "We're gonna make it to America, aren't we, Lord?" He curled up under his quilt for the night.

As the town came alive at sunrise, Phillip determined to set out on this adventure and not look back. He spent the day trudging along the streets near the boat docks on the Rhine. Toward evening, he located the boat landing where he would meet Alban and looked around for a place to spend his last night in Germany. The foul smell of empty containers filled the air. Across the street, he noticed a grassy area with some flowers and park benches. Heading that direction, he heard someone call, "Hey, mate, didn't I see you at the Gasthaus night before last? You have a mind to sail down to Amsterdam tomorrow?"

Phillip recognized the young man from the group that had shown interest the night he met Alban. Across the street, the two met near the little park. "Ja, I plan to find my way to America over the next year or so. I don't have the money for passage, but Alban says he can get me work in Amsterdam to earn enough to go later. What are you doin' here?"

"About the same as you, I guess. Alban must be a good salesman. My name is Trent," he said as he set a small bag on the ground and stretched out his right hand.

"Phillip," was the response, as the two shook hands. "I'm lookin' for a place to spend the night. It could get a bit chilly by morning."

"Same here," Trent said. "Not too many choices. I was here last night and found some protection over by that shed. Join me if you want to. It sure ain't fancy, but we may as well get used to such accommodations if we plan to get to America."

Trent was a man of about twenty but looked much younger. He was short in stature and seemed to have springs in his feet. His long curly hair hung nearly to his shoulders. He wore a small green cap. Phillip was intrigued by his jovial spirit, but sensed he was hiding some pain.

The two men walked in silence, and Trent led the way. As darkness closed in, Trent took out some nuts and fig bars. He offered some to Phillip. Phillip reached in his bag for the apples and shared one. Nourished enough for the night, Trent pulled back some branches and uncovered a knapsack and a coat. They both rolled up in their quilts and prepared to sleep under the bushes.

The night was punctuated by the sounds of the city. Phillip could hear the broom and shovel of someone cleaning the docks. It wasn't long before he heard the deep breathing and occasional snort from his new companion. Sleep came slowly for Phillip.

Phillip and Trent awoke just as the sky started to lighten. They each had a piece of bread and a small cut of cheese before they crossed over to the dock, hoping Alban would show up as he had promised.

At the sounding of the five o'clock whistle, Alban came hustling down the walk. A memorable character, Alban was short in stature and about as wide as he was tall. His head sat on his shoulders as if he had no neck. He was dressed in a dark suit, his pants held up with suspenders and his coat stretched tight around his middle. He wore a black hat that seemed to float above his bushy black hair.

As Alban pulled up, he huffed, "Mornin', men. Glad to see ya. The *Nixie* will sail at six. Want some coffee? A pastry too, I'll buy. Can't have you men goin' hungry."

Phillip knew Alban was making sure they got aboard the *Nixie*. He thought for a moment, *Nixie, doesn't that mean "little water elf"*? He followed as Trent and Alban entered a small shop where Alban pointed to the coffee and pastries.

Phillip and Trent sipped coffee and enjoyed a sweet. Alban paced nervously, waiting to get his "catches" on board the *Nixie*.

At six o'clock, Alban motioned to follow him up the gangplank. His chest stood out with pride. On board, they were guided to some benches on deck and given instructions as to their use of the ship's amenities.

Trent and Phillip rolled out their quilts and made themselves comfortable, disturbed only by the frequent stops at ports along the Rhine. Upon arrival in Amsterdam, Alban directed, "*Amsterdam Shipping* is this way. I'll introduce you to Dietrich. He'll be your boss. Do what he says and you'll be all right." They walked through a long passage way and emerged on the large shipping docks. The smell, a mixture of fish, garbage, and manure, took Phillip's breath away. Remembering his goal to become a landowner in America, he resolved to endure the stench.

Dietrich's "office" was a small building about eight feet square at the edge of the dock. It had once been painted white, but most of the paint had peeled off. The door stood open, and a huge man filled the opening. His upper body was like a box with fleshy arms coming out of the upper corners. He had a round head and a red face with a bent stem pipe between his teeth. He wore a black sailor cap with bushy reddish hair standing out on both sides. His red shirt under his suspenders was partly tucked into his black pants, and his pants were partly tucked into his black boots.

"Dietrich, here are two more dockhands for ya," Alban shouted. "They need a bed in the bunkhouse and a place to eat. I'll check back when they're ready to ship out to America."

Dietrich looked at Phillip and nodded his head slightly. A glint of a smile and head movement from side to side belied his assessment of Trent. He called to a young man just starting up a gangplank, "Joe, take these two over to the bunkhouse and assign 'em bunks. It's 'most noon. Go have chow with 'em and get 'em back here."

Joe led them up some steps above the dock area toward a long narrow white building. Phillip thought, *I sure could use a bath*. The door was on the side opposite from the sea. Inside were rows of bunks with blankets and quilts claiming many of them. The bunks were steel and attached to the floor so they could not be moved. Under each bunk was a metal mesh drawer with a strong padlock hanging from the latch. "Keep your stuff in there and it won't get lost. Guard your key and your stuff'll be safe," Joe advised.

Joe stepped aside. Phillip put his things in the drawer, checked the money in his pocket, and turned ready to move on. Trent skipped along behind as they followed Joe to the mess hall. The food was hot and filling but lacked in taste. Phillip shrugged and thought, *Only a year and I'll be out of here.*

Back at the docks, Dietrich put them to work. Phillip, at six foot one, was strong and wiry. Growing up, he had learned to cut and split wood, and his father expected him to do the family chores. Work was not new to him. He noticed Trent struggling to lift crates and push loaded carts up the gangplanks. Phillip took the heavier loads and gave Trent a hand whenever he could.

One day, Dietrich called Phillip aside. "Hey, man," he said, "you sure are helpin' that kid a lot. I don't know what I would've done with him without your help." The boss hesitated. "I'm in need of a crew boss down the dock a ways. There's a good bonus in pay if you take it on. The men are older, been with me a long time, but I can't trust 'em on their own. Want to give it a try?"

"What's in it for me?" Phillip inquired.

"An extra dollar a day for you and a five at the end of the week if you get her loaded a day early," Dietrich responded.

"What'll the older guys think of a new younger man in charge?"

"They'll give you a hard time for a while, but if you get in there and work hard with 'em, they'll learn to respect ya. I've seen how you get along with the guys. I wouldn't have suggested it if I didn't think you could do it."

Phillip nodded approval and said, "When do I start? What about Trent, does he go with me?"

Dietrich scratched his head and looked across the dock at the young man struggling with a cart load of cargo. "Guess he needs a partner, take him along. No bonus for him."

Phillip walked over to Trent, grabbed his shoulder, and said, "Come on, we're bein' moved down two crafts." The two men followed Dietrich, weaving their way along the docks to the new work site. Six men were waiting for orders to load a steamer making ready to sail. Dietrich spoke to the six. "This is your new boss, Phillip. You answer to him. Any problem, he reports to me. Any reports and you're fired."

Phillip squared his shoulders and gave the order to get started. Andy, a middle-aged man with a graying beard, eyed Phillip with a sneer and turned to start the task. Looking over his shoulder, he quipped, "You're still wet behind the ears. You better watch your hind side and the kid better do his share."

Phillip knew he had to stand up to the men, so he responded, "Do your work as ordered, the kid'll do his. Any problem, you answer to me."

Andy huffed and went to work.

The days dragged on. Phillip could see the job would not be done by the end of the week at the current pace. He was determined to earn the added bonus to help get him to America. He put his shoulder to the work and spoke to the men to move out a little faster. "We don't have all day. Get those crates aboard before we break for dinner." He shouted, "Andy, give Trent a hand with that load over there. Get movin'."

Andy trudged across the dock toward Trent's cart. When he arrived, he gave Trent a shove as he walked past. Trent lost his balance and went sprawling on the dock. Andy gave him a kick as he moved behind the cart.

Phillip slipped around the stacks of cargo and came up behind Andy. "You don't treat men on my crew like that," he ordered. "Do your work and keep it to yourself."

Andy whirled around and faced Phillip. "Are you goin' runnin' to Dietrich and get me fired? If you do, you'll find out what trouble is. I've got friends around here. They'll teach you who's really boss. If you want to see the light of another day, you better back off."

Phillip stepped forward and spoke with a firm voice. "Dietrich put me in charge here and you answer to me. Get that cart up the plank and back for another one, now!"

Andy slid to one side and snarled, "Do you think you can make me?"

Surprised by the action, Phillip snapped back, "Do the job, or I'll fire you on the spot!"

At this, Andy lunged forward with a fist aimed at Phillip's jaw. Phillip flashed a prayer, "Lord help me!" and ducked to one side. As Andy flew past, Phillip brought his knee into Andy's thigh, sending him to the ground. Andy rolled and came to his feet with fire in his eyes. Phillip saw the flash of a blade in his hand. Moving backward, Phillip waited. Andy charged at Phillip, knife in hand, when suddenly, he doubled up and went headlong to the deck. The impact jarred the knife from his hand, slashing Phillip's side as it flew through the air. Trent had thrown his body in front of Andy, tripping him. Phillip felt warm blood soak his shirt, but he knew he had to finish this man off. As Andy went to the deck, Phillip came down on top of him with all his weight. He saw Andy's eyes bulge as his head hit the pavement. While Andy was dazed by the blow, Trent flipped the knife within arm's length. Phillip grabbed the blade and brought it to Andy's throat, applying just enough pressure to start blood trickling around his neck.

"Are you ready to get back to work, or do I take a slice?" Phillip shouted. "You've got five seconds to decide." As Phillip waited, he applied more pressure on the knife.

Andy brought his hands up and whispered, "Back to work."

Phillip released his captive, stepped back, and reached out a hand to Andy to help him up. "Now, do we go together to report this to Dietrich, or do you get to work and see that this load is done by Saturday night?"

Andy looked over at the other five men on the crew, wiped the blood from his neck with his sleeve, and said, "Come on you guys, don't just stand there. Let's get this tub loaded."

Phillip turned to Andy and said, "You won't be needin' this anymore." He slung the knife in the ocean.

The men worked with new determination, and the ship was loaded by noon on Saturday. Trent won the crew over with his humor and antics. Andy suggested having Trent stow the cargo on board and keep count of the crates while the stronger men did the heavier lifting.

Back at the bunkhouse that night, Phillip squeezed Trent's shoulder. "Thanks, friend, for saving my life today." Trent shrugged, his eyes twinkled as he smiled back. Phillip got ready for bed, reached for his mother's Bible, found the passage where Jesus calls us "friends," and prayed a prayer of thanksgiving. In the dimly lit bunkhouse, he held up the picture of his mother and father. Tears came to his eyes as he remembered his mother's love for him.

The next week, Phillip found the bonus in his pay envelope. He thought, *That'll help get me off these docks and on the way to America.* On Monday, when Phillip reported for work, he said to Dietrich, "Thanks for the bonus from last week. It'll help a lot."

"Hey, man, I hear you put old Andy in his place. You got more work out of that crew than ever. Do you want 'em again this week?"

"Sure, give us a job to do." Phillip waited until he had Dietrich's attention. "Hey, remember that Alban guy, the one who's gettin' me passage to New York? Have you seen him around? What'll it take to get on board one of these steamers?"

"Kid, you don't owe Alban nothin'. Steamers are new and not always reliable. Why don't you sail on a cargo ship? If you keep workin' hard like last week with that crew, I'll keep my ears open for a captain who needs a good hand. That way you would have some money when you get there."

Gradually, Phillip and Andy became friends. Since Andy held the power in the group, the rest of the men put their minds to the work. They were all rewarded with better pay envelopes. Dietrich put them to loading larger sailing ships with larger cargo holds. After several months, Phillip began to see his savings grow.

Dense fog hung over the Amsterdam docks when Phillip arrived at work one morning. He found Dietrich standing in the doorway of his shack with a broad smile on his face. "What's with you this mornin'?" Phillip asked. "Did you find the pirate's treasure chest?"

Dietrich glanced at the gangplank leading up to a ship making ready to sail. "She's leavin' for 'Merica tomorrow mornin'. She's called the *Wiebe*. She's made many a trip to New York. Captain Hubrecht's one of the best. Says he could use a lower deckhand. You won't see the light of day much, but it'll get you to 'Merica. Wanna meet him?"

Phillip felt a mixture of fear and excitement in the pit of his stomach. He swallowed hard. "Sure, Dietrich, I'd appreciate that."

Dietrich moved his huge frame out of the doorway, pushed the door shut, and started across the dock. His lengthy stride forced Phillip to move quickly to keep up. "Sir, Captain, here's the kid I told you about. I guarantee he's a good worker. He's lookin' to get to New York."

Phillip looked up at the captain, a large man with powerful arms. He stood straight with shoulders back, a hand taller than Phillip. His dark black eyes displayed a mixture of toughness and kindness. He was dressed in black wool pants with white shirt puffed out around the waist. Golden curls hung below his black cap.

"We sail in the mornin' half past five. Good wind blow'n. One bag's your limit. You'll sleep in the supply room and eat in the galley. Your job will be keepin' the lower deck clean and in order. Buckets and mops are in the supply room. The first mate will show you. Any questions?"

"I'll be here at 5:00. How do I find the first mate?"

"No problem, got one arm. Other one twice as stout."

Phillip turned to leave when it hit him. *What about Trent? He saved my life. Can't leave him behind.* Phillip swung around and saw the captain moving swiftly up the plank. "Captain," Phillip called as he ran after him. Hubrecht stopped, looked at the young man with contempt in his eyes. "Got a request, sir."

The captain hesitated a moment. "What's that, kid?" he snapped.

"Captain, sir, mister, I got this friend, Trent, he saved my life. He needs to go too. Another hand? He works good."

Captain Hubrecht looked past Phillip to the dock below. Dietrich, large hands on his hips, gave a slight nod.

"You call me Captain, that's all. Bring your friend, I need a cabin boy. He sleeps in the supply room with you. Brings my grub and cleans." He turned and disappeared up the plank. Phillip stood there in wonder.

When Phillip reached the dock below, Dietrich was waiting for him. "No work for you today. Go find Trent and go to the 'Merican Office. Your last pay envelope will be at the dock office in an hour. Better get a bath, none on the way. Sleep at the bunkhouse tonight. I'll be here in the morning."

Phillip found Trent and the crew well into the morning's work. "Where've you been?" Trent called. "We're not carrying your load all day."

"I've got some news for ya. Hey, Andy, guys gather around." The men dropped the loads they were moving and stepped over to Phillip. "Trent and I are leavin' for New York tomorrow mornin'. We sail on the *Wiebe* at 5:30. Trent, you'll be the cabin boy, and I'll be the lower deckhand. Andy, you're in charge here. Trent and I need to get our passage papers and get ready to sail. Guess this is good-bye, mates."

Andy reached out his big paw of a hand, "Glad for ya, son," he said with a slight crack in his voice. "You're a good man, Phil. You too, kid," he said as he tussled Trent's head. "The *Wiebe* is a rapid mover, good captain. You'll be in America before you know it."

4

Matilda Mannweiler
Germany
1854

JOHANN MANNWEILER BURST INTO THE kitchen of his home in Ratzin, Germany, on a cold January day in 1854. Throwing an envelope on the table, he turned to hang his coat on a hook by the door. His wife, Caroline, was at the stove preparing supper. She was used to Johann's anger over recent events in Germany. She waited while he washed his hands, knowing he would talk about the contents of the envelope when he was ready. After drying his hands and face, he threw the towel at the hook by the water bucket and watched it fall to the floor.

Turning toward Caroline, Johann shook his head and waved his hand toward the table. "I've been expecting it, but not this much," he snorted. "How much tax can we pay? Ever since the March Revolution in '48, this country has been in turmoil. Even the church has become so political that I doubt it will make any difference in our country. I'm comin' to believe more and more that the Pietists are right. We need more people with hearts warmed by a spiritual rebirth."

Johann sat down at the table and studied the papers. Caroline moved slowly around him and put her hand on his shoulder. He placed his hand over hers and took a deep breath. Finally, he said, "Caroline, it's time! We can't go on like this any longer. If we stay here, we'll be bled dryer than a stuck hog. I stopped to see Arnie Schmitt today. His two sons left for America two years ago. They're in Wisconsin now, and they both have land claims and are earnin' a good livin'. Arnie said they got a letter from them this week. They're buildin' homes of their own. We'll never get ahead here in Germany." He looked up at Caroline and continued, "Arnie said Wisconsin became a state about five years ago and has released land to people who'll live on it and improve it. All we have to do is get to Milwaukee. Thousands of Germans are goin' every year."

Caroline felt her stomach tighten. Johann had talked like this before, but he had never been this insistent. He turned and looked into her eyes, pleading for her support. "Caroline," he appealed, "would you go with me? I'm sixty-four years old. I still have some of the money I earned running the dray for Napoleon when I was a young man. We could sell the cows and the horses. We'd get something for this house and furniture. I'm sure we'd have enough to get to Milwaukee."

The kettle on the stove began to boil over sending Caroline running to push it back on the range. She lingered at the stove, thinking, *My husband is an honorable man. I love him and would do anything to please him. He has been a good provider and father.* She turned, their eyes met, and she spoke. "Yes, Johann, I'll go where you go. I made that promise when we married. But, Johann, we must think of Matilda. She's but a girl, and she's been sick so much of her life. She came home from school early today and went to bed. What'll happen to our daughter on such a journey as this?" Caroline brushed a tear from her eye with her apron and started toward the bedroom.

"Caroline," Johann said firmly, "I would not neglect our daughter. You know that. She's the apple of my eye. But we can't go on like this. Soon we'll have nothing. I'll watch over Matilda and see to her care. We can do it with God's help."

Quietness hung over the family as they sat down for supper. Johann offered his familiar prayer. Caroline had prepared fried chicken, potatoes, and gravy. She put out some small cookies at the end of the meal. Soon Matilda began to carry the dishes to the washstand as her mother prepared the dishpan. Johann cleared his throat and spoke. "Matilda, your mother and I have made a decision. We'll be leaving Germany to live in Wisconsin in America come spring."

Matilda turned to her father with a totally blank expression. "What do you mean, Vati?" were the only words she could speak. She put the dishes down and sent a questioning look toward her mother. Caroline held out her hand, and Matilda fell into her mother's arms.

Johann put his head down on his arms and waited, knowing he needed to give his daughter time to adjust to the news. Mother and daughter went into action washing the dishes and cleaning the kitchen. Johann went to his favorite chair and took up his pipe. He was aware that Matilda had gone to her room and he could hear the clicking of Caroline's knitting needles across the room.

At bedtime, Matilda came to say good night. She lingered a moment and then asked, "Vati, when will we leave?"

"We're making plans to leave this spring. Matilda, I know this is sudden for you, but I can't continue to pay the taxes and still have food to eat. Even the church is controlled by the government. We must do something. I'm going to start selling the cows and horses to gather enough money for the journey."

Matilda nodded. "Good night, Vati," she said as she turned to say good night to her mother.

Matilda lay sleepless most of the night. She thought about how long it would take to get to Milwaukee, how they would travel, and what it would be like to live in a different country. Her stomach hurt. Tears soaked her pillow.

Matilda was small in stature, and sickness often caused her to miss out on events. She loved her father and knew he would make the best decisions for his family. She tried to help her mother with housework, but she tired quickly. The weeks passed slowly as she watched her father sell their property. Two large traveling trunks sat by the wall in the kitchen, reminding Matilda every day of the upcoming move.

One Saturday afternoon, Matilda found her mother knitting a sweater for the trip. "Mutti," she said, "are you glad we're going to Wisconsin? Do you worry about finding our way?"

Caroline put the yarn down and reached out to her daughter. She pondered, *What a lovely daughter, how innocent and frail she is.* "Yes, dear, I do worry. I worry about you and how you'll get along. Your father is a good man, and I trust him completely." Her hand touched her necklace. "Matilda, when you were born on August 9, 1841, your father and I were so happy to have a little girl. In fact, your vati gave me this cross the day after you were born. Vati will see that we all work together to get to our new home."

Matilda whispered, "Thank you, Mutti."

During the winter days of January and February, Johann diligently sought buyers for what little livestock he had. He was especially happy to find a family to purchase his property. He talked with his friend Aldo, who ran a freight business between Ratzin and Hamburg. Aldo said, "Johann, I'll put you on the list for the next time the *Nord Atlantica* sails for Quebec. That steamer is owned by the shipping company that I work for."

Johann responded, "Thank you, my *freund*. We want to leave in early spring so we'll be there in time to get ready for winter." The two men shook hands, and Aldo waved as he drove away.

That night at supper, Johann reported, "I talked to Aldo today. He will arrange for us to sail on the *Nord Atlantica* this spring. It'll take us to Quebec. From there, we'll travel by train to Milwaukee." Matilda took a deep breath as she realized this journey really was going to happen.

On May 5, 1854, Aldo drove up to the Mannweiler house with his freight wagon. Johann and Aldo loaded the two trunks and a personal bag for each member of the family. Matilda packed her bag carefully to get as much in as possible. She took the best clothing she had along with three books, her diary, and a small bracelet her friend had given her. Sadness washed over her as she left the house she had lived in ever since she was born. She stood by the steps for a moment.

Her mother reached to her daughter and said, "Come, Matilda, we're starting a new life. Let's see what God has ahead for us."

The trip to Hamburg took several days. To save their limited funds, the family found a place to sleep near the wagon each night. Caroline had packed a bag with dried fruit, bread, and cheese. Each morning, Aldo offered them a cup of coffee.

It was late afternoon when Aldo drove down a cobblestone road along the ship docks. He made a sharp right turn and stopped at an iron gate. Aldo waved to the gatekeeper who nodded and slid the gate open.

Aldo pointed to the left and said, "There she is, the *Nord Atlantica* ready to sail tomorrow. You can board now and pick a cabin on the lower deck. I'll take you to the boarding area."

Aldo loaded the trunks in the cargo hold. The steamer would take three to four weeks to cross the Atlantic. "Thank you, my *freund*, for your kind help," Johann called to Aldo as he drove away.

A steward took Caroline's bag and motioned for them to follow. They went down through the hatch and along a narrow passageway in the middle of the ship. The steward opened a small door to a little room. Matilda noticed some clumps of cloth or canvas hanging from the ceiling. The steward reached up and swung one of them across the room and placed a ring on a hook. He winked at Matilda and said, "That's your bed."

Later that evening, the steward announced, "Supper's ready, come an' get it!"

The Mannweilers chose to eat out on the deck. "Look," Caroline breathed as the sun painted brilliant colors over the city of Hamburg. "God is blessing us with a beautiful sunset as we leave our homeland." A small German band began to play some familiar folk songs.

Darkness came quickly, and the cool breeze soon drove the family below. They found the toilet down the ramp a few meters. Matilda was pleased that she was feeling well. Johann read some verses from the Bible and prayed the traditional evening prayer. The quiet was interrupted by her father's low snoring and her mother's humming of a hymn. Matilda felt close to God.

The next morning, Johann went to the galley and returned with fried potatoes, sausage, and coffee for breakfast. After morning prayers, they went up on deck. The same German band was gathering on the dock near the gangplank. As the ship moved away from the dock, a cheer went up from the crowd, and the band played a lively tune. Matilda's heart quickened as she felt the steam engines propel the *Nord* out into the Elbe River toward the North Sea on the first leg of their voyage to America. She recorded the departure date in her diary: May 11, 1854.

Once they reached the open water of the North Sea, the motion of the ship caused Matilda to feel nauseated, driving her to their quarters. She prayed that she would gain her sea legs quickly so she could enjoy the voyage.

Early one morning, Matilda woke up in a cold sweat, coughing and feeling miserable. She adjusted her position in her hammock, but the cough kept her awake. Finally, she called, "Mutti, I feel terrible. I'm both hot and cold, and I can't quit coughing."

Caroline put her hand on Matilda's forehead. Heat radiated from her skin. She tried to cool Matilda's body with damp cloths, but the high fever persisted. Her father's snoring stopped. Looking over his wife's shoulder at his daughter, he said, "I'll go find help."

"My daughter's sick with a fever and cough," Johann said with urgency to the steward at the galley.

The steward, still half asleep, responded, "Ja, three others are sufferin' the same. The doctor on board ain't sure what's causin' it. I'll have him see your daughter in the mornin'. Until then, try to get her to drink some tea and rest."

Hours later, the doctor knocked on their door. He was a man of average build. His black pants looked like he had slept in them. His vest hung open over skinny ribs. His beard was sparse, as was the hair on his head. Yawning deeply, he said, "Yup! Same thing as the others. We've got six now. I'm thinkin' its measles. It'll spread through the ship in days. Captain will decide what to do. Hate to think of makin' the whole voyage with a ship full of sick people."

Captain Harold announced an "all hands on deck" for three that afternoon. He appeared to be about sixty years old. Tobacco juice had stained his chin whiskers brown among the otherwise gray beard. Once the people gathered, he moved to the steps leading to the bridge. "I'm Captain Harold," he began. "During the night, we swung to the starboard. We have many passengers with the measles. Liverpool is our destination. The sick will be quarantined there. After a few days, those who are well may stay on board as we proceed to Quebec."

Johann, Caroline, and Matilda were not on board when the *Nord* left for America. Matilda's quarantine lasted six weeks. Johann grew increasingly anxious to get to Milwaukee in time to claim land and build a shelter for winter. Their quarters in Liverpool were comfortable enough, but the unexpected cost was hard on their money supply.

Johann walked into the office of *Liverpool Shipping.* The clerk at the desk was busy looking through some papers and writing down numbers. Johann cleared his throat, causing the clerk to look up. "Can I help you?" he asked with a startled look.

"Ja, my family was on our way to Quebec on the *Nord Atlantica.* My daughter came down with measles. Her quarantine has just been lifted. Your company was recommended to us to get passage to Quebec."

"You came to the right place," the clerk responded. "We have a sailing ship leaving in two days. It'll stop in Dublin and then leave for Quebec. Food and water will be provided, but we have no cook on board, so passengers have to prepare their own food."

The quarters on the sailing ship were crowded. The beds were but shelves that folded down from the wall. The Mannweilers were thankful for their warm quilts as the nights were very cold. The stop in Dublin turned into a week. Johann's anxiety grew.

They had smooth sailing on the Atlantic for several days, but on July 7, Matilda was awakened in the night by loud crashes that sounded like cannons. The ship was rolling and tossing every which way. She took a deep breath as she clung to a small rail at the head of her bed.

She felt her father's arm keeping her from falling to the deck. She heard him speak, "It's all right, Matilda. We're in a storm. The captain has ordered us to stay in our cabins."

The storm raged on for days. Caroline was able to get small amounts of food each morning. The stewards brought drinking water, but the rations became smaller and smaller. Matilda lost track of the days. She thought, *If August 9 has passed, I'm thirteen years old.* Some days the storms let up, but the winds would go calm, causing the ship to lie still in the water. Finally, after weeks of storms, the captain announced, "Today is September 2, 1854. Tomorrow, we will sail into the Gulf of St. Lawrence and land at Quebec."

The Mannweiler family rejoiced at the news. Matilda thought, *If it's already September, we were sailing for nine weeks.*

The next morning, the captain explained the late arrival to the officials at the immigrations office. A boat was secured to take them up the St. Lawrence to Montreal where they could board a train to Chicago. Johann said to Caroline, "I'm starved, let's find a place to get something to eat." After struggling with language, they had a tasty meal in a little Quebec café.

Johann rented a room at a rooming house. He smiled her way and said, "Matilda, you're first to take a bath. But don't take too long, we all need a turn." The warm water brought life into Matilda's body. She wished she could stay in the bath for hours.

Bryson, captain of the boat that would take them to Montreal, was a young man with a spring in his step and a ready smile on his face. "Come on, you Germies, can't let you get your land legs before getting up the Lawrence. Your trunks are on board. Find yourselves a seat and we'll be on our way."

Bryson noticed Matilda standing behind her father. "You there, sweetie, you be first up the plank." He reached out and took her hand and slipped it on his arm as he led the way aboard. Matilda felt her neck turn red at the attention, but she liked the way he made her feel special. She watched for the captain during the voyage, but he was busy steering the boat.

At the dock in Montréal, Bryson came up beside the Mannweilers as they made their way to the train station. He glanced a smile toward Matilda and handed her a small pin with the word *Montréal* printed on it. "This is to remember your boat ride to Montréal." Turning to Johann, he winked. "Bring her back when she gets a little older and I'll ask permission to court her." Johann and Caroline smiled and thanked the captain for the safe trip. Matilda blushed.

That evening, as the train was slowly winding its way toward Chicago, Johann wondered, *Will I be able to find land and build a cabin before winter?* After a simple supper in the diner car, they wrapped themselves in the warm quilts Caroline had made for the journey and slept on the bench seats. Matilda gave thanks to God and fell asleep to the clicking sound of the wheels on the track beneath her.

Next morning, while drinking a cup of coffee, Johann's heart sank when he observed the brilliant colors of the morning sun on the hillsides. He desperately wanted to get a cabin built and a shelter for a few animals before winter set in. He figured he could count on most of October, but beyond that would only be a gift from God. When he returned to his family, he found Caroline folding the quilts and straightening their belongings. Matilda had gone to the toilet. Caroline knew something was bothering her husband. "What is it, Johann?" she asked.

Johann flung his hat down on the seat and kicked at the side of the bench and spouted, "Six weeks with the measles and nine weeks on the ocean and now fall is here and we haven't even found our land. I had planned on getting to Milwaukee long before this. This train stops more than it goes, and we still have to change trains in Chicago. Who knows when we'll get to the land office to take up a claim? We're gonna be in our new home by winter, and that is that!"

Caroline had been observing her husband growing increasingly irritated as the days slipped past. She put her hand on his arm. Johann jerked away and turned to the window. "Johann," she said quietly, "you know we must trust God all the way. He will be with us. That was our promise to each other when we left home. Now we must do what we said. We must not cause Matilda to worry."

"I know," he snorted. "But I get so impatient with all the delays. I just wish this train would keep going."

The conductor came through the car, announcing, "Breakfast is ready in the diner. Next stop is Syracuse, Syracuse next stop!"

The days passed slowly as the train moved through towns with strange-sounding names like Rochester, Buffalo, Erie, Cleveland, and Toledo. Matilda met a girl her age from Norway named Abigail. The two girls spent most of the time together talking and playing games. Caroline was pleased to see Matilda having a good time and that she was gaining strength as the trip went on.

The conductor struck up a conversation with the girls, asking, "Where are you ladies headed?"

Abigail answered, "I'm going to Chicago for a visit, and Matilda is going to Wisconsin with her family to find a new home."

The conductor looked at Matilda, winked, and smiled. "You'll like it in Wisconsin. Lots of people have ridden my train on the way to Milwaukee with plans to take up land. Is your father a farmer?"

Matilda nodded. "We left Hamburg way back in May. There were so many storms crossing the ocean that it took us nine weeks, so we were late getting to Quebec. That's why we're on this train. Do we have to take another train to Milwaukee?"

"Yes, it'll be waiting for you when we get to Chicago. We'll see that you get on the one to Milwaukee." The conductor gave each of the girls a tap on the shoulder. "Keep on smiling and God be with you."

The next morning, as the sun burst up over Lake Michigan, the conductor came through the car. "Chicago, next stop, Chicago. All passengers prepare to leave the train. Your trunks will be on the platform. Chicago, next stop, Chicago."

Transferring to the train to Milwaukee went smoothly. As the Mannweilers were settling into their seats, the conductor shouted, "All aboard for Milwaukeeeee, have your tickets ready for Milwaukee." The train pulled away from the station.

The Late Mate
Le Havre, France
1852

I T WAS A CHILLY MORNING in Le Havre. The porter motioned to Adam with some disgust. "Get on that wagon. It'll take you to *Du Vale Maritime Shipping Company*. The *Robert Harding* is pushing off now." Adam, with his bag in hand, jumped on the wagon. The driver spoke to the horses, setting them on a run down a rutted ally and out onto cobblestone streets. Adam hung on to his hat with one hand and the seat with the other, clamping his bag between his legs. The fog thickened as they went. The driver stopped momentarily at a gateway to shout a message to the keeper. The gatekeeper looked at Adam with a strange scowl. Adam shrugged. The driver guided the team down a slope and around some large containers. They stopped at the side of a beautiful sailing vessel. On the bow, Adam saw the name painted in blue on white with gold trim, *Robert Harding*.

Seamen were at work on the deck, getting ready to hoist sails as they pushed off from the moorings. The driver waved his hat and shouted to the dockworkers. No one seemed to pay attention. He jumped down from the wagon and approached a man dressed in a dark-blue suit, shiny boots, and a sailor's cap. The gentleman shrugged his shoulders and turned to leave. The driver followed and kept talking. The gentleman stopped, waved to a dockworker, and left. The dockworker motioned to Adam and shouted, "Follow me!"

Adam was guided down some steps and along a boardwalk to a small boat. Following the motions of his escort, he stepped into the boat. Two muscular men took to the oars and moved the boat out toward the *Robert Harding*. They maneuvered the small boat alongside the ocean-ready *Harding*. Two sailors dropped a rope down to the oarsmen who put a rope chair harness on Adam. "Hoist away," one of them shouted. Adam clung tightly to his few possessions as he was hauled up the side of the ship and over the railing. Whistles and applause from the passengers and crew greeted him. Though embarrassed by the attention, Adam decided to make the best of it and bowed low with a motion of his hand to the men who hoisted him aboard. A crewman shouted, "Welcome aboard, Late Mate!" The nickname stuck.

With an extended hand, the purser stepped forward and said with a grin, "Welcome aboard the *Robert Harding*, Mr. Late Mate. Follow me to your quarters." Adam was guided down the hatch and along a passageway to his compartment. He took a deep breath and stretched out on his bunk.

Once rested, Adam ventured out on the main deck. The sky was dazzling blue, and the silence was broken only by the creaking sound of the masts and gaffs as they held the sails to the wind.

The *Robert Harding* passenger list was at capacity. Adam found the food to be both sparse and bland. Drinking water was to be conserved. Sanitation was questionable. It was well known that some America-bound ships buried passengers at sea while en route.

Favorable spring winds made for smooth sailing on the Atlantic. The captain held the ship to the wind, tacking powerfully to the port. Then the crew would work in unison to bring the ship about to run with the wind to the starboard. In every direction, Adam could see nothing but the blue of the ocean and the sparkle of the sun on the rolling waves.

On the third day out, Adam took his Bible and nestled down near the bowsprit where he was sheltered from the cool wind. He found the story of Jonah in the Old Testament. As he read, he thought about how he didn't want to go to America. It meant leaving everything familiar. Jonah didn't want to go to Nineveh. In fact, he ran from it. Yet God was in the whole plan and brought about good. Adam sensed the Lord showing him that he would bring about good in this journey too.

He heard a small voice. "Hey, Late Mate, what you doin' there?" Adam looked up into the faces of five children lying on their bellies, looking down from the deck above the forecastle. With smiles on their faces, they began a chorus of "Hey Late Mate, Hey Late Mate . . ."

The initial irritation quickly evaporated, and Adam decided to have some fun with the children. He spoke with mystery in his voice. "Look, you with the blue coat, what's that in your ear?"

Little "Blue Coat" put his hands to his ears in dismay. By this time, Adam was on his feet beckoning the children to come down from their perch. The children ran down the steps to meet Adam on the main deck. The little guy with the blue coat held back with his hands on his ears. Adam stepped up and put his hand by the boy's ear. "Look," he said, "you have a coin in your ear." Adam opened his hand, and there was a silver coin. He turned and put his hand by a little girl's ear and whispered, "Now it's in your ear." He opened his hand, and the coin was gone. The children laughed. "Do it again! Do it again!"

The next day, Adam went to his favorite place to read his Bible. This time, the group of children had grown to a dozen or more. They chorused, "Hey, Late Mate, do some tricks." Adam only knew one more trick, so he decided to save it for another time. The children kept saying, "Mr. Late Mate, show us a trick."

Adam offered, "Today, let's play a game." He remembered the games he played at home with his brothers and sisters. He organized the older children to help the younger children, so everyone was having a good time. When interest waned, they sat and talked until mealtime.

The next day, Adam found still more children and some parents waiting for him. He worried that the parents didn't approve of his games with their children. He started to turn back just as one of the fathers spoke up. "Mr. Late Mate, I would use your name, but that is what the children love to call you. We would like to talk to you." Adam waited. The man continued, "Please come sit with us. We have a request."

Adam approached and sat down with the group. A woman, possibly in her midthirties and obviously the mother of four or five of the children, spoke. "Mister . . . what is your name? I have trouble calling you Late."

"My name is Adam, Adam Utzinger."

"Mr. Utzinger"—the woman smiled—"our children have been so excited about your tricks and games. We're wonderin' if you would be willing to teach the children some readin' and figurin' while we're on board the *Robert Harding*. The children should be in school now. They could be learnin' here on the ship."

Adam swallowed and looked at her with wonder. "I'm not a teacher. I graduated from the Volksschule and from my pastor's class at the church, but I'm not a teacher. I don't have any books or slates or anything. How can I teach your children?"

One of the fathers chimed in, "We've talked together and have decided that we would pay you a half dollar a day if you would teach our children. Please consider our offer."

Still another voice rang out, "We brought some books with us, and some of us have slates. We'll take turns helping you. We need someone the children look up to."

Adam then asked, "My studies included the Bible. Would Bible stories be acceptable for learnin'?"

"Yes, we would want you to use the Bible. We are on our way to America to find freedom in our faith. We are Christians. We believe everyone should study the Bible." Adam remembered what he once read about Pietism. *I wonder, could these people be Pietists?*

It was agreed that the children would come the next morning with their books, slates, and sharp minds. Adam went back to his compartment, wondering, *What have I gotten myself into?*

The next morning when Adam arrived, the children were waiting for school to begin. He started by writing some sums on a slate and watched to see what hands went up. He did the same with words, watching to see how quickly the children responded. Soon he had parents involved, helping the children. The children were eager when he started a word game that challenged their thinking. Some of the children were learning spelling and the sounds of the letters.

When Adam saw that the morning was about spent, he asked, "Did everyone have fun today?" He received a chorus of, "Ja! Ja!"

"Who would like a good Bible story to end the morning?" Again, the children responded with, "Ja! Ja!" He asked, "What do you know about Jonah?"

"He got swallowed by a whale," one student answered. Another said, "He got throwed up by the whale."

Adam went on, "When you left your home in Germany, did you want to go to America?" It got quiet, and some of the children put their heads down. Finally, a little girl said, "I didn't wanna leave my grandma." Another child nearly whispered, "I had to leave my best friend." Others just shook their heads.

Adam said, "Jonah didn't wanna go to Nineveh either. He ran off in another direction. But when Jonah finally went where God wanted him to go, God used Jonah to do something very important. I didn't wanna leave my family and friends, but I'm praying that God will work for good in my life. Let's all watch to see what God is doing in our lives on this journey."

Wilfred, one of the older boys, held up his hand. When Adam nodded, he ventured, "I didn't wanna go to America, but I'm asking God to use my life to help others find Jesus." Adam nodded in affirmation and ended the day with a prayer.

Adam was hard-pressed to think of ways to teach with few books or slates. He thought of stories to tell and games to play. The number of children increased every day as word traveled among the passengers. Parents became acquainted with other families and shared their faith with them. On Sunday, the families gathered for worship. God was at work aboard the *Robert Harding*.

One evening after supper, Adam strolled out on the deck. His mind was circling back to life on the Scharrhof. The moon was full and cast shadows high on the sails. The swishing sound of the hull passing through the waves brought on a bit of melancholy. His thoughts tuned to Aubrey, her quiet innocence and winning smile. *Will I ever find a woman like her?*

Suddenly, his daydreaming was interrupted by a firm male voice coming from the shadows. "Mr. Utzinger," the man addressed, "would you share a visit?" Adam strained to recognize the source of the request. "Here, over here by the rail. I'm out for a bit of quiet, enjoying the moonlight. I'm Ahren, Wilfred's vater. My wife and I are very thankful that you are teaching our children."

The two men shook hands and moved to stand with their elbows on the starboard rail. It had been still for a moment when Ahren spoke. "What's your plan when you get to America?"

Adam simply shrugged. "Don't really know. I had to get out of Germany. With my brother Jacob already in the cavalry, Mutti didn't have the heart to see another son become a soldier. My brother Peter is in New York workin' in a lumber mill. I'll join up with him and see if we can make it together. How about you?"

"We are from the Palatinate in Germany. We're headed for a place called Pennsylvania. Thousands of Germans have moved there over the years. We wanted to get passage to Philadelphia, but all the ships were full until next year. We chose to go on faith and head for New York and find our way from there. You probably noticed we're a group of ten families."

Ahren turned with his back to the rail just as the ship jolted out of a tack to run with the evening breeze. He spoke as he caught hold of the rail to maintain his balance. "Adam, you mentioned your studies with your pastor. Are you thinking you'll become a pastor?"

Surprised at the thought, Adam responded quickly, "No, no thought of that. I'm a farmer. Hope someday to have my own place with a wife and family." It was a genuine smile that he saw on Ahren's face in the moonlight.

"Ever heard of the people called Pietists?" Ahren ventured. Not waiting for an answer, he continued, "A man by the name of Phillip Jakob Spener was known as the father of Pietism back in the 1600s. My family heritage goes back to the early Pietists. As a little boy, I remember my great-grandfather passing on stories that he had heard from the generations before him about this prophet of a preacher. My old grandpa would say, 'Ahren, when Spener was pastor of that old Lutheran church in Frankfurt, he wrote this thing called *Pia Desideria* (Pious Desires), and it set off a movement all across Germany.' Grandpa and my vater after him were staunch believers in Jesus as Savior."

Adam was moved by the earnestness of faith reflected by the moonlight on the face of his new friend.

Ahren went on, "Spener was a Lutheran pastor, but he felt further reform was needed in the church in Germany. He was concerned that people had the head knowledge of salvation by God's grace but lacked the fruit of the Spirit of God. He challenged the universities and seminaries not only to teach theology, but to teach pastors how to demonstrate the holy faith of the apostles. Spener saw that many people had a presumption of God's grace that caused them to take God for granted. I have a heritage that I don't want to be forgotten."

As Ahren was talking, Adam felt a stirring inside. "Ahren"— Adam hesitated for a moment—"when I was studying with my pastor, I always felt there was something more. I have this inner longing for God. Could that be what you are talking about?"

Ahren put a hand on Adam's shoulder. "Adam," he offered, "it sounds like God is at work in your life."

Both men were startled by the twin blasts of the fog horn ordering all passengers below deck. A bond had been formed. As they approached the hatch, Ahren said, "Good night, my brother." Adam nodded the same.

As the voyage continued, Adam observed Ahren and the ten families in his group. He thought, *They have what I have been looking for.*

The days lengthened and warmed as March came to a close. After being at sea for just over four weeks, the captain announced, "This is the fastest trip I've ever made across the Atlantic. We'll sail into the New York harbor tomorrow, March 29, 1852. Once docked, take your bags with you. Good to have you on board."

As the *Robert Harding* moved up to the dock, the passengers crowded toward the gangplank. Fathers, with young children on their shoulders and bags in each hand, were followed by wives and families heavily loaded with baggage. Faces reflected both fear and excitement. Adam followed the flow to the immigration office.

Hearing his name, Adam turned to find Ahren and his family. Ahren squeezed Adam's shoulder and said, "God go with you, my *freund.*"

The Drunken Drover
South Bend, Indiana
1852

ONCE THE McQUILLANS WERE SETTLED in camp near South Bend, Indiana, Jacob and Jake saddled up and headed for town. While tying their horses at the hitching rail in front of the livery stable, a young man approached them. "Can I help you, men?" he asked politely.

Jake answered, "Yep, we're on our way to Minnesota Territory to conscript land. We've got a problem back a mile or so. A wheel hit a rock and broke things up pretty bad. Is there a wagon shop in town?"

"Ya, sure is, just opened up a year or so ago, one of the best in the business. They're sellin' wagons like hotcakes. Go down there to the next corner and hang a left. You'll see the Henry Studebaker Wagon Shop on the right."

Thanking the young man, the father and son headed down the street. They found Henry Studebaker to be very businesslike in manner and willing to help. Noticing the sun was low in the west, Henry observed, "There's not time before dark. Let's go just after sunup in the morning."

At suppertime, Jacob prayed, "Thank you, Lord, that no one was hurt in the accident. Thank you for this food and please help us get the wagon fixed tomorrow." While they were eating, Jacob said, "It looks like we'll be here a couple days. Polly, would you stock up on supplies for the next ten days on the trail? Joe and Sid, would you . . ." Jacob realized Sid was nowhere to be seen. He caught Joe's eye.

Joe hesitated, looked down to the ground, and grunted, "He's gone."

Waiting for more, Jacob looked at Joe. "What do ya mean, gone?" Jacob remembered the times he had seen Sid watching Mary M.

"Gone to town," Joe offered. "Said he needed a drink, didn't say when he'd be back."

Jacob hesitated a minute, and then he spoke. "You children better get off to bed. It'll be dark soon. Jake and I'll meet Henry Studebaker in the morning to get Jake's wagon fixed."

Jacob stayed by the fire while Polly and Catharine put the children to bed. John and Israel were playing by the river. Mary M seemed quiet and slowly walked over to the freight wagon. Jacob wondered if Sid had made advances before he left camp.

After Jake checked the animals, he stopped by the campfire. "Pa," he said, "I hate leavin' my wagon out there on the trail all night with all of our household things in it. I'm goin' out and guard it for the night."

"If that's how you feel, Jake, I'll take your watch. Mary M is sleepin' in the supply wagon tonight. Catharine has Hester with her. Mary M ain't feelin' the best. I'll let her know you left. Lucinda can stay with her for company," Jacob said. Silently, he vowed he would be on watch if Sid came back from town. Jake took his bedroll and rode off to spend the night in his wagon.

Jacob mounted Jenny and made rounds of the camp. Everything seemed quiet. He saw Joe getting into his bedroll near where the animals were tethered. "Joe"—he spoke softly—"Jake's goin' out to watch over his wagon. I'm takin' his watch. If you see Sid, let me know. I need to talk to him. And by the way, thanks for your help gettin' up that riverbank today. Don't know what we'd done without you."

"Sure, Boss, everybody did their best. I'll let you know if I see Sid. Don't know what's gotten into him." Joe rolled over, and Jacob moved on.

The family in the Schooner had settled down for the night. Jacob slipped in over the tailgate. Polly was kneeling by her bed, praying. She turned and reached a hand toward her husband. He went down on one knee beside her. They were quiet for a moment, and then he spoke. "I need Lucinda to spend the night with Mary M. I'm concerned about her. I think Sid is paying improper attention to her. I don't think Mary M knows it, but I've been watchin'. Sid's in town, but I'm afraid he'll come back drunk and try somethin'."

"What can Lucinda do over there? Is it dangerous for her?"

Jacob put his arm around Polly. "I'll tell her to call for me if anything happens. I'll be on watch all night. Jake went out to guard his wagon. I just don't want Mary M out there alone. Lucinda would be a good help."

Jacob moved to the front of the wagon and whispered, "Lucy, I'd like you to stay with Mary M for the night. Jake went out to his wagon, and she's all alone."

Lucinda climbed out of her bunk and took her quilt with her. Jacob moved out over the tailgate and lifted Lucinda down. As they walked to the supply wagon, Jacob instructed, "I don't want Mary M to be alone since Jake left camp. I'll be on watch all night. Call me if you need anything. I know you like spending time with Mary M."

"Ya, Pa, I really like Mary M. We pray together sometimes." Lucinda felt special as her pa lifted her up to the supply wagon seat.

Jacob spoke softly. "Mary M, I brought you some company. Lucy would like to sleep in the wagon with you." Jacob stepped up on the wheel and continued, "Jake wanted to go out and watch over your wagon. I thought you might be lonesome."

"Thank you." Mary M spoke in a soft voice. "I'm not feeling well tonight, and I could use a nurse. Come on in, Lucy. You can sleep on that big trunk behind the wagon seat."

Lucy crawled in and pulled her quilt around herself. "Mary M, do you need anything? Can I get you a drink?"

"No, I'm all right. I'll wake you if I need help. It's different not having our own wagon. Lucinda, you're such a good friend."

It was about 2:00 a.m. when Jacob heard a horse whinny softly. He pulled Jenny into the shadow of a large tree. In the moonlight, he saw Sid tethering his horse. Sid staggered as he walked toward the wagons. He hesitated near big Joe, making sure he was out for the night. He stopped and listened by the supply wagon. Thinking Mary M would be sleeping near the seat, he stepped up on the wagon wheel to the seat. As he pushed the canvas open, he was greeted by a wild scream. "Pa! Indians are attacking us! Pa!" More screams and panic followed.

Startled, Sid jumped to the ground and started running toward his horse. As he went past the lead wagon, suddenly, something wrapped around him like the coil of a snake. His arms were slammed against his sides, and he was stopped in his tracks. Suddenly, he was aware of a man on a horse behind him. As he looked up at the horseman, he felt the coil tighten, taking the air out of his lungs. He spun like a top as the coil unwound. Dizzy both from drink and the spin, he lunged to the ground. His hand went to his gun, just as a huge form grabbed him by both arms and lifted him off the ground. Joe had been awakened by the screams. Jumping from his bedroll, he saw Sid spinning in front of him. Joe held Sid two feet off the ground with his back against the lead wagon.

Jacob approached and took Sid's gun. "Thanks, Joe," he said. "Let's put this guy up for the night while we decide what to do with him." Joe lowered him to the ground. "Take the halter ropes and tie him to that tree down by the river. The mosquitoes will sober him up by morning. Sid, I'll talk to you before breakfast."

Joe put Sid under his arm like a loaf of bread, grabbed some ropes, and headed toward the river. He backed Sid up to a tree and tied his arms around the tree behind him. He took a long rope and made five or six loops all the way around the tree and secured the knot. "I warned you, Sid, that it wouldn't go good for ya with the boss. See ya in the mornin'."

Jacob hurried to the supply wagon. He found Mary M trying to comfort Lucinda. He took his nine-year-old daughter in his arms. "I'm so glad you were here with Mary M. That was not an Indian. It was

58

Sid. He was drunk, and he was going to harm your friend. Joe has taken care of him, and nothing more will happen. You can be sure of that."

Lucinda snuggled in by Mary M. With the assurance of her pa and the calm of Mary M, Lucy soon was asleep. In the morning, Jacob found Sid well tied, sober, and covered with mosquito bites. When Jacob approached him, he was greeted with an oath of foul language. Jacob let him vent. Finally, when the air cleared, Jacob spoke. "Sid, first of all, you're fired!"

"No, I'm not. I quit. Let me out of here and I'm gone," Sid shouted with fire in his eyes.

"Hold it there. You need help. I've been watchin' your glances at Mary M. I knew if you came home drunk, you'd try to get to her. I set you up by putting Lucinda in the wagon. Mary M is my daughter-in-law. Hurting her is hurting me. If I didn't know that my God has been merciful to me and by his grace given me new life, I would condemn you to death right here on the spot. God has taught me that I must love you because Jesus has loved me. My Lord Jesus has forgiven me. You need forgiveness too. So I forgive you for what you were tryin' to do with my family. When I talked to you that day in Delta, I knew you needed a friend. I hoped our family could show you a better way of life, so I gave you a job."

Jacob untied the ropes and allowed Sid to tumble to the ground. "It's your choice. You can leave camp now, or you can make a confession before the whole group, ask forgiveness, and make a new start." Jacob extended a hand to help him up. "What'll it be?"

Sid spit at his hand, rolled over, and got to his feet. "I'll take my horse and go," he spouted. "You can keep your religion to yourself. I'll make my way, you'll see."

Joe was standing nearby as Jacob spoke to Sid. Turning toward Joe, Jacob said, "Tell Polly that I need a bag with a loaf of bread, some cheese, fig bars, and some coffee to send with Sid."

When Joe turned to leave, Sid spouted, "Keep your old vittles. I don't need a handout." With a curse, Sid started toward his horse. He stumbled and almost fell as he wobbled along. Jacob shouted after him, "I'll leave the food on the feedbox. Your pay for the last week will be in the bag."

The family was eating breakfast when Sid stopped for the package and rode away. Jacob prayed that the young man would learn from the experience. He turned his attention to the tasks ahead.

Lucinda noticed Mary M by the supply wagon, leaning against the wheel with her head down. Mary M had not eaten much breakfast. Lucy approached her sister-in-law. "Mary M, are you all right? Can I help you?"

Mary M climbed into the wagon and answered, "Thanks, Lucy. I'm just going to rest awhile."

John and Israel went with their grandpa to help get the wagon fixed. At the Studebaker Wagon Shop, Henry had his team hitched to one of his new wagons. When they arrived at the broken wagon, they found Jake stacking all of the supplies and personal goods on the ground.

Jake said, "I thought I'd make it lighter to get it up off that broken wheel. The fifth wheel under the wagon is badly bent. I'm not sure we can pull it even if we get a new wheel on."

Jacob dismounted and tossed a bag to Jake. "Polly wanted you to have some breakfast. Don't know what she put in there, but she knew you'd need something to eat."

"Thanks, Pa, you can always count on Polly. I still miss Ma, but I'm sure grateful for Polly." Jake turned away as he felt his eyes fill.

The boys were having fun riding among the rocks on a knoll off toward the east. Henry looked under the wagon to see what would be needed. "Banged her up real good, didn't ya? That fifth wheel is the biggest problem. Let's raise the box up so we can get the wheel and the fifth wheel off. We'll take 'em in to the shop for repair." Looking up at Jake, he said, "You and those two boys can load your stuff into my wagon. Don't want it standin' out here for two or three days." With a motion to Jacob, he continued, "Help me get this thing jacked up."

When the boys came galloping down the slope, Jake called, "Come on guys, we've gotta load all this stuff in Mr. Studebaker's wagon." The boys jumped down from their ponies and set to work with Uncle Jake.

Once the load was transferred and the wagon parts hung on the side of Henry's wagon, they headed back to town. Jake climbed up on the seat with Henry. As they made their way back to South Bend, Jake was thinking about Mary M. *I love her so much, but she hasn't been herself lately. I wonder if she's unhappy about going to Minnesota Territory.*

"You seem deep in thought," Henry observed. "We'll get that wagon goin' in a couple days. I need to fashion some parts and make a new wheel. It'll all work out."

"Ya," Jake responded. "Guess I was daydreamin' a bit."

Henry looked over at the young man. "That your wagon or your pa's?"

"Mine. Pa's been helpin' me get started farmin'. I'm gonna take a homestead of my own in Minnesota. I bought that wagon on a sale, and I've been fixin' on it."

"What'd ya think of my new wagon? I could offer a trade, and you could get back on the trail," Henry said as he urged his team to a trot.

"Don't have the cash for wheels like this. Bad enough to have to pay for repairs on the old one," Jake responded.

"I wouldn't mind havin' one of my Studebakers up in Minnesota. It could bring me some business here along the trail. I'd make you a good offer. I'll need fifteen dollars for the repairs, and I'd trade for fifty. All I'd ask is that you put my Studebaker sign on the side so folks would know where you got it."

"Guess I'd have to talk to Pa about that. I don't have the fifty. In fact, the fifteen would leave me near broke." Jake looked around, pulled the canvas aside, and observed the bunks and storage bins. *Mary M would like this. It has a lot more room for our belongings.*

As Henry set the brake on the Studebaker, Jacob rode up and dismounted. "I've been wondering if we should take Jake's things out to our camp so you can have an empty wagon."

"May not be necessary," Henry said, glancing at Jake. Jacob waited while Jake jumped down from the wagon. Henry continued, "Made your boy a mighty good offer, you men better talk it over. I'll get these parts in the shop."

"John and Israel, you boys ride on out to camp," Jacob ordered. "Tell 'em we'll be there soon."

Henry started getting the parts in the shop. Jake motioned to his pa to come to the back of the wagon. "Pa," he said, "Henry offered to trade wagons with me. He wants to get one of his wagons up in Minnesota. Good for his business, he said. Fixin' the old one would be fifteen dollars and he'd trade for fifty. I don't have fifty dollars, but it sure seems like a good deal. All I have to promise is that I leave his Studebaker sign on the wagon as we move on across Indiana and Illinois." Jake stopped and glanced at his pa with a questioning look.

Jacob, looking down the street, saw John and Israel watering their ponies by the livery stable. He motioned for them to come back. "Jake, I need to tell you about something that happened last night. While you were gone, Sid came back to camp drunk and started to get into the wagon where Mary M was sleeping."

Jake's body tightened as he looked into his pa's eyes. "I'll kill that . . ."

"Hold on, son, nothing happened. I'd been watchin' Sid's eyes whenever he was around Mary M. I knew, with you away from camp and Sid in town for a drink, we had the chance for trouble. I had Lucy sleep in the supply wagon with Mary M. When Sid opened the canvas, Lucinda let out a scream. I caught Sid with my whip as he started to run. Joe strung him to a tree until morning. He chose to leave before breakfast. He won't be back. That leaves us in need of another drover. I'll pay you the extra thirty-five if you take on more work with the stock so we don't have to find another hired hand."

"I can do that, Pa. Joe's as strong as two men—and reliable. I'd be glad to work with him. And it would be nice for Mary M and Hester to have the new wagon. Thanks, Pa." Jake thought a moment. "Pa,

I'm worried about Mary M. She doesn't seem quite herself lately. I'm wonderin' if she's unhappy. Maybe this will cheer her up."

Jacob turned to the boys. "There's been a change of plans. You boys ride out to camp. Tell them to get ready to move out. Jake and I will be there soon. I want to make it to La Porte by Saturday."

John and Israel rode off at a gallop. Jacob watched them for a moment, admiring his grandsons. He thought, *Maybe they could take more responsibility on the trail too.*

It was high noon before the McQuillans were ready to start out. Mary M, though she looked a bit pale, was excited about the new wagon. "Wow!" she said. "A spankin' new Studebaker wagon! Thank you, Jake. I'll help so you can spend more time working with Joe. I love you, Jake!"

The wagon train moved steadily on, inching closer and closer to Minnesota Territory. Lucinda asked her pa if she could ride double with him the next time he scouted out ahead. Thursday afternoon, Jacob saw Lucy walking alongside the wagon, reading a book. "Lucinda," he called, "do you want to ride out with me?"

The sun was high in the sky, and the days were getting warmer as April had passed into May. Lucinda tossed her book in the Schooner and grabbed her pa's hand as he swung her up behind him. She felt secure with her arms around her father's strong body. He put Jenny to a single-foot lope out ahead of the wagons. The midafternoon breeze caused her hair to stand out behind her. Down the trail, they came to a clump of oaks and a little stream of clear water. Pa reined in, swung Lucinda down, and dismounted. Pa filled his canteen and offered Lucy a drink and took a deep draft himself. "Let's rest awhile over there on that log."

Lucinda thought for a moment. "Pa, I feel so bad about breaking Jake's wagon. I was driving the bays when we hit the rock. Mary M and I were talkin', and I wasn't watchin'. We almost tipped over. I tried to tell Jake how sorry I am, but he just said it would be okay."

"Lucinda, it could happen to anyone. The animals get so used to following the wagon ahead of them that they cut the corners. The bays cut too sharp, and you didn't see it in time."

"Ya, but, Pa, we lost a day on the trail and all that with Sid and Mary M last night. Seems like it's all my fault. I keep thinkin' Jake's mad at me."

"Lucy, you've asked forgiveness. You are forgiven. God has forgiven you, I forgive you, and I know Jake has forgiven you. The most important thing in my life is that God has forgiven me and has a place for me in heaven. I remember when I was about your age, I went to a camp meeting. Jacob Albright was preachin'. He invited anyone who wanted to trust Jesus as Savior to come up to the front. I knew I was a sinner, so I went up there. Mr. Albright prayed with me, and I knew my sin was forgiven. That is the most important thing in my life." He paused a moment as he put his strong arm around Lucinda's shoulders. He looked down into her face. He thought, *God, what a beautiful little daughter you've given to me. Please, God, help her to trust in your Son.*

They sat quietly for a few minutes. Lucinda felt close to God. "Pa," she asked, "do you remember at camp meeting last summer when Preacher Anders had the children go down by the river with him and Mrs. Anders? I asked Jesus to forgive my sin that day. I do know I'm forgiven. I've been readin' the Bible since then. I don't understand much, but I keep reading. Last night, I read about how Jesus forgave the man they put down through the roof. I do know I'm forgiven."

Jacob drew his daughter close and said, "Thank you, God, for your forgiveness. Thank you for forgiving Lucy and for forgiving me." As he breathed a quiet "amen," Lucy asked, "Pa, do you think Mary M will be all right? Last night in the wagon, she was coughing, and she threw up once. I'm worried about her."

"Ya, Lucy, I've been noticin'."

Jacob mounted Jenny and swung Lucy up behind him. They galloped all the way back to the wagon train. Progress was slowing in the afternoon sun. Jacob announced, "Lucinda and I found a good spot to camp, maybe a mile down the trail. Nice cool stream and a grove of oaks. It looks like we can make La Porte by noon on Saturday."

Polly drew Jacob aside. "Mary M is sick. I had Israel drive for her so she could rest in the wagon. I'm glad they have that new wagon. She's much more comfortable in it. George drove for me so I could help Mary M."

"What do you think's wrong with Mary M?" Jacob asked. "Do we need to find a doctor?"

Polly thought a moment. "I don't know, but I'm worried. I'm glad we're coming to a town. Remember when we were in Toledo last year, didn't we hear that they have a medical school in La Porte, Indiana? That's the next town, isn't it?"

"You're right, Polly, we should be able to find a doctor there."

In camp that night, Lucinda worked extra hard. When things were settled, she went to Mary M's new wagon. "Are you okay, Mary M? Can I help with something? I don't want you to be sick."

"O, Lucy, I don't want to be sic . . ." Coughing stopped her words. Catching her breath, she continued, "I don't want to be sick either. Jake is so proud of his new . . . *cough*, wagon. He wants to work extra to help pay Pa, and here I am, can't even help with supper . . . *cough*."

Lucinda, remembering how her ma would put her hand on her head when she was feeling sick, reached out and touched Mary M's forehead. "Oh, Mary M, your head is hot! You're burnin' up. Once when I was sick, Ma put cool cloths on my head. I'll go get some cool water and a cloth." Lucinda went to the Schooner to get a pail and a cloth. As she went around the corner of the wagon, she said, "Ma, Mary M is really hot. I'm gonna get some cold water from the stream."

When Lucy arrived back at the Studebaker, her mother was there talking to Mary M. She placed the cool cloth on her sister-in-law's forehead. "I'm praying this will help."

"Thank you, Lucy, you're a good nurse." Polly reached out and put her hand on Lucinda's shoulder. "You stay here with Mary M. I'm gonna ask Pa and Jake to check on her during the night."

Polly glanced at Lucinda with a *well-done* smile and left. It was quiet for a spell, and then Mary M coughed so hard she nearly vomited.

Lucinda kept the cool cloth on her head. Mary M spoke softly. "Lucy, I'm glad you screamed the other night. That Sid was a scary guy. I didn't like the way he looked at me. I'm glad he's gone."

When Polly returned, Lucinda asked, "Ma, can I stay here with Mary M tonight? If she gets real sick, I'll come get you."

Polly thought a moment, then nodded. "That's a good idea. I'll tell your pa you're gonna sleep here tonight."

Lucinda got ready for bed quickly and went back to the Studebaker. Polly came to the back of the wagon. "Pa wants you to call for him from the wagon seat if Mary M needs help."

"Okay, Ma, I'll keep a cool cloth on Mary M's head, and I'm gonna pray for her. Good night, Ma."

When Lucinda felt Mary M's forehead, it didn't seem as hot as before. She changed the cloth. A slight breeze moved through the wagon as the two talked for a few minutes. Lucinda saw that Mary M was getting drowsy. The cough had settled, and the young woman fell asleep. Lucinda curled up on the floor by her sister-in-law's bed. Next thing she knew, the morning sun was streaming in through an opening in the canvas. Mary M stirred, "Lucy, did you sleep there all night?" Lucinda nodded and smiled.

John, Israel, and George had caught enough trout for a special breakfast. Pa prayed for the day ahead and asked God for guidance to find help for Mary M. Following the prayer, he said, "Let's get a good start this mornin' so we can make it to La Porte by suppertime."

Polly and Lucinda looked after Mary M during the day. In midafternoon, Jake rode up with news that La Porte was only about a mile away. He reported, "It looks like quite a city. We should be able to find a doctor in that town."

A good camping spot was found near a pond with some trees for shade. As soon as the animals were tethered, Jake said, "I'm gonna ride to town and see if I can find a doctor."

John headed for his pony and announced, "I'm goin' with you, Pa." The two rode away at a gallop.

7
Aboard the Wiebe
Amsterdam
1853

P HILLIP AND TRENT ENTERED THE America office located near the Amsterdam docks. After securing their immigration documents, Phillip considered sending a message to his family but decided against it. *They don't really care about me anyway*, he thought.

The two young men purchased some bread, cheese, chocolate, and dates before heading back to the bunkhouse. They put their belongings in the mesh drawers and sat on their bunks, amazed by the events of the last few hours. Trent, in his carefree manner, soon drifted off to sleep.

Phillip, in the dimness of the bunkhouse, opened his mother's Bible to the story about a man who was helped by a Samaritan. As he read the story, he asked his mother's God to get him safely to his destination in New York. He prayed for Trent and gave thanks for Dietrich's help. When he thought of his father, his throat throbbed in pain, and a tear slipped down his cheek. He shook his head, straightened his shoulders, and vowed not to look back. The night was long, and sleep was short.

At four thirty the next morning, he roused Trent. Phillip secured his travel papers and money, having heard stories of men being robbed in America. With their belongings in hand, they headed for the dock where the *Wiebe* was waiting.

As they approached the *Wiebe*, Dietrich stepped out of his shack. "Mornin', men," he said. "I've been waitin' for ya. I have a favor to ask. My son, Dirk, shipped over to New York on the *Wiebe* a couple years ago. Would you look him up and give him this pouch? I wrote his address on it. Don't lose it. It's for my boy."

Phillip noticed dampness in Dietrich's eyes when he received the pouch. "I'll personally see he gets it," Phillip promised as they shook hands.

The first mate was a huge one-armed man called "Lefty." It was a strange name because it was his left arm that was missing. Maybe they called him "Lefty" because he could do more with his powerful right arm than any other man could do with both.

Lefty said to Phillip, "Keep the lower deck and the latrines clean." Turning to Trent, he ordered, "Keep the captain's cabin clean." That was the extent of their training.

Phillip soon knew why they needed a lower deckhand. The sailors worked a shift, drank a shift, and slept a shift. Their sleeping quarters were in the stern of the ship. Phillip never had to enter their quarters, but the steps, passageways, and latrines were his responsibility. The mixed smell of vomit, urine, excrement, tobacco spit, and body odor was sickening.

Most days, Phillip found time to read from his mother's Bible. Trent never joined him but sometimes would sit nearby. Phillip had told him that his mother died when he was young and that she always read the Bible to him. Trent would tip his head to one side as if he wanted to understand but never asked questions.

On the fifteenth day of the voyage, Phillip woke to Trent's heavy breathing and raspy cough. The room was stiflingly hot. Trent coughed until he gagged, and then he held his breath until he gasped for air. Phillip went to his friend's cot where he found him shaking with fever and in cold sweat. Phillip tried to cool his body with wet cloths on his head and chest. When Trent settled down, Phillip went to the galley where he found the cook frying side pork and eggs for the crew.

Phillip told the cook that Trent was hot with fever and could hardly breathe. The cook shrugged. "You better get Pauwels to see him. His bunk is behind the captain's quarters, the little door to the left. He'll do what he can."

Phillip knocked on the doctor's door. When Pauwels opened the door, he wore nothing but a towel around his waist. His bloodshot eyes told either of too much drink or too little sleep—maybe both. "What'd ya want?" he slurred through a heavy black beard. His hair was matted and dirty. He was about five feet tall and hunched over.

Phillip wondered what this man could do for his friend, but he knew he had no other options. "My friend Trent, the cabin boy, is sick. He can hardly breathe. Please, come help him."

Phillip learned that a ship had its own culture. This little man was known by everyone on board. They called him Doc because he exercised all kinds of cures for all kinds of ailments. Some got better, and some died.

Finally, Doc came out of his room, buttoning his pants, as he tried to tuck in his dirty shirt. He waddled down the steps to the lower deck. Upon arrival at the supply room, they found Trent thrashing about on his cot, struggling to breathe, and wringing wet. Doc stopped in his tracks just inside the room. He put his hands over his head and whispered, "Oh no! This will have the whole crew. Don't let him out of this room. It's the seamen's fever. I'm not goin' in there. You'll stay out if you know what's good for ya." He turned to leave, his hand over his mouth.

Phillip grabbed him by the shoulder. "Doc, you have to do somethin'."

Doc shook his head and kept walking. Phillip followed for a few steps and then stopped with hands on his hips. He returned to the room. *Trent saved my life on the dock. I have to do something for him.* Again, he took the cloths and cool water and tried to cut the fever. Trent settled down some but never said another word. He died before morning. Phillip was heartbroken. He hadn't realized how much that little man meant to him. With tears running down his face, he gathered Trent's belongings and put them in his bag.

Captain Hubrecht was startled out of a deep sleep at Phillip's words. "Captain, Trent, your cabin boy, is dead. Doc said it was the Seamen's Fever. There was nothing I could do."

The captain's face went whiter than a sheet. "We've got to get the body off the ship. You've been in that room. On the top shelf in the store room are some rolls of canvas. Wrap the body in one and bring it to the deck for sea burial. I'll need his passage papers when I return to Amsterdam. Don't tell anyone about this. It'll demoralize the crew."

Phillip's shoulders slumped as he shuffled back to the supply room. Trent's body was cold and wet, but light as a bag of wheat. After spreading the canvas on the floor, Phillip placed the body in one corner and rolled it up, tucking the corners in and tying twine around in two places. He dug in Trent's bag and found his passage papers in a leather pouch along with a large roll of money. *I wonder where he got all of this money?* Phillip paused for a moment. *I could trade my papers for Trent's and be a different person when I arrive in New York. My family could never find me. I could keep the money to claim land in America.* He bowed his head. His mother's words whispered in his mind, "You're a good boy, son." Tears filled his eyes as he tucked the leather pouch in a fold of the canvas, put the body on his shoulder, and headed for the deck.

The captain was waiting, obviously anxious to get this over with. Phillip handed him the pouch. "His papers and his money," he said as he lowered the body to the deck. The captain opened a small book and read some words committing Trent to the god of the sea. Phillip thought of the words that were spoken by his pastor back home when his mother died. "I am the resurrection and the life . . . In my Father's house are many mansions . . ."

"Hoist him in," the captain commanded. Phillip straightened up, gave a slight salute to the captain, lifted the body over the rail, and watched it fall into the foamy sea below. Phillip leaned over the rail until he felt a hand on his shoulder. The captain spoke softly. "He was good friend. You can keep the money. I'll just take the papers."

"No, Captain, take the money to his family when you give them notice in Amsterdam. God will provide what I need."

The captain nodded. "Now we have to deal with that room. Get your personal stuff only. Leave the blankets, the clothes you're wearing, the cots, and all of the kid's things in the supply room. Lock the door. Come to my quarters, take a bath, and put on clothes you had in your bag. You'll stay in the side room off my cabin. If you show any sign of Seamen's Fever, I'll throw you overboard. You got a new job, Cabin Boy."

Phillip followed the captain's orders. The bath felt great and clean clothes even better. Once he was cleaned up and dressed, he sat on the cot, reached in his bag, and found his mother's Bible. He opened and read,

The LORD is my shepherd; I shall not want.

He maketh me to lie down in green pastures: he leadeth me beside the still waters.

He restoreth my soul: he leadeth me in the paths of righteousness for his name's sake.

Yea though I walk through the valley of the shadow of death, I will fear no evil: for thou art with me; thy rod and thy staff they comfort me.

Thou preparest a table before me in the presence of mine enemies: thou anointest my head with oil; my cup runneth over.

Surely goodness and mercy shall follow me all the days of my life: and I will dwell in the house of the LORD for ever.

Tears soaked the page as Phillip grieved the loss of a friend who had saved his life. Yet he wasn't sure which grief was worse—the recent loss of a friend or the emptiness from the loss of his mother. He remembered how she talked about knowing Jesus in her heart. "Son," she would say, "Jesus paid it all." Phillip knew his mother had something more than the catechism and sacraments that he learned about as a child.

Phillip began to pray, remembering how his mother talked to God. "God," he prayed, "I want to know you the way my mother did. My insides hurt for Trent, and I long for Mutti." As he prayed, he felt warmth come over his body. He looked through his tears and thought he saw Jesus with his hand stretched out toward him, saying, "Come, son, I will show you the way."

A pounding on the door brought Phillip to attention. The captain's voice was gruff. "Son, it's time for my supper. Get down to the galley. Bring some for yourself." Wiping his face on his sleeve, Phillip promptly carried out the orders.

After sailing through two days of stormy weather, the *Wiebe* caught stiff winds, making it possible to tack through the waves at great speed. On the twenty-second day out, Lefty called from the bridge, "Land Ho! Land Ho! Ten o'clock over the bow."

Like rats being drowned out of their tunnels, every hand came to the deck. Phillip stepped out of his cabin and fixed his eyes on his new home. The captain took the tiller and guided the ship into the port at New York. Phillip was amazed at the buildings and the expanse of the city. *How will I ever find my way in all of that*, he wondered.

Most of Phillip's belongings were still in the store room where Trent died. *How fortunate I am that I didn't get sick. I could have been left out there in the sea too.* The captain had given him a wool blanket. He still had one change of clothes and enough money for a few days lodging and food.

Once off the ship, Phillip noticed a small building much like Dietrich's shack in Amsterdam. He approached the dock boss. "Hallo, I just came in on the *Wiebe*. How do I find the immigration office?"

The boss pointed. "Get on that wagon. It'll take you to the office over on the passenger side."

Just as he was ready to climb on the wagon, Phillip remembered. He turned back to the dock boss and said, "Do you know Dietrich from Amsterdam?"

"Ja, sure do. He got me this job," the boss answered.

"Do you know his son, Dirk? I have a parcel for him."

"Ja, do." The boss nodded. "I'll get it to him for ya."

"I told Dietrich I'd deliver it personally. Can you help me find Dirk?"

"Sure, come here at six o'clock tonight and I'll take you there."

Phillip shouted over his shoulder as he jumped on the wagon, "Thank you, I'll be here at six."

Hunger pains welled up in his stomach at the smell of pastries as they passed a small bakery. Coming to a stop, the driver pointed toward a large building with people lined up at the door. Phillip jumped down, grabbed his bag and coat, thanked the driver, and got in line at the immigration office.

The line moved slowly, causing Phil to become impatient. He sat on the stone walk, leaning against his bag, making sure his money and possessions were safe. He began to think about owning land and having a wife and children. He had pored over articles in Germany about how to strike it rich in America on good black soil with abundant crops of wheat and potatoes. Suddenly, it hit him. *Today is my birthday, October 26, 1853. I am twenty-one years old in a strange land with strange voices all around me.*

Phillip stepped up to the desk. His papers were in order, and having few possessions, the process went quickly. With his money exchanged for American currency, he heard the clock in the square strike five times, telling him he had one hour to find his way back to the cargo docks. He had watched closely as he rode over on the wagon, so he started to retrace his steps. His bag was getting heavy, and he was tired. A man in a carriage spoke to him in what must have been Norwegian. He could understand some of what he said. Finally, Phillip figured out that the man wanted to give him a ride. "Twelve cents . . . twelve . . . to cargo docks," the man said with motions.

Phillip knew he had some coins in his pocket but was unsure what they were. He held one out to the man but could soon tell it was not enough. "No, no," he reacted, shaking his head. Phil tried another, and a smile came to the driver's face. He jumped down from the carriage and put Phil's bag on the back of the buggy. Phillip watched his bag carefully as he climbed into the carriage.

"Ah ha! Just in time," the boss crowed. "I'm closin' this place and headin' home to my woman and a good supper. I'll drop you at Dirk's on the way. Good man, Dirk. Good vati back home too. Come on, this way."

The boss led the way down an ally to a stable where he hitched his horse to a small cart. "Throw your bag on and jump aboard," the boss urged. Phillip realized he would arrive at Dirk's home at suppertime. He hoped the parcel from home would offset the poor timing. The boss pulled up in front of a small house with green shutters. "Dirk, there, wife and daughter." He extended a hand to Phillip and said, "Glad to help a friend of Dietrich."

Phillip knocked on the door, spoke a brief prayer to his mother's God, and waited. The door opened. Standing in the doorway was an exact, but younger image of Dietrich. The same box-shaped upper body with huge arms coming out of the corners and the same round head and red face with a questioning look. "Ja," he said, "who's there at this hour?"

Phillip was taken back but responded by holding out the pouch. "Phillip Eppard, just arrived from Amsterdam. Your father, Dietrich, asked me to . . ."

The large man melted into tears. "You have word from Papa? Come in, please come in!" Phillip stepped inside the door and watched as Dirk hugged a sweet little blonde woman as they opened the pouch. Money fell on the table but went unnoticed as they unfolded the letter. The woman read as the two of them wept. A small girl held on to her mother's skirts.

After reading the message and gathering the money together, Dirk realized his visitor was still standing by the door. Moving toward Phillip, he reached for his wife's hand and said, "This is my wife, Greta, and our daughter, Anna." It was obvious Dirk had not remembered his visitor's name.

"The name's Phillip, I worked for your father in Amsterdam. He got me a job on a freighter to America and sent the pouch with me."

"Greta, set another place at the table for our guest. Phillip, would you spend the night with us since it is so late? We can talk together about the old country. Life has been good here, but we miss our families so much."

Greta served a tasty supper. Dirk and Phillip talked long into the night. The next morning, Dirk helped Phillip find the wagon from the lumber mills. Waving good-bye to Dirk, he climbed on the wagon and settled in for the long ride north.

A Surprise Doctor
La Porte, Indiana
1852

THE SUN MOVED BELOW THE western horizon as Jake and John rode into La Porte, Indiana. Jake was determined to get help for Mary M. He could see many shops and judged it to be a town of several thousand people. He and John tied their horses at the rail in front of the livery stable. A man with a bushy gray beard spoke from the inside. "Need some help?"

"Ya," Jake responded, "we just pulled in with five wagons. We're camped on the edge of town. My wife is sick. Any chance we could find a doctor here in La Porte?"

"Ya, we got doctors here." The man stroked his unruly beard. His eyes glistened with pride. "Got a medical school too, been goin' about ten years. Your best bet is Dr. W. W. Mayo. William Worall, I guess it is. He's got a place over on Michigan Avenue, over by all those maple trees. His name is on a post out front. He's a little guy but knows his stuff. Graduated a couple years ago from Indiana Medical College, got married, and does some doctorin' around here. He sure helped my pa when he got the gout."

Not allowing the livery man to give him the complete history of the town, Jake grabbed John's shoulder and said, "Come on, let's go find him." They rode off at full gallop toward the row of trees visible against the evening sky. The sign on the front fence was visible in the moonlight, W. W. Mayo, Doctor of Medicine. A young woman opened the door. With a smile, she said, "Can we help you? The doctor's busy with a patient. You're welcome to wait."

A few minutes later, a side door opened, and a couple with a young boy, arm in a sling, came out. The doctor, a man in his midthirties, not much over five feet tall, emerged with them. He was showing some signs of balding, making him seem older than his actual years. Looking up and down John's frame, he said, "What can we do for you, son?"

Jake reacted, "No, Doctor, it's my wife. We're camped on the edge of town. She has a high fever and a bad cough, sometimes hard to breathe. We came to town looking for a doctor. The livery man sent us here. Can you help us?"

Dr. Mayo looked up at the clock and thought a moment. "High fever, huh? Can you bring her in tomorrow morning? I'll need some specimens. We have a microscope at the medical college."

Jake was getting anxious. "Can't you come see her tonight? She's really sick. We need your help."

"Is she coughing up mucus?" the doctor asked. "I could ride out with you now and take a look, but I'll need to go to the college tomorrow. I want to check the specimens with the microscope." The doctor removed his white coat, reached for his hat, and called out, "Louise, I'm goin' on a call with these men, be back in an hour or so." Not waiting for a response, he led the way out the door. "I'll get my horse and meet you by the alley."

Riding his spirited gelding, Dr. Mayo took a shortcut down a backstreet and followed a trail out of town. "Lead the way," he shouted. Jake urged his horse on ahead, and John followed the doctor.

Upon arrival at the camp, Jake led Dr. Mayo to the Studebaker wagon. He lit two candles and set them near Mary M's bunk. The doctor greeted his patient and asked some questions. He took a long tube that looked like a trumpet on one end and a bell on the other from his black bag and held the large end to Mary M's chest and his ear to the other. He moved to several places on her chest, then on her stomach and finally on her back. Noticing the interest on Jake's face, he said, "This is a stethoscope. I just read that an Irish guy named Leared invented a better scope last year. We want to get one for our medical college."

"It isn't pneumonia," he offered. "Lungs are clear. Ears are fine. I want a specimen from your throat and a urine specimen. The baby seems to be doing well. I could hear a strong heartbeat."

"What?" Jake yelled so loud the whole camp could hear. "What do you mean the baby?"

Mary M straightened up and turned to her husband. "Oh, Jake, I didn't tell you. I've missed a couple monthlies, but I wanted to be sure. I didn't want you to be disappointed if it wasn't true. Thank you, Doctor, now we really know. I feel better already."

Dr. Mayo instructed Mary M on collecting the specimens. The whole family gathered, and Jake shared the news that he was going to be a father. That night, Polly had a mother-daughter talk with Lucinda.

The next morning, Dr. Mayo reported that he had studied the specimens under the microscope and found some bacteria. He thought Mary M would be feeling better in a few days. He was proud to have used the valued microscope.

The wagon train pressed westward. April days grew longer and warmer. Often, the evenings were cut short by rain showers. John, Israel, and George became skilled hunters, providing fresh meat for the family. One day, the three boys came riding up to the wagons at full gallop. Their faces were aglow with excitement. George shouted, "Up ahead, there's water as far as you can see. You'll never believe it, Pa, it's just flat water forever." Jacob knew their route would take them along the southern shore of Lake Michigan.

That afternoon, as the wagon train was moving steadily along, Joe rode up beside Jacob. "Boss," he said, "been meanin' to talk to you."

"Sure, Joe, what's on your mind?"

"You know, Boss, that mornin' you talked to Sid after he was makin' an attempt on the young lady? If'n that had happened to one of my kin, I think I'd a put him down. When you told me to tie him to that tree, I was mad enough to put a rope around his neck. When I heard you talk to him about bein' forgiven, I could hardly believe my ears."

"Joe, just a few days ago, I was tellin' Lucinda that I asked Jesus to forgive my sin at a Jacob Albright camp meeting when I was only ten years old. But a few years later, when we still lived in Pennsylvania, I was sowin' my wild oats a bit. My ancestors came from Ireland, and they were farmers. Then German people started comin' from the Palatinate, takin' up land around us. We wondered how we would get along with 'em. I went to school with their kids, and the boys became my friends. They were great people. One of the neighbor girls caught my eye, and I started to play up to her. One of the German boys had his eye on the same girl. The German guy got jealous and started to push me around. Having a bit of an Irish temper, I pushed him off. He kept at me until one day, I lost control and broke him up pretty bad.

"That night, his pa came over to our place, askin' to talk to me. I wanted to run, but my pa made me take my medicine. That German man walked up to me with a smile on his face and said, 'Young man, you were hard on my son today, fightin' over that pretty little neighbor girl. You know, I could have the sheriff pick you up for breaking Andy's nose. But I'm not gonna do that. Back in Germany, when I was young, my family joined up with some people called Pietists. They talked about a guy named Spener and the things he had written. I was on my way to trouble, but these people knew God, and I saw somethin' in them that I wanted. My family went to their meetings, and one night, I trusted Jesus Christ to forgive my sin. Instead of runnin' you in, I want to invite you and your family to come to our house for a prayer meetin' tomorrow night.' He turned and talked to my pa awhile and then rode off.

"Joe, as that man rode away, I remembered what I did when I was ten. We went to that meeting and more after that. I recommitted my life to Jesus and asked him to live in me. Jacob Albright died when

I was about twelve, but the Evangelical Association continued on. Class meetings were held in our home through the years. While I was on watch after you tied Sid to the tree, I started thinkin' about forgiveness. I knew my sin was forgiven, and I knew Sid could be forgiven. That's why I gave him that chance."

Joe swallowed, looked down, and rode quietly for a while. Finally, he said, "These last few days, I've been thinkin' about people I've hurt pretty bad. Sometimes I forget how big and strong I am. I can't do much 'bout it now, but I sure would if I could. Could I get to know this Jesus too?"

Jacob pulled Jenny to one side. "Let's go over under those trees until the wagons come along." The two men dismounted and let the horses graze. Jacob took a deep breath and then said softly, "Joe, every one of us is a sinner. We need God's forgiveness and new life. What we need to do is confess our sin to God and ask his forgiveness. Once we're forgiven, it's like he takes our sin and gives us his life. You can have that too." As the wagon train was approaching, the two men bowed in prayer; and when Joe opened his eyes, he knew something had changed.

Later, as the wagon train came around a curve, the sun burst forth its evening beauty, reflecting off miles of crystal. "Lake Michigan," Lucinda breathed, "it's beautiful!" The Illinois border was not far away. At supper, Joe gave thanks for his new life and shared what had happened while talking with Jacob that afternoon.

The next day, the McQuillans were aware of Lake Michigan off to the right. At times, they could see the white-caped waves. The cold wind bit into their faces. One stagecoach driver said, "It's best you take the territorial trail that goes northwest toward Elgin and on to Rockford. Keep your eyes open along there, you might see the *Pioneer*."

"What do you mean the *Pioneer*?" Jacob questioned.

The driver tipped his head and responded, "The *Pioneer* was the first locomotive to go to the town of Chicago when the *Galena & Chicago Union Railroad* started runs about four years ago."

A few days later, as the train tracks ran close to the wagon trail, a locomotive came chugging up the slope. Smoke was puffing out of the chimney, and once in a while, it let off a blast of steam. The children ran alongside the wagons, yelling and laughing as the engine approached.

Adam, concerned that the train might spook the mules, called to Israel, "Tighten the reins and bring 'em to a stop." The drivers were alert in case one of the draft animals would bolt.

Lucy was driving so Mary M could rest. She called, "Mary M, the train is coming." Lucinda gave good attention to the bays, but she got a chance to see the locomotive. As the wagon train and the locomotive met, the engineer and the fireman waved to the children. The children waved their hands and shouted greetings. Hester jumped up and down and waved his arms as the train passed by. When he was a little ways past, the engineer gave three short toots of the whistle, careful not to cause a runaway. Lucinda recorded the excitement of the day in her diary that night.

9

Staking a Claim
Wisconsin
1854

THE MANNWEILER FAMILY STEPPED OFF the train in Milwaukee, Wisconsin. Matilda nudged her father. "Look, Vati, over there, that sign says *German Immigration Office*, and it says *Welcome New Arrivals*. Let's go there, Vati, come on!"

"Ja, daughter, but we have to get our trunks first. They're over there on the platform." Just as Johann spotted the trunks and started toward them, a porter waved. "We'll bring 'em to the office. Meet you there."

The man at the desk in the immigration office was sleeping on the job. The sound of the door startled him awake. "Wel . . . Welcome to Milwaukee," he said. "Looks like you're lookin' for a claim. Middle of September's a little late to get started."

Johann spoke firmly. "Yup. No time to waste and not much money left. We started out from Hamburg in early April. Measles, delays, and storms have taken all this time. Now we need some help to get to a claim. I want some good land with a chance to make a livin' for my family. Can you help me?"

The middle-aged man stood up and put his thumbs under his suspenders as if to say, *I'm in charge here*. He spoke with a huff. "Hans is the man to help you. He's busy just now. Have a seat over there and I'll get him when he's done. Have some coffee and sweets if you wish."

The sweets tasted good, and the coffee was much appreciated. Hans came in the side door and moved quickly across the room. A smile showed through his reddish beard. He extended his hand to Johann as he said, "Welcome to Wisconsin. We represent the Wisconsin Land Agency. I understand you've had delays in getting here. We'll do everything possible to help you. Land is going at $1.25 an acre. We recommend the Princeton area. A wagon is leavin' for Princeton early tomorrow mornin'. You're welcome to stay in the bunkhouse out back tonight."

Johann spoke with urgency. "With all the delays and added expenses, my funds are nearly gone. Is there a place where I can get a loan?"

"Many families come to us with no money in hand. We do have loans available, but the land reverts to us if you're unable to firm up the claim. You'll be able to sign a loan in Princeton." As Hans turned to leave, he said, "A driver'll be here at five in the mornin'."

Johann spent the night tossing and turning in his bedroll, thinking about everything that needed to be done to be ready for winter. Early the next morning, he urged, "Let's be ready when that wagon arrives to take us to Princeton."

The coolness of the September night put a chill in the bunkhouse. Caroline hurriedly dressed and got some bread and dried meat out for a quick breakfast. The hot coffee from the office tasted good at that early hour. Matilda dressed in warm clothes and repacked her bag for what she hoped would be the last part of a long journey. "Vati," she inquired, "will we get to our new home today?"

"No, the man said it would take several days to get to Princeton. Hurry now, we want to be ready when the wagon arrives." Johann grabbed two of the bags and rushed out.

The team and wagon pulled up in front of the office. Johann waved and called, "Hello! Are you takin' us to Princeton?"

"Yup, I'm your driver." The young man spoke with an inviting voice as he jumped down over the wagon wheel. "Name's Arnold. I live in Princeton. I just put my ma and pa on the train. They've been here for a visit. Glad to have some company on the way back home."

Johann responded, "We're the Mannweilers, just in from Hamburg. We're anxious to get settled on some land. It's gotten late on us, so we want to get to Princeton as fast as possible. My name's Johann, and this is my wife, Caroline."

Soon the team was at a steady trot. Matilda snuggled under her quilt for a morning of reading. Arnold knew his team and made the necessary stops for rest and water. The maple trees were in full color, and Matilda noticed a large flock of birds flying in a huge V formation. "Geese," Arnold remarked when he saw Matilda's questioning look, "they're heading south for the winter. Good eatin', I hunt 'em in the fall."

Johann took advantage of the time with a local resident and asked, "Arnold, do you farm near Princeton?"

Arnold urged the team to a faster pace. "Yup, me, my wife, and two kids. Been there three years now. Ma and Pa came from Germany and spent the summer with us. We built a farmhouse. Another young one is due in a few months. Needed more room. You got family here?"

"Nope, it's just the three of us. We heard about Wisconsin Land Agency and decided it would be a good place to take up land. Got any advice for us?" Johann ventured.

"We live south of Princeton along the Fox River. There are some small streams and springs down there. You'll need a team and wagon, a plow, and tools to get started. You could live in a wagon for a while, but come mid-October, you'll need a cabin." Arnold pulled up on the reins, bringing the team to a walk. Looking over at Johann, he lingered a moment and spoke. "Have you thought about winterin' in Princeton and startin' out in the spring?"

Johann looked around, observing the beauty of the September day. The trees glowed in the sunlight in reds, oranges, and russets. A light breeze and a little whirlwind sent some dry grass and leaves spinning upward along the trail. "Got my mind set on takin' land this fall. The weather's still good. Don't wanna waste time."

Arnold nodded and pulled the team off the trail to give the horses a rest. He pulled a cloth bag from under the wagon seat and offered to share. Matilda noticed dried fruit and nuts. She sent a questioning glance toward her mother. Receiving a positive nod, she took a handful. They tasted good after living on bread, cheese, and dried meat for many days. Matilda wondered what it would be like to live on a claim. *Will I have any friends? Will I go to school and church?*

Arnold announced, "We should get to Princeton by suppertime. I'm stayin' in town tonight. I have to get supplies tomorrow before headin' home. You can camp by the agency tonight."

The agency office was on the main street of the town of Princeton. Johann pointed down the street. "Look, Caroline, there's a store. Take Matilda with you and buy some food for supper and breakfast. We'll camp by those trees. The weather looks good, and we need to save every cent we can. I'm goin' down to the livery to see if I can find a team and wagon for sale. We can't go any farther without a wagon. Tomorrow, we'll see about a claim."

Arnold was unhitching his team by the livery when Johann arrived. "Come on, I'll introduce you to Fred. Maybe he'll know where you can buy a team and wagon." They walked through the gate and past a row of stalls. "Hey, Fred," Arnold called, "I got you a customer here."

A man of about fifty came out from one of the stalls. Fred took off his hat and rubbed his head. "I can't keep up with all the work. Farmers are comin' to town to sell crops, wantin' a place for their horses. When it rains, it pours around here. What can I do for ya?"

Arnold answered, "This is Johann Mannweiler. I just brought him and his family from Milwaukee. He's lookin' for a team. He wants to get started on a claim yet this fall. Got somethin' for him?"

"Sure glad you asked," Fred said with a grin. "Just today, a farmer came in with his family. They're givin' up and movin' back home. He had to sell his stuff in a hurry. I bought the whole thing. Got it cheap and I'll sell it for ten bucks over what I paid."

"Give me a look," Johann responded as he felt a flutter in his chest. "I may be interested. I need to get started right away to get set up for winter."

Arnold shook hands with Johann and wished him well. "Fred'll show you the road to the south. Stop by sometime. It's the place with the red barn back to the east about four miles down."

Fred led the way through the back gate. Darkness was settling in quickly, but Johann could see a covered wagon with tattered canvas draped over wooden hoops. "Canvas is shot, but the hoops look good. Look in the wagon. There's a plow, some tools, broadax, grub hoe, shovels, about everything you'll need. Emmitt, the blacksmith, could sharpen the plowshares for ya. Look, it has a coulter to cut the sod, that's a big help. You can cut sod for your cabin with that one. Always good to use some sod at the bottom for warmth. Emmitt's a good one. He can set you up with new canvas too. I'll sell you the whole thing as is for fifty bucks."

"What about a team?" Johann asked. "I'm wonderin' if I should have horses or oxen."

Fred rubbed his head again and responded, "Oxen can work harder and longer than horses. It's good to have a horse to ride as well as work. The team that came with this wagon is in the stable. They look good and strong. They're yours for ten bucks."

Johann wondered if God was blessing him with everything they would need. The two men walked back to the stable. "Right there in that stall," Fred said with a motion toward a pair of sorrels. "I drove 'em on a delivery today. The owner said the mare is bred to foal in the spring. The gelding is strong and good to ride."

Johann reached a hand to Fred. "Will a handshake keep 'em until noon tomorrow? I need to go to the agency office and work things out. I'll be here before noon."

Supper was ready by a little campfire when Johann arrived. He prayed the well-known prayer but ended with, "Thanks too, God, for bringing us here and please help us get everything we need tomorrow."

As they ate the fried eggs and bread, washed down with fresh cups of coffee, Johann told them about the possible deal at the livery.

Before going to sleep, Johann counted the little money he had. He could make a down payment on the land, buy the team and wagon, and have a little left for household supplies. He decided he should ask for a loan so he could buy some lumber for the floor, loft, and door for a cabin. He needed feed for the horses and seed for spring planting. Finally, fatigue took over, and he slept soundly through the night.

"Good morning, Vati," Matilda said with a smile when her father finally opened his eyes. "We thought you were gonna sleep the day away. Come, breakfast is ready."

As they were eating, a man dressed in brown trousers, a tan shirt with a string tie, a vest, and a brown hat rode up on a pinto pony. "You must be the family wantin' to get out on a claim yet this fall," he said with a shrug. "Come on in and we'll talk."

The office was a small room with a desk in the center. Johann approached the desk. "I'm Johann Mannweiler. We just arrived from Hamburg. We had delays on the way with measles, storms, and missed connections. We meant to be here by July. We need to get on a claim soon to be ready for winter."

The agent offered his visitor a chair and sat down behind the desk. "My name is Bert, representing Wisconsin Land Agency. We have claims all right, but it is terribly late to get started now. Have you considered wintering in Princeton?"

"I don't have the money for lodging. With all the delays, my funds have run short. In fact, they told me in Milwaukee that I'd be able to get a loan to tide me over. I have enough for a small down payment on the land. I have a good deal on a team, wagon, and equipment over at the livery. We need a loan to cover supplies for the family and some lumber for buildin' a cabin."

"Winters can get pretty mean around here," Bert responded. "We could help you find a place for the winter, and you could get on a claim in the spring."

Johann scratched his head and looked down at the floor. "You know, I've had my mind set on gettin' that land. Now we're here, I can't bring myself to wait. Can you see my thinkin'?"

"Well, it's your doin' and your family. We don't recommend it, but if that's your decision, you can get a quarter section for $200. We need $20 down, and you have five years to pay off the rest. It's hard for some, but most make it."

Bert walked over to a map pinned on the wall. Pointing, he said, "You can take your pick. South of here is a good choice right now. A claim with both open land and trees provides logs for a cabin and firewood, as well as land that can be broken for crops."

Johann stammered a little and said, "Wh . . . what about a loan?" He hated feeling like he had to beg for help.

"The bank is down Main Street a piece. They'll answer that question. I can draw up some papers that you can take with you to the bank. The $20 will be due on May 1 if you've found a claim and built a cabin to live in."

Johann squared his shoulders and walked with determination to the family camp. "Matilda, stay here with our things while Mutti and I go to the bank. We shouldn't be gone long." He motioned to Caroline, and the two of them headed for the bank.

During the trip, Matilda had learned how to be content. She was getting interested in a story in her book when she heard a small voice. "Hallo, hallo, are you all alone?" Matilda turned to see the source of the words. "Over here," the voice continued, "by the well. My name is Helga. I live down there in that rooming house."

Helga was dressed in a plain blue dress with a sash tied around her waist. Brown curls hung below her matching blue bonnet. She spoke broken German but was easily understood. She walked slowly toward Matilda. "I saw you arrive last night on that wagon. I've been watchin' you this mornin'. I saw your ma and pa leave and thought we could talk."

Matilda wondered what her parents would think if she talked with a local girl. Yet she couldn't see any harm in it. She offered Helga a seat on a trunk and poured two cups of coffee. "Helga, that's a pretty name. I have a friend in Germany named Helga. My name is Matilda, Matilda Mannweiler."

"That's a nice name too," Helga said in what was nearly a whisper. "I'm thirteen. We came here when I was ten. My vati died last year, and we moved to town. Mutti couldn't keep the land. She works in that café down there. We get to eat at the café, and they pay for our room at the rooming house. Guess that's okay." She stopped and looked at her new acquaintance with a questioning look.

Matilda responded, "We just got here last night. We had a long trip from Hamburg. I got the measles and had to wait weeks in Liverpool, and then our sailing ship went through weeks of storms. I thought we would never get here. My vati wants to take a claim here."

"I go to school here in Princeton during the winter," Helga shared. "We go to church too. It's Methodist. The preacher comes once a month. We meet at the Lange's house on Sundays." Matilda wondered, *Will I get to go to church and school when we get settled?*

Matilda put her hand on Helga's arm. "Helga, I'm so glad to meet you. I hope we can see each other often. Maybe I can go to school or church with you sometime. I'd like that."

Caroline returned to the campsite. Matilda jumped up and said, "Mutti, I have a new friend. This is Helga. She lives over there, and we've been visiting." Caroline spoke to Helga and thanked her for visiting her daughter.

Helga excused herself and left for home. Caroline turned to her daughter. "Vati went to the livery and will be coming for us soon. He bought a wagon and a team, and we're gonna go find a claim. We need to get everything ready to go."

Johann arrived at the livery just as the sun was straight up. Fred greeted him, "Wondered if you changed your mind on the deal I offered. I'd like to get rid of those two. Got plenty of hay burners around here."

"Arrangements on land took longer than I hoped," Johann said hurriedly. "I'm sure interested in the team, all right. I'd like another look at the wagon in the daylight."

Out back, Fred lifted the wagon tongue and swung it back and forth. "Fifth wheel seems in good shape. Wheels need grease, and the iron tires could use some work. With new canvas, you got a good rig. Emmet will treat you right."

Looking inside the wagon, Johann found it full of tools and even some corn in the box under the seat. "You got yourself a deal. Let's get that team hitched. Where's that blacksmith located?"

"You'll find him down at the end of the main drag, just off to the left." Fred took a horse collar from a peg, gave the mare a pat on the rump, and said, "Get over there, Maud." As he buckled the collar, he spoke to Johann. "The mare is Maud, and the gelding is Louie. Call 'em what you want, but that's what the owner said."

Johann spoke to his newly acquired team and, with a wave to Fred, swung up the street to get his family. Finding Caroline and Matilda ready to go, he circled around the camp and said, "Whoa, Maud, whoa there, Louie." Smiling, he turned to his family. "How do you like the names of our new horses?"

Matilda thought she could think of better names, but Maud and Louie would do. Johann jumped down from the wagon, scratched his head, and pondered, "Guess we may as well leave our things here. I need to take the wagon to the blacksmith for repairs. We'll stay here another night." He climbed back on the wagon and said, "I'll be back soon. Let's have supper at that little café tonight. I'd like to get a room and a place to take a bath before bedtime." That sounded good to Matilda.

Caroline took out some mending, and Matilda went back to her book. Suddenly, a thought popped into Matilda's head. "Mutti," she said, "Helga lives in that rooming house down there. Maybe we could find a room there for tonight. Her mutti works at that café. Could we see if they could help us?"

Caroline responded, "Maybe, we'll need to see what Vati says when he gets back." Matilda looked toward the rooming house, wishing Helga would come back.

Johann found Emmet pounding out some plowshares on his anvil. Johann shouted above the noise, "I need some work done on my wagon. Could you get at it today?"

Emmet doused the share in the cooling tank, sending up a cloud of steam. "Ja, been expectin' ya. Fred said he was sendin' you over. What can I do for ya?"

"Well, you better look the team over and see if they need to be shod. The wagon needs new canvas, and the plowshares need to be sharpened. The wheels need repairin'. If you can get started, I'll look through the rest of the stuff and see what we need."

Emmet spit a stream of tobacco juice into his forge, raising a smelly sizzle. "Ja, I know this outfit. Too bad the Beckers couldn't make it. Ague took their children, and the missus was frail. Had to hang it up." Johann's heart jumped at the story, but he didn't let himself consider the consequences of what he was doing.

Johann urged, "I need to get out to take a claim soon. Winter is not far away. When can I come back for the wagon?"

With another spit in the forge, Emmet nodded toward a young man in the back of the shed. "With Eddie's help, we'll get you out of here before noon tomorrow."

Johann nodded and said, "Much obliged! I'll be back at noon." He walked back to his family, watching for a rooming house along the way.

Matilda ran up to her father. "Vati, Helga came over here this morning. She is thirteen just like me. Her vati died, and her mutti works at that café. They live in that roomin' house down there. I could find Helga and see if we could get a room where she lives. She's really nice and seems to need a friend. Could I, Vati? Could I?"

"Whoa, just a minute! Who's Helga?" Johann looked down at his daughter. He thought, *She sure is growing up fast. Guess she needs a friend. It'll be lonely out on a claim.*

"Helga's my *freundin*. She lives right down there," Matilda urged. "Let's go see if we can get a room for tonight." Both father and daughter walked away toward the rooming house. Caroline watched them and considered, *Like father, like daughter. They even walk alike.*

A room was rented, the baths were refreshing, and the sun was setting in the west when Helga led the way to the little café on the main street of Princeton. As they entered the café, Helga turned to the Mannweilers and said, "My mutti's name is Olinda. You'll like her."

Helga moved to a table in the back of the café. "This is where we eat. You can sit here too. Mutti will come over here when she has time." Johann observed the men making rude remarks to the waitress at a table across the room. One of them reached out and patted her on the thigh. She backed away and continued to take their order. In a few minutes, she came to see who had come in with her daughter.

Helga jumped up and met her mother as she approached the table. "Mutti," she said, "these are my new friends. They were camping by the agency office. Matilda is thirteen just like me. They have a room for tonight at the rooming house. Can they eat with us?"

"Slow down, Helga," the mother cautioned. "Yes, they can eat with us, but . . ."

Johann stood and put a hand on Caroline's shoulder as he spoke. "We are Johann and Caroline Mannweiler. We just arrived last night from Hamburg. We're going out to take a claim tomorrow. We need some food and will be stayin' at the roomin' house tonight. Helga and our daughter, Matilda, met at our camp this morning. It looks like they're becoming friends. We'd be honored to have supper with you."

"Please be seated. Olinda is my name. I'll bring your food as soon as I serve the other table." Helga's mother left with a little nod toward Caroline.

The food tasted so good after days of bread, cheese, and dried meat. All three Mannweilers ate until they could eat no more. At the rooming house, Johann and Caroline went to their room, while Matilda asked if she could go with Helga. The girls spent the evening talking until Helga's mother came home from work. Olinda asked Matilda, "Do you think your vati and mutti would like to come to our room for coffee before they go to bed?"

"Oh," Matilda responded, "that would be so much fun. I'll go see."

Soon Matilda and Caroline returned. "Vati was too tired, but Mutti wanted to come for a visit." Olinda invited Caroline to the table in the corner of the room as she poured two cups of coffee.

"I understand you're headin' out to take a claim tomorrow," Olinda remarked.

Caroline took a swallow of coffee. "Yes, Johann is so anxious to get land. He's had a hard time in Germany and just can't wait to have his own place. Everyone tells us it's too late to get started, but my husband is set on findin' our place and buildin' a cabin before winter. He bought a team and wagon today. Tomorrow, we'll leave to go out south of Princeton to find a claim." She looked up at her new friend with a worried look in her eyes.

A lump came up in Olinda's throat as she remembered her own experience on a claim. "It is late all right. If weather stays good, you could get a cabin up in a few days. You'll find that your neighbors will be inquisitive and want to help. Spring would be better, but I know how these men are once they get their minds made up. My man was that way. He was a good man and a man of God too. I miss him, and Helga misses her vati."

The two women sat quietly for a moment. Caroline ventured, "Would I be too bold if I asked what happened to your husband?"

A tear slipped down Olinda's cheek. She took a deep breath. "It was that ague that went through here a couple of years ago. He got a high fever and would shake the whole bed with the shivers. I tried everything to help him. The doctor came but couldn't do anything for him. We lost two children too. Only Helga and I are left. I would go back to Germany, but there isn't anything there for me. I'm just glad to have work at the café and a place to live. Sometimes the men get a little fresh, but I ignore them. God has been my help."

Caroline and Matilda spent the next morning buying supplies at the general store. Johann made some necessary purchases at the hardware store. Emmet had the team hitched and ready to go when Johann arrived at noon.

Maud and Louie were willing to take them along at a steady trot. Once, they shied to the side when a flock of prairie chickens flushed out of the tall grass. Johann spoke to them and kept them at their pace. A gentle breeze whispered through the oak trees along the trail. Fall definitely was in the air. Johann daydreamed as he sat with his wife and daughter on the wagon seat. *Someday, I'll have a beautiful home, a big barn with a herd of cows. We'll have a church and a school. God will help us.*

After crossing a little stream, Johann stopped in the shade of an oak tree. Caroline and Matilda had been dozing on their quilts in the wagon. Both mother and daughter put out some lunch while Johann gave the team a drink. He wondered, *How will I know we are there? God, I need your guidance.*

Louie let out a soft whinny, and Maud's ears leaned forward as she looked off in the distance. Matilda said, "Vati, there's a wagon down there. It's comin' this way."

It was a team of blacks on a light wagon moving at a fast pace, but it slowed when the driver spotted the Mannweilers. The driver was dressed in black with a large black Stetson hat. The approaching rig pulled to a stop across the trail from the Mannweilers. The driver set the wagon brake and jumped down over the wheel. As he walked across the trail, he spoke in a strong German voice. "Mannweiler, by any chance? I heard you might be comin' today." He stretched out a hand to Johann and continued, "My name's Eldwin Bauer. I live down the trail a piece. Welcome to Green Lake County."

Bewildered by the sudden arrival of a young man he had never met yet knew his name, Johann stepped forward and accepted the handshake. "Yup, I'm Johann Mannweiler. How'd you know my name way out here? I never expected to see anyone, let alone someone callin' my name."

"I saw Arnold last night," the man responded. "He lives just down the trail. You'll see his barn when you pass. I live just beyond him on the next claim. Arnold and me, we watch the place for the agency. We don't want any claim jumpin' or any bad blood. Arnold said you're good folks. I'm wonderin' if I could help you find a spot. I've been prayin' for you."

"That would be mighty kind of you. I've been wonderin' how to know what's taken and what ain't." Johann paused. "Oh, Mr. Bauer, is that the name?" Getting a nod from the young man, Johann continued, "This is my wife, Caroline, and my daughter, Matilda. We're anxious about our late start, but I want to get on our land. Your help would be much appreciated."

Eldwin offered, "I'll turn my rig around and lead the way. The claims are surveyed out in 160 acres each. I'd suggest another mile down. You'll need a source of water and some trees for logs and firewood. This area all drains down to Green Lake."

Johann nodded and jumped up on his wagon. Eldwin turned around and started down the trail. After about a mile, Johann noticed Eldwin pointing off to the left toward a farmstead couched against a hillside. "Must be Arnold's place," Johann assumed.

The trail veered to the right and up a steep hill, following a ridge through a stand of maples. They came to a clearing that opened into a vista of autumn beauty, stretching down a gentle slope toward a lake far in the distance. The fluffy white clouds in the afternoon sun cast shadows on the prairie. About a quarter of a mile to the south was a row of willows and aspen crowned with golden leaves. Johann said, "Must be a pond or a stream down there."

Eldwin turned and motioned to Johann to pull up beside him. "I'd suggest you camp down by those willows tonight. You'll have water there for the horses and protection from the wind. It's gettin' late, and I want to show you the lay of the land. Have your wife take your wagon down there and come ride with me over to the corner markers of the claims."

Caroline grew up driving horses in Germany. The flurry of a flock of prairie chickens caused Maud to jump against Louie, and the load in the wagon shifted. Caroline took a tighter hold of the reins as they approached their destination.

Johann and Eldwin made a circle along the hardwoods. Eldwin pointed out a large boulder that had been rolled into position to mark the corner of the four sections of land. "You could take your choice of any one of the quarter sections from here. The southeast corner includes the aspens down there. They would be good for building a log cabin. I'm not wantin' to decide for ya, but I know how long it takes to build using hardwood logs. You need some shelter for the team as well as your family and plenty of grass to put up for feed for the horses for winter."

Johann answered, "Let's drive across to the far corner so I can see if we have any hardwood trees on that corner." Eldwin nodded and urged his team to a trot toward the far corner. Johann was watching Caroline and Matilda as they made their way toward the willows. He could see a good site for a cabin on a slope near the aspen grove. "Look," he said, "I think those oaks over there would be on this quarter."

Eldwin drew the team to a stop. "Yup, you're right. This quarter would give you prairie to break up for crops, a stand of hardwood for later building and firewood, as well as a great homesite with protection down by the stream."

Johann said, "I think we just found our new home. From that big rock, I would have a half mile each direction, making a square. What do I do to claim this piece?"

Eldwin smiled. "*Freund*, all you need to do is build a cabin and live on it and make a livin' for your family. I'll take you down to your family and hightail it for home."

The sun was setting in the west when Eldwin waved good-bye. "Arnold and I will stop over in a few days to see how you're doin'. By the way, do you have a rifle with you? I'm sure deer will be comin' to the stream for a drink in an hour or so. Good eatin' this time of year."

"Ja, I picked up a supply of bullets in town, and my gun is in one of the trunks in the wagon. I'll give it a try soon as we get unpacked. Much obliged for all your help."

Johann looked around for a level place to park the wagon. "Come on, Maud and Louie, let's get this wagon in place. It'll be our home for a month or more."

The Mannweilers fell into a three-way embrace. Johann affirmed, "We're home! I'm gonna build a log cabin over there on that slope. It'll be safe from flooding in the spring. We'll have the morning sun and protection from the north wind." He bowed. "Thank you, God, for bringing us to our new home. God, please give us strength to prepare for winter. Your Word says, 'I can do all things through Christ who strengthens me.' We need your strength right now."

Working far into the evening by the light of a full moon, they unloaded the plow and tools from the wagon, making room for sleeping. They cut prairie grass to fill the mattress ticks. Caroline remembered the geese they had seen during the day and realized it would take a long time to get enough down to make a feather bed. She thought, *This will have to do until we have something better.*

It had been a long hard day. After one last hot cup of coffee, the Mannweilers climbed into their wagon home and pulled their quilts up against the night air.

The Lumber Camp
Upper New York
1853-1855

P HILLIP PULLED THE COLLAR OF his heavy wool coat up around his neck as the wagon moved slowly toward the upper New York lumber camp. *Now I'm glad I lugged that coat all this way*, he thought. About sixty men were at the tables for supper that evening. He and the other newcomers were given work orders for the next day.

Phillip soon learned that lumbering happened in two seasons. In the colder months of the year, the men worked in the forests, cutting down trees and sawing them into logs to be floated down the rivers to the sawmills after spring thaw. In the warmer part of the year, the men were transferred to the sawmills to make boards and dimension lumber from the logs. Both the forest and the sawmills were dangerous places to work.

The next day, after choosing a heavy double bit ax and a set of files for sharpening, Phillip jumped on the wagon that shuttled the men to the work site. As he boarded the wagon, Bruno, a large bearded man in bibs and red plaid shirt, stuck out his foot, causing Phil to lunge forward and sprawl out on the wagon floor.

"Lookie here"—he laughed—"we got us a German with his shiny new ax. He's as green as the trees we cut. Hey, guys, we better train him in good this mornin'."

Phillip pulled himself up and found a place on the bench on the side of the wagon. He decided he would make friends with that big guy as soon as possible. At the work site, Phillip noticed a small wagon with vats of hot coffee. He drew a large cup. The first sip of the strong brew made his eyes water.

He heard a loud voice. "Eppard! Get over here! Put your hones in that box, cut your name in it, and get ready to go."

Using his pocket knife reminded him of his father. His throat tightened as he carved his name in the wooden box that would become the only private thing he had while working as a lumberman.

"You're on the trimmin' crew," the foreman ordered. "When a tree is down, you strip off all the branches. Work with the guys on your team. You start on one end, someone else on the other. Okay, let's go!"

Three other men were starting to strip logs. Phillip had done this many times back home, having used an ax since he was a child. Straddling a log with his long legs, he started swinging his sharp new ax, severing branches with each blow. He soon slowed down to a steady pace, keeping up with the crew.

Glancing to one side, he saw Bruno with his partner measuring off a sixteen-foot length of the tree they just stripped. The two men started cutting through the log with a crosscut saw. Bruno looked over his shoulder at Phillip and shouted, "Pretty handy with that ax for a greenhorn. Your hands will show it by night." Phillip knew what he meant when he removed his gloves at quitting time. Blisters had broken, and blood oozed from the sores.

January of 1854 brought cold days with steady snow, turning the woods into a winter wonderland. Pay envelopes held about twelve dollars a month. Phillip could see he was making little progress toward his dream of land ownership. He had earned the respect of the lumber crew, and even old Bruno had become a friend.

It happened when Bruno's partner came down with a high fever and couldn't work. Bruno asked the foreman if Phil could take his partner's place. As it turned out, a scarlet fever epidemic was attacking the camp. When the fever hit Bruno, Phillip brought him an extra quilt and bathed him with cool water. Then Phillip woke one morning with a burning fever and a dry, inflamed throat. In a few days, his neck and chest were covered with a rough rash. While Phillip was dreadfully sick, a traveling evangelist walked into the quarantined area of the bunkhouse, standing tall with a broad smile showing through his bushy whiskers. He moved from cot to cot speaking with the sick and dying men. He approached Phillip, placed his hand on his shoulder, and prayed. Phil's throat tightened as he was reminded of his mother's prayers. He wondered if he soon would join her in whatever lies beyond this life.

After about three weeks, the rash began to clear, and Phillip's appetite returned. For some reason, his head had gone bald as a result of the fever. Finally, both he and Bruno regained their strength and went back to work in the woods. The evangelist moved on to another camp, but his visit left Phillip with a renewed desire to read his mother's Bible.

One evening, Bruno came past Phillip's cot. "Is that the Good Book you're readin'?" he asked as he plunked down on his friend's cot. "Read a little for me. I could use some too." Phillip read the story about some men who let a paralyzed friend down through the roof so Jesus could heal him. The man left carrying his bed and his sin forgiven.

Bruno started to make a habit of coming by when Phil was reading. One night, Phillip handed Bruno the Bible and said, "Why don't you read this time?" Bruno jumped up and stammered, "Got . . . got to . . . got to go to bed."

The next day, out in the woods, Bruno sat down next to Phillip during lunch. "Hey, partner, sorry about last night. Guess I need to get honest with ya. Never had a chance to learn to read, feel pretty dumb. My pa ran off when I was a kid, and I've been supportin' my ma ever since. I send 'er most of what I make here at the camp. Too late for book learnin' now, but I sure like to hear you read."

"Sure, Bruno, I understand. Stop by any time." The two men became good friends.

Winter

Princeton, Wisconsin
1854

T HE SHIP PITCHED AND ROLLED. Water gushed over the bow. Matilda gripped the starboard rail with all her might. Cold water splashed on her face. Startled, she woke up in a cold sweat, her hands clasped to a hoop of the covered wagon. It took a moment to realize she was not on a ship on the Atlantic, but sleeping on a grass-filled mattress in a covered wagon in Wisconsin. Then she heard her pa's voice. "Get up there, Maud!" She wondered, *What's he doing with the horses this early in the morning?*

Finally getting her bearings, Matilda found her mother by the fire, making buckwheat cakes. "Come, Matilda, coffee's ready. Did you sleep well?"

"Oh, Mutti, I had a terrible dream. I was on a ship in a storm out on the ocean." She poured a cup of coffee. "What is Vati doing with the horses at this hour?"

"He's been workin' since four o'clock this mornin'. He cut the grass where the cabin will be, and he's using the plow to cut the sod and dig into the hillside for the cabin. We need to fix a good breakfast for him."

Johann worked with all his might through the whole day until darkness closed in. By the fire, Caroline noticed Johann rubbing his hands. She asked, "What's wrong with your hands, Johann?" He opened his clasped hands, revealing huge blisters and draining sores. "Oh, Johann! We must do something or you'll get an infection." Caroline melted some venison fat to use as a salve on her husband's hands. Over the next days, his hands became callused for hard work.

The weather held for the next week. Johann worked from dawn to dark every day. He dug into the hillside to make most of one cabin wall. He cut aspen logs and laid up the walls to about seven feet. Caroline and Matilda cut grass into short pieces and mixed it with clay and sand to chink between the logs.

As time passed, Matilda kept track of the days and dates in her diary. It was a beautiful Saturday morning in late September. The dew sparkled like diamonds in the sunlight. Pa was notching a log with his broadax as Ma hung venison to dry above the fire.

At the sound of a low whinny, Matilda wondered what had caught Louie's attention. Maud's ears lay forward as she looked to the northwest. Matilda called, "Vati, look! A wagon is coming!" Johann looked up briefly, wiped the sweat from his face onto his sleeve, and resumed chopping the notch in the log.

Caroline thought immediately, *I have no food to share with company.* She put the coffeepot on the fire.

As the wagon drew closer, they recognized Arnold's team. A woman was sitting next to the driver, and others were in the wagon. Matilda noticed Eldwin in the back of the wagon along with a woman and several children. Johann put the broadax down and stepped over to welcome the visitors. *I'm too busy for visitors,* he thought, *but it's good to see some people.* "Good mornin'!" he called. "Welcome! Come have a cup of coffee. We don't have much of a place to sit," he apologized.

Arnold set the wagon brake, jumped over the wheel, and helped an attractive woman down. Eldwin stepped off the rear of the wagon and gave a hand to assist his wife. Four children jumped to the ground.

After proper handshakes and greeting, Arnold said, "Hey, man, you've got quite a cabin goin' there. Looks like you've been workin' day and night. Looks good!" Arnold turned and took his wife's arm as he noticed Caroline approaching. "This is my wife, Adelle, and our son, Alvin. And that's our eight-year-old daughter, Berta, over there runnin' after a butterfly. She never stops." Caroline noticed that Adelle was with child and obviously close to delivery.

Eldwin stepped up and said, "And this is my wife, Dagmar, and our twin daughters, Gerda and Gertrude. They're eleven and have been dyin' to meet Matilda."

Johann introduced his family and invited the visitors to have a cup of coffee. As he turned to lead the group over to the fire circle, Arnold spoke up. "Johann, we don't want to take you away from your work. We came to help with your cabin. We brought some tools, and Adelle and Dagmar brought food for lunch. Gerda and Gertrude love to go fishin'. Maybe Matilda would like to give it a try. What can Eldwin and I do to help?"

Johann was taken aback by the generosity. Then he grinned. "Well, I've been wonderin' how I was gonna get the roof on alone. I have the cross logs ready, and the logs for the rafters are about ready. I have to split some clapboards for shingles. Here, let me show you what I'm thinkin'."

As the men discussed the cabin, Caroline invited Dagmar and Adelle over to the fire circle. They spent the afternoon talking, and the neighbor ladies gave Caroline pointers about preserving meat and tanning the hides for rugs or robes. Caroline was so thankful to have some women to talk to.

The four girls scrambled through the trees to the stream. Dagmar called after the twins, "Keep an eye on Berta down there!"

Matilda watched as Gerda put a worm on her hook. Gertrude walked along the stream, ready to try her luck. Matilda held the stick and line in her hand, wondering what to do. She felt squeamish about putting a worm on the hook. Gerda looked up at her and said, "They won't hurt ya, just poke the hook through it. Here, like this," she said as she slipped the hook through a juicy worm.

About that time, Gertrude let out a scream. "I got one! I got one!" she shouted. "It's a big one, a really big one. It's a trout!" Gertrude cut a forked willow stick and threaded it through the gills of the trout.

Then she stuck one end in the bank of the stream and let the fish lay in the cool water.

Soon Gerda caught a trout and added it to the stick. Matilda was not having any luck until Gertrude gave her some help. Soon she added two fish to the catch. By noon, they had eight large trout on the stick. Gertrude ventured, "Let's see if Mutti will clean these, and we can have fish for supper."

Holding up the willow stick, Gertrude announced, "Look, Mutti! We caught eight trout, nice big ones. Can we have fish for supper?" Dagmar glanced at Caroline, wondering if she had a skillet for frying fish.

Through the day, Arnold and Eldwin cut and set the rafters in place. Johann laid the floor of the loft. Alvin, with froe and mallet, split enough clapboard shingles to cover the roof. By late afternoon, Johann breathed a sigh. "Thank you, neighbors, now I know we'll have shelter for the winter." Arnold offered to come back next week to help lay up a chimney for a fireplace.

The fried fish along with the food the Maiers and Bauers had brought made for a feast. The three families gathered by the fire. Johann prayed his traditional prayer and added thanksgiving for new friends. Matilda took a plate of food and sat on the ground by their wagon. The twins joined her. Alvin hesitated and then took a place near the three girls. Matilda looked up from her plate to see Alvin smiling at her. She felt her face flush as she looked down again.

The Bauers and Maiers climbed into the wagon to head for home. Matilda noticed that Alvin glanced her way just as he stepped up on the wagon wheel. As they drove away, Johann called out, "Thank you! Thank you, friends, for your help!"

Arnold kept his promise to help with the fireplace chimney, and the fire felt good in the cabin on frosty October mornings. Johann worked hard every day, chopping wood for winter and cutting and stacking prairie grass for the horses. Louie and Maud now had protection from cold and wind in a small lean-to. The horses' coats grew thicker as the cold came on. Maud began to show that her colt would come in early spring.

Caroline and Matilda helped Pa cut wood and stack it alongside the cabin. Sometimes Matilda went hunting with him to help drag a deer home. Matilda learned to snare rabbits and butcher them.

In spite of Johann's hunting success, Caroline was concerned about having enough food for the winter. She wished they had a cow and some chickens for fresh milk and eggs. Knowing how hard Johann was working, she didn't burden him with her worries about the food supply. The flour was more than half gone, and they were down to the last bag of potatoes. To make sure Johann and Matilda had enough food, she determined to eat less herself.

One day Johann complained, "Caroline, I work hard every day, I need more meat and potatoes for dinner. I get hungry cuttin' wood. I saw a flock of turkeys bunchin' up in a grove of willows upriver. Tomorrow, I'll take my gun and go get a couple."

Caroline slowly took a deep breath, knowing how the food supply looked, and agreed, "Bring as many turkeys as you can. It's getting cold enough to keep the meat frozen." She wanted to tell Johann about her worries, but she decided to wait once again.

The next morning, Johann took his gun and walked upriver, looking for the flock of turkeys. He found where they had roosted for the night, followed the tracks, but came up empty-handed.

By evening, a dark cloud bank had formed in the northwest. The damp chill in the air was a sure sign a storm was moving in. Johann brought a wagonload of wood to the cabin. "Matilda," he called, "looks like a storm is comin' on. Get a good supply of wood in by the fireplace in case of a blizzard."

"Okay, Vati," she responded. "Did you get some turkeys?"

Johann unhitched the horses and took them to the stall in the lean-to. "No, they had moved out before I got there. I'll try again this evenin'."

By the time the wood was unloaded, the wind blew at gale force. Caroline served a meager supper. Neither Matilda nor her pa noticed that Caroline ate only a crust of bread and drank some water. She busied herself at the fireplace, adding wood to get as much warmth as possible. The wind whistled through the trees and tugged at the door. Johann prayed his traditional prayers and added, "God, please keep the roof on our cabin."

Matilda watched her father bank the fire for the night. She climbed up the ladder and crawled into her bed in the loft. They rolled up in their quilts and deerskins against the cold of the night. Matilda burrowed down in her bed, covering her ears to hold out the sound of the wind. Johann added wood to the fire every hour. By morning, the supply in the cabin was gone. Caroline found a thin layer of ice on the water bucket when she went to make coffee, using the grounds from the previous day.

"I'm gonna get some wood," Johann said as he opened the cabin door. The snow was banked waist-deep in the doorway. The wind blew in with force, causing a flurry of sparks to swirl up the fireplace chimney. He quickly pushed the door shut to keep the fire from going out. "Caroline," he urged, "get your big cookin' kettle and put the coals we have in it. We have to keep them alive while I dig my way out to get more wood."

Caroline used a small shovel to gather the last coals into the kettle. As she worked, her body shook with cold. She covered the kettle, leaving an opening for air. When she straightened up, she had to catch herself with one hand on the trunk that was used as a table. The room started spinning before her eyes. Hunger gnawed at her stomach. Cold possessed her body. She wanted to lie down, but she knew her family needed her.

"Matilda," Pa called, "open the door and hold it while I dig my way out." Without fire, the cabin had already taken in the cold of the morning. Even with warm boots, Matilda's feet were freezing. She responded to her pa's request. Her hands stung with cold. She used all of her strength to hold the door until she heard her pa say, "Let it shut, but be there when I get back."

Johann rounded the corner of the cabin and trudged toward the woodpile. The wind tugged at his coat, threatening to take him to the ground. He caught his breath and moved to pick up an armload of wood, only to see that snow had covered the entire pile. He tried to kick the snow aside, but it was too deep. His tools were in the lean-to. It was only fifty feet from the house, but the blowing snow hid it from sight. Bracing himself against the wind, he made his way to the lean-to. Maud and Louie stood close against each other in the shelter of the log wall. They whinnied as Johann arrived. He dragged a supply of prairie grass hay to each of them, then found his shovel and made his way back to the woodpile.

In the cabin, Matilda asked, "Mutti, what's takin' Vati so long to get wood? Should I go help him? He's been out there a long time."

Caroline was having trouble thinking. Her head hurt above her eyes, dulling her thoughts. "No, he'll come soon. Matilda, please get me a cup of water." They waited.

Matilda covered herself with her quilt and began to pray the prayers she had learned as a young child. Finally, she heard a pounding on the door. She leaped across the room and pulled the door open. Johann emerged from the white cold, his face red from the wind. Snow and ice clung to his cap and coat. His eyebrows were caked with ice. His arms clutched to snow-covered sticks of wood. Once he was in, Matilda closed the door and helped her pa take the wood to the fireplace.

The wood he carried seemed so meager against the hours that lay ahead. He thought, *Who knows how long this storm could last?* Trip after trip to the woodpile finally produced a stack by the fireplace that would last some hours.

Taking a dry stick and his knife, Johann whittled a small heap of tinder. Using the coals from the kettle to light the wood shavings, Johann coaxed the fire into flames of warmth. He spent the entire day getting wood and feeding the fire. Caroline heated water and made coffee and used some of her precious flour and oil to make pancakes.

They ate some dried venison. Caroline took a small amount but made sure her husband had more.

Johann asked, "Caroline, do we have any dried fruit or preserves?"

Caroline knew she must tell her husband the truth. "Johann," she said, "we have no dried fruit, nor preserves. Only a little flour, some lard, and a little dried venison. That's all we have. I've been relyin' on the turkeys. I'm so sorry, but there's no more. Johann, I didn't want to bother you when you were workin' so hard cutting wood."

Johann brought in more wood and filled the water bucket. He announced, "I'm goin' to get some food. I'll take Louie and make my way to the Bauers'. If they can help me get to town, I'll bring all the food I can carry on Louie. It may take me a few days. Use the wood I brought in and what food we have. I'll hurry as fast as I can."

Louie seemed ready to go when Johann swung up on his back. Maud whinnied as the horse and rider left the lean-to. The drifting snow made it nearly impossible to see the landmarks to get to the neighbor's house. Louie was willing to go on the run in the open where much of the snow had blown away, but some of the time he had to lunge his way through the belly-deep drifts. Johann wondered, *Does this horse know we're going to the neighbors?*

Johann leaned down close to Louie's neck as they moved against the driving snow. He talked to Louie as they went, "Come on, Louie, that a boy, take me to the Bauers' place." As they proceeded along the ridge, Johann could see a cluster of oaks that he knew was near the trail to the Bauers' house. "There you go, Louie," he coaxed as they made their way through the storm. Johann could feel his legs going numb. He let the reins fall in front of him over Louie's neck and tucked his hands under his arms. The force of the frigid wind penetrated his body. "God," he prayed, "I need food for my family, or we'll die. Help me, God."

Could I have lost consciousness? Where am I? Johann realized his mount had stopped. He nearly fell off when Louie put his head down. Then came a voice, "Johann, is that you? Come on in. You need to get warm. Have some coffee." Dazed, Johann shook his head and then realized that his horse had indeed taken him to the Bauers' house.

Eldwin helped Johann down from his mount and guided him into the kitchen. "Gerda, Gertrude, get your coats on and go put that horse in the barn. Give him some hay and oats. Brush him down good. There's a horse blanket on the bench."

Johann's mind began to clear as the coffee started to warm him from the inside. "Thank you," he said. "I guess that horse remembered the way over here. Thank you for takin' care of him."

"What brings you over here through this storm?" Eldwin inquired. "Is your family sick?"

With his head down, Johann answered, "Eldwin, I have been working so hard to be ready for winter. The cabin seems to be warm enough. I have a good supply of wood, but I didn't know we were nearly out of food. Caroline said she didn't want to interrupt me from cuttin' wood, so she didn't tell me the food was low. She said she thought we would get deer and turkeys before the bad weather. She has snared some rabbits, but the supplies are nearly gone. I need to get to town and get supplies. I think Caroline is weak from lack of food."

Eldwin scratched his head, turned to Dagmar, and questioned, "What do we have in the smoke house? Can we send some bacon or ham to the Mannweilers? How is the flour supply? Can you get some things together to take over there? Take some laudanum along for Caroline." He then turned to Johann. "We'll take the team and sledge tomorrow and get some food to your family."

"Oh, you don't have to do that. I just need to get to town. I can get supplies and get back home. You have done so much for us already. Just let me warm up and—"

"You're not goin' back out in this storm. As soon as it lets up, we'll take food to your family. We'll be goin' to town before Christmas. You and your family can go with us. We have food enough to share until then. The twins are taking care of your horse. You get some hot food in you and warm up."

*　*　*

"Mutti," Matilda pleaded, "are you all right? Mutti! Wake up! Mutti! We need to keep the fire goin'." Caroline didn't move. Matilda put on her boots and coat. The cabin was cold and dark. She could see some coals glowing in the fireplace, but the flame was gone. She carefully cut shavings from a stick of wood and gradually brought the fire back to life. Slowly, she added wood and could feel the warmth begin to creep out into the room. "Mutti," she whispered as she moved near her mother's bed. "Mutti, are you all right? I got the fire goin'. It's dark out, but Vati has not come home."

Caroline rolled over and moaned weakly. "Matilda, come here, my daughter. Can you bring me some water? My head hurts." Matilda put her hand on her mother's face. It was hot and clammy. She broke the ice in the water bucket and dipped a cupful for her mother. She found a cloth to dampen and gently placed it on her mother's forehead. Fear began to well up in her thirteen-year-old heart. *Oh, Vati, we need you, please come home. God, please help my mutti. She is really sick. Help us!*

Matilda spent the rest of the night tending the fire and changing the cool cloths on her mother's forehead. It seemed an eternity before the sun rose in the east. She opened the door just an inch or two. Her heart quickened when she realized the snow had stopped and the wind was calm. "God," she prayed, "please bring Vati home soon."

The cabin warmed slowly, and Caroline drank a cup of coffee. Matilda brought her a small piece of a pancake she was able to fry from the dwindling supply of flour and oil. "Oh, Mutti, when will Vati come home? We'll run out of wood before long. What are we going to do? Mutti! Can you get up?"

Caroline whispered, "Matilda, we must pray for God's help."

As they prayed, they heard a stirring outside. "What's that?" Matilda said excitedly. "Mutti, I hear voices! Vati must be here, and someone is with him! Oh, thank you, God!" Matilda ran toward the door to fling it open, but just as she touched the latch, she felt someone pushing it open against her.

112

Johann stepped into the room, carrying a wooden box. He turned and spoke. "Come in, Eldwin. Come in, Dagmar." The neighbors crossed the threshold, lingering to allow their eyes to focus in the darkness.

"Vati, you were gone so long. I have been so worried. Mutti is sick, and we don't have any food. I've been trying to cool her fever, and I gave her what food we have. Did you bring food?"

Dagmar had moved across the room to Caroline's bed. She put a hand on her forehead. "Caroline"—she spoke quietly—"are you in pain? I'll fix you some broth and hot tea."

Matilda helped Dagmar heat water for tea and coffee. They set the broth to heat by the fire. The aroma of the food cooking made Matilda aware of how hungry she had become.

Pa set the box on the trunk in the middle of the room. Dagmar took out bread and cheese. She moved deftly by the fire as she fixed a meal of bacon and potatoes to go with the bread and cheese.

Johann and Eldwin replenished the wood supply in the cabin. Johann noticed the pile beside the cabin was dwindling. He knew he must cut more wood soon.

Caroline was able to eat some broth and bread, but she was too weak to sit up. She held her head, and her eyes seemed sunken and dark. Dagmar gave her some laudanum to help with the pain.

The morning passed quickly. Eldwin helped Johann bring in a load of wood. Matilda and Dagmar washed the dishes, straightened up the cabin, and put away what food they had. Dagmar remarked, "Matilda, you have grown up so much since we saw you last fall. You sure are your mutti's helper. I'm proud of the way you took care of her."

At her neighbor's words, Matilda began to weep. "Oh, Dagmar, I was so scared. I didn't know what to do. The fire was nearly out when I woke up. Mutti couldn't get out of bed. I cut shavings with Vati's big knife and got the fire going. It was so dark, and I couldn't find a candle." She sobbed. "Dagmar, is my mutti going to die? What would we do without her? I don't think Vati knows how sick she is. He just keeps working to get wood and food." Choking back the tears, she fell into Dagmar's arms. "I'm so glad you came. Vati was going to catch some turkeys, but they got away." Exhausted, she sobbed and sobbed in her neighbor's arms.

Caroline slept through the day. She seemed more comfortable having taken the laudanum. Finally, she awoke and whispered, "Matilda, please bring me some warm tea and a little of that broth. Is Dagmar still here? She is an angel bringing us that good food."

"Yes, Mutti, Dagmar is here, and she is an angel." Dagmar went to Caroline and realized the fever had broken and her color was better. She helped Caroline sit up and pulled a quilt around her shoulders.

Soon the men came in from hauling wood. Eldwin said, "Dagmar, it's getting late. We need to get home. I asked the girls to do the chores, but I need to close things up for the night." Dagmar looked at Eldwin with a concerned look. Eldwin glanced at Caroline and back to Dagmar. Noticing a slight nod from his wife, he said, "We'd like the three of you to come and stay with us until Caroline is feeling better. We can make room for you. We could make it a neighborly party." He glanced at Johann to see a slight frown on his friend's face.

"Thank you, but no," Johann replied steadfastly. "We'll stay in our cabin. This is our land, and we'll live here." He continued with a smile. "We're so grateful for your help today, but we'll be stayin' right here," Johann said firmly as he moved to open the door for the Bauers to leave. "Thank you for your kindness. We would like to go to town sometime before Christmas though." Eldwin and Dagmar reluctantly said their good-byes to Caroline and Matilda and drove away in the sledge.

On their way home, Dagmar leaned close to her husband for warmth. "Eldwin," she whispered, "I'm worried about Caroline. She's so thin and weak. I'm afraid she won't make it through the winter." Eldwin put his arm comfortingly around his wife's shoulders as he urged the team on toward home.

The Runaway
Crossing Illinois
1852

ADAM ZEDEKER AND HIS BOYS John and Israel rode in to Elgin to check out the Fox River crossing. Adam inquired at the general store, "How's the river crossing? We've got five heavy covered wagons headin' up to Minnesota Territory."

"You shouldn't have any trouble," the storekeeper assured. "The ford has been improved since the *Galena & Chicago Union Railroad* came to town a few years ago, opening a market all the way to Chicago. The farmers cross the river every day with their wagons bringin' their products to market."

Adam and the boys rode across the river to get a feel of what to expect the next morning. Everything looked good to Adam, except the steep slope on the far side. He knew it would be a hard pull for the draft animals.

In the morning, after a hearty breakfast, the men prepared the teams for crossing the Fox River. They harnessed the spare team of horses and yoked the extra pair of oxen.

Adam was confident his mules could pull his wagon across the Fox, but for safety, he had Joe hitch the spare team ahead of Ben and Birdie. Taking the four reins in his hands, he talked to the teams in a steady voice. The mules' heads came up as if to meet the challenge. "Come on now," Adam urged. "Get up there, Ben, Birdie, get up now!" The heavy wagon cut into the riverbed, bringing sand up with the wheels. The teams were in up to their bellies. Adam held a steady rein and continued to urge them along. When they came to the far side, the teams came up the slope, slipping some, but able to keep moving. Joe saw a slight hesitation, so he jumped down in the knee-deep water and grabbed the spokes of the rear wheel. With a mighty twist, the wagon moved forward, home free.

With a third yoke of oxen added, Jake and Joe took the freight wagon across without a problem. Jake's Studebaker was next with Jacob's four blacks ahead of Jake's bays. Jake, with six lines in his hands, spoke softly to the horses. The lead blacks leaned into their collars with the other four following. Jake ordered, "Get up there, Jack, Jill, lead out there." The six horses pulled together to bring the Studebaker up the slippery slope. Jake, Adam, and Joe worked together to yoke up the six oxen to bring the supply wagon safely across the Fox.

Knowing the Schooner was the heaviest wagon of all, Adam hitched his mules ahead of the four blacks. Unaware of the engine switching cars in the railroad yards next to the trail, Jacob took up the six reins. At the exact moment that Jacob gave the command for his team to "get up," the Pioneer sounded two loud blasts of the train whistle. Ben spooked and lunged forward, taking Birdie with him. The four blacks had no choice but to follow. Jacob tightened the reins to bring the teams under control. He reached for the wagon brake handle to slow the wagon just as the Pioneer set off another blast of the whistle. All six animals burst forward, with Jacob hanging on to the seat with all his might. When the wagon hit the river, the water rushed up over the front, nearly washing Jacob off the seat. Jacob struggled to hold the teams on the ford and keep the wagon upright. The mules went headlong up the slope on the other side, nearly dragging the horses behind them. All four blacks kept their footing up the slope. Jacob recovered enough to get all six reins in hand, but the teams wouldn't respond. Thinking quickly, Joe caught up with the teams on his saddle horse and gradually calmed the mules and brought the runaways to a stop. Shaking, Jacob collapsed on the seat and put his head in his hands. "Thank you, God."

"Amen, brother!" Joe added, grinning ear to ear.

With the wagons back in order, the men brushed down all of the draft animals and saw that they had water and feed. The Schooner had to be unloaded and things hung out to dry. Fortunately, it was a nice day with bright sun. Lucinda helped her brothers and sisters get their quilts and clothing hung over the bushes. By midafternoon, the camp was settled. Lucinda recorded the runaway story in her diary.

Joe mounted his horse and said, "Boss, I'm gonna ride back to town. I'll be back for supper." By sundown, the bedding had dried, and the Schooner was restored for sleeping. Polly started preparing supper, and Mary M and Catharine came to help. John and Israel had shot some prairie chickens, and the aroma of creamed prairie chicken gravy filled the air.

The family was gathering for supper when Joe rode into camp. He quickly tethered his horse, washed his hands, and joined the group. He had an impish smile on his face. Lucinda asked if she could pray. Her pa nodded. She began, "Dear God, thank you for helping Pa when the horses ran today. Thank you they stopped. God, I was afraid for Pa. We love each other and don't want anyone to be hurt. Thank you for the prairie chicken gravy. Please help us move on to our new home in Minnesota. Amen."

Lucinda was ready to start washing dishes when she heard Joe speak. He said softly, "Boss, I thought we were gonna lose you today. If you fell off that wagon, you woulda gone under the river and woulda been a goner. Boss, I was prayin' for ya all the way. I know God brought you through. Back in town, I found this little shop where a man sells things he makes out of brass. Here, Boss, would you nail this to the Schooner?"

Jacob received a black bag from Joe. When he lifted a shiny brass cross out of the bag, his throat tightened. His head went down as he whispered, "Thank you, Joe. Thank you, God." After a quiet moment, Jacob stood and walked up to Joe, threw his arms around

117

the huge man, and pounded him on his back. Everyone around heard the sniffles from both men. "Thank you, Joe, thank you!" They all watched as Jacob tacked the cross to the side of the Schooner.

Joe caught his breath and spoke again. "I wanted to get somethin' for all of you. You've made me a part of your family. All I could think of was these." He held out a bag. "Enough for four pieces for each of the children and a taste for the rest of us." He handed the bag to Lucinda who found it full of wrapped hard candies.

"Oh, Ma," she said, "we never get to have sweets." She helped each of the children, including John and Israel, to get four pieces. They all treasured the candies and put them away carefully.

Little Matilda ran over to Joe and climbed up in his lap. Looking up into his eyes, she said, "Thank you! Thank you . . ." Waiting a long moment, she continued, "Can I call you Unca Joe?"

The big man put his huge arm around her and choked out the words, "Sure you can if it's 'right with your pa." Jacob nodded, and Matilda said it again, "Unca Joe, I love you."

Mid-May brought out a dazzling display of flowers along the trail. Longer days soon produced the heat of summer. The ford at the Rock River was in much better condition than the Fox River crossing. Crossing went smoothly, and they replenished supplies at the general store in Rockford, Illinois.

On the way up the hill out of the Rock River valley, a stagecoach came up behind them. Jacob rode Jenny alongside the coach and shouted, "Mornin' to ya." The driver returned the greeting. Jacob continued, "What's the trail like ahead? We're on our way to Minnesota Territory. Got any suggestions?"

"Pretty much farmland between here and Galena," the driver returned. "Best you take the north route from Galena and stay up on top until you get close to Dunlieth. Make sure your wagon brakes are in good shape after Galena. You'll hit some hills, and the slope to Big Miss is steep. You'll get the ferry at Dunlieth. Guess they call it East Dubuque now. I like to take Gregoire's boat. He's in a big fight with

Fanning. May go to the Supreme Court, they say. Gregoire has good boats. You can get your wagons on without unhitchin'."

The driver slapped the reins to his wheel horses and passed on by. Jacob shouted, "Much obliged," as he waved in appreciation.

The territorial trail took them through miles of prairie land that was being prepared for spring planting. Mary M was feeling better, though she still had uncomfortable mornings. Lucinda was her constant companion and nurse. Lucinda tried to spend some time each day reading the Bible and writing in her diary.

They reached the town of Freeport on Saturday evening. A kind gentleman gave Jacob the latest copy of the local newspaper. On the back page was an announcement of Sunday services at the community hall. Following Saturday night baths and a good rest, the McQuillans arrived at the hall just in time for the opening hymn. The folks were much like the German people in Pennsylvania and Ohio. At a picnic following worship, Lucinda met a girl her age, and all the children had fun playing games. That evening, Lucy said, "Thank you, Pa, for taking us to church today."

The next morning, Rusty announced the dawn with his healthy crowing. Old Rusty was lucky the prairie chickens were plentiful, or he would have been long gone by now. The terrain gradually changed from farmland to rolling hills. They passed through the beautiful Apple River Valley as they moved toward Galena.

As usual, Jacob stopped at the local livery stable. "Where'd ya get the name 'Galena'?" he inquired of the bearded old man sitting on a bench out front.

The old man stood up and stretched his muscles. "It's those lead mines out there that gave us our name. The Indians had been usin' the lead for war paint for years. Now they ship it down the river for good money. Town's been growin' ever since. Most fourteen thousand hangin' out here now."

"How did lead mines name the town?" Jacob pursued.

"That's the name of the ore they get the lead from. It's called Galena Ore," the old man said as if everyone should know that. "Can I help you with somethin'? Need some repairs, feed, harnesses?"

Adam spoke up. "We hear we'll be comin' into hills ahead. Our leather brake pads need replacin'. Any chance you'd have some heavy leather?"

"Ya, got just the thing you need. You betcha, gotta have good brakes going down to Dunlieth. Trail's good, but you gotta keep on the brakes or the wagon will run up on the critters."

Adam was pleased with the quality of the leather and the good price he paid. That night, Adam and Jake repaired the brakes on all five wagons and made sure the brake levers were set and strong.

Lucinda was both excited and anxious when they started out the next morning. She still remembered the runaway team at the Fox River. The trail took them through rolling hills, giving a view of the Mississippi River winding its way southward. Lucinda called to her pa, "How will we ever get across that big river?"

"We'll go on the ferry," her pa answered.

"What's a ferry?" Lucy questioned.

"It's a big boat. We can take a team and wagon on all at once. It's a steamboat," Pa answered. "It'll be exciting."

The campsite that evening was a clearing on a ridge above the Mississippi. They were treated to a beautiful sunset showing through thin clouds in the west. Lucinda spent the night with Mary M while Jake took watch. Sleep came slowly, and her mind was filled with visions of runaway wagons going down steep hills.

The next morning, Jacob rode out ahead to check the descent. Coming back, he reported, "The livery man was right, we'll need a man on the brake of every wagon as we go down the hill."

When they came to the slope, Adam called, "Israel, jump up and drive the mules on the lead wagon. I'll use both hands on the brake." They made it down the slope without difficulty.

Joe stepped to the seat of the freight wagon, and John took a whip and walked to the left of the oxen. Joe had to work hard to keep the heavy wagon from running up on the oxen, but they made the decline safely.

Jake said, "Come on, Lucy, let's take the bays down. You take the reins, and I'll hold the brake." Lucy was uneasy, but she trusted her older brother. At the bottom of the hill, Jake nudged his little sister and said, "Good job, Sis."

Now Jacob was the only man left up top. He said, "George, here's my whip. You command the oxen, and I'll take the brake on the supply wagon." They successfully joined the others at the bottom.

Jacob drew the group together and said, "I talked to Gregoire this morning. He's expectin' us by midday. Adam, lead the way to the ferry and get started taking these four wagons across. Catherine is up there waiting with the blacks. Joe and I will ride up and get the Schooner."

Catharine had a snack ready when Jacob and Joe arrived at the Schooner. Once the teams were hitched, the two men climbed onto the wagon seat. Catharine mounted Jenny and led Joe's horse behind.

Jacob knew Mit and Missie would be able to hold steady, but the heavy Schooner would be a challenge. He took the reins, and Joe was on the brake handle. They made the first slope and curve just fine, but the next one was steeper and sharper. As they started down, Mit slipped and lost his footing. By the time he recovered, the wagon had gained speed. Joe held on to the brake but was unable to slow the wagon. To keep from running over the horses, Jacob let the team go to a trot. They made it around the curve, but they were gaining too much speed. "Joe!" Jacob yelled. "Hold on! We're almost to the runaway trail!" They hit the runaway trail hard, but the upward slope slowed the wagon down. When the dust settled, everything was still intact, but now they were headed the wrong way on a one-way trail. Jacob tried to get Mit and Missie to back the wagon up enough to get back on the trail, but the load was too heavy. Joe left the brake and jumped down from the seat. He went to the rear wheel and yelled at Jacob to try again. As the horses pushed backward, Joe made a mighty twist on the wheel and moved the wagon a few feet back. After five or six attempts, the wagon was in place to move forward. Joe bounded up on the seat as Jacob allowed the team to start down the slope. Back on the trail, they moved faster than they wanted to. But between Joe's braking and Jacob's skilled driving, they brought the Schooner safely to the bottom.

"Boss, I sure was doing some prayin' up there," Joe breathed. "Thank God for some mighty good horses. Them blacks are the best."

When Jacob, Catharine, and Joe arrived at the ferry dock, Lucinda came running. "Are you all right, Pa? What took you so long? Both ox teams are across, and the ferry is coming back. I was worried about you."

Jacob answered, "We're all right. Mit slipped, and we had to pull off on the runaway trail to keep from gainin' too much speed. Thanks to Joe, we were able to back out and get goin' again. That man is a moose. I'm mighty glad he's with us!"

13

Alone on the Streets
New York
1852-1855

A DAM UTZINGER WALKED OUT OF the Immigration Office with one thought on his mind—finding a good meal in New York City. He headed across the street toward a café that looked inviting. As he turned to his left, he tripped over a boy who was sprawled on the ground. Adam tried to speak words of apology as he fell, but then a man tumbled on top of him, and still another person stumbled onto the pile. After some untangling, the four of them stood, nodded to one another, and went in their separate directions.

Adam brushed himself off, picked up his bag, and continued toward the café. Unbuttoning his coat, panic struck like a bolt of lightning. The money pouch was gone. His throat tightened, and he began to shake uncontrollably. All he could do was breathe, "God, help me!"

Hunger pains were immediately replaced by fear. A strange city with a strange language stretched out before him. Loneliness held him in a breathless stranglehold. Adam walked the streets, hoping to find help from someone. The sun broke through the cloud cover briefly before darkness descended over the city. Adam gravitated toward an open lot where some low bushes provided shelter from the wind, and his quilt gave some warmth. Between fear of possible danger and the hunger in his belly, Adam was unable to sleep.

After a long night, the city gradually came to life. A milk wagon rattled past. People appeared on the streets, mechanically making their way to jobs in shops and factories. Adam walked aimlessly looking at people, longing for someone to notice his need. He heard a voice. "Adam, is that you, Adam?" A middle-aged man was walking toward him. "Adam Utzinger, what are you doin' here?" The face seemed familiar, and the man spoke again. "You are Adam, aren't you?"

Stunned, Adam began to stammer, "Ja! Ja! . . . I . . . I'm Adam." Recognition broke through. Adam breathed, "Mr. Lehmann . . . Terrell Lehmann?" Memory took him back to his village in Germany where the Lehmann family had operated a small table and chair factory. They had left for America four or five years earlier.

Terrell inquired, "What are you doin' on the streets of New York? How long have you been here?"

Adam was embarrassed but decided to be honest. "I came in on the *Robert Harding* yesterday. Unfortunately, three people rolled me on the street and took my money pouch. I had it tied around my waist and under my belt, but somehow, they lifted it."

"Ja," Terrell said, "they're good at that around here. The police don't do much about it either." He paused with a thoughtful look. "You must be hungry. My factory is just down the street. Come along while I get the shop open and the workers started. Then we'll go have a good breakfast."

Adam walked with Terrell to a small diner near his shop. They took stools at the counter. The smell of frying sausage brought on urgent hunger pains in the pit of Adam's stomach. In a matter of minutes, two plates loaded with well-seasoned eggs and sausage landed in front of the customers, with plate-sized wheat cakes on the side.

Once the hunger was satisfied, Adam smacked his lips and said, "Thank you so much, Mr. Lehmann. I don't know what I would have done without your help." The two men polished off their breakfast, finishing up with a third cup of coffee.

Out on the street, Adam offered a hand to his friend. "Mr. Lehmann, I can't thank you enough for your kindness."

Terrell looked straight into Adam's eyes and said, "Adam, where are you goin' from here?"

Fear moved into Adam's chest, and his eyes found the sidewalk. "I really don't know, but God brought me to you this morning. Guess I'll be trustin' him out ahead. Eventually, I hope to find my brother Peter. He's workin' at a sawmill in Fulton County. I'm plannin' to contact him and get work at the mill."

Terrell nodded. "Why don't you work for me as an apprentice while we find your brother? There's a cot at the shop you can sleep on. I'll pay you enough for your food."

Adam felt like a beggar, but the plan sounded better than any alternative. He straightened up and said firmly, "I'll work hard for ya. I learned hard work at home at the Scharrhof."

Mail service was slow, but the Utzinger brothers finally made contact. Peter was assigned to drive a team of mules hauling a wagonload of lumber from the mill to New York City. The two brothers met on a New York street on a Saturday morning. Seeing each other, they hesitated and then ran into a brotherly bear hug. Adam said good-bye to Terrell and joined his older brother on the wagon headed to his new home at a lumber camp in Fulton County, New York.

Out on the trail, the mules fell in pace with the caravan. Peter questioned, "How are Mutti and Vati? Are they well? I had to leave so fast, with the draft and everything; I hardly had a chance to say good-bye."

Adam paused, then responded, "Mutti and Vati are well. It's been hard on 'em knowing how Jacob has suffered in the cavalry. He still writes about the rough treatment. Crops have been good. I think Mutti still grieves the death of Thekla. Yet she still hums the hymns while she works in the kitchen. It was hard for me to leave, but Mutti is determined not to have another son in the German army."

Adam turned to face his brother. "Peter, I'm in a jam. I don't have any money. Just after comin' out of immigration, a boy tripped me on the street. Two men piled on top of me, and when I got up, my money

125

pouch was gone. I happened to meet Terrell on the street. He let me stay in his shop and do some cleaning and odd jobs for my keep. I don't have tools or warm clothes to get started."

"Don't worry, they'll have tools for ya. The food's good at the mess hall. The bunkhouse is warm. Not the quietest place, but you'll be tired enough to sleep. The problem is you never get paid enough to save anything. I want to get out of here to go west to take up a land claim, but I never get ahead. I hear things are good in Wisconsin, but I don't know how we'll ever get there."

"Vati thinks we'll have a better chance workin' together. He made me feel responsible for the two of us, but I don't see how that makes any difference."

Peter lifted his hat and scratched his head. "Believe me, it'll be great havin' you with me. It'll help the loneliness, but it won't help the finances. They keep you poor so you can't leave. I have my eye on a pretty little gal at the camp. Her name is Carolina Buchardt. She came here from Rhienland-Pfalz with her family as a young girl. Her vati is a foreman, and her mutti is the cook. The family is well established. I don't think they'd be happy if I asked to court Carolina."

The crickets began their evening song, and darkness came quickly. The brothers spent the night in their bedrolls under the wagon. Sleep was interrupted early by the baying of the mules. Adam appreciated the hearty breakfast of bacon, eggs, potatoes, and lots of hotcakes. The coffee was strong enough to jolt anyone awake.

Once the wagons were on the trail, Peter asked, "*Bruder*, what brought you to America? Just before I left home, you had graduated from the pastor's class. You were interested in studyin' and all. I thought you'd be headin' for the university and maybe the seminary."

The wagon jolted over a rocky stretch in the trail while Adam collected his thoughts. "I did join the Lutheran church, but I've been growin' more and more troubled with the church. It's become so controlled by the government. I've done some readin' about Pietism. A couple hundred years ago, a man by the name of Jakob Spener led a movement in Germany, calling Christians to live out what they believe. He wrote about the heart warmed by the Spirit of God. I met some Pietists on the *Robert Harding*; genuine, caring people. They asked me to teach their children. Peter, I have a longing for something more. I want to have a farm and a family, but I'm also searching for God."

At nineteen, Adam looked every bit of twenty-five. When Peter introduced him to the mill boss, he quickly found a place for a new hand. Peter arranged for his brother to bunk next to him in the bunkhouse. The sauna was heated up three nights a week. A plunge in the river was good for cooling down after a hot day.

As Adam put his empty tray on the wash table, he heard his name. "Hey, Utzinger," the deep voice echoed. "Young Utzinger, what's the name, Adam?" Turning toward the sound, Adam recognized the saw boss. "We're puttin' you on slab detail. You'll be at the mill every mornin' at 4:30 sharp. The old engine needs to be hot when the cutters arrive at 6:00. While she's heatin' up, I'll teach ya how to grease and oil the mill and stoke the boiler. The pay is twelve dollars a month, includin' all you can eat and a place to sleep."

Snoring and other sounds in the bunkhouse made for little sleep that night. Worry about being late for work kept him aware of the time all night. He was surprised by the voice of the saw boss. "Utzinger, you've got twenty minutes to be at the mill. Late and you're fired."

By lantern light, Adam arrived at the sawmill, gloves in hand, ready for his new job. He learned how to feed the fire in the steam engine to generate the power to spin the saw blade through the logs. When the steam whistle blew, the men were ready with a log on the carriage that moved the log through the saw blade. Day after endless day, Adam's job was to drag the slabs to the steam engine, cut them to length, and feed the fire.

After a long hot summer at the sawmill, the men were moved to the lumber camp upriver. Foreman Buchardt assigned the Utzinger brothers the task of swinging the double bit axes to remove the branches from the logs. Peter was most interested in winning the favor of the foreman because of his attraction to his daughter, Carolina.

One winter evening, after a tasty supper, Peter and Adam wandered out to the kitchen. Mrs. Buchardt was scrubbing the pots and pans. Her daughter, Carolina, was washing dishes. Peter spoke up. "Mrs. Buchardt, this is my younger brother, Adam. He's new in camp, just arrived from back home last spring. We're on Mr. Buchardt's crew this winter."

The cook, a woman of about fifty, with slightly graying hair pushing out around her white cook's cap, smiled at Adam. "Welcome to our camp. We've got a big crew this year. They sure put away the vittles."

Adam nodded in response. "Mighty good food, Mrs. Buchardt. Sure appreciate your good cookin'."

By this time, Peter had gravitated toward the dishwashing stand, his heart pounding against the back side of his ribs. Carolina looked up from her work. When their eyes met, Peter stammered, "Not . . . not much interested in the cards and partyin' out there. Could you use a hand? I'm pretty good with a towel."

He noticed Carolina glance toward her mother. Receiving a positive nod, she answered, "Ja, that would be nice. Not many men would offer. There's a towel on that hook."

Adam wandered toward the back of the room where he noticed a door to a back porch. It was a clear, cold evening. In the stillness of the night, he looked up into the sky. The stars sparkled brightly in the winter darkness. *I wonder what Vati and Mutti are doing. Can they see the same stars?* He thought of Aubrey. *Would she be my wife now if I were at home?* He shivered as he came back to the reality of a New York lumber camp.

As the two men left the kitchen, Mrs. Buchardt wiped her hands on her apron and waved. "*Tschuss*, it'll be apple pie tomorrow. Stop after and I'll save you a second piece."

Peter smiled toward Carolina. "I'd be pleased to hear more about your trip back to Thaleischweiler. I still miss home, but no chance to return. Guess I'm a lumberjack now. Good night." He carried her smile in his mind as they made their way to the bunkhouse.

"I can see why you're interested in Carolina," Adam said. "It looks like her mutti is clearin' the way."

"Ja, Adam, I sure wish I could get some money saved up. I'd like to ask her vati's permission to court her. Twelve dollars a month gets you nowhere. If only . . ." His voice trailed off.

The brothers made a practice of visiting the kitchen for a generous slice of pie and some conversation. Carolina tried not to be obvious when she slipped off her long white apron and settled in a chair next to Peter. She was tall and straight in stature, though graceful and feminine. Most striking were her deep blue eyes that seemed to sparkle when she smiled.

As winter gave way to spring, Boss Buchardt was pleased that production was up considerably from previous years. One day, during lunch break, Peter noticed the boss sitting on a log, drinking his coffee. He ventured, "Mind if I join ya for a bit, Mr. Buchardt? I've got a question for ya."

"Ja, sure. I've got an extra cookie straight from the cook." The boss grinned as he handed Peter the oatmeal morsel. "What's on your mind?"

Peter accepted the cookie and held it in his left hand. He glanced around to see if any of the men were within earshot. "Mr. Buchardt, I would like to ask your permission to court your daughter, Carolina. I find her to be a woman of honor, and I would ask the privilege of getting to know her better."

The boss waited until the two men's eyes met. He smiled. "According to her mutti, you're doing a good job already with all the pie and coffee you've been consumin'. I've been wonderin' when you'd ask. My wife and I have talked about this, and we agree that we would be pleased for you to court our daughter. Carolina is most special to me, and I will expect you to treat her with respect."

Peter wasn't sure what to do or say, so he stuck out his hand toward the boss. As they shook hands, Peter said, "Mr. Boss, you can count on me to honor and respect your daughter. Thank you for your permission." That afternoon, Adam noticed that Peter swung the ax with more power than ever before.

Adam found himself spending more time alone now that Peter was taking evening walks with Carolina. He still would get an occasional extra dessert and coffee in the kitchen. He even took over some dishwashing to give Carolina a break, and he had some long talks with Mrs. Buchardt.

Word circulated around the camp that some men had moved to Wisconsin where they got jobs on farms that paid much better than the logging camps. They heard of men who took over farms and were able to build homes and have families. Adam and Peter longed for the chance to move west.

After a productive summer at the sawmill, the crew returned to the logging camp for the winter. One bright spot was the week that a traveling evangelist visited the camp. Adam soaked up the preaching of the Word and stimulating conversations with the preacher.

January was unusually cold with constant wind and blizzard conditions. One miserable day, the wind was blowing at gale force. In spite of whiteout conditions, the company insisted the crew report for work. Adam and Peter started moving along two trees, removing the branches as they went. They had to bend down and feel their way. Adam took a hefty swing at a large branch. His wet mitten slipped on the ax handle. The sharp bit came down on his shin, bringing Adam face forward into the snow. He could feel the hot blood fill the leg of his wool pants. Pain took his breath away. He called, "Peter, help me! I can't get up!" No response. "Peter, Peter, come help me!"

Peter reached the end of his log and chopped off the top. He turned expecting Adam to come up beside him. Peter started back, trimming off branches as he went. Then he heard his name muffled by the wind. "Peter, Peter, come help me!"

Peter removed his woolen scarf and twisted a tourniquet around Adam's upper leg. Adam writhed in pain as Peter and the boss carried him to the sledge. Peter covered his brother with the wool horse blankets for warmth against shock. He shouted, "Boss, I'll make sure the sledge is back for the crew at the end of the day." The team knew the way back to the bunkhouse, but the snowstorm forced them to move slowly.

Peter urged the team toward the kitchen entrance. He called to the stableman to take care of the horses. With Adam's help, he managed to get his brother's body up on his right shoulder. Blood dripped from Adam's ankle. Carolina came to help guide Peter to a cot by the fire.

"What happened?" Carolina gasped. "I'll get some warm water. Peter, cut his pant leg off. This is when we need a doctor. Mutti, ya better get your needle ready." Ma Buchardt had sewn up many a woodsman in her day. She was the closest thing to a doctor in the whole territory.

Adam seemed drowsy from the heavy bleeding. Peter removed his boot and sock while Carolina bathed the wound with soap and hot water. Then she pressed the wound together and held it with a warm towel. Adam winced and gritted his teeth to keep from crying out. "We need to get this cleaned up to ward off infection."

The blood was clotting, but Ma Buchardt was not satisfied. She said rather calmly, "This is gonna hurt." Adam took a deep breath and stuck his mitten between his teeth. Ma swabbed the cut with a solution of water and alcohol that she used as an antiseptic. Adam doubled over and released an "aaowwwooooo!!" The cook-doctor, with a curved needle and a strip of gristle, neatly sewed the flesh and skin together.

Carolina tore some old dishtowels into strips and heated them in the oven. When her mother stepped back, Carolina carefully wrapped Adam's leg from ankle to knee. Peter smiled as he watched her gentle fingers caress the bandage in place on his brother's leg.

Peter returned to the woods with the team and sledge. Boss Buchardt stepped up to the front of the box and asked, "Did the cook get him patched up? She's a good doctor." Peter responded with a nod and a touch to his cap.

Adam slept on a cot by the kitchen fire for the next few nights. Peter found comfort in an old horsehair-stuffed chair. He kept the fire going through the night but was expected to be at work early in the morning.

The pain gradually let up, and Adam started to have cabin fever. The cooks put him to work peeling potatoes, chopping cabbage, or pressing cookies on large tin sheets. They soon accused him of getting fat and lazy. Bouts with infection and slow healing caused Adam to be unable to work in the woods or the sawmill for several months. The company manager informed Adam that he would have to pay for his board and place in the bunkhouse. "No loafers around here. You work or you pay. That's our way," he announced.

Adam appealed, "It was your order to work on that stormy day. You caused the accident. You owe me something for lost time." The manager just shook his head and left. Each month instead of pay, Adam got a bill. By the time it was over, Adam was out about a hundred dollars.

The Utzinger brothers stayed on through the logging season and moved back to the sawmill in the spring. Adam was able to get back to work on slab detail. They made plans to leave for Wisconsin the following spring after one more winter in the woods. While Carolina's parents were disappointed to think of their daughter living so far away, they were thankful that she had found an honorable man for a husband. They were ready to help plan a wedding the next time the evangelist came to camp.

Several weeks later, following a long day at the mill, the men returned to the cook shack for supper. Peter gasped with surprise when the evangelist started playing hymns on his accordion while the men filled their trays. After supper, he made his way to the kitchen lean-to. Carolina was aglow. She cried, "Peter, Vati talked to the preacher, and he is stayin' a couple weeks. We can have our wedding here at the camp."

With Adam as best man and Carolina's sister as maid of honor, Peter and Carolina were married on August 27, 1854. A day and a night at the little cabin by the river was their honeymoon, reminding themselves that the trip to Wisconsin the next spring would be the real thing.

Following their last winter in the lumber camp, Adam and the newlyweds moved downriver with the crew. But this time, they caught a ride on a lumber wagon to Albany, New York. In the Albany train station, Adam pointed to the ticket prices. "Look, Peter, I think we have saved just enough to get to Milwaukee, Wisconsin."

"Young man, where ya headed?" a middle-aged man in a cowhide jacket and a broad brimmed hat asked abruptly.

"Milwaukee. My brother and I are plannin' to take claims out there."

"Want a free ride?"

Adam was interested, knowing the condition of his finances. "What do ya mean?"

"I've got five cattle cars on the next freight train out of here. I'm lookin' for some men to ride with me and help feed and water the cattle. We have a mess car, and one guy cooks. Not much of a place to sleep," the man offered.

Adam took hold of Peter's sleeve and pulled him out of the line. Peter caught Carolina's arm as they moved toward a corner of the room. The gentleman pulled four chairs into a circle.

"The name's Hofmann, Strom Hofmann. The farmers out west need cattle to start herds. I buy heifers and ship 'em to Wisconsin. Once they're bred and ready for a farmer's herd, I get a good profit, and the farmer gets the cow and calf. It could take two weeks or more to get to Milwaukee. Your pay would be the ride, the food, and a place to crawl into your bedroll at night."

Hofmann caught Peter's attention and asked with a nod toward Carolina, "Your wife?" Seeing Peter's nod, he continued, "Not much of a ride for a lady." He paused.

Carolina spoke up. "I've cooked for a lumber camp. What's that mess car like? Could it use a woman's touch?"

"The mess car ain't much, but I'd like to see what a lumber camp cook could do with it. It has a stove and water supply, and garbage goes out at every stop. I provide cash, and you shop in the towns where we overnight." With a shrug, "That's about it."

"I'd like to . . . ," Carolina started, but Peter interrupted. "Carolina, are you sure you want to get into this?"

"What's wrong, Pete, don't you trust my cookin'?" Carolina answered with a smile. She asked, "How many in your crew?"

"I'll be on board and three other workers. With the three of you, it'd be seven. Ja, seven of us."

Carolina chuckled. "Nothin' compared to a loggin' camp."

The agreement was made, and Strom led the way. The engine was just backing the train on the switch toward a group of cattle cars. With a sudden bump, the cars were attached, and the train lurched forward.

Hofmann jumped up the steps of the first car. "Put your stuff in the mess car and make yourselves at home. There should be some supplies on hand. You can stock up again at our stop tomorrow night."

The mess car was the front part of one of the cattle cars. Carolina found supplies and soon had stew on for supper. They organized things in a small pantry room to make a place for Carolina and Peter to sleep. Adam staked claims on a spot by the cookstove.

On May 25, 1855, the train pulled out of the Albany station. At bedtime, Peter said, "Come on, my bride, we're on our honeymoon. Let's go to bed." Adam rolled his eyes and pulled his quilt around his shoulders.

Strom had planned stops along the way to purchase more heifers. This meant long hours for Adam and Peter loading the new heifers and adding to the feed supply. Carolina shopped at markets to replenish her supplies as they slowly made their way west.

The trees on the slopes of northern New York were in full leaf, announcing the coming of summer. Carolina started to experience some morning nausea as she prepared breakfast. Food lost its appeal, but she was able to see that the men were well fed. She looked for times to rest while the men were tending their chores. She had not had a monthly since February.

They spent an overnight in the Syracuse rail yard and again in Buffalo and then on to Cleveland. After Cleveland, they passed through miles of farmland dotted with farmsteads with treeline windbreaks. Seeing the houses and barns with livestock grazing in the pastures caused Adam and Peter to long for the day they could have places of their own.

Adam marveled at how Strom got his cattle cars through the busy train yards in Chicago and transferred on to Milwaukee, Wisconsin. Carolina poured another cup of coffee for the men after a hearty meal. Strom and his men returned to their bedrolls. Adam stepped out of the mess car on an errand. Carolina sat down next to Peter and leaned her head on his shoulder. She put her hand on her husband's chest. With a tender smile, she ventured, "Peter, I'm so proud to be your wife. I miss my vati and mutti, but I'm happy to be with you. I'm glad to work for Mr. Hofmann so we can save our money for a place in Wisconsin." She paused. "Peter, I think I'm with child. If I'm right, we'll have a baby by the end of the year."

Peter spun around, threw his arms around his wife, kissed her, and then caught himself saying, "How do you feel? I'll do your work for you on the way to Milwaukee." He stopped, and looking into Carolina's eyes, he said, "You are so beautiful." His heart was racing, causing him to hyperventilate.

Carolina chuckled and said, "Peter, calm down. This has happened to thousands of couples. I'm healthy and comfortable. I can do my work. All that's happening is that we're going to have a baby."

Adam returned to the room with some laundry to do in the kitchen sink. Immediately, he was aware that both Carolina and Peter were staring at him with mouths half open. He looked down at himself to see what was attracting attention. Peter and Carolina looked at each other. Carolina whispered, "He's your brother."

Adam said, "Ja, we're brothers, but where's that cat that swallowed the canary? Come on, out with it."

Peter stood up, bowed to his brother, and announced, "From now on, you will be known as 'Uncle Adam' in our household. This lovely lady"—he put his hand on Carolina's shoulder—"is with child."

Taking a moment for the news to register, Adam let out a, "Yiippeee! I'll work at being the best uncle ever."

The rest of the trip to Milwaukee was uneventful. After getting the heifers unloaded and into the care of the drovers, the three Utzingers found a room for the night where baths and beds seemed like a luxury after the long journey.

The next day, they purchased a team and a light wagon. Zelig was a big headstrong gelding and Zelda, a sturdy well-built mare. Adam bought a black and white pinto named Rowdy. They traveled two days north where they found jobs working for Jed Stewart near Brandon, Wisconsin. The pay was minimal, but Jed gave them the use of a log cabin as part of their pay. Carolina spent the fall days lining the shelves of the fruit cellar with quarts of tasty vegetables and dozens of jars of jam and jelly made from berries she found in the woods along the river. The small Utzinger clan had begun to build a new life in Wisconsin.

Gathered at the River
On through Iowa
1852

THE CAPTAIN OF GREGOIRE'S FERRY motioned for Adam Zedeker to bring his mules aboard. Adam spoke to Ben and Birdie and urged them down the ramp. When the team reached the deck, Ben set his feet and would not move. "You stubborn mule," Adam muttered as he climbed down from the wagon. He pulled on Ben's bridle to lead him ahead. Ben leaned back and would not budge. Adam reached up and patted Ben's neck and talked to him quietly. Ben stood his ground. Adam yelled, "Jake, put some blocks in front of the wheels. Let's bring your team up here." The men switched the teams, and Daisy and Dolly pulled Adam's wagon onto the ferry. The ferry pushed off.

Jake and Joe put blinders on Ben's bridle and hitched the mules to Jake's wagon. When the ferry returned, Joe was ready on the seat of the Studebaker. He spoke firmly to Ben and Birdie, urging them down the ramp. They moved forward slowly, but when Ben came to the deck, he stopped dead still. Joe jumped down and tugged on Ben's bridle. Ben refused to step on the deck. Joe stood back a pace, got Ben's attention, and reached up with both hands and took the mule by both ears. He spoke so softly that only the mule could hear. Joe started onto the deck. Ben shook his head, put his nose to the ground, sniffed the deck, and walked up behind Joe.

Jacob drove the Schooner aboard. On the way across the Mississippi, Jacob said to Joe, "What did you do to get Ben up on the deck?"

Joe smiled. "I squeezed and twisted his ears good and hard and told him if he didn't get goin', I would drag him on board by his ears. Guess he decided to come along."

The May flowers were withering, and June brought the rapid growth of the prairie grass. Jacob was anxious to arrive in Minnesota with time to build cabins and barns before winter. They stopped at a livery stable in Dubuque, Iowa, where a stagecoach was making ready to head east. "What's ahead for us?" Jacob asked. "We're on our way to Minnesota."

The stage driver shrugged and responded, "Iowa became a state a few years ago. The goin's good on the territorial trail upriver to Guttenberg. Lots of Germans have been comin' under that Western Settlement Act out of Cincinnati. Since that Lussiana purchase back in '03 and settlin' things with the Indians in '33, settlers have been comin' through every summer. From Guttenberg, the trail goes west and north toward Minnesota." He pointed to a fork in the trail. "Over there is the trail upriver."

"Much obliged." Jacob nodded. "A blessed day to ya."

On the way through Dubuque, Polly noticed a building with a belltower and a cross on top. "Look!" she exclaimed. "That must be a church over there." The sign in front announced services at the Dubuque Methodist Church on Sundays at 10:00 a.m. Being late Saturday afternoon, they found a place to camp upriver from town. Sunday would be a day of rest for both the animals and the travelers.

Before bedtime, Polly approached her husband. "Jacob, did you see that little Methodist Church in town? Do you remember back in Pennsylvania that Jacob Albright was once a preacher with the Methodists? Seems like they said the only thing that kept him from being Methodist was the rule by Francis Asbury that he was not allowed to preach in German. It isn't far back there, could we go to church tomorrow?"

Jacob lifted his hat and scratched his head. "Polly, I'm so focused on getting to Minnesota that I didn't see a church. What time is the meeting?"

Polly reached out and put her hand on her husband's arm. "Jacob, you are so tired, and I love you so much. We all need this Sabbath rest. Come, let Joe go on watch and you settle in for a good sleep."

Even Rusty the rooster was lazy the next morning, delaying his crowing until the sun cast reflections over the Mississippi. Jacob shook his head, hardly able to believe he had slept close to ten hours. His body was stiff, but well rested. The smell of coffee brewing brought everyone out of the wagons.

"Hotcakes are ready," Polly announced. As the family gathered, Jacob began to pray, "Lord, thank you for bringing us this far. Thank you for getting us across the river yesterday. We give thanks for this beautiful day. Thanks for the food we are about to receive. Amen!"

While he had everyone's attention, Jacob continued, "We passed a church back a piece yesterday. Polly and I and our children will be attendin'. Everyone's welcome. Let's eat!"

After swallowing a tasty bite of the sausage, Jake spoke up. "Pa, you could hitch the spare team to the Studebaker to drive to church. That would give the bays a day off."

"Good idea," Jacob agreed. "You and Mary M are welcome to go."

"Since I ain't never gone to church, I'll stay with the stock," Joe offered.

Adam chimed in, "Catharine and I'll be stayin' here in camp. Joe, you should go, it would do you good to hear some good preachin'. I'll watch the stock, and maybe the boys and I will try a little fishin' in the Mississippi."

It was settled. Everyone piled in the Studebaker for the trip to church. Upon arrival, Jake proudly parked his new wagon in the row with others at the hitching rail by the street. When the McQuillan family approached the front entrance, a middle-aged couple reached out a hand. "Welcome to worship this morning."

Jacob responded, "We're the McQuillan family. We're passin' through Dubuque on our way to Minnesota."

Inside the building, they sat on benches a few rows from the back. Matilda crawled up in her pa's lap and snuggled against his strong chest. George was sullen, having wanted to stay in camp and go fishing. Lucinda was excited to be at worship. Joe looked uncomfortable, hunched forward like he was trying not to be seen.

A tall, skinny boy of about thirteen dressed in bib overalls six inches too short got up and started pumping a handle on the organ that looked like a pump handle. A round-faced woman not much taller than she was wide approached the swivel-topped stool. She sat down and swung in toward the instrument. Between her full-length skirt and the folds of her body, the stool was completely out of sight. Her stubby fingers were challenged to reach the octaves. With no hymnbook in sight, the notes rang out clear and crisp. She moved from "Rock of Ages" to "When Morning Gilds the Skies" to "Sweet Hour of Prayer" without the slightest hesitation. The faster she played, the faster the lad pumped.

The sexton, gold watch in hand, gave a mighty pull on the rope just as the hour hand reached straight up. The belfry creaked as the bell rang out over the city. The pastor entered from a side door. He was a man of middle age and medium height. His hair was thin on top and a bit disheveled. His black suit had seen many Sundays. His long coat was fastened together by one button over a slightly plump stomach. He approached a table in the center of the platform, knelt for a few moments, and sat down on a chair with a dark-red padded seat. The organ stopped abruptly. The pastor stepped to the pulpit and welcomed the people who had gathered.

Lucinda joined in the singing of a hymn she had memorized. Her heart was warm within her as the pastor prayed. She followed along as he read the Scripture from Philippians 3:12-14. The sermon was about pressing on toward God's goals in our lives. Lucy was encouraged about pressing on to a new home in Minnesota.

As the service drew to a close, the pastor stood at center stage and held out his hands, gently offering an invitation to receive new life in Jesus through faith in his sacrificial death on the cross. It was quiet for a long moment. Then a shuffling sound and heavy steps came from the back of the room. Joe, walking tall, moved up the aisle. He approached the pastor and said in a clear voice, "Preacher, I just met Jesus last week talkin' with my boss on the trail. I want to settle things with Jesus here and now."

The pastor, overwhelmed both by the sudden response and the size of his candidate, reached his hand to Joe's shoulder and began to pray. Tears rolled down Joe's face as he went down on his knees. Sniffles were heard throughout the church.

Joe stood and turned to go back to his seat. The pastor said, "Wait, young man, would you like to be baptized? We could gather at the river this afternoon. Might be a bit cold, but I'm willin'."

Joe nodded his head. "Guess that would be fittin'."

The pastor announced, "We'll meet at Fred and Nan's by the river this afternoon at 3:00. Everyone come! The service is over. God bless all of you."

The people were friendly as the McQuillans headed back to the Studebaker. A young man came up to Jake. "Mighty nice wagon you got there. Where did you come by one like that?"

"Back in South Bend, Indiana, at the Studebaker Wagon Shop," Jake answered. "Had some problems with my old one and traded with Henry Studebaker. We like it a lot." The young man nodded and walked away.

Jacob got directions to the baptism. When the McQuillans arrived back in camp, the fire was burning, and the fish were ready for the frying pan. At dinner, Joe was quiet, withdrawn, and obviously nervous. Jacob talked to the family group about baptism and that Joe was doing one of the most important things in a lifetime.

Between dinner and the time to leave for the baptism service, members of the family got some needed rest. Lucinda read from the Bible in the book of Acts where Philip talked to an Ethiopian man and he was baptized. Lucinda felt that same warmness in her heart that was there at church in the morning. She climbed down from the wagon and found her pa sitting by the fire. "Pa," she said, "I've been reading the Bible, and I'm wonderin', you know, I've never been baptized. Could I be baptized with Joe?"

Jacob put his arm around his daughter and looked down into her eyes. "Don't see why not, if the preacher's willin'."

All fifteen McQuillans set out for Fred and Nan's for what would be one of Lucinda's most memorable days. When the pastor and Joe walked toward the water, the pastor turned to Jacob and said, "Best you help me with this man or we'll lose him if I can't bring him back up." Laughter came from the gathering. The preacher spoke loudly. "Joseph, I baptize you in the name of the Father, the Son, and the Holy Spirit." Joe went under and back up. Cheers and applause sounded from the believers. Since Jacob was in the water, the pastor invited him to stay for the baptism of his daughter. When Lucinda came up from her baptism, her face glowed with joy.

The ladies put out sandwiches and lemonade for everyone. The pastor sat next to Jacob, enjoying the refreshments. "It was good to worship with your people this morning, Pastor. Surprised to find a church here in Dubuque," Jacob commented.

"Ya," the pastor responded, "been here since 1834, started by the Methodists as a part of that Pietist movement with John Wesley in England. It's the first church built in all of Iowa."

Jacob shared, "Our roots are in the Evangelical Association started by Jacob Albright in Pennsylvania. Guess he was influenced a lot by the Methodists. It seems a lot the same as your church. Thanks for being willin' to come out here for Joe and my daughter."

"Wouldn't miss it for anything. It's been good for our people to have you with us. God bless you as you move on to Minnesota."

Lucinda was too excited to sleep that night. She slipped out of her bunk and found her way to Jake's wagon. She spoke quietly. "Mary M, I can't sleep, could we talk?"

"Sure, Lucy, come on in. Hester is sleepin'." She told Mary M about the warm feeling she had in church and other times during the day. Mary M shared, "That's one way the Holy Spirit makes himself known to us. You've had a special day today. You'll remember this day the rest of your life."

A Smile on Her Face
Princeton, Wisconsin
1854

T HE FOOD SUPPLY WAS DWINDLING, and the rabbit snares were empty. Matilda was worried. The days following the Wisconsin blizzard turned bitter cold. Johann cut wood every day to keep a fire in the open fireplace. Eldwin rode in on his saddle horse as Johann finished stacking the last of his load.

"Come in, my friend, let's have a cup of coffee," Johann invited. "What brings you out this cold day?"

Caroline poured two cups while the men visited. "We're goin' to Princeton tomorrow. I thought you'd like to go with us. We'll leave early in the morning."

After a short chat, Eldwin stood up and tipped his hat toward Caroline. "Much obliged for the coffee." As he stepped over the threshold, he said, "See you in the mornin'."

Johann stood in the doorway and waved good-bye to his friend. "Thanks, Eldwin, we'll be there early."

The Mannweilers were up before daylight. Caroline fixed coffee and bread for breakfast. Johann hitched Maud to the small sleigh he had fashioned using a pair of old runners. He put some warm horse blankets in the sleigh. "Come on, Caroline, Matilda, we need to get to the Bauers'," he urged. "Wrap that hot iron in a gunnysack and bring it to keep our feet warm. Hurry!"

Matilda had her boots and heavy coat on, but Caroline just sat by the fire, wrapped in a blanket. "Matilda, tell your vati that I can't go. I'll stay and take care of the cabin. I have food, and the wood is in. You go with your vati. Go on now!"

Matilda went to her mother with her hands out. "Mutti, you can't stay here alone. I'll stay with you. Either you come with us or I will stay with you."

By this time, Johann was impatient. "Come," he insisted, "the Bauers will be waiting for us. Caroline, you must get your coat and boots."

"No, Johann, I'm not goin'. You and Matilda go along now," she said quietly. "I'm not goin'. I'm too tired. I'll be too much trouble for you."

Matilda considered, *I need to stay here with Mutti, but I so wanted to see Helga.* "Vati," she said, "I'll stay with Mutti. You go and get the supplies."

"No, Matilda, you've been lookin' forward to seeing your friend. I will not deny you that. I'll bring in more wood, and your mutti can stay. She'll be all right for only two days." Johann doubled the wood supply and kissed his wife good-bye.

Maud went at a trot all the way to the neighbor's house. The Bauers were ready to leave when they arrived. It was a bright, sunny day, cold, but clear and still. The only sounds were Johann's and Eldwin's low voices and the gliding of the runners in the snow.

Helga let out a screech when she saw Matilda come into the café. The two thirteen-year-olds were thrilled to have the afternoon together. Once they caught up on all the news, Matilda's shoulders slumped, and her countenance fell. "What is it, Matilda? You look so sad," Helga asked.

"It's my mutti, she's been really sick. Just before we left home this morning, she refused to come with us to town. I'm worried about her out there in the cabin alone. Vati said she'll be all right, but I'm afraid for her."

Helga took Matilda's hand in hers and shared, "That's what happened to my vati. We need to pray for your mutti."

Johann went to the bank and borrowed a little more money. "Matilda," he said, "I need your help purchasing household supplies. We must get the food your mutti will need."

They stayed at the rooming house that night, planning to head home the next morning. However, as often happens, a second blizzard followed the first. When Matilda looked out the window at dawn, she exclaimed, "Vati, look at the snow, it's a blizzard. I can't see the building across the street. Vati, we have to get home to Mutti."

Johann's heart nearly stopped. *We would never find our way home in that storm.* "Matilda, don't worry, we'll go as soon as we can. Your mutti will be all right."

Matilda and her pa trudged through the snow to the café. Upon arrival, Eldwin said, "With this storm, we'll not be startin' for home until the weather clears. Dagmar isn't feelin' good this mornin', and the twins are sleepin' in."

Matilda was torn between worrying about her mother and the chance to spend more time with Helga. She could feel the worry in her father's quietness. "Vati," she ventured, "I'm worried about Mutti. She isn't strong enough to get more wood. Isn't there some way we can get there to help her?"

Johann took hold of his daughter by both arms, looked straight into her eyes, and said, "Matilda, I'm gonna rent a horse at the livery and ride home. I want you to spend the day with Helga. I'll take some food with me. You must bring the things we bought at the store. Eldwin will help you hitch Maud to the sleigh so you can drive her home from the Bauers'. I'm not leavin' Mutti alone another night."

"Olinda," Johann said as he paid for breakfast, "Caroline is home in our cabin alone. She hasn't been feelin' well. I'm gonna ride home today. I'd be obliged if Matilda could stay with you."

As Olinda put the payment in the drawer, she felt a slight flush move up her neck. She admired the courage of this man. She thought, *Though older, he is much like my husband.* Unconsciously, she put a hand on

147

his arm and said, "Oh, Johann, of course Matilda can stay with us. Do be careful. I'll pray for you."

The walk from the café to the livery convinced Johann that this was a real blizzard. He knew it would be nearly impossible to see, but he was not going to leave his wife alone. He breathed a simple prayer and walked in to find Fred. "Hey, Fred," he called. "Fred, I need to rent a horse, a strong and reliable one."

Fred appeared from behind a fork full of hay. "Ja, who is that out there? No one in his right mind would be renting a horse today. No beast of mine goes out in this storm."

"It's Johann Mannweiler. I bought that team and wagon last fall. My daughter and I came to town for supplies, but my wife was too weak to travel. I need a horse to get back to my place. My wife's not strong enough to make it through another night. I need the best horse you have."

"You're crazy to go out in this storm. A horse might make it, but you'll never survive. I'm not lettin' you go out there and then feel guilty the rest of my life over your foolishness. No horse from Fred's Livery!" he vowed and walked away.

"All right, Fred, it's either a horse from you or I start walkin', and that seems more foolish. A horse or I walk. Take your choice." Johann started to leave in a huff.

"Wait up," Fred returned, "puttin' it that way, I reckon my gelding could get you there. You ain't dressed for a ride like that though. I'll let you take the horse, but you're puttin' on wool pants and a drover's coat. You need some wool socks and boots too."

"Ain't got the money for duds like that and you know it. Where's the horse? I don't have time to lose."

"I'll loan you my stuff. Get yourself dressed if you want a horse from me. Besides, I'm not chargin' you rent, and I'll be prayin' ya through."

Johann was so bundled up in Fred's clothes that he could hardly get in the saddle. Once he was on his mount, Fred pulled a heavy wool blanket around his back and over his shoulders. "That gelding's been out that way lots of times, Barney will know the way."

The wind came in mighty gusts. Johann thought, *I'm glad that northwest wind is at my back.* After what seemed like an eternity, Johann pulled his mount up in the middle of a grove of pines. Barney pawed in the snow for a few bites of grass and ate some snow for a drink. Johann took a few bites of the jerky and some cheese that Olinda handed him as he left the café. From time to time, Barney would put his nose to the ground; and on occasion, he would whinny softly. Johann wondered if the horse sensed other animals in the area. "Please, God, don't leave me out here after dark."

When Eldwin heard that Johann had left for home, he was both worried and angry with his friend. He saw no way that Johann would make it to the cabin. "This wind is more than any man could survive," he told Dagmar.

Dagmar was worried for another reason. "Eldwin, I must tell you that I can't go home tomorrow. I think the baby will be born before we leave. You may have to take the girls with you and come back for me and the baby."

Fred's clothes kept Johann tolerably warm. He couldn't tell if snow was still falling. When he saw the grove of hardwoods at the corner of his claim, his heart began to beat faster, knowing he soon would be there for Caroline. He urged Barney on across the prairie toward home. Darkness began to move in as he approached the little log cabin. Johann breathed a sigh of relief as he spoke to his mount. "Good job, Barney, good job."

Louie whinnied when Johann entered the lean-to. He untied Louie and led the two horses to the open water below the rapids for a drink. Back in the lean-to, Johann tossed a forkful of hay to each of the animals. Barney shook and stretched when Johann removed the saddle.

Panic struck as he approached the cabin. His heart shuddered in his chest. "Oh no!" he cried out loud. "No smoke coming from the chimney." He pushed the door open. The cabin was cold and quiet.

"Caroline!" he shouted. "Caroline, where are you, Caroline?" He stumbled across the room in Fred's big boots. His eyes slowly adjusted to the darkness. Finally, he found her wrapped in her quilt on their bed. *Could that be a smile on her face?* He felt her cheek. Cold! "Caroline, I can't go on without you. You can't leave us now. We are just getting our land. What will Matilda do without her mutti? Oh, God, don't let this be happening. It can't be!" He fell down on the bed beside her and sobbed. "How can I tell Matilda? How?"

Grief moved to necessity. It took all the energy he could muster to get the fire started. Gradually, the cabin warmed. He made a cup of coffee and broke off a piece of bread. He sat on his old chair by the fire, allowing his heart to break. *O, my love, how can I go on?* His body went numb from grief and fatigue. The night passed slowly.

At daylight, his mind began to clear. The immediate struck him. *What will I do with Caroline's body?* Johann straightened his shoulders, put on his coat and boots, and went to the lean-to. The horses whinnied softly but received no attention. He dug behind the hay pile and found some boards that he had stored away. Returning to the cabin, he fashioned a simple coffin with hammer and nails. He took the coffin back to the lean-to and pushed it up against the log wall. He trudged back to the cabin, took his wife's body in his arms, and carried her to the lean-to. Placing her in the coffin, he gently wrapped the quilt around her and straightened her hair with his mitten. Once again, he noticed the smile on her face. Tears streamed down his face as he nailed the cover in place. Louie nuzzled his owner as Johann broke into sobs. "O, God, what am I going to do?"

The snow had stopped. The sun was moving toward middle sky. Johann banked the fire and prepared to ride to the Bauers' home and wait for them to return from Princeton. As he put a small lunch in a cloth bag, he noticed Matilda's open diary on the shelf. He read, "Five days before Christmas." He could cry no more. The pain was too great.

Upon arrival at the Bauer home, Johann found the fires well tended and the stock cared for by a trusted neighbor. He dug the sleigh out of the snow and watered Maud to be ready to leave as soon as Matilda arrived.

With nothing to do but wait, Johann's body felt empty and limp. He sat down on a stool and leaned back against the barn wall. The warmth from the stock in the small barn caused weariness to come over him. He dozed off only to be startled by Fritz barking at the arrival of the family. Johann was glad they had arrived, but how could he tell them?

Johann stepped out of the barn as the team and sledge came to a stop. "Vati," Matilda shouted, "I'm glad to see you. How did the ride go? Is mutti all right?" Johann's head went down. *How can I answer her questions?* He stood there as if paralyzed. Matilda jumped down from the sledge and ran to her father. "Vati, what is wrong? Vati, answer me!"

Johann straightened up, drew a deep breath, and answered, "Oh, Matilda, your mutti is dead. The fire was out when I arrived, and she was dead. There was plenty of wood in the cabin. She was in her bed. She must have died in her sleep. I'm so sorry, Matilda."

Matilda's knees buckled as she fell against her pa. He held her up as she sobbed and sobbed. "Vati, what will we do without her? How can we go on? I knew I should have stayed home with her. I could have helped her. It's all my fault, Vati."

"No, Matilda, it is not your fault. She knew this was going to happen and wanted to shelter you. She had everything she needed. Matilda, your mutti knew how sick she was, and she chose to die while we were gone. You have to believe me, Matilda. It was God's way. She had a smile on her face when I found her."

Looking around, Johann asked, "Where is Eldwin and, and . . . Dagmar? Did you girls drive home alone?"

Gerda answered, "Mutti is having the baby. Vati wouldn't leave her, so he sent us home to take care of the stock. He knew we were expected home today, and no one would be here. He was concerned about you and Mrs. Mannweiler too."

Gertrude had the team watered and in the barn. "Come, let's make some coffee and lunch. You need to eat before you leave for home."

The twins worked together to kindle the fire in the cookstove and set out a tasty lunch. Johann and Matilda did not feel like eating, but they forced a few bites down to sustain them for the ride home. Matilda hugged each of the girls as she and her pa made their way to the sleigh.

Maud moved out at a steady pace. Louie was on a lead rope behind. Matilda sat close and leaned against her pa, feeling the warmth of his body. The only sound was the slight jingle of the harness. As they approached the cabin, the sun had moved low in the western sky. The cold of the evening and the brightness of the snow were punctuated by sun dogs on either side of the blazing red sun. *Does Mutti know the pain that is in my heart? Why, Mutti, did you have to leave us now?*

It didn't seem like home to Matilda as they unhitched Maud and fed and watered the horses. Matilda carried the supplies to the door and waited. Johann approached. She fell into his arms and sobbed. They held each other for a long time. Johann reached and opened the door. "Come, Matilda, we must make some coffee and eat something."

"Where is she?" Matilda whispered as if someone were sleeping. She looked over at the bed. "Vati, where is she?"

Johann forced his words through the lump in his throat. "I made a coffin. She is safe by the wall of the lean-to. We'll dig a grave in the hardwood grove next spring when the frost is out. Maybe we can find a preacher to say some words for us."

Johann stirred the coals in the fireplace, added wood, and brought it to flame. The hot coffee tasted good but did not dull the pain. After supper, Matilda took her diary by the candle and read her last entry. "Five days to Christmas!" A deep breath filled her lungs, and it felt as if she could not let it out. "Vati," she cried, "day after tomorrow is Christmas. Mutti and I were planning a special dinner. We had saved a ham the Bauers gave us. We kept some potatoes, and we were going to make a cake. I can't face Christmas without Mutti."

Across the room, Johann was sitting on the edge of the bed, head in his hands. She saw his shoulders slump but knew he could not answer. She realized his pain was as deep as hers.

Matilda turned the page of her diary. She saw a loose piece of paper tucked between the pages. She read, "Dearest Matilda, I love you. I know my time has come. I saw Jesus! He smiled at me. I smiled back at him. Please keep smiling!" Tears flowed down her face, and the lump in her throat stopped her breath. "Look, Vati, Mutti left a note in my diary."

Johann stood and moved slowly across the room. He went down on one knee and read the words slowly in a whisper. "Dearest Matilda, I love you. I know my time has come. I saw Jesus! He smiled at me. I smiled back at him. Please keep smiling!" Matilda felt her pa take a deep breath. "Yup, Matilda, she has a smile on her face." After a long pause, he spoke with resolve. "Matilda, we have to keep going. We will keep the claim!"

The Coffee Mill
Minnesota
1852

A S THE McQUILLAN WAGONS HEADED northward out of Dubuque, Lucinda knew something special had happened in her life at her baptism. She thought, *Mary M was right, I will remember this day the rest of my life.*

Lucinda continued the routine of helping her mother with the younger children and doing the needed chores. She was determined to read from the Bible each day. "Ma," she asked, "will I go to school when we get to our new home? Will we have a church?"

"I know you always liked school, Lucinda. We'll have our own school for our family. We could get started right here in our Schooner. I brought some books along. You could help the little ones with their reading. Melissa and Ezra got a good start last year. Once we get settled, we'll see that all the children go to school and we'll always worship together."

Returning from scouting the trail, Jacob warned, "Just ahead, we'll start downhill to the town of Guttenberg. Be ready to use the wagon brakes on the way down."

"Guttenberg," Lucy asked, "didn't he invent some kind of type for printing?"

"You're right, Lucinda," Jacob said. "This town is named after him, and they have a copy of a Bible that was printed using his type."

From Guttenberg, the trail angled to the northwest, leaving the river valley. Lucinda saw log cabins and barns surrounded by fields planted with corn, wheat, and oats. Lucy asked, "Pa, are we getting close to Minnesota? Will our place be like these?"

Jacob answered, "We still have a long way to go, maybe a couple of weeks."

The storekeeper at the Decorah Mercantile made it clear. "This is the last store on the trail to Minnesota. You get it here or you go without. Them winters in Minnesota can get mighty long," he cautioned as he carried a bag of potatoes to their wagon.

Jake checked the tools and purchased everything they would need for building their log cabins. He noticed a two-man crosscut saw hanging on the wall. "Pa," he said, "let's get that saw. It sure would speed up building our cabins. Like the man said, them winters get mighty long, and I promised Mary M a warm home for the baby."

"That's a good idea, Jake," Jacob responded. Turning to Polly, he said, "Have the girls help you stock up on staples for the kitchens. We may not get to a store again before spring."

Adam called to Jake, "Let's go over to that mill and buy some wheat and oats for seed. I want to get some plowin' done and some winter wheat planted yet this fall."

Jacob remembered how hard it was to plow the virgin prairie when they arrived in Ohio. He was regretting his decision to leave his sulky plow back in Ohio. Adam and Jake returned from the mill all excited about seeing something called a grasshopper plow. Jake urged, "Pa, it's made for breakin' up the prairie sod. Come, have a look."

At the blacksmith shop, the smithy said, "This plow was made by a blacksmith over in Illinois by the name of John Deere. He's been makin' 'em for about fifteen years. The settlers around here swear by 'em. They say they can break three times the sod as any other plow. Some have hauled 'em all the way from Illinois."

Jake said, "That plow is a necessity." Adam and Jake rearranged the wagons and loaded the Grasshopper on the back of the freight wagon. It made for a heavy load, but they were determined to get the plow to Minnesota.

Rusty the rooster announced the dawn of another day. Lucinda went to spend some time with Mary M. "How are you feeling today?" she inquired.

"I'm much better now," Mary M said with a sigh of relief. "I'm getting more excited every day about the baby. Polly assures me that everything will be just fine."

Lucinda shivered her shoulders. "I can hardly wait. I want a little niece. Boys can be a pain sometimes."

The draft animals pulled hard to move the wagons up the hill out of Decorah. Leveling off, the trail meandered through rolling hills and farmland. Jacob was tempted to look for a claim in Iowa, but he was determined to get to Minnesota where they would have no neighbors.

The days of June were unpredictable. One day would be hot and sunny, the next cloudy with cold rain pelting the faces of the drivers. On rainy days, the children spent most of their time in the wagons reading or doing their arithmetic.

On a pleasant June afternoon, the trail curved a little to the left past a grove of oaks. Suddenly, John and Israel began to shout. Israel jumped down from the lead wagon and started to run as fast as he could out ahead. Lucy wondered what had caused the excitement. As the wagons moved ahead, there it was. A log had been split in half and, carved on the flat side, was the word *Minysota*.

Joe and the entire family gathered by the sign. Jacob bowed. "Thank you, God, for bringing us this far. We look to you to show us our new home."

Harvey spoke up with a loud voice. "Pa, is this where we'll live? Where will our house be?"

Jacob lifted his son to his shoulder and said, "No, son, not right here, but God will let us know where we are to stop."

In midafternoon of the next day, Jacob took Polly's arm and said, "It's a beautiful day, come, ride out ahead with me." Jenny and Jake's saddle horse sensed the adventure as they galloped away. When they were out of sight of the wagon train, Jacob led the way up a slope into a grove of hardwoods. He dismounted, stepped over, and put his hands on Polly's waist as she swung down to the ground. He turned her and drew her into an embrace. "Polly," he said softly, "I love you. I'm so glad I saw you at the picnic that day back in Delta. I've been noticing the beautiful rolling hills and flowing streams. I think we're getting close to our new home. I want you to pray with me, asking God to show us where we are to live."

Taking Polly's arm, Jacob stepped over to a grassy area. They sat in quietness. Jacob prayed, "Lord, you have been with us on this journey every day. Your provision has been full. Thank you, God. We need your guidance in choosing a place for our new home. We wait upon you, Lord, for clear direction. Thank you, God."

Jacob turned to Polly and drew her close. They kissed. He looked out across the meadow. He started to stand. Polly took his arm. "Wait." She drew him back. "I've been waiting to tell you, I'm sure now that I'm with child. It should be a month or so after the new year."

Jacob held her for a moment. "You and Mary M about the same time. Good reason to get the cabins built and warm for winter. Polly, you're a good mother." They returned to the wagons with new resolve.

Even old Rusty the rooster sensed the McQuillans were getting close to their new home. His crowing was louder and earlier each morning. June rains caused muddy trails, but the greater problem was the overflowing river ahead. The only option was to camp and wait. The next morning, Joe said, "Boss, look how much the river went down overnight. Other travelers have put large logs in the river to get their wagons across. I can rearrange the logs and add some more so we can move on."

Thanks to Joe, the crossing was successful. The land flattened out to a slightly rolling plateau. Jacob could see miles of prairie grass, as tall as the horse's backs, flowing in the wind. Lucinda shuddered and asked, "Pa, are we lost? I don't like that tall grass. I can't see anything."

"No, Lucy, we're still on the trail." He waited. "Lucy, do you have your diary calendar? Is it July yet?"

"Yes, I looked this morning." Lucy answered, "It's July 2."

That evening, Jacob and Adam were sitting by the fire with a cup of coffee. Adam said, "Did you notice today that very few wagons have made their way through the prairie grass?"

"Ya," Jacob responded, "I think we're well beyond any settlements in Minnesota Territory. We'll be watchin' for a place any day now."

On July 4, 1852, despite the heat and humidity, Jacob woke up filled with anticipation. He said, "Polly, I have a feeling we'll find our new home today."

Polly turned, looked into her husband's eyes, and answered with excitement, "You know, Jacob, I woke up with the same feeling. Let's get these wagons rolling."

During a midmorning rest stop, Jake said, "Look, Pa, down to the right. That gentle descent must lead to a river flowing off to the east. That rise off in the distance must be on the other side of the river."

Gazing off to the north, Jacob answered, "Yup, I think you're right, son. I'm gonna take a ride and check that out. Bring the wagons down that way once the teams are rested."

Jacob mounted Jenny and rode down the slope. Beyond the river, he saw two clumps of trees a few rods apart that looked like oases on the prairie. He urged Jenny to a gallop as excitement rose up in his chest. As he crossed the river, Jenny stopped for a drink and wanted to linger in the cool water. Jacob pulled her to attention and moved on, feeling drawn to the clusters of trees on ahead. Jenny veered to the right and came to a stop. There in front of him, hidden by the tall grass, was a stream of clear water only a few feet wide. Jacob followed the stream a short distance and found a pool about thirty feet across. The sand in the bottom of the pool was bubbling. He remembered hearing about boiling springs. He dismounted. Rather than being hot, the water was extremely cold. He realized it was a spring bubbling up clear cool water.

Jacob reasoned, *There must be another spring that feeds this stream.* Taking Jenny's reins, he walked along the little stream toward the other clump of trees. He found another spring much like the first. It was the source of the little stream. Jacob knew he had found their new home.

Jacob set Jenny to a gallop back toward the wagons. He could not hide his excitement but wanted Polly to have the same discernment. He called to Adam, "Lead the wagons down the slope and across the river. We'll camp by those trees on the left tonight."

It took a couple of hours to guide the teams down the hill and across the river. The animals lingered for a long drink. Jacob led them through the prairie grass to a stand of oaks. With the teams resting in the shade, Jacob said to the family, "Come with me, I want to show you something very unusual." He led the way to the edge of the spring. "Polly," he said, "put your hand in the water." She hesitated and then touched the water with one finger.

"Oh," she exclaimed, "I thought it would be hot, but it's very cold. Jacob, this is our new home. There's good water, plenty of grass for our stock, and shade for hot summer days."

Jacob exclaimed, "This is it! Polly, go get the coffee mill from the Schooner!" Jacob turned to Adam with a smile. "Adam"—he winked—"bring me a hammer and two nails." Adam was puzzled but brought the requested items.

When Polly arrived with the coffee mill, Jacob walked about a hundred yards up the slope and nailed the coffee mill to a sturdy oak tree. Turning to the family, he said, "This is our claim, unhitch the critters. We're home in Minnesota Territory."

Supper that night was the usual prairie chicken meal, but Polly added a tasty salad of watercress from the spring. The McQuillans gave thanks to God for his grace and love bringing them to their new home. Lucinda climbed up on her pa's lap, gave him a hug, and said,

"Thank you, Pa, for getting us home." She wrote in her diary, "July 4, 1852—we're home in Minnesota!"

Next morning, Rusty the rooster crowed louder and longer than ever before. Lucinda said, "I think Rusty's happy to be home in Minnesota."

Jake added with a chuckle, "He's happy because he sees all this prairie grass and knows we'll have plenty of prairie chicken to eat."

After breakfast, Jacob called the family together. "We're home. Now we must work hard to be ready for winter."

That day, the women rearranged the wagons as their homes for the next few months. Polly asked, "Jake, would you make a shelter and set up my cookstove so I can bake my favorite bread?"

Jake rubbed his stomach and said, "It'll be done by sundown."

Adam added, "The boys and I will start cutting the prairie grass on the slope to the west. I want to get the Grasshopper goin' to turn some sod. I'll plant potatoes and vegetables that we can harvest this fall."

"That sounds good," Jake offered. "Joe and I could get started cuttin' logs for the cabins in that grove of poplar over to the west of the river crossing. Three cabins will take lots of logs."

Jacob interrupted, "Good ideas, let's get the supply wagons unloaded so you can get started."

Before long, the place was like a beehive. Everyone found a job, and everyone was willing to work. George asked if he could work with Jake and Joe. Lucinda, Melissa, and Ezra went exploring along the stream. They came back with an apron full of wild strawberries. "Ma," Lucy said with excitement, "we found trees full of crab apples and plums. We can make sauce and jelly forever."

Work went on from dawn to dark every day, but Sunday was always a day of worship and rest. The three men worked out an agreement that Jacob would take the western spring and the land to the west and Jake would take the eastern spring and the land to the east of it. Adam found a choice property a little to the northeast of Jake.

Each day, grass was cut, dried, and stacked. The Grasshopper never stopped as the men took turns behind the plow and the draft animals were changed every few hours. Sod was stacked row upon row to make walls for a barn. Logs were cut, hauled, peeled, and notched for cabin walls.

One late summer morning, Polly noticed her husband putting the morning's milk to cool at the spring. She startled him when she said, "Good morning, Jacob, you were up early this morning. You're working hard these days."

"Each day draws closer to snow and cold. I promised you a warm place for the children come winter. You're working hard too." He patted her tummy and remarked, "I want you to take good care of that little one. I love you, Pol." He drew her into his arms.

The women made tallow candles for the long, dark winters. They canned and dried plums and crab apples. Venison was cut in strips and dried in the sun and over the fire. They made cheese and butter from excess milk. Clothes were passed down from one child to the next, adding a few more patches each time. Bare feet in summer saved the shoes for winter.

Polly made fresh apple pies for supper on September 7, 1852. After supper, Jacob asked his daughter to come and stand by him. "Lucy," he said, "remember the day you took a step of faith in Jesus and were baptized at the river along with Joe?" She nodded. "Your ma and I have something special for you on your tenth birthday." He handed her a package wrapped in brown paper.

Lucinda received the gift and pulled the paper back. With a squeal of delight, she cried, "My very own Bible. Pa, I'll read it every day, I promise."

"One more thing"—Jacob lifted his hand for attention—"Ma and I have some news for the family. Come January, we'll be having a new McQuillan. You kids will have a new brother or sister." He looked at Polly with a smile. She nodded and smiled at the children.

Matilda screwed up her face in thought. "What do you mean a new McQuillan? We've got enough McQuillans." She put her hands on her hips and gave a huff.

Lucy reached for her sister's hand. "Matilda, Mommy is going to have a little baby. It might be a boy, or it might be a girl."

The little girl huffed, "Well, I don't know where she's gonna get that baby, but it better be a girl. I don't want any more boys around here like Harvey."

September brought shorter days and cooler nights. Log after log had been put in place as the cabins came closer to completion. Joe, with his great strength, would hoist the logs in place. The children helped mix chopped prairie grass with clay and sand to make mud to chink between the logs. Soon the rafter logs went up. Roof boards were made by splitting logs and shaving them smooth. John, Israel, and George spent hours with the froe and mallet, splitting clapboard shingles.

The maples broke forth in brilliant reds and oranges, and the poplar and cottonwoods added yellow to go with the russets of the oak trees. October was passing rapidly. Potatoes were dug and stored in the root cellar along with jars of fruit and jam. Combs of honey were brought in from a beehive in an old hollow tree.

Wood was cut and stacked by each of the cabins. The outer walls of the cabins were banked with prairie grass to add warmth. Polly chided, "You better get that stone chimney done and my stove set up if you want me to roast a turkey for Thanksgiving." A few weeks later, the stove was ready, and John and Israel snared two birds for Thanksgiving dinner.

Lucy recorded each event in her diary, keeping track of the days on her calendar. On Sundays, Jake would play his fiddle for the singing of the familiar hymns. Joe sang loud and off-key, but no one matched his joy and enthusiasm.

In the cold of winter, the stoves and fireplaces demanded large supplies of wood. Adam hitched his mules to a sledge he had made to haul loads of wood to each cabin. The boys continued to bring in elk and deer for fine cuts of meat. Christmas was the celebration of the birth of Jesus, and the family found ways to make gifts of love for one another.

Early one January morning, Jacob awakened to the sound of pounding on the cabin door. Opening the door, he found Jake in his boots with his coat pulled over his nightshirt. "We need Polly quick. It's happening." Jake turned and ran back to his cabin.

Jacob woke Polly, now large with child herself, and walked with her to Jake and Mary M's cabin. Jake was boiling water at the fireplace. Father calmed his son while Polly assisted Mary M in the delivery of a fine baby boy. They named him Edwin.

Not many days later, January 24, 1853, Catherine was called to assist Polly with the delivery of Franklin Pierce. Even though Matilda wanted a sister, she soon warmed up to her little brother.

Lucinda, at the young age of ten, became a constant helper to her mother. She learned quickly how to cook, knit, sew, and care for babies. Mostly, she looked forward to every chance she got to spend time with Mary M and baby Edwin. Lucinda was blessed to have godly mentors as she grew toward womanhood.

Old Tom for Christmas
Princeton, Wisconsin
1854

A FTER BREAKFAST, MATILDA HEARD HER father leave with the team and sleigh to cut wood. Loneliness enveloped her. She cried until she could cry no more. How she wished her father had taken her with him, yet she knew he needed to stay busy to relieve his pain. She forced herself to do the needed work around the cabin.

A little before noon, a light knock came on the door. Matilda's head came up as she nearly spoke out loud, *Who could that be?* She opened the door just a crack and peered out. "Gerda," she cried with surprise, "what brings you here? Come in, my *freundin*, please come in." Opening the door wide, she looked out. "Are you alone?"

Gerda entered the cabin but seemed unable to speak. Matilda pulled out a bench and offered her visitor a seat. She poured two cups of coffee and sat down. She waited.

Finally, Gerda looked up at Matilda and spoke just above a whisper. "I feel so bad for you, Matilda. I don't know what I would do if my mutti died. Gertrude and I are home alone. Vati and Mutti haven't come home from Princeton yet. Tomorrow is Christmas, and we may be home alone. We want you and your vati to come for dinner. Gertrude is preparing food, and we don't want you to be alone on Christmas."

Matilda didn't know what to say to her kind neighbor. She ventured, "Vati is out cutting wood. We would have to ask him. Gerda, I'm so glad you came. Vati is so sad, and I can hardly talk with him. We both hurt too much." Matilda paused a moment, took up the paper her mother had left, and handed it to Gerda. "Mutti left this for me in my diary."

Gerda read the note and burst into tears. The two girls held each other and cried. Gerda straightened up and said, "I rode Ginger over here. You could ride with me to ask your vati about tomorrow. Then I need to go home to help my *schwester.*"

Ginger shied a bit as Gerda helped Matilda up behind the saddle. They followed the sleigh tracks to find Johann. The cold wind in her face stimulated Matilda. They found the team and sleigh with the halter ropes tied to a willow. Gerda said, "Look, the tracks lead into that aspen grove." They followed the tracks toward the river. A gunshot and then another echoed through the woods. In a few minutes, they saw Johann walking toward them, carrying a turkey in each hand.

"Vati," Matilda shouted. "Vati, Gerda came to visit."

Johann approached with his gun slung over his shoulder, a turkey in each hand, and a slight smile on his face. "I've been after that Old Tom for two weeks, and I got me a hen at the same time."

Gerda swung her leg over Ginger's neck and slid down in the snow. She dropped the reins to the ground and walked up to Johann. "Mr. Mannweiler," she said, "we don't want you and Matilda to be alone for Christmas. Mutti and Vati are still in Princeton, but Gertrude and I want to fix dinner. We would like you to come."

Stunned by the sudden question, Johann looked down at his catch and said, "Can we dress Old Tom and have him for dinner?"

Gerda looked from one turkey to the other and asked, "Which one's Old Tom? We can dress him. We've done it before when our vati shot one. We'll stuff him with sage dressin', and he'll be right good."

Matilda slid down from Ginger, and the three of them trudged back through the snow to the sleigh. Johann put Old Tom in a gunnysack and hung him over Ginger's back. Gerda waved as she rode off across the prairie.

Father and daughter spent the bright part of the day cutting wood and stacking it on the sleigh. When the sun was well to the west, they climbed up on the seat and headed back to the cabin. It had been healing for them to work together.

Again, the night seemed long and lonely without Caroline. Following the blizzards, the little cabin creaked and cracked from the bitter cold. Pa got up several times in the night to keep the fire burning. Matilda heard her pa sobbing as he sat by the fire. She wanted to comfort him, but she had little comfort to give. Eventually, she heard his deep breathing and soft snoring. Memory after memory of her mother rolled through her mind. "God," she prayed, "please comfort Vati and please hold Mutti close. And, God, please take away this hurt in my heart."

Christmas morning arrived still and cold. Johann put six potatoes and some cheese in a cloth bag to take to the Bauers. While Matilda was at the outhouse, he dug down to the bottom of one of the trunks and found a small gray box. When he slipped the lid off, tears streamed down his cheeks. He swallowed to try to still the pain in his throat. With his thumb and finger, he held up a small gold cross on a gold chain. With tear-filled eyes, he remembered the day he gave it to Caroline. It was the day after their baby was born, and they named her Matilda. He replaced the cross in the box and tucked it safely in his pocket.

After a light breakfast, Johann hitched the team to the sleigh. Matilda put on her best dress, warm coat, and boots. With grief so close to the surface, few words were spoken on the sleigh ride across the prairie and along the ridge to the Bauer home.

Fritz barked a friendly greeting as they drove up to the barn. Matilda ran to the house while Johann took the horses to the barn. He looked around and said to himself, *Someday, I'll have a barn like this with some cows and chickens, maybe some pigs.* He gave Louie and Maud a good rubbing with brush and curry. He wondered what it would be like having Christmas with three young girls.

In the house, Gerda and Gertrude were scurrying about fixing the Christmas meal. The smell of fresh-baked bread welcomed Johann as he pushed the door open. "Come in, Mr. Mannweiler," they said in chorus. The bright smiles on the twin's faces warmed his heart. Matilda was peeling potatoes, and the turkey was roasting in the range oven. "How do you like the smell of Old Tom?" Gerda asked. "I hope you're hungry for a Christmas treat."

Johann marveled at all the cooking Gertrude and Gerda had done along with doing the barn chores. Warmth from the cookstove soon brought drowsiness to Johann as he sat by the window. He jumped when Fritz went barking across the yard to welcome an approaching sledge.

Gertrude and Gerda grabbed their coats and ran out the door. "Mutti and Vati are here!" they shouted as they ran through the snow. Johann and Matilda went to the door and waited. Steam floated above the horses' backs, indicating they had been running at a fast pace. Johann went out and took care of the team.

Matilda got her coat and went to greet the Bauer family. She heard a familiar voice. "Oh, Matilda, I'm glad to see you." The voice came from a girl riding on a big black horse.

Matilda screeched, "Helga, I didn't expect you here today! And your mutti too. What brought you here?"

When everyone settled down, Eldwin spoke. "We have a new baby in our family. His name is Gerard to go with the other two Gs. Mutti was not ready to travel, but she wanted me to come home to have Christmas with the twins. Dagmar and Gerard are at the rooming house. Olinda didn't have to work today, so I invited them to come with us for Christmas."

Johann led the horses to the barn. Helga followed with her saddle horse. While Johann was giving the horses a rubdown, Eldwin came in the door. He brought hay for the animals and gave them some oats. Louie whinnied, so Eldwin gave him a treat as well. "Johann," he asked, "how is Caroline doing? How was your ride in the blizzard? I was worried about both of you that day."

Johann took a deep breath and spoke to his neighbor. "Caroline didn't make it." That was all he could get to come out of his mouth. He worked to keep the tears from flowing.

"Johann, what do you mean Caroline didn't make it?" Eldwin questioned. "Did you get home that day? Did that horse get you through?"

"When I got home, Caroline was dead," he answered. "She must have died in her sleep. The fire was out, and she was in bed. She left a note for Matilda. Said she knew she couldn't go on."

The two men met near the door. Eldwin put his arm around his neighbor's shoulders. "I'm so sorry, Johann. We'll help in any way we can, my friend. I'm so glad the twins invited you over today."

"I didn't know what to do with myself yesterday so I went out to cut wood. Took my gun along and shot a couple of turkeys. When Matilda came lookin' for me with Gerda, I sent one with her for dinner. Your girls got a good thing goin' in there."

"Ja, those girls can do most anything." Eldwin opened the door and waited for Johann to step out. "Dagmar has trained them well. We lost two babies since the twins were born. We're glad to have a son."

The two men came in and stomped the snow off their boots. The aroma of roast turkey brought their hunger to the surface. "Wow!" Eldwin said. "Smells like dinner is about ready."

Gertrude touched her vati's arm and said, "Vati, we are ready. Would you carve Old Tom and we can sit down for dinner?"

"Old Tom, who's Old Tom?" Eldwin wondered.

Matilda spoke up to answer the question. "Old Tom is a turkey Vati has been after for weeks. He finally got him yesterday."

Eldwin chuckled. As he started carving, he quipped, "Hope he ain't too tough from runnin' away from the hunter."

Once seated at the table, a quiet came over the room. Eldwin bowed his head. *How do I pray for my neighbors on this Christmas Day?* He opened his mouth, and God gave him the words.

Dear God in heaven, thank you for the birth of your Son, Jesus. Thank you too for the birth of our son, Gerard. Thank you for bringing our neighbors to be with us today. God, please bring comfort to Johann and Matilda today. Our dear friend Caroline has come to be with you. Thank you that she is with you now and that you surround her with your love. Father, it would comfort our hearts if you would be with us here at the table. Help us to take care of each other. Amen!

When Eldwin finished the prayer, Johann looked up. As he brushed a tear from his cheek, he glanced across the table and noticed Olinda doing the same. The thought ran through his mind, *She knows what I'm going through.* Food was passed, and conversation turned to the great job Gerda and Gertrude had done preparing the meal.

When everyone had eaten their fill, Eldwin presented silver bracelets to his twin girls and their friends Helga and Matilda. The girls felt elegant with their new gifts. Then Johann reached into his pocket and drew out the small gray box. Struggling to control his voice, Johann said, "Matilda, I have a gift for you." He cleared his throat and kept going. "I gave this to your mutti the day after you were born." He held the box in his huge rough hand as if he wanted to preserve it forever. His voice cracked as he said, "My daughter, may you wear this to remember your mutti." With his head down, Johann walked around the table to his daughter's chair between the twins. She swallowed hard as she received the gift from her father.

Matilda opened the box. Everything in the room stood still. She put her slender fingers in the box and brought out the gold chain and allowed the gold cross to swing beneath. She drew a deep breath and exploded in tears of joy and sorrow mixed with love. She stood on wobbly legs and embraced her father. He held her with eyes full of tears.

After a few minutes, Helga broke the silence. "Matilda, I have my vati's gold watch, and I treasure it more than anything. Now we have something special to share as *freundins*." Johann noticed that Olinda wiped a tear on her apron.

The afternoon passed quickly. When Johann and Matilda were ready to leave, Johann asked, "Olinda, how are you gettin' back to town?"

"Helga and I will ride Ebbe, our black mare," she answered, wondering why he was asking.

"Would one of you like to ride the gelding I borrowed from Fred? I need to get him back to town."

"Sure, we'll leave tomorrow about noon. Can you bring him over?" She saw him nod as the Mannweilers drove away.

That night, a deep loneliness came over Matilda as she lay in her bed. *O, Mutti, why did you have to leave us just as we were getting started? I miss how we worked together. I need you to teach me how to be a woman.* She cried herself to sleep.

The winter days of January and February passed. Conversation between father and daughter was limited. They both tried to avoid talking about Caroline to keep from causing the other pain. Yet the quiet reeked with pain. Matilda knew her pa was spending long hours cutting wood just to stay busy. On stormy days, he brought a harness in for repair, or he worked by the fireplace making a chair or a shelf for the cabin. His steps were slower and his shoulders slouched.

One day, as they were eating turkey soup, Johann turned to his daughter with a look of defeat. "Matilda, we should give up and go back home. I never should have brought you here. This is all my fault." His head went down on his arms, and his shoulders shook, but tears would no longer flow.

At thirteen, Matilda did not know how to respond to a grown man's grief. Her pain over the loss of her mother now turned to fear that her father would give up and they would have nothing. All she could say was, "No, Vati, we must prove our claim for Mutti."

Silence reigned. Johann finally straightened up. "If you can, I must," he said. He left the cabin. Matilda wept.

Heading West
Muskegon and Racine
1855-1856

AFTER TWO BACKBREAKING YEARS IN the New York lumber camps, Phillip's savings were meager. Rumors about opportunities in the mills in Michigan drifted through the camp. One day, seeing no future in New York, Phillip said good-bye to Bruno, joined two other men, and hopped a freight train heading west. Traveling by train, horseback, and sometimes on foot, they kept pressing on until they arrived at Muskegon, Michigan.

About a year later, in the spirit of adventure, Phillip jumped aboard a lumber barge and crossed Lake Michigan to Racine, Wisconsin. Refreshed by a bath and a good night's sleep in a Racine hotel, he stopped at a little café for breakfast. A tall lanky man in a business suit was sitting at the counter. The waitress addressed him as judge. As she topped off his coffee, Phillip heard him say something about needing a hand to work on his farm.

When the judge stood up to leave, Phillip stepped forward and said, "Excuse me, Judge, sir, I overheard you say that you need a man to work on your farm. I just arrived from the New York lumber mills and need a job. I grew up workin' hard in Germany. I'm sure I could do a good job for ya. I wouldn't need much more than some food and a place to sleep. If I learn fast, we could settle on wages later."

The judge looked up and down Phillip's frame. "You look like you could do a good day's work. Be here Saturday mornin', ready to go out to the farm. My farm manager, John, and his wife, Isabel, are livin' on the place. John'll get you started. Isabel's a good cook. The house is small, so you'll sleep in the loft in the barn."

"Thank you, Judge, I'll be ready on Saturday." Following a sturdy handshake, the judge departed.

The judge arrived as scheduled the following Saturday, driving a pair of blacks on a plain buggy. After some bacon and eggs, the two men headed out of town. The landscape opened to rolling meadows and fields being prepared for planting. Phillip breathed in the freshness of the spring morning. The judge held the blacks to a steady pace until they turned up a lane to a farmstead with a small house and a barn with a lean-to.

Stepping down from the buggy, the judge said, "John, this is Phillip Eppard, just in from out east and ready to go to work. You'll have to get him started."

A young woman, stout in stature with an attractive, cheerful countenance, stepped out on the porch. The child on her hip looked to be about six months old. She called, "Good mornin', Judge. Thought you'd be out today, so the coffee's hot." The judge introduced her to his new farmhand.

The kitchen was small, but clean and neat. Hot cups of coffee were served along with slices of bread and jelly. Putting his cup down, John said, "Well, Phillip, might as well get you started."

Phillip nodded toward Isabel. "Much obliged for the coffee."

The barn was built in a hillside. The lower level was for the livestock. The upper level had a large sliding door, making it possible to drive in with a team and wagon. John had Phillip put his bag in the loft. With a shrug, he said, "Make yourself at home. Get water over at the well." With a nod to one side, he continued, "We're buildin' a covered wagon for the judge. He's got plans to move to Minnesota and take up some of that good land. Since that Mendota Treaty with the Indians, people have been flockin' to Minnesota."

The months passed quickly. Phillip worked diligently on the wagon. He shaped and assembled the wagon box and made the hoops for the canvas top. He took care of the cows and did the milking morning and night. Queen, the dappled gray mare, seemed to take to him as he took rides in the hills in the evening.

One Saturday morning, Judge Felch and his wife, Hannah, drove in with his team of blacks. Isabel welcomed Hannah and led the way to the house. Phillip noticed the judge and John in a lengthy conversation. Phillip wondered if John was dissatisfied with his work.

Finally, Judge Felch and John walked into the barn. The judge circled the wagon with an approving nod. "Eppard," he said, "I've been talkin' to John. He says you're good with the animals, especially that dappled mare, Queen. How'd you like to ride her shotgun on my trip to Minnesota Territory? We'll be takin' an extra wagon to haul some farm equipment, a few chickens, and some seed to get started on the new claim. Six bucks a week for the trip and a job on my land when we arrive. John will stay here to keep this place up."

With his heart in his throat, Phillip croaked, "You . . . you got a rider! When do we leave?"

"Next Saturday. I've hired a guide who's made the trip before. His name is Johann Wolf. He goes by Johnny. You'll be workin' with him, standin' watch at night, takin' care of the horses, and such as that. You'll pack your personal things and a bedroll on your horse."

The judge looked around the barn as he considered further plans. "John," he continued, "we'll be takin' the big farm wagon for supplies and equipment. Have the blacksmith check it over. We'll take the sorrels, Lark and Lady, on that wagon."

Mr. Felch walked to the door and looked across the yard. "I want that sod-breakin' plow with us. Get a new one so you'll have one here next fall."

The judge started to leave. "Hannah and I will drive the blacks on the covered wagon. Hannah wants to take some furniture and personal things. We'll load that wagon in town." He tipped his hat and left.

John turned to Phillip with a smile. "I guess you're goin' travelin' next week."

"Ja, John, it looks that way." Phillip waited and then went on. "Did you want to go to Minnesota?"

"No, we're happy here. We have the baby and lookin' to have more. Life is good here for Isabel and me. I wish you well on the journey." John grinned and bumped Phillip on the arm. "You better have a good hat along or you'll burn that bald head of yours."

Phillip chuckled and responded, "Yup, you're right. That scarlet fever took my hair, and it never came back."

It was early morning when Phillip woke up on May 25, 1856. He lingered under his quilt, allowing his mind to drift. *What would Vati be doing just now? Does he ever think about me? How I miss Mutti.* He shook himself out of his daydreaming and straightened up with resolve. *I'm on the way to Minnesota!* The old rooster crowed. It was quiet, and he crowed again. Phillip thought, *If he's ready, I better get going too.*

While Phillip was putting the last hen in the crate on the supply wagon, a rider came up the lane. Once the dust settled, a stout man with a reddish-gray beard swung down from his big gray gelding. He wore a brown leather vest over a black shirt loosely tucked in his black denim pants. A gun in a holster hung from his waist. He swaggered across the yard toward Phillip. "Johann Wolf's the name. Call me Johnny and we'll get along good. I'm the wagon boss for the judge goin' to Minnesotie. The judge sent me to fetch a kid named Phillip and a team of sorrels on a supply wagon."

Surprised by the abruptness of this stranger, Phillip stammered, "Ja, ja, the wagon's loaded and ready to hitch the sorrels. My name's Phillip, Phillip Eppard. I'll be ridin' Queen and helpin' you on the trail."

The dark black eyes of the wagon boss drilled into Phillip's face before he spoke. "Just remember who's boss."

Phillip ignored the comment and hitched the sorrels to the supply wagon. As he was snapping the hame snaps in the neck yoke rings,

John came out of the house, carrying a canvas pouch. "Isabel didn't want you goin' hungry on the trail."

"Thanks, John, that's mighty fine of her." Out of the corner of his eye, he saw Isabel on the porch. Phillip tipped his hat and shouted, "Much obliged, Isabel, I'll miss your cookin' on the trail."

In town, the judge was waiting with his blacks hitched to the covered wagon. Hannah appeared to be a few years younger than her husband. Her straight black skirt hugged her slightly rounded figure. The white ruffled blouse seemed out of place for a day on the trail. A black bonnet framed her light-complexioned face and silver-blonde hair. Her deep blue eyes sparkled as she stood with hands on her hips, making her impatience known.

Judge Felch remarked, "Phil, you remember my wife, Hannah. She's a good cook. You'll be helpin' her with the fire and gettin' the supplies." Phillip touched the brim of his hat and nodded a greeting.

Hannah smiled and stepped forward. "Charles has been telling me about this young man who'll be traveling with us. I'm pleased to meet you."

The judge continued, "And this is my son, David. He'll be handlin' the sorrels on the big wagon. Looks like we're ready to pull out." The judge turned toward the wagon seat and remarked, "Come on, Hannah, let's get to Minnesota and find our new home." He took her hand, assisted her over the wagon wheel, and stepped up behind her.

Johnny spurred his horse out front. Sitting tall in the saddle, he made a powerful wave of his right hand. "Move out!" he shouted. "Get those wagons on the roll."

Judge Felch led with his team, and David followed with the supply wagon. In midafternoon, they met three drovers taking a small herd of cattle to market in Racine. Suddenly, a steer vaulted from the herd and ran between the judge's wagon and the team of sorrels, causing the drovers to lose control of the herd.

The judge saw what was happening and called, "Johnny, get back here and help with these critters."

At that, Johnny turned in his saddle and spouted, "I'm the boss here, not a cow puncher. That young bald-headed punk can run the cows. I'm runnin' a wagon train."

Passing the reins to Hannah, the judge jumped from the seat and sprinted toward Johnny. "You get off that horse and get over here."

Johnny responded, "You get on that wagon seat and follow up. You hired me to boss this trip, and boss it, I'll do."

"You get down here now, and we'll get it straight who's the boss around here," Judge Felch barked.

Johnny swung down from the saddle, dropped the reins, and turned toward the judge. "I'm not about to fight ya, but I'll be boss or I'll be out of here."

"You'll help with the cows, or I'll have that horse, saddle, and boots that I bought for you as payment for the trip. Let's get this straight, I'm the boss. I pay the bills, and you do what I say. Do you understand? Now get those cows out of here and let's get on the trail."

Johnny kicked the dirt, cursed, and swung into the saddle. He reined his horse to the right and yelled, "Hey, kid, circle back and I'll bring these two along." Soon they had the herd back under control.

That evening, Hannah came out of the covered wagon wearing a denim dress, her hair up in a bun, ready for work. Phillip started the fire and brought a supply of water. Soon they shared a tasty supper. Johnny stayed to himself, sulking after the episode earlier in the day.

The judge walked down by the stream where they had watered the horses. "Johnny, you're gonna get awfully hungry if you don't get up there and join us for supper."

Johnny kicked the dirt and huffed, "Not hungry! Don't need none of your grub!"

By breakfast time, he had changed his mind and gobbled down six pancakes and several mugs of hot coffee. Johnny brought in some prairie chickens for supper the next night.

Late afternoon of the third day, Johnny rode alongside the judge's wagon. "We're goin' a little longer today so we can reach Whitewater.

It's a good place to camp. I recommend spending a rest day there. It's called Whitewater for the white sandy bottom of the river. We can catch some fish for breakfast too."

"Good," Charles responded, "we need a day of rest."

After supper, with the wagons secured and the animals tethered, Johnny said, "Hey, Phil, let's go to town for a drink and some fun. We get the day off tomorrow."

"Naw, that's not for me. I'm gonna take a good bath in that river and get some sleep." Phillip knew Johnny was in for trouble and wanted nothing to do with it.

After a bath, Phillip sat by the fire and pulled out his mother's Bible. He was reading about the farmer who went out to sow his seed and how it fell on different kinds of soil. He wondered what kind of soil he would be. He remembered his mother, how she told him about the change Jesus had worked in her life. He breathed, *God, why did you take her away from me? Sometimes I feel so alone.*

The stars were just coming into view and a gentle breeze brought the cool of the evening. "Phil, are you enjoying the evening quiet?" Phillip spun around, startled by the voice.

"David! I guess I was way off in a bit of dreamin' here by the fire. How are things goin' for you? Are you doin' all right drivin' Lark and Lady?"

David sat down on a stump across from Phillip. His eyes fell on the Bible on the log next to Phil. "Do you believe the stuff in that book? I sure don't. It talks all about this God of love and all that, and then he takes my ma dead. And my *bruder* Ben, he killed him too. Do you call that love?"

Phillip put his hand on the Bible and put his head down. "I guess it doesn't seem like it, does it? What happened, Dave? With your mutti and your *bruder*, I mean."

"Well, it just ain't fair. With Wisconsin becoming a state in 1848 and the university starting in Madison the following year, I had plans to go to the university and maybe become a doctor or somethin'. Now this! Pa has Hannah, and she talks about havin' more kids. Not much place for me anymore. It just ain't the same."

Phillip knew from experience that anything he said about God or the Bible would fall on deaf ears. He waited. David drew a deep breath and continued, "It was a terrible accident. Ben was only seven. Pa had him ridin' in front of him in the saddle. They were bringin' some cows in. Pa got off to close a gate. I guess the cows were turning the wrong way and the horse thought it was his job to stop 'em. When the horse started runnin', Ben fell, but his foot was caught. His head hit a rock and broke his skull. Pa still has nightmares about it. Then only a few months later, my ma was having a baby and had trouble. The baby died, and a couple of days later, she died. You see, it just ain't fair. You can keep your old Bible stuff."

The boy's voice choked, and his shoulders shook with grief. Phillip put a hand on the lad's shoulder and said, "I understand your grief . . ."

"No, you don't understand," David spouted as he walked away. He slurred, "You can read your old Bible, but it just ain't true."

Stunned, Phillip opened his mouth, but nothing would come out. He sat there in his own grief until weariness sent him to his bedroll. He tried to pray for David, but thoughts of home prevailed.

Everyone was slow starting the next morning. Johnny still had not returned from town. Hannah fried some side pork and eggs to go with the hotcakes. The judge was working with some papers on the wagon tailgate, preparing for some business at the capital in Madison.

The sun was nearly straight up when David crawled out of bed. Hannah poured him a cup of coffee and gave him some bread and cheese. "You're too late for breakfast, so this'll have to hold you 'til supper," she said.

David nodded and mumbled, "Not hungry anyway." He took the bread, walked down by the stream, and sat on a stump.

Phillip came by and said, "Dave, let's make a gunnysack net and catch some fish for supper." David shrugged him off. Phillip took two old feed sacks, sewed them together, and attached them to two sticks.

Pushing the net along the deepest side of the river soon produced a nice trout. "I got one," he shouted. "Come on, Dave, take one end of this thing and we can get our supper."

The excitement got David going, and the two young men soon had a nice catch. Hannah came down to the stream with a knife and announced, "You guys caught 'em, you can clean 'em. I'll fry 'em."

David was cleaning a large trout when Phillip spoke. "I've been thinkin' about what you said last night. I suppose it would be hard for anyone to understand your feelings about your mutti and *bruder*. I spoke too hastily."

"Let's forget it, okay. I don't want to talk about it. It just hurts all the more." David tossed the remains of a fish toward the river where the birds flocked to it for a meal.

Phil drew a deep breath. "I can't forget it, David, because I hurt a lot too. You see, my mutti died when I was eleven years old. One day, she just died. No good reason for it, she just died. She meant the world to me. That Bible you saw last night, it was her Bible. I read it to remember her." He stopped and drew another breath.

"Ja, but you still got a pa. God took my ma dead, and my pa has his new wife, and I'm alone. I don't have anything left. You think that's fair?" David threw the knife down and started walking away.

"Do you want to hear the rest?" Phillip urged. He picked up the knife and started cleaning another fish. When he looked up, David was facing him with a questioning look on his face.

"Well, go ahead, I'm listenin'," David sneered.

Phillip put the knife down and reached out to touch his young friend's shoulder. "I know I can't feel all of your pain, but neither can you feel all my pain. You see, about a year after mutti died, my vati married a younger woman. She didn't care a wit about me. All she did was have babies. Six of 'em! All girls. She was always complaining, and my vati kept trying to satisfy her. I moved down in the cellar by the coal bin. I lost my vati too. When I left home to come to America, he only grunted when I asked for his blessing. I'll never see him again, and I don't care. Now can you understand me?" Phillip looked down and realized his hands were shaking, and he had to gasp for breath.

David took Phil's hand and then stepped into an embrace. Both of them struggled to keep back the tears.

The fish made a tasty supper. While they were eating, the judge said, "Well, I guess we've lost our guide. Johnny must've found better things. Even if he comes back, I'm lettin' him go. Phil, you'll have to do the scouting out ahead." He looked up. "David, can you help Phil out with the horses?"

"Yup, I'd like to do that. Did you know that Phil's ma died too? We can work together."

Mosquitoes moved in as the sun was setting, driving everyone to their beds. A short time later, Phillip heard loud voices near the horses. He slipped out of his bedroll and walked along next to the wagons. It was the judge talking to Johnny. "About time you showed up. You look in tough shape."

"Ain't your business what shape I'm in. You gave me a day off, and I took it. I'm back and will be ready to lead out at sunup," the wagon boss spouted. "You just go back to that pretty little lady of yours, and I'll get some sleep."

Phillip waited. The judge spun around and faced Johnny with fire in his eyes. "You don't speak of my wife in that tone. You're fired. Here's fifteen dollars for your time. Leave the horse and saddle here. You can keep the boots. Get out of here and don't come back."

With that, Johnny charged toward the judge. Being unsteady from drink, when the judge stepped to one side, Johnny went sprawling in a heap on the ground. When the wagon guide started to stand up, Phillip saw a shiny reflection in his hand. He yelled, "Judge, look out for his gun!" Distracted by Phillip's voice, Johnny fired toward Phillip, giving Judge Felch the break he needed to grab Johnny's wrist and bring a knee to his stomach. The gun fell to the ground. Johnny gasped and went down.

"Where did you come from?" the judge asked Phillip. "I'm sure glad you were there."

"I heard the commotion and came to see what was goin' on. I wasn't sure what to do, but when I saw the gun, I just called out."

Johnny tried to get up but staggered back to the ground. Felch picked up the gun and stuck it in his belt. "Phil," he said, "get a bucket of water from the river and cool him off."

When Johnny was able to walk, the judge and Phillip took him to town and had the sheriff lock him up for the night. The sheriff agreed to give Johnny the money and his gun in the morning with sound instructions to head back to Racine.

As they were riding back to camp, the judge said, "Thanks for sounding the warning. I didn't think about that gun he was carryin'. Since I ended up with this horse and saddle, I'd like to give you Queen and the saddle. It's a small thing for savin' my life."

"Thanks, Judge, it all happened so fast, I didn't even think about what to do."

Three days later, they arrived in Madison, the state capital. While Judge Felch took care of his business, Phillip and David visited the university. David saw more books than he ever dreamed existed.

The livery man said, "You should make it to Prairie du Chien over on the Mississippi in six or seven days. The trail follows the course of the *Milwaukee & Mississippi Railroad.*"

One unusually hot day, the judge called to Phillip, "You better find a place to camp before long. That cloud in the northwest looks like it holds some wind and rain."

Phil put Queen to a gallop. Around a curve, he saw a cluster of oaks by a small pond. The prairie grass was trampled down by earlier travelers. Phillip motioned to the judge and David to pull in close to give protection against the weather. As they unhitched the teams, the temperature dropped suddenly. The horses huddled together with their heads down and their hindquarters to the northwest. An eerie feeling pervaded the campsite.

"Come in our wagon," Judge Felch beckoned to Phillip. "This could be trouble. The horses will have to fend for themselves. Let's put some struts up to help hold the canvas."

Phillip turned toward the judge's wagon just as a mighty flash of lightening split the sky down to the horizon. He heard a scream off to his right. In the near darkness, he saw movement by the supply wagon. A loud crash of thunder followed. Then he heard another scream, now farther away. Phillip's hat flew off in the wind as he started to run toward the distress. The near darkness of the storm made it hard to see where he was going. More screaming and sobbing followed. Phil's long legs carried him past the wagons. He could still hear the sobbing. Then it was quiet. Large, freezing cold raindrops began to fall on Phillip's bald head. He heard heavy breathing by a large limestone ledge.

Finally, Phillip saw David shaking and sobbing. "David," he called, "what are you doing out here? You need to get in the wagon with your ma and pa. Come with me, hurry!"

"No, no, I ain't goin' in there. Don't take me there," the boy begged.

Phillip reached down and pulled the boy to his feet. "You can't stay out here in this storm." Hailstones started to beat against the ground. "Look, it's hailing now. We have to get under cover." David started to kick and pound on Phillip's body. "I ain't goin' in there. I ain't!" he screamed.

The rain and hail were coming down in sheets. Phillip lifted David off his feet and carried him to the wagon. He shoved him over the tailgate and climbed in behind him.

Judge Felch grabbed his son and held him while the wailing continued. Hannah brought a quilt and put it around his shivering body.

Phillip was soaked to the skin. His body shook with cold. Blood ran down his face from a gash on his head. Hannah handed him a towel and a blanket. "What was that screaming about out there?"

Once David warmed up, he said, "The lightening and that loud flash, I thought the wagon was on fire. I didn't know where to go. I thought God was gonna kill me too." He tried to hold the tears back. The wind caused the wagon to shudder as the rain and hail pelted against the cloth. Water spewed down from slits in the canvas. Then came a calm followed by a powerful gust of wind. The judge yelled, "Everyone get to this side!" as the wagon began to tilt to the left. Then they felt it settle back on the wheels.

Finally, what had felt like the darkness of night was washed away by piercing rays of evening sunshine. The travelers stepped out of the wagon just as the last sprinkles of rain fell. "Look," Hannah called, pointing at the eastern sky, "what a beautiful rainbow. It's double, reaching all the way to the ground."

The evening was spent drying out and rearranging the wagons. At supper, Phil said, "May I say a prayer thanking God for his protection? That's what my mutti would have done." David removed his hat and bowed his head.

Scouting out ahead the next day, Phillip guided Queen up a rise; and suddenly, he could see for miles over the Mississippi River Valley. Below was the settlement of Prairie du Chien. A plume of dust rising from the trail caught his attention. With a whip in hand, a stagecoach driver was pressing his six-horse team up the slope at a full gallop. Phillip moved out and lifted his hat in greeting. When they met on the trail, the driver reined in to stop.

"Hallo," Phillip called, "*Gutten tag* to you."

The driver waved and returned the greeting. "That's a long steep climb. I'm glad they have a fresh team for me just ahead. Where are you headed this fine day?"

"We're on our way to Minnesota. We've got an eye on some land up that way. How's the trail up ahead?"

"The trail's good. Stay on your brakes on the way down. Since land opened up in Iowa and now in Minnesota, folks are flocking in to take claims. We've been adding coaches to keep up with the demand," the driver answered.

Phillip inquired, "How is it crossin' the big river at Prairie du Chien?"

"No problem! They have plans to push on west with the railroad. Bridging the Mississippi is far in the future, so they'll be usin' big barges to ferry the train cars across the river. You'll be able to get your wagons on a barge." The driver cracked his whip and, with a wave of his hat, set out to the east.

At Prairie du Chien, the judge secured passage on a barge. With the wagons safely loaded, the steam tug brought them to the Iowa side.

As the stage driver had said, the trail from Prairie du Chien to Decorah, Iowa, was well traveled. The tracks were hardened by horse's hoofs and iron wagon tires. The judge called to Phil, "Let's let these horses run for a while. I'm gettin' anxious to get to Minnesota."

Phillip passed the word to David, and they picked up the pace. That evening, at supper, Phil cautioned, "If we keep goin' at this pace, we'll end up wind breakin' one of the horses. Tomorrow, we'll move out in the cool morning, but we have to take rest stops in the heat of the day."

In Decorah, Iowa, the judge urged, "Hannah, this is the last store on the trail, so you need to stock up for at least a couple of weeks. I've got some business to do at the bank."

Back on the trail, the afternoon sun came on with blistering heat. Phillip made numerous stops for water and rest. At one stop, David cautioned Phillip, "Pa's getting pretty hot under the collar. He's complaining about all the stops you're making."

"If we go any faster, we'll have a dead horse on our hands. Lark and Lady have a heavy pull on the freight wagon. Lady is breathing hard already. I'm pulling off for the day the next place we find water." Phillip mounted Queen and called out, "Let's get goin'. We'll camp for the night at our next stop."

An hour later, Phil rode up next to the judge and pointed off to the right. "We'll be campin' down by that cottonwood."

The judge responded, "No, we can keep goin' another hour or so. No need to stop this early."

"If we go any further, that sorrel mare will go down. I'm pullin' off!" Phil said firmly.

"Young man, you better listen to me, or you'll be out of a job," the judge returned.

"Out of a job or not, Lady's not goin' any farther pullin' that heavy load," Phillip insisted. "Pull off by that tree, we'll have fresh horses in the morning."

"Have it your way," the judge grumped. "You better be ready for the trail at sunup tomorrow or I'll have your hide." He reined his blacks to a stop. He turned to Hannah and barked, "Get off this wagon and get some supper goin'!" Hannah knew her husband's temper, so she moved quickly.

Phillip went to unhitch the horses and found Lady lying on the ground. "Judge," Phillip called, "we've got a sick horse on our hands. I need your help! The sorrel mare is down. Unbuckle the hames and pull the harness up. I'll get the collar off. We have to get her up and moved to the shade by that tree. Now get around her, and when I yell, everyone guide her over by the tree." Phillip cupped his hands around Lady's ear and shouted as loud as he could. The horse jumped and rolled up on her feet. David and his pa put their shoulders to the mare's rump, and she took enough steps to reach the shade. Phillip said, "Okay, Lady, stand there, steady now."

Phillip breathed a sigh of relief. "Bring buckets of cold water. We need all the water we can get."

Phillip poured water slowly over the mare's shoulders to help cool her heart. David came with more water. Hannah brought water in the cook kettle.

"David," Phil called, "see if she'll take a drink from a bucket." David responded quickly, and the horse sipped a few swallows. Gradually, Lady seemed to relax. "I'll take care of Lady. You men need to unhitch and water the other horses. Don't let 'em drink all they want. Pull 'em away after one good drink."

A low cloud in the western sky moved over the bright sun. Evening cool started to move in. Hannah rang the supper bell. When they were together, David bowed his head and said, "Thank you, God, for helping us with Lady. Thanks that Phil knew what to do."

After supper, they watered the horses again and tethered them for the night. David called, "Phil, look, Lady's grazing with the others. It looks like she'll be all right. That was a close call." The mosquitoes drove everyone to cover. Phil rolled out his quilt under the wagon.

"Son," a whisper came from one side, "I owe you an apology. Thanks for gettin' us off the trail. I was too anxious to get to Minnesota. How did you know what to do with that horse? I would have let her die."

"Well, when I worked in the sawmills in New York, I watched the teamsters with their horses pulling heavy logs and huge loads of lumber. When they saw a horse overheating, they poured water over them. So that's what I did," Phillip answered.

"And that yell in the ear, how did you know that would work?" The judge chuckled.

Phillip laughed too. "I saw an old veterinarian do that with a cow one time, and I hoped it would work with the mare. I'm sure glad it did. We would've lost her if we couldn't get her in the shade."

Morning brought another sunny day with promise of heat and humidity. Lark seemed to be willing to pull a little extra that day, giving Lady a lighter load. In the cool of the morning, they made good time over the hills and across the sloughs and rivers of northern Iowa.

It was midmorning when Phillip noticed a pile of rocks at the side of the trail and a sign scratched in a board, "Minnesota Territory." "Judge," he shouted, "here it is, we're in Minnesota!"

Phillip met two farmers resting their teams on the way to Decorah to do some trading. "Do you mind if we pull these wagons in here and join you for a rest?" he asked. "It's starting to get hot already. We had a mare go down yesterday, so we're more careful today."

"Ya, we've been pushing pretty hard, so we decided to rest awhile. Where ya headed?"

Judge Felch arrived just in time to hear the question. "I'm Judge Charles Felch. We're headed for Brownsville to see about buying some land at the Federal Land Office. Will this trail take us to Brownsville?"

One of the men stood up. "No, Brownsville is east of here. This trail connects Decorah with Manterville on up the territory. It goes through the town of Hamilton. That's a good little town with a store and hotel. Land is going fast on west of there."

The other farmer broke in, "I heard they moved the Federal Land Office to Chatfield just last month. All the claims had been taken from the big river on west for twenty-five miles or more. I recommend you go on to Hamilton and ride saddle horses to Chatfield. It's about twenty miles or so."

"That seems like good advice," the judge agreed. "Hamilton, here we come."

That evening, a dark cloud formed in the west and brought a cool breeze and a gentle shower. With cooler weather and the dust settled, the Felch group arrived in the little town of Hamilton in the afternoon of June 28, 1856.

The Funeral
Princeton, Wisconsin
1855

As Johann tossed a log on the fire, he said quietly, "Matilda, tomorrow we must go to Princeton before the spring rains turn the trail to mud. We'll get supplies and see about gettin' a preacher so we can bury Mutti." Quietness covered the cabin the rest of the evening.

Matilda fixed an early breakfast. Johann gave his daughter a hand as she stepped up to the wagon seat. Each knew the other was in thought about a funeral for Caroline. They said little.

The Princeton streets were busy with farmers getting ready for spring's work. Johann made the necessary purchases. He found his funds limited and considered another loan to meet the $35 land payment.

Matilda stopped at the café to find Helga. Olinda sent her to the rooming house where Helga was doing her studies and housework.

Helga shrieked, "Hallo!" when she saw her friend. "Matilda, what brings you to town? Can you stay with me tonight?"

"We're goin' home today, but we have a little time until Vati finishes his trading," Matilda answered.

The two friends had so much to talk about that they had to make every minute count. Matilda finally said, "Helga, Vati says we need

191

to bury Mutti soon. She's in a coffin in the horse lean-to. Could you come?"

Helga took a deep breath. "I remember when we buried Vati. It was summer. The preacher came and read from the Bible and talked to us. I cried a lot, but it really helped me. Let's walk over to the Langs' and see if they know when the preacher's comin'."

The two girls walked the short distance to the Lang home, talking quietly as they went. Mrs. Lang came to the door. Helga spoke. "Mrs. Lang, this is my *freundin*, Matilda. She needs the preacher to bury her *mutter*. When's he comin'?"

Mrs. Lang shook her head. Turning to Matilda, she said, "I'm so sorry, my dear. Your name is Matilda, Matilda what?"

"I'm Matilda Mannweiler. We live on a claim south of town. My mutti died three days before Christmas. We need to have a funeral. She's in a coffin in the lean-to at our claim."

Mrs. Lang began to see the need. "Preacher Wagner's comin' this Saturday. We'll have church on Sunday. I'm sure he'll help you, maybe next Monday?"

"Thank you, Mrs. Lang," Helga responded for her friend. "We'll tell Matilda's vati."

As Helga and Matilda walked back to the rooming house, they saw Johann's team and wagon by the general store. "Let's go tell Vati," Matilda urged. At the store, Matilda pulled at her father's sleeve. "We talked to Mrs. Lang, and Preacher Wagner can come next Monday. Is that okay?"

Johann knew that would push him to have the grave ready. "Ja, that's good. When I finish here, we'll go talk to the Langs. Pick out some kitchen supplies and help me get loaded. We need to start for home soon."

On the way home, they stopped to tell the Maiers and Bauers of the funeral plans. Matilda fixed supper, while Johann unloaded the supplies and finished the evening chores. As Johann banked the fire for the night, Matilda noticed a lighter feeling in her breast. Her father seemed freer, and they talked about plans for Monday. The neighbors said they would bring food for lunch after the burial. Matilda finally asked the question that had been on her mind all day. "Vati," she waited. At his nod, she continued, "Could I see Mutti?"

Johann took a deep breath and nodded.

The next morning after coffee, without a word, Johann took his hammer and motioned for Matilda to come. In the lean-to, Maud's and Louie's welcome went unnoticed. Johann pushed the hay away from the coffin. He pulled the nails with the claws of his hammer. When he lifted the lid, he said, "Caroline, your daughter wants to say *auf wiedersehen.*" He stepped back, and Matilda looked down on her . mother's still body. Tears filled her eyes.

It was quiet. Matilda whispered, "*Auf wiedersehen*, Mutti, I love you." She turned to her father. "She's smilin', isn't she?" Johann nodded and waited quietly. His hammer rang notes of finality.

Both father and daughter knew what was next. Johann tossed his shovel and pick into the wagon. Louie and Maud broke into a trot as they headed toward the hardwoods. Without words, they chose a site. Johann turned a shovelful of earth. He handed the spade to his daughter. She did the same. They embraced. Johann loosened the hard soil with his pickax. Matilda dug it away. By Saturday, the grave was ready.

That evening, Johann looked across the trunk they still used as a table. When Matilda's eyes met his, he announced, "We're goin' to church tomorrow. Leavin' at sunup!" Matilda nodded.

How good it was to sing an old hymn and hear the Word of God. Matilda remembered how stiff and solemn her church in Germany was. These people seemed filled with joy and peace. The preacher spoke with great power, yet she felt love. At the end of the service, the preacher announced that the burial would be held six miles south of town the next day.

Monday morning, Johann trimmed his beard and brushed his hair. Matilda heated her curling iron by the fire and made long curls below her bonnet. She reached back on the shelf and brought out a small gray box. "Vati," she said softly, "would you help me?"

Johann's huge fingers struggled with the tiny latch as he placed the cross around his daughter's neck. Tears filled their eyes as they embraced. "Remember, my daughter, she's smilin'." Matilda forced a smile through the tears.

As the sun approached mid-sky, the Maiers and Bauers arrived. Arnold and Eldwin helped load the coffin on Johann's wagon. Adelle and Dagmar started to set the food out on a makeshift table. Other wagons and riders came across the prairie. Fred and his wife arrived in a small carriage pulled by Barney, the big gelding. Emmett, the blacksmith, and his wife, a jolly heavyset lady, followed. The Langs' wagon was filled with people from the church, among them Helga and Olinda. The food tables were loaded, coffee and lemonade aplenty. And still people came.

Preacher Wagner stood by the coffin. With his head bowed, he waited as the people gathered. It was still. Matilda felt grown-up next to her father. The preacher's strong voice sounded, "I am the resurrection and the life: he that believeth in me, though he were dead, yet shall he live: And whosoever liveth and believeth in me shall never die. Believest thou this?"

Matilda's heart was pounding within her. She struggled to concentrate on the preacher's words. He invited the people to trust Jesus, reminding them that Jesus is the way to life in a place prepared in heaven for them. She kept thinking about her mother and the smile on her face. She remembered the note her mother left for her. She reasoned, *Mutti must be in that place prepared for her if she saw Jesus.*

Then she heard the preacher say, "Earth to earth, ashes to ashes, dust to dust; trusting in God's great mercy and looking for the resurrection of the dead and the life of the world to come."

Preacher Wagner stepped forward and reached for Johann's hand and put his other hand on Matilda's shoulder. His kind voice brought comfort. "She's with our Lord. May God bring you his peace."

Johann spoke softly. "Thank you, Preacher Wagner."

Matilda watched as the men took two ropes and lowered the coffin into the grave she had helped dig. Without a word, the men went to their wagons and brought shovels to close the grave.

Matilda felt a tug on her arm. Turning, she heard Helga say, "My *freundin*, the pain will be less, but you will never forget your mutti. I remember the day we buried my vati. His grave is on the claim we had north of town. I go there sometimes."

Olinda was standing alone, watching the men shovel earth over the coffin. Johann reached out to her. "Memories?" he asked. "We share the same."

She took his hand. A tear ran down her cheek. "They get better, but never leave," she answered. "Yes, we do share the same. Our daughters do too. They are *freundins*." They watched Matilda and Helga as they walked together toward the cabin.

Preacher Wagner gave thanks, and the people moved past the food tables. Johann and Matilda were amazed at the words of love and hope that were offered to them. Before leaving, the men organized a barn raising for late June. A sawmill owner offered to trade the lumber for the barn for some oak logs on Johann's claim. It was settled.

That evening, after supper, Johann sat down in his chair by the fire with a long board in his lap. With knife, chisel, and hammer, he carved a C, an A, and an R . . .

It was time for spring's work. The river was flowing freely. The cardinals began their spring mating call, and Matilda learned how to gather eggs from the prairie chicken nests, leaving some to hatch. Gerda and Gertrude taught her what greens she could cook or eat fresh. Matilda became skilled at catching trout and bass for supper.

Johann watched Maud closely, knowing that her foal would be born soon. One evening, just after sundown, the mare was wandering about with her head down sniffing the ground. He left Louie tethered and brought Maud to the lean-to. He scattered fresh prairie grass for clean bedding. Johann opened the cabin door and called, "Matilda, I'm gonna spend the night with Maud. Looks like her colt is coming."

Matilda came down the ladder from the loft. "Vati, can I stay with you? I want to see the new colt. Please, Vati."

Johann stepped in over the threshold. "Come if you want, but a horse givin' birth can be messy. Do you have the stomach for it?"

Matilda got her warm coat and brought some cookies she had baked that afternoon. Johann called back over his shoulder, "Bring those two deerskin robes. It could be a long wait, and the night has a chill in it."

It was about midnight when Maud became very restless. Before long, the water broke, and the head of the foal appeared. Matilda was worried and wanted Johann to help the delivery. "No," he said, "best we just let Maud take her time." The horse gave a mighty push, and with a gush of water and afterbirth, the foal came into the world. Maud turned in the stall and sniffed her new born. Gradually, the mother nudged the baby into action.

Matilda begged, "Vati, should I get some water to give the baby a bath? Look, it's all wet and bloody."

"No," Johann cautioned, "Maud will clean her. I see we have a little filly. You'll have to think of a girl's name for her." Maud licked the foal clean and kept nuzzling her until she stood on wobbly legs.

Then Matilda squealed, "Look, Vati, the baby is nursing from her mutti."

On a sunny morning following a refreshing rain shower, Maud was grazing in the pasture. Her colt was running circles around the mare. Matilda took a lump of sugar and held it out to the filly. "Here, little colt," she called, "come, have a treat." The baby came close but jumped and scampered away on spindly legs. Matilda thought, *How peaceful and free is that little colt.* A name popped into her mind for her friend. "I'll call her Winnie. It means 'peaceful friend.'" Watching Winnie run and play with abandon and freedom brought some healing to Matilda's heart. That evening, at supper, she announced, "Vati, I named the filly today. Her name is Winnie."

"Ja," Johann responded, "she is a peaceful friend, isn't she? That's a good name."

At daylight, Johann yoked his oxen to break new sod to get ready for planting. At midmorning, Arnold arrived with his team and harrow, ready to spend the day breaking down the newly plowed sod for a good seed bed.

Matilda brought them coffee, bread, and cheese for lunch. Johann said to his neighbor, "It's mighty kind of ya comin' over to help like this. Ya really wouldn't have to do it, ya know. Kind of humblin' to have my neighbors helpin' me firm my claim."

Arnold bumped his friend on the shoulder and responded, "Not one of us would ever firm a claim without the help of neighbors. When I first got here, the neighbors came and helped me. Now I can help you. That's how it works. We're lookin' forward to the barn raisin' come later June. You'll want to get some stock before fall and some chickens."

Johann shrugged. "Gotta get this plowin' done now," he breathed as he moved toward his oxen.

That spring, Johann planted some corn and oats. The barn went up in two days. By fall, he had enough wood cut for winter, and he bought a small stove for the cabin. He still faced the necessary payments on the land and supplies. The bank was unwilling to make further loans. He bought two cows, eight laying hens, and a rooster. Matilda left three of the hens to bring out a brood of chicks. Some would be butchered for fryers, and some became layers for the next year. As Johann pondered their progress, he found many reasons to be hopeful about the future.

20

A Near Gunfight
Minnesota
1854-1856

S PRING BROKE EARLY IN MINNESOTA in 1854. Jacob McQuillan announced at breakfast, "It's time to get that grasshopper plow goin'. Plantin' time is close." He lingered a moment. "I nailed that coffee mill to that old oak, but now that the federal survey is completed, the government's gonna want us to sign some papers for our land. It's time to get over to the Land Office in Brownsville."

Joe offered, "Boss, I can keep the Grasshopper goin' while you're gone. The boys and I can do up the chores."

A few days later, father and son set off on the seventy-mile ride to the Federal Land Office in Brownsville and filed claims to the land they had chosen. They returned with papers marked Abstract of Declaratory Statements, with number and entry attached. That evening, Jacob announced, "We're now officially land owners in Minnesota Territory." They gave thanks to God for his provision.

However, the McQuillans were in for a huge surprise. One beautiful June day, a man with an attorney at his side came looking for Jacob McQuillan Jr. Jake came in from his field, wondering, *What's this about?* The man extended his hand, saying, "My name's Daniel Booth. This is my lawyer. He has something to tell you."

"I'm Jake McQuillan. What do you have for me?"

The lawyer unfolded a sheaf of papers. "Mr. McQuillan, we understand you filed claim to this quarter section of land on April 9, 1854. According to the records at the Federal Land Office in Brownsville, the Federal Survey was finalized and the land released for claim by the president on June 1, 1854. That is obviously after you filed. Is that true?"

Jake was stunned and could hardly answer. Finally, he said, "My father and I are in this together. I need to get him before we discuss this matter."

The attorney responded abruptly. "This is a matter regarding Jacob McQuillan Jr. Is that your name?"

"Yes, that's my name, but, my father, Jacob McQuillan Sr., is my partner," Jake insisted.

"I disagree, Mr. McQuillan. This matter concerns Jacob McQuillan Jr., and I must show you the rest of this document." He unfolded the papers further and proceeded. "I have in hand documents filed by my client, Mr. Daniel Booth, proving that he holds claim to this property. Here is the *Abstract of Declaratory Statements* dated June 5, 1854, which falls after the land was released for claim. Mr. McQuillan, you will have to vacate this property immediately since it belongs to my client, Mr. Booth. Here is a copy of this notice. Good day." Stunned, Jake took the copy, and the two men turned on their heels and walked away.

Jake found his father by the barn working on the fence. "Pa, did you see the visitors that just left my place?"

"No, I guess I was too busy workin' on this fence. What did they want?"

Jake unrolled the papers and handed them to his father. "This is what they brought to me. It seems Mr. Booth has taken claim to my land, saying the land had not been released for claim by the president when I filed. He's takin' my land!"

Jacob took the papers and studied them. "We'll get an attorney and fight this. We'll not let that scoundrel put us off our land."

The litigation was in stalemate for months. Jake decided to move on and took another claim a mile to the east. Confident he would win in court, Jacob employed Mr. Ropes, a professional surveyor, to plat Section 6 as the town of Elkhorn. Mr. Ropes recorded his survey on April 26, 1856. Jake McQuillan was appointed postmaster of the Elkhorn Post Office.

Not to be outdone, Daniel Booth drew his own plat of the same Section 6 and had it recorded on July 4, 1856, as the town of Hamilton. Booth and his partner Mr. Randall opened a general store with a $3000 inventory. Soon other stores, a blacksmith shop and a sawmill, opened for business. Booth applied for a post office for Hamilton.

The competition between Booth and the McQuillans caused tension throughout the community. People took sides along the lines of friendships. A group of Jacob's friends decided to force Booth out. About twenty men, rifles in hand, met at Jacob's farm, ready to end the controversy.

Jacob said, "I've been thinkin' and prayin' about this all night. We must start by sending out two unarmed men to let Booth know we mean business and that he must return the land to Jake."

Two men volunteered. They started walking down the trail toward Booth's store. When they were about ten rods away, two men came out of the hotel with rifles ready. The four men moved closer and closer to each other. Just as they met, a large group of armed men came out of the hotel. The four men talked for a few minutes and then retreated.

When Jacob's friends returned, they said, "They'll make no compromise. It's give up the land or shoot it out. They have at least forty men with rifles."

Jake stepped up to his father. "Pa, it's not worth bloodshed. We must be willin' to forgive. Remember what Jesus said after givin' the Lord's Prayer in Matthew? If we are unwillin' to forgive, God will not forgive us."

"Son," Jacob answered, "I know you're right. It's just the principal of the thing. We came here early and broke the trail, then to have some upstart with big ideas take the best land away from us. I know

201

it's not worth dying for, and that's what would happen if we try to shoot it out. My money's gone. I can contest no longer. I guess we're done."

"Pa, I have a half section just a mile east. Let's claim the other half. We can do well with six hundred acres between us. You've made a new start several times in your life. Let's make another one now and God will be with us. Come, Pa, go with me to talk to Mr. Booth and ask him to set our differences aside."

Father and son walked down the trail approaching the hotel. Again, the same forty men came out with guns in hand. The two McQuillans stopped and held their hands out. Jake spoke. "Mr. Booth, would you ask your men to put their guns away and come and hear our proposal?"

Booth and his attorney stepped forward. Booth commanded, "Put 'em down men," and advanced toward the McQuillans. "What ya got to say?" he snapped.

Jake took the lead. "We've got a good community here. We need to get along and help each other. We'll contest the land no longer. In the Bible, God taught us to forgive, and we offer you our forgiveness. You pay me back the $1.25 an acre that I paid and somethin' for the improvements and the land is yours. We only need one town and one post office. I'd like to be the Hamilton postmaster, if you'd agree to that."

Booth stuttered, "I . . . I . . . I don't know about forgiveness, and I don't know about God, but I do know the land is rightly mine. Like we said in the papers we filed, I'll pay you $1.25 an acre and an agreed amount for the improvements you've made."

Jake started to extend a hand in agreement when Booth turned to Jacob. "What about you, old man, you're the one who put this in litigation, can you agree to this settlement?"

"Mr. Booth, you know that Jake had squatter's rights to the property. You also know you wanted the property because it's the choicest piece in Fillmore County. It's only my faith in God that makes it possible to forgive your actions. Tom Corey wants to rent my place.

I'll move over to Sumner Township by Jake and start over, God being our helper. I'll put this behind, and I'll be in your store to do business with you in the future."

The three men shook hands. The attorney stood there like an uninvited guest. Booth shouted as he returned to his friends, "Drinks are on me," as he led the way to his place behind the store.

That night at the supper table, Jacob leaned back in his chair and announced, "Today, we settled the dispute with Mr. Booth. Jake has turned the land over to him, and they have made an agreement. I'm proud of Jake for the way he is able to forgive Booth." Lucinda was proud of her older brother and her father.

Jacob eventually sold his claim and developed a half section next to Jake's, a mile east of town. Lucinda was happy to live close to Mary M. She completed eighth grade with high achievement at School District No. 125 in Hamilton.

Publicly, Jacob tried to put the land dispute behind him. But privately, he was deeply discouraged by these events. Every time he saw Dan Booth, his emotions threatened to go out of control. Then one day, as Jacob was plowing in his field, he saw a lone rider leading a pack mule up his lane. The rider continued toward the field. Jacob commanded his oxen and plowed on toward the rider. At the headland of his field, the two men met.

"Hallo," Jacob called, "who's my visitor today?"

Without answering, the man slid down from his saddle. His shoulders slumped, face covered by the brim of his black hat. In a low voice, he spoke. "I'm lookin' for Mr. Jacob McQuillan."

"That's me, what can I do for ya?"

"The name's Sid. I've been ridin' for days lookin' for ya. I'm the guy who tried to rape that woman and nearly shot ya to death. I went back to Delta, did some drinkin', got in trouble, and sat in jail for a few months. I did a lot of thinkin' and couldn't get your words out of my head about forgiveness. I came to ask you to forgive me." He paused for a breath.

Jacob reached out both arms. "I forgave you the mornin' you left, and that's not changed."

Sid fell to the ground, sobbing. Jacob knelt next to him, an arm around Sid's shoulders.

Time passed. Lucinda approached her father with his lunch. "Pa, are you all right?" Lucinda shook her father's shoulder. "Pa! What's wrong?" she demanded.

"Lucy, this is Sid. Remember him? He came to ask us to forgive him. Did you bring lunch?"

"Yes, Pa, and coffee too."

"Pour him a cup, and give him some bread."

Jacob shook Sid and urged, "Sid, here, have some coffee and bread. Lucinda brought you some lunch."

Sid's eyes met Lucy's. "Lucinda, I've thought of you so many times. I'm glad you screamed that night. I don't know what I may have done to the lady if you hadn't been there. Lucinda, will you forgive me?"

"Yes, Sid, I forgive you. You look hungry. Here, have some cheese and nuts."

Sid started to wolf down the food. When his mind started to clear, he realized he had eaten all of Jacob's lunch. "Sir," he said, "I'm sorry, I ate all your lunch. Don't know when I last ate."

Jacob said, "Sid, you'll have supper with us tonight. Take your horse and mule to the barn. Give 'em water and fodder. You can sleep in the loft tonight."

That evening at the supper table, Mary M said to Sid, "Many times, I've dreamed about what could've happened in that wagon if Lucy hadn't been there. It's by the grace of God that I've been able to forgive you. Sid, have you truly asked God to forgive you?"

"I'm not sure I know how to do that, but I want to," Sid responded. That evening, with the assistance of the McQuillan family, Sid made peace with God.

Just before he went out to sleep in the loft, Sid asked, "By the way, where's that big guy that tied me to a tree? Guess I need his forgiveness too."

Jacob responded, "You mean Joe? He got word that his mother was sick and hopped the stage back to Ohio. Haven't heard from him since." Sid nodded and left.

Sid got a job at Booth's sawmill where he worked until he had the money to return to his family in Ohio. He left Hamilton a new man.

One evening at bedtime, Jacob mused, "Polly, I was in the store today. Funny thing, I don't resent Dan like I did before Sid came. We may have taught Sid to forgive, but he has taught me forgiveness as well." Polly drew her husband close.

Work in Wisconsin
Brandon, Wisconsin
1854-1855

ADAM AND PETER UTZINGER WORKED for Jed Stewart through the fall harvest season. Jed's wife, Leona, and Peter's wife, Carolina, became good friends. Carolina found comfort in having an older woman, who had raised a family of nine, as a mentor as she awaited the arrival of her firstborn. One brisk November morning, Carolina put a couple of jars of canned tomatoes and several glasses of grape jelly in her basket and headed over to visit Leona.

The two women were in the middle of a conversation about the expected arrival when Jed walked in with the two Utzinger boys. "Coffeepot on?" Jed called as they came in through the woodshed. "I got a couple thirsty boys here."

Leona slid the coffee to the burner and replied, "All the time, it'll take a few minutes to hot up." She turned to Carolina and motioned. "Wanna pull the wax out of one of those jelly glasses? I'll slice some bread." Soon the five were sitting around the kitchen table, sipping mugs of hot coffee and devouring slices of whole wheat bread.

Jed pushed back from the table, patted his stomach with pleasure, and waited for the attention of the other four. With his hands behind his head, he spoke. "I've been wantin' to talk with the three of you Utzingers. Our agreement was that you men would work for me to get the crop in and put away. That's done now." He paused.

Adam took a deep breath, fearing Jed's next words. He and Peter had wondered what they would do when Jed decided he didn't need them any longer.

Jed continued, "You seem pretty comfortable in that old cabin. We kept warm there a lot of years before we built this house. How would you like to stay for the winter? You could cull out the dead trees down by the river for firewood. I could use your help with the chores. Would you be interested?"

Stunned by the offer, Peter stammered, "That . . . th . . . that would be great. We would work hard for you, Jed. I noticed you have some posts set for a lean-to by the barn. We could cut some logs and slice shingles to finish that job."

Jed nodded approval as he waited for a response from Adam.

Before Adam could speak, Carolina leaned toward Jed with tears slipping down her cheeks. "Oh, Mr. Stewart, it would please me to have a warm place for the baby. And, Leona, I miss my mutti so much. Would you teach me how to take care of the baby?"

Adam tried again, but Leona scurried around the table and put her arms around Carolina. "Yes, my dear, I'll help you, but you'll be a wonderful mother. God just shows us how to love our children."

Finally, Adam jumped in. "Jed, Peter and I want to get land of our own someday. We've not been able to save enough to get started. Would it be possible for us to have a few cows and maybe some chickens?"

"Ja," Jed responded, "we can work that out." He stood up, and with a swing of his hat, he said, "You guys better get cuttin' wood and stackin' grass for the winter. Snow could come any day now."

The days shortened, and the mornings were greeted by frost-covered prairies and ice in the water troughs. At the supper table, Adam said, "I'll be ridin' in to Princeton tomorrow to get some supplies. I hear there's a good church there that I'd like to check out on Sunday."

Peter, a bit surprised by Adam's sudden announcement, responded, "Why don't you take the team and bring the things Carolina will need in the kitchen?" By bedtime, they had a long list of items needed for winter, along with what Jed and Leona added.

The sun was peaking over the eastern horizon as Adam urged Zelig and Zelda to a steady trot on the trail to Princeton. A rooster pheasant cackled as he lifted into flight and gracefully glided out into the cornstalks. Adam was looking forward to some time alone. He thought, *Maybe I'm jealous of my brother and his wife.* Near noon, he rolled into Princeton, set the brake, jumped down, and tied the team at the hitching rail in front of a little café on Main Street.

Adam held the café door for a family of four and stepped in behind them. Tobacco smoke hung from the ceiling. He spotted an empty stool at the counter across the room. He hung his jacket and hat on an old hall tree by the door and pushed his way to his destination. Feeling a bit crowded by the huge man who hung off all sides of the stool next to him, Adam waited to be served.

A young woman dressed in a plain blue dress drawn around her slim waist by the tie of a red and white apron said in a quiet, nervous voice, "My name's Matilda. You'll have to bear with me. I'm helpin' my friend Helga on this busy Saturday. What would you like this morning?"

"I'm new in the area. What do you recommend for a hungry farmer?" Adam felt the squeeze on his side as the big man on his right turned on his stool and peered down at him. He fixed his attention on the waitress.

"Helga's mutti makes some right good cinnamon rolls, and the coffee is the best in town," Matilda offered. "Or if you're ready for dinner, the roast beef is a good choice." Suddenly, she noticed how directly her customer was looking at her. Her right hand went to the gold cross on the chain around her neck. She felt a flush move up the side of her neck.

"I'll have the roast beef please and coffee while I wait, if you have time." A sudden thought crossed Adam's mind: *It would be nice if she were a few years older.*

As the waitress left, Adam's neighbor turned toward him and said in a rather loud voice, "New in the county, huh?"

"Yup," Adam responded as he adjusted his weight to the far side of the stool under him.

"Thought so, no one ever sits on that stool. I give Helga an extra two bits for takin' up two spots. Thanks for savin' me a quarter." By this time, a snicker was heard throughout the café. Adam was relieved when the man to his left stood and motioned for Adam to move over.

Matilda arrived with a steaming mug of coffee. "Here's your coffee. Cream and sugar are on the counter. Roast beef will be out soon."

As she turned to leave, Adam again noticed the gold cross at her neckline. *Still too young*, he affirmed. "Thanks, looking forward to it."

Adam dumped a heaping spoonful of sugar in the mug, stirred it gently, and allowed it to cool. Thankful for less crowded conditions, he prepared to enjoy his coming meal. The stool creaked under the weight of its occupant as his neighbor turned his way. "Where ya farmin'?"

Trying not to be interested in the conversation, Adam shrugged. "Workin' for Jed Stewart east of here."

"Sorry for bein' rude, my name's Halgrave," the big man offered as he stretched out his fleshy hand.

Adam felt his hand disappear when he reached to shake. "Utzinger, Adam Utzinger is the name. Pleased to meet you, Mr. Halgrave. My brother Peter and I helped Jed with harvest and will be staying the winter."

"Ja, I know Jed. I have a quarter section of good land on north of his place. Jed tells me you brothers are right good workers. Said he always gets a good day's work for a day's pay."

Matilda arrived with a steaming plate of roast beef, potatoes, gravy, peas, and carrots with two slices of bread and butter on the side. "Here's your dinner, mister . . ." Her voice waited for a response.

"Ah, ja, Utzinger, Adam Utzinger, thanks for the service." Their eyes met, and again, he noticed the gold cross.

"You're welcome, Mr. Utzinger, hope you have a pleasant stay in Princeton."

"Thanks, I'm findin' it a friendly town." His eyes followed her as she moved down the counter to serve another customer.

Halgrave observed Adam's interest in the waitress and spoke in a whisper. "Fine girl, that Matilda. Her mother died a couple of years ago. She's helpin' her father firm his claim. Arrived too late in the fall and winter got the woman."

Adam felt a twinge of sadness. He wiped up the last bit of gravy with a piece of bread and washed it down with a long draft of coffee. He started toward his jacket when he heard Halgrave's voice.

"Utzigger, I'd like to make you an offer. Stop over to my wagon back of the livery stable," the huge man said, now standing a head taller than Adam.

"Utzinger is the name. What do you mean an offer?"

"Ja, that's right, Utzinger, a business offer for you and your brother if you're interested. Over by the livery in a half hour?" Halgrave turned, ducked his head, and went through the kitchen door.

Adam slipped into his jacket and held his hat until he was outside. He scratched his head with one hand as he pulled his hat on with the other. *What kind of business deal could this be?*

"Come on, Zelig and Zelda, I'm gonna get you some fodder and a good drink." Adam noticed the general store down the street and the livery just beyond.

At the stable, a middle-aged man with a limp in his right leg stepped out to meet him. "I hope your critters ain't as mean as the last ones I took in. The bronc kicks like an ornery mule. What can I do for ya? My name's Fred. Best livery in town. That's cuz it's the only one." Fred smiled.

"I'm Adam Utzinger. I just arrived from New York last summer. I've been workin' for Jed Stewart for the harvest. I'll be in town 'til Monday noon. I need a place for these nags."

"You'll find room out back to park your wagon. You can water 'em at the tank by the back door. Do you want me to give 'em hay and oats?"

Adam started to drive around the building. He spoke over his shoulder. "Thanks, Fred, I have oats in the wagon. Just a good feedin' of hay will do." Adam parked the wagon, pulled off the harnesses, and led the team to the trough. As he approached, Fred met him with a hand out to take the halter ropes.

"Nice team you got there. They'll be in good hands 'till Monday."

"Ja, the gelding's Zelig, and the mare's Zelda. You should remember the two Zs." Adam touched the brim of his hat and turned toward the general store. He heard a familiar voice.

"Utzigger, come on over to my wagon and I'll make you that offer." Mr. Halgrave beckoned with his hand and moved down the row of wagons.

Adam wanted to get at his business, but the man's size and insistence made it hard to resist. "Utzinger is the name," he insisted as he followed.

"Ja, Utzinger, come on, you'll like what I have to say."

Halgrave stepped up on the tailgate of a brand-new covered wagon and motioned for Adam to follow. The inside of the wagon was customized as an office and living room. The mahogany woodwork was polished like a shining mirror. The wagon rocked from side to side as the big man moved to sit down at a built-in desk. "Have a seat," he said, motioning toward a padded side chair.

"Quite a place you have here," Adam said as he sat down.

"Ja, made by a man named Studebaker down in Indiana." The big man leaned back in his chair and stretched his arms above his head. "Now for the offer," Halgrave said with eyes set on his visitor. "I know Jed Stewart very well. I know what he says is reliable truth. Jed told me that the Utzinger brothers are good workers."

Adam nodded as the man continued, "I have a quarter section off northwest of Jed's place. It's good land with a house and a barn. I have a herd of ten milk cows and some chickens. The claim is paid and firm. I need someone to farm it for me on shares. I furnish half the seed, and the renter does the work and takes half the crop. I provide the herd, and the renter takes half of the milk, cheese, butter, and eggs. Half of the increase of the herd stays with me, and half goes to the renter. The renter lives in the house and cuts his own wood for heat and takes good care of the buildings. Are you interested?"

"Who's been farmin' the place this year? Do you have a renter now?"

"I took the claim about eight years ago. My kid and I have been farmin' it, and it's produced well. My kid took sick a year ago and died last winter. I invested in the café with Olinda and Helga, and I have some other plans here in Princeton. I need a good farmer to take over the farm."

"I'd like some time to talk it over with Peter when I get home on Monday. How can we get back to you?"

"I have a man taking care of the chores. I go out every week or so to see how he's doin'. I'll stop at Jed's the end of the week. It'd be a good start for you Utzinger boys."

"We'll be lookin' for you end of the week. You've caught my fancy. Have to see what Peter says."

Adam spent the afternoon gathering the items on his list at the general store. Since it was getting late, he arranged to pick up the supplies on Monday morning. The café was still open, so he stopped for a light supper, thinking he might see the young waitress with the gold cross.

When he entered the café, another young woman met him. "You just made it under the wire. I'm lockin' up for the night, but I'll serve you while I clean up. How about some chicken and dumplings? Just one servin' left in the pot."

"Sounds good," Adam answered, "and a piece of pie and coffee." Once he was served, he said, "You must be Helga. I heard about you from Halgrave today."

"Quite a man is Barrett. Generous as the day is long. He's part owner of the café. We wouldn't have made it without his help. He told me how he about sat in your lap today. Matilda had a good laugh too."

Adam finished the dumplings and started on the apple pie. "Helga, I'm in town for the weekend, and I'd like to go to church tomorrow. Do you know of a service?"

"Sure do!" she responded with enthusiasm. "We have a Methodist service over at the Langs' house. The preacher's in town, and we're expecting a big crowd. It's the white house just the other side of the land office. Starts about 10:00, potluck dinner afterward. Come join us. We've got a good preacher."

The night had cooled as Adam made his way to his wagon. He threw a straw tick down under the wagon and rolled up in two wool horse blankets. The ground was hard and cold by morning, and thoughts about the Halgrave offer made for a sleepless night.

As the sun broke through a rim of clouds in the east, roosters began an antiphony back and forth across the town. He found a thin layer of ice on the watering trough when he filled his bucket. A cup of hot coffee, brewed on a small campfire, started to warm him from the inside. Three slices of bread with Carolina's plum jam along with some dried fruit prepared the young farmer for morning worship. Feeling lonesome, Adam sat down on a small stool, pulled a blanket around his shoulders, and read his Bible. He remembered the days he spent studying with his family pastor back in Germany. *I wonder what my parents and brothers and sisters are doing back home.*

Adam's mind rolled back to the children on board the *Robert Harding*. The conversation with Ahren about the Pietists and the teachings of Jakob Spener came clearly to mind. *There must be more to faith in God than knowing the catechism and repeating the prayers*, he thought. Adam looked down at his Bible and started to read. The words from Colossians formed in his mind as a prayed,

> *Giving thanks unto the Father, which hath made us meet to*
> *be partakers of the inheritance of the saints in light: Who hath*
> *delivered us from the power of darkness, and hath translated us*

into the kingdom of his dear Son. In whom we have redemption through his blood, even the forgiveness of sins: Who is the image of the invisible God, the firstborn of every creature: For by him were all things created, that are in heaven, and that are in earth . . .

What do all of these words mean? Here I am, 23 years old. I don't have a wife. I don't know what I believe. Loneliness came over him like a dark cloud. He quickly brushed a tear from his cheek with the back of his hand. Startled by his melancholy, Adam stood up and gave his body a shake. *I need to find the Langs' house.*

Beyond the land office, Adam saw a large white house with several wagons and buggies in the backyard. Three men were leaning against a wagon in conversation. As Adam approached, one of the men reached out a hand of welcome. "Good mornin', I'm Arnold Maier. Don't think I've met you."

Adam received the handshake and noticed the friendly smile. "Utzinger, Adam Utzinger. I'm in town for the weekend. I heard there's preachin' here this mornin'. Thought I'd take it in before headin' for home."

"You sure are welcome." Arnold continued the handshake as he offered an introduction. "Here, meet Eldwin Bauer and Jake Lang. This is Jake's place. We meet here when the preacher's in town."

After the welcoming handshakes, Jake said, "Make yourself at home, Adam. We're always glad to welcome a visitor. What brings you to Princeton?"

"My brother and I just arrived a few months ago after workin' in New York for a spell. We've been workin' for Jed Stewart out east of here. I came to town for supplies and thought I'd see if I could find a Sunday meetin'."

A middle-aged woman dressed in a black dress with a white fluffy blouse opened the back door and shouted, "The preacher's ready to start. Come on in and find a place." Her eyes circled the yard and fixed on a group of four young girls sitting on the grass by the stable. "Come on, girls, we need you to help with the singin'."

The girls jumped up and ran toward the door. Adam noticed Matilda and Helga in the group. The other two looked like they could be twins. Again, a thought flashed through Adam's mind. *It'd be nice if they were a little older.*

Adam was pleased to hear some good preaching. He especially noticed the mention of John Wesley and his heart-warming experience at Aldersgate in England. The preacher said, "We all need a heart warming, a heart change. That's the mark of true biblical faith." Adam considered approaching the preacher and asking about Pietism, but he let it pass for now.

The people were friendly and the food much appreciated since the café was closed on Sunday. When Adam turned to leave, Jake Lang offered, "Come again when you're in town. The welcome mat's always out."

Adam was glad to see clear skies and a brilliant sunrise on Monday morning. Zelig and Zelda whinnied a welcome when he stepped into their stall. Fred met him by the watering trough with a sleepy, "Good mornin', Utzinger, you're up and going early."

"Yup, early bird gets the worm as they always say. What's the damage for the keep of these nags?"

He paid his bill, hitched his team, and headed for the general store to pick up his supplies. The crates and barrels nearly filled the wagon box. A stop under an oak in the afternoon gave the team time to rest and graze. Adam had some lunch and caught a nap leaning against the tree trunk.

The sun was ablaze in the west, and the evening had settled before Adam pulled into the yard at the Jed Stewart farm. Peter came out to meet him, signaled by the barking of Jed's big collie. "We've been wonderin' about you. We thought you found yourself a girlfriend and decided to stay in town."

"No girlfriend. It just took time to do the business, and it's a long way home. I need to water and feed Zelig and Zelda. I'm mighty hungry myself."

Peter and Adam settled down at the table while Carolina dished up the meat and potatoes with lots of gravy and several slices of fresh-baked bread. Adam prayed one of his familiar prayers and savored the home-cooked meal. The combination of a full stomach and the warmth of the cookstove brought drowsiness. "Guess I'll be off to bed. I didn't get much sleep under that wagon. I'll be sharin' some things in the mornin'."

Next morning, when the chores were done, Jed said, "Pete, go get Carolina and we'll all have coffee together. Leona has the pot on and some caramel rolls to go with it." On the way to the house, the men watched a flock of Canadian honkers heading south in full flight. A gust of north wind brought down a swirl of leaves from the maples by the barn. "Feels like snow in the wind," Jed commented. "It's a good thing we have wood in and hay for the stock. I'm obliged to you men for your help this fall."

"We're glad to have work and a warm place to live," Adam responded. "We need to get the lean-to finished so we have shelter for the animals this winter."

Carolina poured five cups of hot coffee while Leona took the caramel rolls out of the oven. Once all five were seated at the table, Jed rubbed his hands together and said, "Thanks, Lord, for the rolls and coffee and for friends to share it."

The caramel had cooled, and everyone was ready to sip some coffee through the sweetness. Adam took advantage of the quiet to ask a question, "Jed, do you know a man by the name of Barrett Halgrave?"

Jed's head jerked up like a puppet on a string. "Ja, everyone knows Barrett Halgrave. How could you miss him? He's big enough for two men. I hear tell he takes up two stools at the café counter at mornin' coffee."

"Tell me about it," Adam replied with a belly laugh. "I made the mistake of takin' the stool next to him, and he spilled over like yeast bread left too long in the bowl. The whole place was laughin' by the time the guy next to me took pity."

Peter, wondering at the mystery, asked, "Hey, you two, would you let us in on who this Barrett is?"

Jed offered, "Barrett Halgrave is a huge man of about fifty. He has a farm northwest of here. His son died suddenly last winter. I understand the memories of his son make him want to get off the farm. They say he's makin' some investments in Princeton."

"That's where we come in," Adam said. "He made Peter and me an offer to work his farm on 50/50 shares. He claimed he had heard from you, Jed, that the Utzinger brothers are good workers and called me over to his wagon to make the offer. He's gonna stop here later this week for our answer."

Peter put his cup down and pushed his chair back from the table. "Adam, are you sayin' we have an offer to farm this man's land? How much land is it? What about equipment, horses, stock, and all that?"

"First, we have to know from you, Jed, can this man be trusted? I confess I was so overwhelmed by his size that I found myself doubtin' his character."

Jed looked across the table at Leona with a smile. "What do you think, Lee, can Halgrave be trusted?"

Leona responded, "Without a doubt, you can trust him." She went on to say, "One day, I was drivin' home from Brandon, and old Max went lame. I pulled off the road, wonderin' what to do, when along came this huge man. He patted Max on the neck, lifted his front leg, and dug a stone out of his foot. He smiled, tipped his hat, and went on down the road. A year or so later, we met Barrett and his wife. He recognized me and said, 'You sure looked scared the day I got that rock out of your horse's forefoot.' I blushed and asked how he knew Max was lame. With a little smirk, he said, 'Horses don't usually stand on three legs.'"

Jed took a long drink of his coffee. "Barrett Halgrave is a kind and generous man. You can trust him to keep his word, but he expects other people to do the same."

Mr. Halgrave arrived as promised about noon on Thursday. He urged the Utzinger brothers to meet him at his farm the following day. They came to an agreement to move to the Halgrave place the first of March to begin the 50/50 arrangement.

On the day after Thanksgiving, a heavy black cloud hung in the northwestern skies. By noon, the air felt damp and cold. The stillness brought on an eerie feeling of anticipation. At about four in the afternoon, Jed ordered, "It's time to get the stock fed and the milkin' done. There's a good one brewing in the northwest. I'm gonna put a rope up from the house to the barn. You better put one up from the cabin too."

"What are the ropes for?" Adam asked.

Jed responded, "A couple years ago, old Charlie, our neighbor, lost his way in a blizzard goin' out to the barn. The next spring, they found what was left of him out in a grove of trees a half mile from the barn. We put up ropes every winter now."

Carolina didn't sleep much that night with the wind whistling around the cabin. She knew her baby could come anytime now. Peter reassured her and encouraged her to rest.

Adam slept like a hibernating sow bear despite the howling wind of the winter storm. He woke up as daylight began to filter through the window above the washstand. He understood what Jed meant about ropes when he opened the cabin door. He was glad for warm mittens as he grasped the rope with one hand and the milk bucket with the other. The wind and driving snow almost took his breath away. Jed's bay mare welcomed him with a soft whinny when he stepped through the barn door. The cows stood up and stretched in their stalls. The old rooster released his morning crow as if he was the one who allowed a new day to begin.

Sensing the welcome of the beasts and even the smell of hay, chopped corn, and manure made Adam muse, *I sure would like to own a place like this with a wife and children.*

By midafternoon, the wind died down, and the sun broke out with brilliant sun dogs on either side. Carolina continued to fret about the arrival of her baby and whether the midwife would get there quickly enough when her time came.

It was early morning on December 11, 1855, that Carolina began to experience labor pains. She waited awhile before waking Peter from his deep sleep. They sent Adam to get the midwife, and Carolina asked Peter to fetch Leona. Her water broke just before the midwife arrived. It was afternoon when Peter heard the soft cry of their little girl.

"Peter, are you disappointed? I wanted to give you a son," Carolina asked with concern.

"No, not at all. I'm happy our little daughter is here and that both my wife and daughter are safe and well."

The birth of Maria changed the life of the Utzingers. Adam worked at being an attentive uncle, but many a night, he chose wool blankets in the hayloft over his bed in the corner of the cabin. He watched his older brother bond with his baby daughter. It heightened his feelings of loneliness. He made more frequent trips to Princeton, especially when he knew the preacher was in town. He met new people and saw a joy and excitement in their lives while sensing emptiness in his own heart.

The Utzingers made the move to the Halgrave farm on March 1. They began to work the soil to prepare for seeding. Hours in the fields walking behind the team gave Adam time to think. He had a growing desire to read the Bible. He saw the wonders of God all around him as springtime broke forth with new life. The cattle seemed vigorous as they were released into the pasture. Little calves were born, and the old sow gave birth to ten piglets. New life was all around him, yet Adam longed for something more.

A Warmed Heart

Princeton, Wisconsin

1854-1856

MATILDA AWAKENED IN THE DARKNESS of the night. Her head was pounding with pain. She was shaking with chills, yet burning with fever. She called out, "Vati, Vati, I need your help. My head hurts!"

Johann, awakened from deep sleep, responded, "Hu! What is it Matilda? Are you all right?" He rolled over and lifted his head, hoping he was dreaming. He listened. He heard it again. "Vati, I need help." Slipping into his boots, he made his way across the room and put a couple of sticks of wood in the stove. He touched a candlewick to a burning log. "Matilda," he whispered, "Matilda, what do you need?"

"Vati, my head hurts. I'm cold and hot at the same time."

Johann put his hand on her forehead. It was burning hot. "I'll get some cool water." He felt her body shivering, so he pulled a wool blanket over her. She groaned.

He placed a cool cloth on her forehead and brought her a cup of water. Matilda's body was shaking so violently that she couldn't hold the cup to her lips. "Oh, Vati, I hurt all over. What am I going to do?"

When the sun came up, Johann hoped his daughter would be feeling better. Matilda tried to help with breakfast but was driven back to bed by severe pain.

As Johann brewed some coffee, he remembered the laudanum the Bauers brought when Caroline was sick. "Here, Matilda," he assured, "a spoonful of this will help the pain." He tucked the blankets around her. Matilda drifted off to sleep. While she slept, Johann went to do the morning chores. The cows greeted him with soft lowing, waiting to be milked. Sitting on the stool, filling the milk pail with foamy white, his mind went to Caroline's sickness and death. *Could this happen to me again?*

Johann returned to the cabin with a bucket of milk and five eggs. Matilda was still sleeping, so he took up the harness he was repairing and busied himself for the morning. Around noon, Matilda stirred and called, "Vati, are you here?"

"Ja, Matilda, I'm workin' on the harness. Are you feelin' better?"

"Vati, I was so sick. I feel better now, but I still feel tired," Matilda said as she slipped into her robe. She poured a cup of coffee and sat down by the table.

Johann looked up from his work. "There are some eggs in the basket. Want a couple for breakfast?"

Bouts of fever, headaches, and chills continued night after night. A dose of laudanum would bring relief, but only temporarily. Finally, Johann affirmed, "Matilda, we're goin' to see the doctor in Princeton."

Doctor Schulz scratched his head and said, "We've got another case of ague. We know what it is, but we haven't found a treatment. I'll send more laudanum with you. But remember, it will make you feel better, but it is not a cure."

Both father and daughter returned home discouraged. The sickness came and went over the next two years. Matilda tried hard to help on the claim. Sometimes she would sit and weep. Gerda and Gertrude took turns coming to bake, prepare food, churn butter, and all the other needed chores. Matilda's love for these two girls deepened.

It was a nice day, so Matilda gathered her strength, took the lunch basket, and walked out where her pa was thrashing wheat. While

222

they were eating lunch, a man on horseback came galloping across the prairie. "Well"—Johann shrugged—"I wonder who's out this way today."

The rider left the trail and called out, *"Gutten tag!"*

Johann waved his hat in welcome and responded, *"Gutten tag."* Then he recognized Dr. Schulz.

The doctor swung down from his saddle, speaking before he touched the ground, "Got good news for you, Matilda. We found a medicine that will cure your ague. A doctor in Milwaukee found it, and we now have it in Princeton. I brought you some. I want you to try it and let me know if it works."

Johann reached a hand to the doctor and said, "That is good news, Doc. I'm not sure I have the money to pay you, but I sure want my daughter to get well."

Dr. Schulz shrugged and replied, "I'm not chargin' for it until I know it works. It sure won't hurt ya, and I'm told it will help."

Matilda offered Dr. Schulz a cup of coffee. After a bit of small talk, the doctor mounted his horse and rode away.

The medicine tasted bad enough to cure a horse of the mange. After a few days, Matilda began to feel much better. Slowly, she started to help with the chores and was able to get back to grinding floor, baking bread, curing cheese, and all the household tasks. Feeling better and now fifteen, she wondered, *What's the world like out there?*

The bread was about ready for the oven when a knock came on the door. Matilda jumped with surprise and opened the door. "Oh, Helga," she shrieked. Forgetting to invite her friend in, she lunged over the threshold and threw her arms around her visitor. "Helga, Helga, I'm glad you came. I've been so discouraged and lonely. Thank you for coming." Matilda realized her lack of hospitality and said, "Oh, Helga, please come in. I'm making bread. It'll be done soon, and we'll have some with coffee."

The two fifteen-year-olds visited like a couple of chatterboxes. The time flew past like a whirlwind. It was quiet for a moment. Matilda drew a deep breath and confided, "Helga, I dearly love my vati, but

I get so lonesome. I wonder what it would be like to live in town and have friends. Sometimes I wonder if I'll ever have a husband and children. I would like to study and go to church and be grown-up."

Helga smiled and reached to touch Matilda's hand. "I know what you mean. I wonder those things too. There's a boy in town I really like. I get all flustered and my face turns red when I see him. My mutti says that's the way with girls and boys."

Harvest had been good. The grain bin in the barn was full, and the wagon was loaded with wheat to sell in town. With arrangements for the Bauer twins to do the chores for three days, Matilda and her father left early in the morning for Princeton. Louie and Maud set the pace. Winnie, now a two-year-old, ran along the pasture fence, fussing at being left behind. Johann couldn't help but think how fast the colt became a horse. *The same is true of my daughter. She's becoming a woman.*

The wheat brought a good price. They made a payment on the land, and the father and daughter had supper at the café. To their surprise, Helga came to their table. "Hallo," she said politely, "welcome to our café. What would you like today?" Then she leaned down and whispered to Matilda, "I have to say that, but I'm glad to see you. Mutti owns the café now, and I'm her waitress. Can I see you after work?"

They gave their orders, and Helga left for the kitchen. Johann rented a room at the rooming house for the next two nights. He knew Matilda would want to stay with Helga. Johann realized, *I can't keep her out in that cabin forever.*

That evening, Olinda invited the Mannweilers to coffee. Johann was self-conscious but went with his daughter. After coffee and sweets, the girls slipped away to Helga's room. Johann slowly relaxed as he realized how easy it was to talk with this woman, though twenty years younger than himself. They talked about the death of their mates. On occasion, a tear slipped down Olinda's face, and Johann choked back a lump in his throat.

Feeling comfortable, Johann ventured, "Mrs. Hartmann, I . . . I'm thinkin' . . . that Matilda is growin' up. I don't know how to help her grow up. I keep treating her like my little girl. She needs to grow up . . ."

"Ja," Olinda answered, "I have that problem too. I want Helga to be my little girl. It must be even harder for you bein' a vati. Helga is wantin' to go to a church camp meeting down at Fox Lake next week. An evangelist is comin', and I don't want to let her go. Mrs. Lang says they'll take good care of her, but . . ."

The hour was getting late. Johann stood. "Thank you, Mrs. Hartmann, I have things to do tomorrow, best I get some rest." He called, "Matilda, I'm goin' now. Are you stayin' with Helga?"

The two girls came out with big smiles on their faces. "Vati, we've been talkin', and Helga and I would like to go to the camp meeting at Fox Lake next week. Can we, Vati?"

Johann gave Olinda a knowing look. He shrugged. "I guess Helga better talk to her mutti about that."

The two parents nodded to each other, and the decision was made. Matilda looked into her father's eyes with the charm of a young woman and said, "Thank you, Vati, thank you so much. I'll stay here with Helga tonight. Good night, Vati."

Johann, moving toward the door, said, "Thank you, Olin . . . Mrs. Hartmann, for the coffee. I think our daughters are two excited young women." As he reached for the latch, Olinda put her hand on his arm. "If I can help your daughter as a woman, I'm willing."

Johann felt a slight flush on his neck and said, "Much obliged."

"Mrs. Lang," Helga said with excitement the next day, "Matilda and I can go with you to the camp meeting. Her pa and my ma said so last night." Mrs. Lang was pleased when she heard the news. She told them what to bring and that they would be camping in a covered wagon.

"Matilda, I want to talk with your vater before he leaves town."

"He'll have dinner at the café today. Could you join us there?" Matilda asked. It was agreed, and the girls ran back to the rooming house. Helga had to work at the café for the lunch hour, so Matilda found ways to help Olinda in the kitchen. For a moment, Matilda wished she could live in town and get a job, but she knew she needed to help her pa firm his claim.

Mrs. Lang arrived and found Johann seated at the table in the far corner. "Hallo, Mr. Mannweiler, how good to see you. Have you had your lunch?"

He stood and greeted Mrs. Lang, "Nope, too busy around here. Matilda has been busy in the kitchen. Would you have a bite with us?" Mrs. Lang was dressed in a drab black dress and black bonnet, but the blonde curls above her forehead and winning smile told of a caring woman. He thought, *This is a woman I can trust to care for my little girl.* He changed his thought to . . . *my maturing daughter.*

"I'm so pleased that Matilda and Helga are going to the camp meeting with us. We'll leave early next Thursday. Preacher Krause will be the evangelist. He comes from the Evangelical Association. They are starting a church in Brandon not far from Fox Lake. He was converted as a youth under the preaching of Jacob Albright in Pennsylvania. Albright was the founder of the Evangelical Association." Johann nodded approval but was obviously anxious to get started for home.

There was a touch of fall in the air as the father and daughter made their way out of town. Johann urged Louie and Maud to a steady trot. He put his arm on Matilda's shoulder and said, "We didn't do anything to celebrate your fifteenth birthday on August 9. Let's think of your trip to Fox Lake as your growing-up trip."

Matilda worked hard the next few days baking extra bread, picking greens, churning butter, and cleaning up the cabin. She altered two of her mother's dresses and put them in her bag along with other necessities for her trip. On Wednesday, Helga arrived on black Ebba. When the girls were ready to leave, Matilda smiled at her pa. "Thank you, Vati. Don't forget to feed the hens. They're setting on some eggs." Johann waved good-bye to his daughter. His throat tightened when he noticed the gold cross hanging around her neck. *She really is growing up. Sure reminds me of my Caroline.*

It was so much fun riding in the Langs' wagon on the way to Fox Lake. When they arrived, they were warmly greeted. Anticipation of the first preaching meeting hung in the air. Matilda had never heard so many shouts of, "Praise the Lord," as she did that day.

The meeting that evening was a total surprise to the young fifteen-year-old. The rousing accordion and violin music left her in mouth-opened awe. People, sitting on blankets or small chairs around a rough wood pulpit, sang with wide smiles on their faces. Matilda had never seen so much joy.

A tall man dressed in a thread bare suit with long tails stood up to preach. His voice filled the air with power. Matilda felt something strange happening inside her breast. It frightened her at first. This was so different from her church in Germany. As she tried to listen to the preacher, she remembered her father talking about a man named Jakob Spener and the people called "Pietists."

Matilda and Helga spread their bedrolls under the wagon. They could hear the voices of people around them joyfully visiting. Sometimes they would hear a quietly sung hymn. She felt close to God. Matilda wondered about the people who had gone to the front at the end of the meeting. *What were they doing?*

Saturday was filled with preaching meetings. They had a huge smorgasbord at noontime. In the afternoon, the girls joined the young people in some games.

That evening, Preacher Krause appealed, "Jesus gave his life for your life. He has taken your life of sin and exchanged it for his life of righteousness." The preacher's strong voice quieted, and Matilda felt he was talking directly to her. He said with conviction, "Jesus Christ is the Way, the Truth, and the Life. He is the only way back to the Father. In him, you can have a spiritual birth. Unless your heart is warmed and your sins forgiven, you will not have eternal life."

Matilda's mind wandered. *Unless your heart is warmed* . . . She felt warmth in her chest. Suddenly, she heard the preacher saying, "Anyone who wants to know your sin is forgiven, come here, come up front. We will pray with you. Come now!" The violin started to play. Matilda's eyes filled. She saw people moving toward the preacher. Without more thought, she started walking forward. She felt a hand in her hand. With a quick glance, she knew it was Helga. Near the front, they fell to their knees with tears running down their faces.

A hand rested on Matilda's head. She heard the voice of the preacher saying softly, "Do you confess that you are a sinner?" She nodded. "Do you trust Jesus to forgive your sin and save you to eternal life?" She nodded again. He continued, "Pray this prayer with me."

That night, Preacher Krause led Matilda and Helga into the presence of the Savior. He gave them a small booklet and urged them to read the Bible and pray each day.

Walking back to the wagon, Matilda noticed that the moon was brighter than ever and her steps lighter. She knew something very special had happened. The two girls were quiet as they prepared to get into their bedrolls. They heard a voice. Mrs. Lang whispered, "A very special night for the two of you." She prayed with them and said, "Good night, my Christian *schwestern*."

It was quiet for several minutes. Matilda whispered, "Helga, are you awake?"

"Ja, I can't sleep," came the answer.

"Helga, now I know my mutti saw Jesus. I know why she was smiling."

Sunday at the camp meeting was a festive day. Preacher Krause closed the morning worship by saying, "Remember, there's a meeting every Sunday morning and evening at the Muller house in Brandon. Come any time you can."

Back home, Matilda fixed supper. She was quiet as they sat at the table. Johann waited for his daughter to tell him about the camp meeting. Matilda waited for him to ask. Johann spoke first. "Matilda, you're quiet, did you have a good time?"

That was enough to bring a burst of words from the fifteen-year-old. "Oh, Vati, it was wonderful. Vati, I have a warmed heart. I know Jesus as my Savior." She looked at her pa. Seeing his questioning expression, she went on. "You know how you sometimes talk about

Jakob Spener and warm hearts? That's what happened to me. My heart is warm with Jesus. Vati, I now know that Mutti saw Jesus. I know why she was smiling."

Johann felt some distance between himself and his daughter. He lingered in thought. *She's growing up, and now it feels like she's growing away.* He could not speak.

Quietness reigned in the cabin that evening while Johann worked on a chair he was building. Matilda dug the family Bible out of the trunk and read for a few minutes. She didn't understand much but was determined to do what the preacher suggested.

The trees started to display their fall colors as Johann continued to break new sod to expand his grain fields. His herd of milk cows increased. But loneliness hung over him like a pall in the quiet of the night.

One Saturday morning at breakfast, Matilda asked, "Vati, could I ride Louie to town tomorrow and go to church at the Langs' home?" She saw his head go down, and she waited.

"How'd it be if we both go and drive the team? We could do chores early in the morning and get back for evening milkin'." He looked at his daughter for a moment and then continued, "Matilda, I want to hear about this . . . this warmed heart that you talk about."

Matilda's heart raced. "O, Vati, I would love to go to church with you. I want to see Helga and the Langs and some other friends I met at the camp meeting."

It was a beautiful September morning. A rooster pheasant cackled and ran into the thicket. Matilda was daydreaming, sitting by her pa on the wagon seat, when they pulled up in the Langs' yard.

The living room was full of people. Matilda moved in to sit with Helga. Johann sat on a milk can by the kitchen door. He returned a nod when he noticed Olinda across the room. Fred gave him a hearty greeting and sat next to him. He knew some of the hymns, and the Bible reading was familiar.

After the service, Mr. Lang approached Johann, "How's your daughter doin' these days? She had a powerful conversion down at Fox Lake. Has she told you all about it?"

Johann hesitated, "Ja, she's excited. I'm not sure what to say to her. Guess I don't really understand. It seems different than our church back in Germany."

Mr. Lang and Johann stepped out in the backyard. The two men talked for a long time while everyone shared a picnic lunch.

On the way home that afternoon, Johann interrupted Matilda's thoughts. "I'm glad for ya, Matilda, your conversion, I mean. Mr. Lang helped me understand what you mean by a warmed heart. I'm glad."

23
Soundly Converted
Methodist Camp Meeting
1857

O N A BEAUTIFUL JUNE DAY in 1857, Adam Utzinger arrived at the Methodist camp meeting on the Fox River north of Princeton, Wisconsin. His loneliness of heart was soon washed away by the genuine welcome of the people. Tables full of food and pots full of coffee drew the people together. Anticipation filled the air.

After supper, everyone gravitated toward a grassy hillside. Families, sitting on quilts and blankets, centered their attention on a rough-hewn pulpit at the bottom of the slope. About a dozen men, dressed in black suits, were on their knees with elbows on split-log benches and heads down in prayer. The men stood up. A hush came over the gathering, and a tall man with a black beard approached the pulpit. He looked up toward the heavens and started to sing in a mellow voice. His arms came up as if to draw words from the mouths of the people. Hymn after hymn, the atmosphere thickened with oneness in worship.

Stillness covered the meeting. The song leader yielded the pulpit to a heavyset man. "I am Louie Lehmann, presiding elder of the Fox River Circuit. Welcome to the Fox River Camp Meeting of 1857. It is my privilege to introduce the evangelist for our camp meeting, Elder George Shaffer of the Menomonee Circuit of the Evangelical Association. We are always pleased to have evangelists from the association since their founder, Jacob Albright, had his start as a Methodist. We are fellow Pietists. Elder Shaffer is known across Wisconsin as a man of God and a powerful preacher of God's Word. Brothers and sisters, I present Elder George Shaffer."

There it is again, that word Pietists, Adam thought as he leaned against an old cottonwood off to the side of the crowd. He raised his left foot and set the sole of his boot against the tree behind him. With arms folded in front of his chest, he waited upon the words of the preacher. His mind held a mixture of defiance and anticipation. On one hand, he was attached to the teachings of his German pastor; and on the other hand, he longed for something more.

Elder Shaffer stepped to the speaker's stand. His deep-set, piercing eyes scanned the crowd. Thick reddish-brown hair migrated down his face into a graying well-trimmed beard. Love and kindness could be felt in his demeanor. Adam sensed a holy presence move over the people like dew on a warm summer morning. A baby ceased crying. Quietness reigned.

The elder bowed his head and spoke in soft, audible words. "Let the words of my mouth and the meditation of my heart be acceptable in thy sight, O Lord, my strength and my Redeemer." When he looked up, Adam felt he was looking directly into his heart. The impact caused Adam's left foot to fall to the ground as he slid down the tree trunk to a sitting position. Adam's ears tuned in to the words of the preacher as he quoted from Philippians chapter 2, verses 5-11:

> *Let this mind be in you, which was also in Christ Jesus: Who, being in the form of God, thought it not robbery to be equal with God: But made himself of no reputation, and took upon him the form of a servant, and was made in the likeness of men: And being found in fashion as a man, he humbled himself, and became obedient unto death, even the death of the cross. Wherefore God also hath highly exalted him, and given him a name which is above every name: That at the name of Jesus every knee should bow, of things in heaven, and things in earth, and things under*

the earth; And that every tongue should confess that Jesus Christ is Lord, to the glory of God the Father.

As Elder Shaffer unfolded these words of Scripture, Adam felt warmth come over him like a blanket. Never before had he felt so close to Jesus and so aware of his death on the cross in obedience to the Father. The preacher urged, "Let your knee bow at the name of Jesus. Right now, you are in the presence of Jesus. Let your knee bow to him."

Adam felt small in the presence of Jesus. His heart raced, and sweat broke out on his neck. He realized he was leaning forward on one knee, listening intently. "Let your tongue confess that Jesus is the Lord of your life." The preacher continued, "Make your confession, now! Trust Jesus as your Lord, now!"

Suddenly, Adam took control of himself and backed away into the shadow of the cottonwood. He reached for his red handkerchief to wipe the perspiration from his face. He tried to move away out of hearing distance from the preacher, but his feet were planted to the ground. A battle raged in his mind. He was drawn in two directions at the same time. Slowly, he placed one foot in front of the other until he was back by his pinto pony. He cinched the saddle in place, mounted, and rode out of the campgrounds. He allowed Rowdy freedom to run. Darkness settled, and the night mist was cool on his face. The tree frogs sang a haunting melody of rising and lowering crescendo. Loneliness consumed him as he tied Rowdy to a tree branch and found a place to crawl into his bedroll. Half asleep, in his mind, he heard the gentle words of the preacher's invitation, only to be crowded out by thoughts of his family and the formality of religion back in Germany. The tug-of-war in his mind produced pain.

At first morning light, Adam mounted his pinto. He allowed Rowdy to set the trail and the pace. Adam's mind returned to the preacher's words from the night before. "Make your confession, now. Trust Jesus as your Lord, now!" No one seemed to notice when Adam dismounted and watered and fed his pinto. He was greeted with a hot cup of coffee and an invitation to have pancakes and sausage.

"Hey, Adam, good to see you," came a friendly voice from a covered wagon. "That's a good lookin' pinto you're ridin'."

"Thanks," Adam answered, looking to see who was speaking. "Oh, hallo, Jake. Ja, I just arrived. Looks like a nice day for the meetings." Jake Lang's friendly welcome made Adam feel more at home.

Jake reached for his hat from the wagon tailgate and said, "It's my job to set up the mourner's benches down front. How about givin' me a hand? Grab one of those planks over there and I'll bring some blocks to put under it."

Adam felt less self-conscious now that he had a part in the activities. The morning Bible study challenged his thoughts, and he was stimulated by the conversation over coffee with other men.

At the evening meeting, Elder Shaffer approached the pulpit. Adam hung on every word as the preacher quoted, "Come unto me, all ye that labor and are heavy laden, and I will give you rest." He continued, "Many of you in this gathering have heavy burdens. Jesus invites you to come to Him. In Jesus you will find rest for your soul."

Adam had an inner sense of the truth of the message. The resistance he experienced the day before began to return, but he pushed it aside. When the elder issued an invitation to "come to Jesus," Adam made his way forward. He went down on his knees as Elder Shaffer put his hand on his shoulder and prayed. During the prayer, Adam experienced the release of his burdens. He knew he believed and that his sin was forgiven.

"Mr. Utzinger," a strong voice called as Adam, bedroll in hand, was looking for a place to sleep. "Could we visit for a moment?"

"Ja, Elder Shaffer, it'd be my pleasure." The two men sat on a log near the horse corral.

"Jake Lang told me you've been attending meetings in Princeton lately. He said you're farming the Halgrave farm with your brother." The elder put his leather bag down and continued, "I saw you leave during the meeting last night. I knew two forces were warring inside of you, so I started to pray. I prayed you'd come back. You know, Mr. Utzinger, the Holy Spirit of God draws us to himself, and Satan tries to hold us back. You made the most important decision in your life tonight. Satan will still try to win you back, but you have the power of the living God at work in you."

Adam wondered how this man knew so much about him. He decided to tell the elder his story. "Sir," Adam began, "I grew up on the Scharrhof in Germany. I took the formal training at my church with our pastor. I thought I knew what I needed to know to be a Christian." Adam drew a deep breath and continued, "I keep meeting people with a joy and peace that I never experienced in my studies with my pastor. On the ship coming over to New York, I met some families who were filled with excitement for God. I believe the things my pastor taught me, but it seems like there is something more. I feel like I'm betraying my pastor and my family, but I have a longing for the things of God."

"Adam, we are now brothers in Christ. I want to encourage you to read your Bible and seek the Lord in prayer. Let me give you a little history that may help you understand what's happening in your life. About two hundred years ago, Philip Jakob Spener, a Lutheran pastor, led a revival in the church in Germany. It triggered a pietistic movement across Europe and has carried on here in America. Spener felt that the teachings of Martin Luther instructed people in the knowledge of faith without the transforming power of the Holy Spirit. Under Spener's leadership, people of like faith drew together in small groups to study the Bible. They wanted to know Jesus as well as know about him. Spener became known as the father of Pietism.

"That's the word the people on the *Robert Harding* used, *Pietism*," Adam said with a questioning look.

"I'm an elder in the Evangelical Association. We are Pietists. You see, Spener's godson, Count von Zinzendorf, helped spread an evangelical awakening all over Europe through the Moravian Church. The Moravians influenced John Wesley, and Methodism spread here in

America. Jacob Albright, the founder of our Evangelical Association, started out as a Methodist but wanted to reach the thousands of Germans who came to Pennsylvania. Since the Methodists insisted upon preaching in English, Albright set out on his own, holding meetings among the German folks in Pennsylvania. He traveled from place to place, holding meetings in homes. As the movement grew, it was necessary to train preachers and provide direction through an association. It came to be known as the Evangelical Association. It has spread now across Ohio, Illinois, Wisconsin, and into Minnesota Territory."

The two men talked far into the night. Adam felt a new freedom and peace. "Mr. Shaffer, I want to thank you for spending this time with me. I must go home tomorrow and tend the farm so my brother and his wife can come to the meetings. It's been a privilege to talk with you."

"You are most welcome," the elder said as he extended a hand to the new convert. "Adam, we have a small Evangelical Association group over in Brandon. You sure would be welcome, and I'm sure they would have things you could read to learn more about Pietism and our association."

The next morning, Adam rode out of the campgrounds as a new man. His burdens were lifted, and his heart was at peace. Back home, he tried to tell Peter and Carolina about his new life, but they were consumed by the farm and their little daughter. Adam said, "It's your turn to go to the camp meeting. I'll take care of the farm."

Adam and Peter continued to work the Halgrave farm. Their share of the increase provided a reasonable living. Little Maria did not gain as rapidly as she should have and often had bouts of earache, high fever, and cough. Dr. Schulz, in Princeton, could not come up with answers. It didn't seem to be ague, though he tried treating it as such.

One Monday, Adam stopped at the Brandon General Store and inquired about Evangelical Association meetings in town. The storekeeper responded, "The Muller family would know if anyone does. Their house is just down the street and around the corner. He's the smithy in town."

Adam jumped to the wagon seat and urged Zelig and Zelda down the street to the Muller home. Several children were playing in the backyard. Adam knocked firmly on the door. A woman, who appeared to be in her thirties, a baby in her arms, stepped into the doorway. She wore a neat cotton dress with a navy-blue sash around her waist. Her blue eyes sparkled as she greeted the visitor with a smile. "Hallo," she said, "my husband is in his shop. You'll find him next door."

Adam stammered, "Perhaps, ah, maybe you can answer my question. They told me at the store that you would know about meetings of the Evangelical Association in Brandon. My name's Adam Utzinger. I was converted at the Fox River Camp Meeting with Elder Shaffer. He suggested I might find some things to read about Pietism and the Evangelical Association here in town."

The woman's smile broadened and invited Adam to take a seat on the porch. "Our preacher is in town and will be holding a Bible study at the Gahringer home this evening. You'd be most welcome."

The baby whimpered, taking the woman's attention for a moment. Adam hesitated and said, "I'm sorry to impose on your family. I need to get home for chores, but I was hoping I could find something to read."

"Preacher Krause is at the Gahringer home now preparing for the meeting. They live out on the west road about a mile, the trail that leads to Princeton." She comforted the baby as she spoke.

"That's on my way home. How will I know the place?" Adam spoke as he moved toward the steps.

"It's on the left side of the trail, a white house, a small barn, and a row of poplars along the lane." She shrugged and said, "That's about it. The preacher's name is Krause."

"Much obliged, Mrs. Muller," Adam responded with a nod of respect. "I'll be comin' to your meetin' sometime soon."

A black dog greeted Adam as he drove up Gahringer's lane. A tall, slender man with a black book in his hands was sitting on a chair in the shade of an oak tree. Adam set the wagon brake, jumped to the ground, patted the dog on the neck, and addressed the gentleman. "Might you be the preacher, Rev. Krause?"

The man closed the book and uncoiled his lanky body into a standing position. "That's my name. Who is it that I have the honor to meet?"

"Utzinger, Adam Utzinger's my name. Do you by chance know Elder George Shaffer of the Menomonee Circuit of the Evangelical Association?"

The two men walked toward each other and shook hands in greeting. "Most certainly do, a good man and a great preacher. What brings you here asking about my friend George Shaffer?"

"I was converted at the Methodist camp meeting on the Fox River under his preaching. I talked with him about my struggles between the teachings I received back in Germany and things I've been hearin' about Pietism. Elder Shaffer suggested I might find some reading materials here in Brandon."

"You came to the right place. My great-grandparents came to Pennsylvania from Germany. My family helped form the Evangelical Association. Yes, I have the books we use to train the exhorters that lead our class meetings. They include a section on the history of Pietism back in Germany under a leader named Jakob Spener. I would be pleased to share them with you."

Mr. Krause returned from the house and handed Adam a cloth bag, saying, "I pray you'll find answers to your questions in these books. I'll be back in Brandon in three weeks. I'd be pleased to visit with you after you have time to do some reading."

"Thank you very much, Rev. Krause. It would be my pleasure to meet with you."

As the men shook hands, the reverend said, "We're havin' a prayer meetin' tonight. You'd be welcome."

"Would like to stay, but my *bruder* is expecting me to help with the chores." Adam tipped his hat as he spoke to the two Zs.

During the next three weeks, Adam spent every possible moment poring over the materials he found in the cloth bag. He sensed Spener's burning desire to bring about change in the church in Germany through revival of true Christianity. Since, at that time, the church and state were basically one, political leaders were seen as "Christians," but their lives did not reflect the Word of God. Spener also called the clergy to be role models of true Christian faith for the common people. He urged the universities and seminaries to include, along with their emphasis on scholarly theology, teaching that would equip the clergy for ministry among the people.

Adam noticed that one of the first things Spener did as a Lutheran pastor was to call the people to gather in small groups where they could share with one another and support one another in living out their faith. Spener taught that every believer should study the Bible and grow in their understanding of what it is to be a Christian by the principles of God's Word.

Adam was amazed at the influence Mr. Spener had all over Europe. He was excited to see how one of Spener's associates, Francke, inspired George Muller to care for orphans as an act of simple faith and prayer. He saw how Spener's teachings stimulated a young man named Count Zinzendorf to give leadership to the great Moravian movement to evangelize the world. The Moravians in turn influenced John and Charles Wesley who were called Methodists in England. Adam was thrilled when he found out that vital Christian faith came to America with Pietists who were seeking greater Christian freedom.

The more Adam read, the more he saw that the Evangelical Association was a part of a wide-ranging revival. He treasured visits with Preacher Krause as he prepared to be a class leader and a regular participant in the Evangelical Association in Brandon, Wisconsin.

24

The Birth of a Township
Minnesota
1856-1858

PHILLIP EPPARD AND JUDGE FELCH walked into the Hamilton General Store. "Pretty nice store for this little town," Felch observed.

"Welcome to Hamilton," a hearty voice came from the back of the store. "My name's Booth. You won't find a better store for miles around. What can I do for ya today?"

"We just pulled in from Racine, Wisconsin," the judge responded. "I'm Charles Felch. We're lookin' to buy some land in the area. Do you have any suggestions?"

Booth came around the counter and shook hands with the men. "I don't do much in the land business, but my partner, Mr. Randall, has a print shop down the street. Since the Land Office moved to Chatfield last month, he's been printin' deeds and legal papers by the score. It wouldn't hurt to pay him a visit."

At the print shop, they met Mr. Randall, a short man of slight build. Thick glasses dominated his round face. His beard was thin and graying. He wore black pants and a white shirt with a black string tie, all covered by a blue denim apron heavily smudged with printer's ink.

"*Gutten tag*, gentlemen, I see you just made camp by the river. I could lay a bet that you're lookin' for land. I don't sell, and I don't buy, but I sure can help those who do," the little man boasted.

"We're in the buyin' mood," the judge answered. "Do you know of claims that are up for outright sale?"

"Sure do, have a look at sale bills on the wall over there. Some good places up for cash."

They browsed through the papers, made a few notes, and prepared to leave. "All sales go through the Federal Land Office in Chatfield. All I can do is let you know what may be available. Once you have the sale papers, I'd be obliged if you'd called on me to do your printin'."

Hannah had supper ready when the men returned. That evening, the judge announced, "Phillip and David, I need the two of you to stand guard here at the camp all day tomorrow. They say the natives are friendly but are inclined to steal and destroy. I'll ride on west and take a look at the properties owned by Joseph Robb and J. D. Gregory. Word is that they want to sell and make a move over into Fillmore County."

Phillip and David were sitting on the wagon tailgate the next morning. Phil said, "Look here, Dave, according to this paper I picked up at the print shop, all it takes to make a claim is to clear a half acre, fence it, and live on it for thirty days, and you can file a claim. The cost would be $1.25 an acre. Workin' for your pa, I could save enough to do that come fall."

David looked up at his older friend with a smile and said, "If you do that, you'll have to find yourself a wife."

"Ja, I guess I would," Phil said, giving his friend a poke on the arm. "I hope to have a wife sometime, don't you?"

After a long pause, David said, "I don't see any good in havin' a wife. I can cook and all that for myself."

Mr. Felch returned shortly after noon. "I've made up my mind to purchase two claims over west of here. They both have log cabins and small shelters for livestock. They're fenced and have crops growin'. I'll be ridin' to Chatfield tomorrow to close the deal."

Hannah stepped down from the wagon with hands on her hips. "Charles! What am I supposed to do while you're riding around the countryside? I've already spent more time in this wagon than I bargained for."

The judge reached a hand to his wife. "We'll get a room for you at Corey's Hotel. You can rest and have a warm bath. I'll be back in a couple days and join you there."

"It's just what I thought it would be, stuck in a little hick town all alone," she huffed and returned to the wagon.

"I'll get a room for her on my way out of town," the judge said with a little smile. "Phil, you and David hitch up tomorrow and take the wagons on west three or four miles and find a place to camp. When I get back from Chatfield, we'll move into one of the cabins and bring Hannah out later. Don't leave the wagons unattended."

With deeds in hand, the judge returned. They moved onto the Robb claim. Phillip took the cabin on the Gregory claim. He set to work building and mending fences and weeding the gardens the former owners had neglected. He cut and stacked prairie grass hay for feed in winter. In the evening, he read from his mother's Bible. He worked hard for the judge, but he dreamed about having a place of his own.

In late summer, Phillip chose a quarter section, cleared a half acre, and put up some fence rails. David helped him build a small cabin and a shelter for Queen. He lived in his cabin enough to qualify for the thirty days. In September of 1856, Phillip rode to Chatfield and filed a claim to a quarter section in Township 104 about two miles west of Hamilton. The same day, William Kalhofer, Gustaav Maas, and Peter Mier filed claims for neighboring properties.

The winter of 1856-57 topped them all for blizzards and cold. Phillip was hard-pressed to take care of the judge's cows and have enough feed for Queen. Hours were spent cutting wood to heat his cabin. The lack of warm clothing and boots caused discomfort. Sometimes, he wrapped his feet in rags inside his shoes for warmth. Then to top it off, 1857 turned out to be a financial recession. Many people lost their claims. With the help of Judge Felch, Phillip weathered both the winter and the financial storms.

The songs of the meadowlarks announced the bursting forth of new life in springtime. A lull after spring planting left Phil feeling tired and lonely. He rode over to the Felch place. "Judge," he said, "I'm feelin' the need of a little time off. I'm goin' in to town for the day. Is David around? Would he like to go with me?"

"Ja, that would be fine. David's down by the creek. I'm sure he'd like a chance to get away for a while."

Despite the nearly ten years difference in age, Phil and Dave had a growing friendship based partly on the fact they both had experienced the death of their mother and felt neglected by their father. They seldom talked about it, but the trust was building.

Riding along the trail, David asked, "What you gonna do in Hamilton, look for a wife? I haven't seen many women around here. Slim pickins, if you ask me."

"Didn't ask you, but you seem to have it figured out anyway. Ja, I would like to find a wife and settle down on my claim. Soon I'll have enough money to build a nice little farmhouse."

"Then you really would need a wife," his young companion jibed.

"You sure want to get me married off, don't ya?"

"You have to admit it gets pretty lonely out there."

Phillip spurred Queen to a gallop. "Let's get on to town."

At Hamilton General Store, Phillip bought a box of bullets for his rifle and a couple of apples. At the counter, the storekeeper took the money and returned with change. As he put the coins in Phillip's hand, he glanced up with a questioning look. "Ain't you the young fella that works for a judge, Judge Felt or somethin' like that?"

"Ja, it's Judge Felch, Judge Charles Felch. He bought the Robb and Gregory claims. We're workin' on 'em now. This is the judge's son, David."

"I'm Dan Booth. I platted the town and have this store and the sawmill down by the river. We plan to start a gristmill. We already have the hotel and the post office. Men around town have been talkin' about gettin' the township organized and electin' a township board. Bill Campfield and O. B. Morse live across the line in Mower County.

They'd like to talk to the judge about helpin' get started. Some of us on the Fillmore County side could use some help too. Have him stop in some day when he's in town."

Next stop was the village post office. Phillip asked, "Any chance you'd have mail for Phillip Eppard or Judge Charles Felch?"

The postmaster flipped through a stack of letters and dropped one out, then another and another. "Yup, three letters here for Felch, none for Eppard. You must be the people that bought the Robb place. Robb was in the other day and said he was movin' on."

As they talked, in walked a girl in her middle teens, a boy a little younger, and another girl of about twelve. They moved off to one side and waited. The postmaster looked past his patrons and said, "Lucy, do you need somethin'?"

Lucy answered, "I saw Preacher Hammeter at the store this mornin'. He asked me to let you know he'd be holdin' services at your house this Sunday." The three youth nodded politely and walked out. Phillip's eyes followed her as they left.

The postmaster stepped around the counter. "I'm Jake McQuillan. I keep hours here at the post office a couple days a week and farm out east of town." He offered a hand and said, "And you are?"

Phil responded, "Phillip Eppard, and this is David Felch, the judge's son. I couldn't help but overhear about the services on Sunday. Would that be in German by chance?"

Jake leaned back against the counter. "We have a small group of families that meet at my house out on the farm. Preacher Hammeter is an Evangelical Association circuit rider. He's about as German as they come. He shows up every three or four weeks. We'd sure welcome you. It's just a mile east of here and around the curve to the left. Our house is in the grove of oaks on the left side of the road. My pa lives further on about forty rods or so."

"I came from Germany about five years ago. I understand German best. I may see you Sunday. Thanks, Mr. McQuillan, I'll see the judge gets these letters."

On their way back to the horses, Phillip glanced up the trail to the east and saw the three young people walking toward home.

The two friends lingered around town, checked out the sawmill, and took a ride along the river. They circled back to the west road to head home. On the way, David said, "Phil, are your eyes all right?"

Puzzled by the question, Phillip asked another, "What do you mean, are my eyes all right?"

"I was wonderin' if you hurt yourself the way your eyes followed that girl when she left the post office. I thought I was gonna have to pick 'em up off the floor." Dave let out a huge guffaw. "Then out in the street, you about lost 'em again lookin' up that trail to the east."

"Aw, keep your thoughts to yourself. She's more your age than mine. I admit I'm lookin, but I need a woman, not a girl."

On arrival, Phillip noticed smoke coming from the chimney of the Felch cabin. He thought, *I wonder if Hannah is baking bread or maybe a pie. I may linger long enough for some supper.* He tied Queen by the fence. The judge came out of the cabin. "Welcome home, you two travelers. Did you have a good day?"

David grinned at Phillip. Phillip answered to keep David from saying what he knew he was thinking, "Ja, it was good to get away a bit. Here are three letters we picked up at the post office. Mr. Booth wants you to stop at the store next time you're in town. He's talkin' about organizing a township board."

"Hannah says for you to come in for supper. She's been cookin' and bakin' all day."

During supper, Phillip ventured, "Judge, I've been thinkin' about my future here in Minnesota. I'd like to break some sod on my claim and get some wheat planted this fall. I want to build a small farmhouse in a couple years. I plan to buy a yoke of oxen or a good team of horses. With the economy the way it is, I think I could get some good prices."

"That would be a good investment for you, Phil. I need your help here on these two places, but you could have some time to keep improving your claim."

Phillip pushed back from the table. "It's gettin' late, and I need to do some chores over on the Gregory place before dark. Thanks, Hannah, for supper. I'm afraid I made a pig of myself."

"See," David teased, "I told ya, you need to find a wife."

Phillip gave his young friend a gentle nudge. "Don't you worry, my friend, I'll get a wife when God answers my prayers, not when you think it should happen. And that reminds me, Judge, I'm goin' to church at a home over east of Hamilton on Sunday," Phillip said as he mounted Queen and rode away. The thought of the girl in the post office kept returning to his mind as he did the chores.

Nerves welled up in Phillip's stomach as he approached the Jake McQuillan farm on Sunday morning. He saw three men standing by a wagon, talking. It looked like a safe place to enter. He rode up to the barn and swung down from the saddle.

"*Gutten morgen.*" The oldest man of the three spoke. "Would you be Phillip Eppard by chance? My son told me we could be expectin' you today."

"You guessed that right," Phillip responded as he flipped the reins around the gatepost. "Jake McQuillan invited me at the post office the other day. I thought I would check out the German preachin'."

"I'm Jake's pa, Jacob, and this is George Santes and Frank Peters." The men all shook hands, and Phillip started to feel welcome.

Movement toward the back of the house caught Phil's attention. Two women were standing at a rough board bench, husking garden corn. "Lucinda," Jake called from the doorway, "Ma wants to know how long it'll take with the corn. She wants it ready to boil when the services are over."

"Just three ears left. We'll be done in a minute," the young woman answered. The two scurried to finish their task, gathered the husked ears, and started for the house.

A light came on in Phillip's head. *That's the girl I saw at the post office the other day.* He watched as she moved across the yard, carrying a basket of corn. He felt his heart skip a beat. She was wearing a light-blue dress with buttons down the front. The skirt flared at her slender waist down over her hips. He considered, *She isn't as young as I thought. I'm going to watch her for a year or so.*

Jake extended a welcome and invited everyone to stay for dinner. Elder Hammeter bowed his head. A hush came over the people. He prayed, "God of all creation, come meet with us today. Fill our hearts with your holy presence." As the preacher prayed, Phillip remembered his mother's prayers when he was a child. He was moved by the preaching of the Word of God. Phillip left knowing this was where he belonged.

The weeks passed. Phillip made friends with the people in the little Evangelical Association. He continued to notice Lucinda and found times to speak to her on a casual basis. Wednesday night prayer meeting was frightening when everyone prayed and he could only remain silent.

One rainy day, Phillip was in the lean-to splitting fence rails when a lone rider, hunched against the weather, came into the yard. "Hallo, Preacher Hammeter," Phil called, "let me tie your horse in the stall by Queen."

In the house, the preacher shook the rain off his coat and hat. Phillip chided, "It's kinda rainy to be out tendin' your flock."

"Not at all," the preacher returned, "I find people home with time to visit on rainy days." He continued, "It's been good to have you worship with us at Jake's house."

"Ja," Phil said, "I sure like the German preachin' and singin' the old hymns."

It was silent as the two men sipped a swallow of coffee. The elder broke the quiet. "Phil, tell me your story. How you came to the Lord and all."

Phillip recoiled a bit. "I . . . I don't know what to say, Preacher. My mutti died when I was young. I just remember how she prayed and sang hymns. I have her Bible. My vati married again, and all that was lost. We didn't go to church anymore. I remember my mutti talking about how we can know God. I know that she knew God. I finally left home and came to America. I've kept prayin' to my mutti's God and reading her Bible. I guess that's about it."

"You've told me about your mutti's faith. What about your own? What do you believe? Where would you go if you died?" the reverend pressed.

It was still for a long time. "I'm not sure. I just know there's a God and my mutti knew him." Phillip reached for the coffeepot and filled the cups. He was getting anxious and wanted to find a way out.

"Phil, you mentioned that your mutti knew God. I'm an elder in the Evangelical Association. Our association has roots in Pietism, a reform movement that spread across Europe a couple hundred years ago. Jakob Spener, a German Lutheran pastor, taught that true faith is not just what we know in our heads, but that we can know Jesus in the heart. You can have the same faith that your mutti had. You can ask God to forgive your sin and give you a transformed life in Jesus. Do you want that, Phillip?"

"Preacher, I think I've always wanted that, but I don't know how to get it." Phillip hung his head and felt tears fill his eyes. "I guess I'm really angry at my vati for having another wife and all those little girls." His shoulders shook as he felt the preacher's hand grip his upper arm.

The conversation continued softly, and then the two men went down on their knees, and Phillip made the step of faith into God's eternal kingdom.

The next day, David looked at Phillip, scratched his head, and asked, "Hey, Phil, did you find a girlfriend or somethin'? I've never seen you so cheerful. I hear you hummin' a tune all the time."

Phillip knew his friend wouldn't understand, so he passed it off. "No girlfriend yet, but I got one in my sights."

A few days later, Judge Felch rode into town for supplies at the general store. "*Gutten tag*, Judge Felt," Dan Booth welcomed. "I've been wonderin' when you'd show up. I asked the Eppard lad to have you stop by. We've been talkin' around town about organizin' the townships. Would you . . ."

249

The judge interrupted, "The name's Felch, Judge Felch, and I'm wonderin' why you're talkin' to me about the townships. I'm a probate judge. I'm a citizen of the township, and I'm interested in seeing the township prosper, but not because I'm a judge."

Booth was taken back and stuttered, "Well . . . well, I just thought that since you are a judge, you'd know what we have to do to organize."

"Oh, I can help you with that. All you have to do is call a meetin' of the citizens, elect a moderator, and have a vote to organize. Then you would elect a town board with officers to serve the township. We could start by notifying the citizens of a meeting."

Notices, printed at Randall's Print Shop, were delivered to the citizens residing on the thirty-six sections of the township. On May 11, 1858, the people crowded into the Hamilton Methodist Church. Judge Felch was elected moderator. He saw that election judges were chosen and a proper vote taken to organize the town board. The question came up regarding a name for the new township.

Someone in the back of the room called out, "Judge, you and that young Eppard are from Racine, Wisconsin, why not call this Racine Township?" That day, Racine Township was born with Judge Felch as chairman of the board and William Campfield and Eli Leonard as supervisors. Other officers were: O. B. Morse, clerk; Jonathan Stewart, assessor; and John Martin, treasurer. H. S. Bailey and Loren Dutton were chosen as Justices of the Peace. At the close of the meeting, Judge Felch announced, "This is a historic day, not only for our township, but also for our state. Today, by decree of President Buchanan, Minnesota has become the thirty-second state in the union."

* * *

One bright Sunday morning, Phillip thought, *It's a great day for a ride down to the McQuillans' for church.* Chores were done, and Queen seemed to have a bit of spring fever the way she wanted to run.

As Phillip was tying Queen to the gatepost, Jake called from the steps, "Mornin', Phil! Put that mare in the barn, rub her down, give her a measure of oats, and come on in." *Good people the McQuillans*, Phillip mused. He did as invited.

Mary M handed Phillip a cup of coffee while hanging on to Ella's arm to keep her from running off. "Go in by the fireplace and make yourself at home while we get these kids dressed."

Hester followed and leaned against Phillip's leg to see the pictures in the New York catalog that Phillip was thumbing through. Not to be outdone, Edwin pushed in by his brother to get a look.

The door opened. Lucy rushed in, red-faced and breathless. "I'm sorry, Mary M, I wanted to get here to help you with Ella, but Ma needed my help with Walter. What do you want me to do?"

Phillip noticed her maturing figure when she reached to hang up her coat. He inhaled when she turned with a beautiful smile and said, "Oh, Mr. Eppard, how good to see you here for worship this morning."

Stunned, Phillip responded, "Thank you, Miss McQuillan. It's a wonderful January day to be out." He knew his face reddened a bit. He took a sip of coffee. He caught a glimpse of flush as she hurried to help with the children.

Distracting thoughts whirled through Phillip's mind during the worship service. He struggled to concentrate on the preacher's words. Lucinda was sitting on the floor with three children around her. Her father had Frankie next to him, and her mother was holding little Walter. Some arithmetic went through his mind. *That man must be at least sixty, and his wife can't be more than forty-five.* He forced himself to listen to the preacher. He heard his mind say, *She has to be at least fifteen, and I'm twenty-six. I'm going to ask her vati for permission to court his daughter,* he decided firmly.

Following worship, he watched for an opportunity to talk with Mr. McQuillan. He was surprised by his feelings when Lucinda brushed past him as she served dessert to the guests. He approached her father. "Mr. McQuillan," he said, "I'd like to ask you about that dappled mare

I ride. She has an open sore on the inside of her right front leg. I've treated it, but it's gettin' worse. Would you please take a look at it and give me your advice?"

Phillip held the barn door for the older man and stepped in behind him. They looked at the sore and talked about possible treatments. Then Phillip straightened up and looked directly at Lucinda's father and said, "Mr. McQuillan, I'm concerned about the sore on Queen's leg, but I have another question to ask you." He took a deep breath and continued, "It's about your daughter Lucinda. I find her to be a fine young woman. If she would be willing, I would ask your permission to court her with the intention of asking her to be my wife."

Jacob gasped. "O, my . . . my daughter, she is but a girl. How could she be old enough to be your wife? I . . . I would have to pray a lot about that." He moved toward the door.

"Mr. McQuillan, I thought the same thing until this mornin'. In church, I noticed that you must be about fifteen years older than Mrs. McQuillan. It seems I may be about ten years older than your daughter." Phil felt his knees shaking as he talked.

"That is very different, young man," Jacob stated. "We were in our adult years when we married. Lucy is just a little girl."

"I beg your pardon, sir, but to me she is an attractive woman. And, sir, you must have been married before to Jake's mother. How old were the two of you when you married?" Phillip wondered if he had gone too far.

Jacob turned back toward Phillip and took a deep breath. "Young man, when you get older, you get wiser. I do see you as a man of Christian character, but I need time to get used to this. I'll take it to prayer and will discuss it with my wife. I'll give you an answer when we reach a decision." He paused. "I must say, you have called my attention to the fact that my daughter is growing up."

"Thank you, Mr. McQuillan. I too will be in prayer as I wait for your answer." Phillip saddled Queen and let her run on his way home.

Jacob went home, pondering, *Is my daughter that grown up, and is she ready for a husband?* He was unable to rest that afternoon. Polly was reading by the fire. "Polly, please come to our room, I need to talk with you."

Polly marked her book and followed her husband. With the door closed, Jacob turned to his wife and said, "Polly, is our daughter old enough to get married?"

In total shock, Polly reacted, "Whatever do you mean by that? Our girls are but children. Where did that thought come from?"

"That young Eppard who's been comin' to church asked me for permission to court Lucy. I told him Lucy was too young, but he had the nerve to tell me that he figured I'm fifteen years older than you are. He even questioned how much older I was than Elizabeth. I have to admit he was right."

Being a practical woman, Polly responded, "Jacob, Lucy is sixteen, and men have a way of noticing a good woman. Phillip has shown nothing but good manners and respect toward our family and the church. He has come to know the Lord and is a growing Christian. He has worked hard and has a claim already. He works for Judge Felch and saves his money. Maybe his bald head makes him seem older than he is."

"Yes, but, Polly, she's my little girl." He paced back and forth. "I guess I'm gettin' to be an old man. I don't want things to change. The way Booth took Jake's land and how he runs the town makes me think about movin' on. But on the other hand, I really want to settle in and keep things the same. Now this!"

After much prayer and many tears, Jacob and Polly went in search of Lucinda.

25

Courtship and Marriage
Minnesota
1858-1861

LUCINDA LOOKED FORWARD TO WORSHIP every Sunday at the Jake McQuillan home. She loved to listen to God's Word when Reverend Hammeter came to preach. She was feeling mature, more an adult than a child.

With questions on her mind, Lucy walked across the field to visit Mary M. Cradling a cup of coffee in her hands, Lucy said with a smile, "Mary M, remember when we would talk while driving Jake's team on the Studebaker on our way to Minnesota, I would dream about having a husband and children. You told me to pray, and God would give me the desire of my heart."

Mary M refilled the cups. "Yes, I remember, and I've been watching you grow into a beautiful young woman. One of these days, some young man will come along and you'll know."

"That's just it, Mary M, there is a man, only he's much older than me. But I think he's noticing me. I have this feeling inside when I see him." Lucinda put her elbows on the table with her chin in her hands.

"Oh, Lucy, I think I know who you mean. I've seen Phillip's eyes follow you a few times." She smiled at her young friend.

"Do you mean you've been watchin'?" Lucy waited. "But he is older, and he came all the way from Germany, and he works for a judge. His bald head and gray beard make him look even older. He never would be interested in me."

Mary M smiled. "What about Willie Santes? He's just a year older than you. He pays attention to you, doesn't he?"

"Oh, Mary M, he's so childish. Sometimes I wish he would grow up." Lucy made a big huff. "Mr. Eppard is a gentleman."

Walter woke from his nap. Lucy watched Mary M cuddle and nurse her child. "Mary M, I would like to have children and love them the way you do." She bid her friend good-bye and walked slowly back home.

The next Sunday, Lucy arrived at Mary M's house to help prepare for worship. She rushed in and hung her coat on a hook in the corner. When she turned, she was startled to see Phillip with the boys looking at a catalog. Words popped out of her mouth, "Mr. Eppard, how good to see you at worship this morning." She knew she flushed a little as she took Ella from Mary M to relieve her mother.

Reverend Hammeter started to sing a hymn off-key, but vigorously. Lucy gathered three children around her and sat down on the floor. The Scripture was read, but she had trouble concentrating. She had to work hard to keep from looking across the room where Phillip was sitting. Once, when she took a quick glance, he quickly looked away. *I don't understand these feelings inside me*, she thought.

After the service, Lucinda helped serve dessert. She was startled at her feelings when she moved past Phillip with plates for the Peters. Later, she wondered what he was saying to her father by the door, and then she saw the two men step outside together. She helped Mary M clean up. She walked home, puzzled.

In the afternoon, she tried to read her Bible, but her thoughts kept returning to the morning. *Is he noticing me, or am I just wishing I were grown-up?*

Her thoughts were interrupted by her father's voice. "Lucy," he said with a questioning tone, "would you come here? Your mother and I want to talk to you." In her parent's bedroom, Polly was sitting on the edge of the bed with a serious look on her face.

The stiff atmosphere made Lucinda nervous. Her father spoke. "Lucinda, that bald-headed young man that was at church this morning drew me aside and asked me for permission to court you. Do you know anything about that?" He leaned with his back against the closed door.

Turmoil flew through Lucinda's whole body. "No, Pa, I haven't done anything wrong." Tears started, but she struggled to stay in control.

"I didn't say you did something wrong. I just wondered if he had talked to you. Your mother and I are concerned for you when a man ten years older is showing interest in courting you. We have thought of you as a little girl, and now we realize you are a sixteen-year-old woman." He stepped forward and reached toward his daughter. Lucinda fell into her father's arms and let the tears flow.

Polly stood and put her arms around them in a three-way embrace. "Lucinda," she said tenderly, "have you been aware of Mr. Eppard's interest? Did you know he wanted to court you?"

"No, Ma, I didn't know, but I did see him watching me. I talked to Mary M about my feelings, and she told me to pray and I would know. I've been prayin', but I don't know."

Jacob put his hands behind his head and walked over by the window. "Lucy, I think Mr. Eppard is a fine Christian gentleman. I believe he would care for you and make a good home for you. Your mother and I want you to be happy. Would you like me to give this young man permission to court you?"

Lucinda took a deep breath, lingered, and finally spoke. "Yes, Pa, I would, but I'm scared stiff."

Jacob prayed, Polly cried, and Lucinda wondered, *God, is this the way you are giving me the desire of my heart?*

Jacob kept asking, *God, am I making the best decision for my daughter?* He tried hard to see her as a young woman ready for marriage, homemaking, and children. He determined to ride out and visit with young Eppard later that week.

Phillip was at his claim clearing dead trees and making fence posts when a rider came off the trail. He recognized the horse as that of Jacob McQuillan. Phil's nerves quickened as he walked toward his cabin to meet his visitor. The two men shook hands in greeting. Phillip spoke. "Welcome, Mr. McQuillan. Let's go in the cabin. It's a bit chilly out today. It's a bachelor's place, but the coffee's on." Phillip held the door while Jacob stepped in. "Hang your coat there, while I put a log on the fire."

Phillip set out two cups of coffee. Silence was broken by conversation about the economic slump. Finally, Jacob straightened up and said, "Phillip, I have come to give you an answer to the question you asked me last Sunday. Mrs. McQuillan and I have had a talk with our daughter. It seems Lucinda was not aware of your interest, but she did say she thought you were looking her way now and then. I can say, she was surprised at your thought of courting her."

A silence followed, then Phillip spoke. "Mr. McQuillan, I want to assure you of my high regard for your daughter. I would never do anything that would bring harm to her."

"I believe that," the older man responded. "That is why her mother and I are giving permission for you to begin courting Lucinda."

Air went out of Phillip's lungs. "Mr. McQuillan, thank you."

"Son," Jacob said with resolve, "you treat her with respect and honor, or you'll hear from me."

The tension released, and both men broke into laughter. Jacob went home lighthearted, and Phillip cut more wood that day than ever before.

On Saturday, Phillip rode over to the Felch home. Hannah was working in her kitchen, and the judge and David were relaxing by the fire. After proper greetings, Phillip started, "Judge, I have permission to court her, and I would like to borrow your driving team and cutter tomorrow to go to church."

"Hold on, young man," the judge said with his mouth hanging open. "Start over, to court who and what else?"

David started to laugh, and Hannah dropped her mixing spoon. Phillip put his hands on his hips in disgust. "Well, it ain't funny. Lucinda is a good woman, and I have permission to court her, and I would like to use your team and cutter."

"Permission granted," the judge announced. "Let's have a cup of coffee and you can tell us more."

"Ja," David put in, "tell us more, Phil, about the little girl you saw in the post office one day."

"You can just quiet down, David, she may have been a little girl then, but she's a grown woman now, goin' on seventeen."

That afternoon, Phillip mounted Queen and headed for the McQuillan home. He knocked on the door and listened as footsteps approached on the inside. Lucinda's mother smiled and greeted, "Mr. Eppard, please come in. We were just to have coffee, would you join us?"

"No, thank you, Mrs. McQuillan, I came to ask your daughter a question." Phillip turned his hat in his hands as he waited.

"Well, do come in and I'll call Lucinda." She held the door, and Phillip stepped inside.

Polly called, "Lucinda, Mr. Eppard is here and would like to talk with you."

There was a long pause. Lucinda came into the kitchen wearing a plain denim dress. Her hair was up in a bun with stragglers fluttering around her face. Brown wool stockings could be seen below the hem of her dress, but most important of all was the genuine smile on her face. "Hallo, Mr. Eppard, did Ma offer you a cup of coffee?"

"Well, yes, but since your pa has given permission, I came to ask if you would please sit with me during the service tomorrow and if you would accompany me for a ride in the country in the afternoon. I have the use of the judge's team and cutter."

"Why, Mr. Eppard, it would be my pleasure to sit with you, and a ride in the country would be grand. Thank you."

Phillip twisted his hat and stepped back. He fumbled at the door handle and said, "*Gutten tag*, Miss McQuillan." He leaped into the saddle and turned Queen loose all the way through Hamilton.

Sunday morning arrived cold, but bright. Phillip finished his chores and hitched the Felch blacks to the cutter. With Lucinda at his side, he was aware of the glances of the neighbors as Jake led in worship. They stayed for dinner and then excused themselves and left for their afternoon ride.

Lucinda was dressed in a warm winter coat and a wool cap tied down around her face. Judge Felch had left the heavy woolen lap robe in the cutter. The blacks were a spirited team. The harnesses had a row of red rings down each side of the hindquarters. Red tassels flowed from the top of the bridle straps. Phillip saw the curtains pulled back from the windows and faces following them down the trail.

Lucinda listened to the swish of the cutter runners and the jingle of the harnesses. She wondered how long it would take this gentleman to speak. She waited.

Phillip cleared his throat. "Miss McQuillan, I'm not much of a talker, but I'm pleased to be with you. I've been watchin' you for a year or more. I'm pleased that you are willin' for us to spend some time together."

"Mr. Eppard, I've been praying about what God has for my future. I want to follow him the rest of my life." She left it there.

Phillip spoke to the team, setting them to a faster pace. "How long has your family been here in Hamilton?"

"We were the very first ones to arrive here back in '52. My pa nailed a coffee mill to one of the oak trees by the Hamilton Spring. It was scary at first with no neighbors." She pulled the robe closer and put her arms under.

Phillip noticed and offered her more of the cover. "I just came in from Wisconsin two years ago along with the judge and his family."

Lucinda lingered and then probed, "Mr. Eppard, do you have a family? You seem to be alone, except for the judge."

"Nope, no family!" he said abruptly.

She felt his answer but left it. They crossed the river and circled up the hill and back down to the east crossing.

At Lucinda's home, Phillip stepped down and came around to her side and offered his hand. She took his hand, stepped down, and looked up into his face. "Thank you, Mr. Eppard, it was an enjoyable day."

"Maybe next time we can be Phillip and Lucinda," he said with a smile. She nodded.

They walked to the door. He held the door, and she entered. Phillip let the blacks run on the way home. He wasn't sure what to make of the feelings inside.

The next months brought them together for prayer meetings, church services, a basket social, springtime walks in the woods, summer picnics, and the like. They became more at ease with each other. Eventually, Phillip opened up more, telling of his home in Germany, the sawmill in New York, and the trip west.

It was early August. After church, Phillip said, "Get that little sorrel mare of yours and let's take a ride."

Lucy ran home, changed to her denims, and saddled Jenny. They set out on a steady gallop. Phillip broke the silence. "Lucy, would you like to ride out and see my claim? It's not much, but I'm gettin' a start. I've got thirty acres of wheat growin' and potatoes and vegetables in the garden."

"Yes, I would like that," she responded. Phillip thrilled inside at the smile and quick response. He watched the wind in her hair and abandon in her body as she leaned forward in the saddle.

He observed her mature figure as she swung down from the saddle in front of his cabin. "Well, this is it. You must remember this is a bachelor's place. I'm plannin' to work for Felch another couple years and then build a house here. I pay as I go and intend to owe no one."

They looked at the garden and walked out to see the field of wheat. Back by the horses, Phillip asked, "Lucy, would you like to see the Felch place where I live now?"

With a nod, she flipped the reins over Jenny's neck. Phillip stepped up to help her to the saddle. She put her hand on his arm, and their eyes met. She smiled. Phillip reached for her shoulder and drew her toward himself. She did not resist. He moved closer, and their lips touched gently. They embraced.

Phillip stepped back. "Lucy," he said, "I would like to ask your father for your hand in marriage. With his blessing, would you accept?"

"Phillip," she responded with a smile, "I care a lot for you. Mary M and I are special friends. She always tells me to pray about whom I would marry. I need to do that, and then I will answer you."

They mounted their horses and rode to the Gregory place. Phillip showed her the new house the judge was building. "I'll have this place for two more years, and then I'll settle on my own claim."

Back at the McQuillans, Lucinda said, "This was a wonderful day. Thank you for showing me your place. I like it." Her smile said good-bye.

The next day, Lucinda had a woman-to-woman talk with Mary M. They prayed, and the following Sunday, Lucinda leaned close to Phillip and whispered, "I've prayed. You can ask Pa."

After worship, in the Jacob McQuillan kitchen, with Lucinda at his side, Phillip spoke up. "Mr. McQuillan, I have come to know and respect your daughter, and I now ask for her hand in marriage and for your blessing upon our lives together."

Jacob seemed not surprised. He turned to his daughter. "Lucinda, do you love this man?"

"Yes, Pa, I love him."

"Do you trust him?"

"Yes, Pa, I trust him completely."

"Well then, you better marry him. You two have my blessing." He put his arms around the two young people. Then he continued, "Let's have a cup of coffee."

Summer moved on into the days of harvest. Phillip hauled a load of wheat to Winona and got a fair price. The house was completed on the

Gregory farm as they approached the wedding date. Polly baked plumb pies to celebrate Lucinda's seventeenth birthday on September 7.

On October 23, 1859, at the Jacob McQuillan home, Lucinda McQuillan, adorned in a dress she borrowed from her sister Catharine, and Phillip Eppard, dressed in black pants, white shirt, and string tie, were married in a ceremony led by Loren Dutton, Justice of the Peace. The marriage was blessed by the prayers of Lucinda's family and the neighbors who came to share the day.

After sharing a special meal and many expressions of congratulations and well-wishes, Phillip lifted his bride to the seat of his wagon and drove home to the new house on the Gregory farm. That evening, as Phillip read from his mother's Bible, a picture fell on the table. "What's that?" Lucinda asked.

"Oh, nothin'," Phillip breathed as he started to put it back in the book. Noticing the look on his wife's face, he handed her the photo, saying, "It's my mutti and vati. She's dead, and I won't see him again." His abruptness ended the conversation.

For the next two years, Phillip worked for the judge, saving every penny he could. At the same time, he was proving his own claim. He bought a good team, a pair of big geldings named King and Captain. The wheat was cut with a scythe and cradle, thrashed with a flail, and winnowed with a scoop shovel. He made three trips to Winona that fall with loads of wheat for market. He slept under the wagon and ate bread and cheese to save money. He returned with some cash and the supplies they would need for the winter.

Lucinda planted a large garden and picked and canned fruit, vegetables, and berries. In the evening, her knitting needles were never idle. She milked the cows, tended the chickens, baked bread, and did all the things that were expected of a wife. When Phillip was gone with a load of wheat, she cared for everything on the Gregory place as well as Phillip's claim.

In the course of a visit with Mary M, Lucinda said, "Mary M, I don't know what's wrong with me. I seem to be tired, and in the morning, I don't feel like eating breakfast. I even feel like I'm going to vomit. I have trouble doing all of my work."

Mary M smiled. "Maybe you're going to have a baby. Sure sounds like the way I feel when I'm with child."

Lucinda gasped. "I never thought of that. What should I do?"

Mary M put her arm around her young sister-in-law. "Let's just wait awhile. See if you have a monthly. Then you can tell Phillip."

A few weeks later after conferring with Mary M, Lucinda, while eating supper, said, "Phillip"—she waited until he looked at her—"we're going to have a baby."

Phillip took another bite of potatoes and gravy, chewed, and paused as if in deep thought. "When will this be?" he asked, hoping it would not be during harvest and wheat-hauling season.

"Mary M thinks it will be at Christmastime or maybe New Year's," Lucinda answered, feeling some disappointment in Phil's lack of excitement.

"That would be good, not bein' in harvest, I mean." He went on with his supper.

Lucinda felt a tear form and finally asked, "Well, aren't you even excited?"

"Ja, I'm excited, but I'm scared out of my skin. We've never done this before." He stood up and went around the table and put his arms around his wife. "Are you feeling all right? Do you need help or anything like that?"

"No, Phil, I just need you to love me. Sometimes I feel weak and tired." Tears came, but she smiled up at her husband and said, "I want to give you a child, maybe a son. This is a gift from God, and we'll raise him to know Jesus."

"Do you know if it is a son?" Phillip asked.

Lucinda laughed. "No, Phil, we won't know until our child is born."

Come fall, Phillip made his trips to Winona with abundant loads of wheat. He cut countless loads of wood for winter, making sure the little one would not suffer cold. Christmas passed, and Lucinda, small in stature, was wishing this kicking child would appear. On January 6, 1861, Polly and Mary M were summoned, and baby Mary Elizabeth Eppard arrived with strong lungs and good health. Phillip and Lucinda gave thanks and committed their firstborn to God.

At first signs of spring, Phillip began the process of building a house on his claim. Lumber was hauled from the sawmill. A cellar was dug, and rock walls were laid up for a foundation. The neighbor men organized a workday to raise the walls and set the roof. Phillip hired Matt Engel to do the finishing and build the cupboards.

On October 1, 1861, Phil completed his agreement with Judge Felch and moved his family to the little house on his own claim. That evening, Lucy was nursing little Mary in their new home. Phillip knelt by the rocking chair, kissed his daughter on the head, and whispered, "We're home at last on our own land."

26

A Complicated Courtship
Brandon, Wisconsin
1858-1859

ADAM'S DESIRE TO ATTEND THE meetings of the Brandon
Evangelical Association took second place to his commitment
to be the best uncle ever. The excitement of the birth of Peter and
Carolina's baby, Jane, in January, was diminished by the fact that two-
year-old Maria continued to weaken from fever and a retching cough.

On the morning of April 23, 1858, Peter and Adam were doing the
morning milking. The barn door flew open, and Carolina screamed,
"Peter, come quick, it's Maria." Peter dropped the milk bucket and ran
to the cabin, only to find Maria's still body in her bed.

Adam fashioned a small coffin out of some oak he found in the
hayloft. Maria's body was laid to rest, but everyone knew she was in
the new home that Jesus had prepared for her.

One day, Adam took his plowshares to Emery Muller to be
sharpened. Emery was a man of deep but very simple faith. Adam
grew to admire this genuine Christian who loved his wife, Berta, and
their six children. His bib overalls were black with soot and his leather
apron pockmarked from sparks that flew from the forge and hammer.
His arms were like the iron he forged, and his hands were callused
tough.

When Adam arrived at the smithy's shop, he heard Emery's
friendly voice. "Mornin' to you Adam, what can I do for you today?"

"I have some plowshares for you to sharpen." Adam leaned against a post as Emery continued shaping a horseshoe. He shook off a touch of envy when he compared himself to this man with a good business, an attractive wife, and lots of children. *That's old Adam thinking*, he reminded himself.

When Emery straightened up from the forge and dipped the horseshoe in the cooling tank, Adam offered, "I'm stayin' in town tonight. I'll stop for the shares tomorrow."

"Great," Emery responded, "I'm pretty busy these days, and besides, we're havin' a prayer meetin' at our house tonight. Why don't you stop in about 7:00?"

That evening, in the Muller home, a group gathered around a large dining table with Bibles open. Emery prayed a hearty prayer appealing to the Lord to move mightily during the meeting. Mike Gahringer read from Ephesians 1:15-23. Adam felt the presence of the Holy Spirit. Emery, in a single motion, turned and knelt with his arms on the seat of his chair. As if they were attached to each other, everyone turned in the same way. Adam felt clumsy, but he followed. His knees were getting sore by the time the last prayer was offered.

Berta nodded to Mary. The two women went to the kitchen and returned with cups, coffee, and cookies.

As coffee was being served, five children came quietly in the back door, followed by a young woman carrying a baby. The children, in order, kissed their father's cheek and said, "Good night, Vati."

Emery put a huge arm around each child and said, "Good night." The young woman leaned forward and held the baby out for the father's good-night kiss. Adam inhaled suddenly when he noticed a gold cross swing from a chain on her neck. *Could this be the waitress from the café in Princeton?* He hoped the others didn't notice how his eyes followed her as she walked across the room. Just as she entered the hall, she glanced back, and their eyes met for an instant. His heart jumped in his chest.

The next day, when Adam went to Emery's shop, he lingered by the door as Emery counted out his change. "Emery," Adam asked, "who was the young woman with your children last evening? Seems I may have met her before."

"Ja"—Emery smiled—"I saw your eyes follow her all the way across the room. What do you mean you may have met her before?"

Adam put the change in his pocket. "I was in a café in Princeton a couple of years ago. I'm next to sure she served me at the counter. The gold cross caught my attention."

Emery swung his iron stool around and motioned for Adam to take a seat. Emery said, "Sure could be. She's from Princeton. Her name's Matilda Mannweiler. Her vati took up a claim south of Princeton about four years ago. They got in from Germany late in the fall. Old Johann worked so hard he didn't notice his wife's failing health. She died just before Christmas. The cross was a gift from Johann to his wife back in Germany when their daughter was born. He gave the cross to Matilda for Christmas a few days after her mutti died. Can't say I've ever seen her without that cross."

"Ja, I'm sure it was the same girl in the café in Princeton, only she's much more a woman now. Emery, I trust you as a friend. I felt a strong attraction to her last night. Would it be out of line to consider courting her? I know she's much younger than me . . ." His voice trailed off.

Emery punched his friend in the bicep with his brawny fist. "Matilda's a wonderful Christian woman. She was converted a couple of years ago at camp meeting under the teaching of Elder Krause. Soon after she got saved, we asked her to help us when Erika was born. Burke was eight then. He didn't like having a hired girl and gave her a hard time. One day, she up and left and walked the thirty miles to her vati's cabin in one day."

A drop of sweat rolled down Adam's back. "Emery, I don't know what to do. I've never felt this way before. I've often thought I would like to have a wife and family, but I don't know what to do next."

Emery smiled through his bushy beard and chuckled. "What makes you think you should get through this easier than any of the rest of us? The first time I talked to Berta, I stumbled over my own tongue and turned as red as the summer beets in the garden. When Jesus brings a man and a woman together, it works a mighty change in the soul. It looks like it's happenin' to you."

"So what do I do next?" Adam got up and kicked the dust on the floor.

"Tell you what I'll do, my friend. I'll ask Berta to fix a nice supper next time you're in town. We'll have the kids there with us, and Matilda will be helpin'. It'll give you a chance to meet her and maybe talk a little. Once the children go to bed, maybe she'd accept an invitation to take a walk or sit on the porch with you. If things go well, you could arrange to meet her father and ask to court his daughter."

Adam reached out a hand to his friend. "Scares the daylights out of me. I plan to be in town again next week. How would Tuesday be?"

When Tuesday finally came, Adam packed a small bag with his best pants and a clean shirt. He polished his boots and went to the barbershop for a haircut and a beard trim.

Upon arrival at the Muller home, Adam handed Berta a cloth bag. "Carolina sent this for your family. We cured some hams from butcherin' this spring. Carolina uses brown sugar and hickory wood. Mighty good taste."

"Thank you, Adam," Berta responded as she received the gift. She turned and said, "Matilda, would you put this in the pantry, please." She held the ham for a moment. "Oh, Adam, this is Matilda Mannweiler. She's such a help with the children. Matilda, this is Adam Utzinger."

Matilda flushed a little. "Ja, I know, I met Mr. Utzinger in the café when I was helpin' Helga. Who could forget the name Utzinger?"

Not sure how to respond, Adam finally chuckled and said, "That was the day Barrett Halgrave sat in my lap."

The laughter cut the tension. At the table, Emery cleared his throat. The children folded their hands, knowing their father would pray. Matilda helped Berg and Erika as food was passed. Adam observed her tenderness as she talked to the children.

The meal ended with large pieces of apple pie. Berta and Matilda took the dishes to the kitchen. Emery offered Adam a seat by the fireplace. When Emery sat down, Erika crawled up in his lap and snuggled against his chest. Emery's large dark hand nearly covered her as he patted her tummy.

At a little after eight, Emery said softly but with authority, "Time for bed, children. Tell Mr. Utzinger good night." Each one in turn spoke to Adam and then gave their pa a kiss on the cheek and went to their beds. Adam felt a deep sense of respect and appreciation for his blacksmith friend.

When Berta and Matilda finished doing the dishes, Berta said, "Matilda, you've had a busy day. Just have a seat in the parlor and I'll see to the children tonight." Matilda started to reject the offer, but Berta put out her hand and went to care for the children.

"I have some bookwork to do for the shop," Emery commented as he moved to the desk in the corner of the room. "It would be nice and cool out on the porch. Maybe the two of you would like to sit awhile."

Adam spoke up. "Miss Mannweiler, Emery told me about your conversion at the camp meeting a couple years ago. I had the same experience at the Methodist camp meeting last year. I'd like to hear your story." Adam stood up and waited. Matilda looked toward the children's rooms, then over at Emery. Getting no response, she reached for her shawl. Adam held the door for her.

Matilda swung the shawl around her shoulders and sat down. Adam leaned against a post, facing the young lady. In the moonlight, he saw the reflection of the cross at the neckline of her blouse. The silence lingered until Adam spoke. "A great family, the Mullers. You do well, with the children, I mean."

Matilda tossed her head with a slight chuckle and said, "We get along now, but Burke drove me out of here two years ago. I walked all the way home."

"Emery told me about that when he told me about your conversion. I'm pretty new as a Christian too. In fact, I left the meeting the first night last year in confusion. I didn't intend to go back, but I guess the Holy Spirit won the battle and here I am. What was it like for you, being converted, I mean?" Adam waited.

Gradually, the two of them relaxed as the conversation continued. When Matilda stood and stated that she had to go in, Adam stepped between her and the door and said, "Miss Mannweiler, thank you for this visit." He lingered. "The cross, the gold cross around your neck, I saw it at the café in Princeton and again at the prayer meeting last week. Miss Mannweiler, to be truthful, Emery invited me here tonight so I would have a chance to talk to you. I would like to get to know you better. Would you be willing if I were to ask your vater for permission to court you?"

A rush of memories flooded Matilda's mind. In an instant, she remembered how she had blushed when their eyes met at the café. How she wished she were older and ready for a beau. She even told Helga her feelings, and they laughed together. Once she collected her thoughts, she straightened her body to full height and said, "Mr. Utzinger, I will consider your request in prayer. I'll seek Mr. Muller's advice and give you an answer when I'm ready."

Adam put his hand on the door latch and responded, "A man couldn't ask for more than that." He smiled down at her as he pulled the door open. He felt the brush of her dress as she moved inside. Over her shoulder, Adam said in a firm voice, "Thank you, Emery, and, Berta, for the delicious supper. Best pie I ever had! I'll see you next week." After a brief pause, he said, "Good night, Miss Mannweiler, thanks for the visit." He drank in her beauty as he closed the door.

Rowdy was ready to run on the way back to the Halgrave claim. Adam worked hard each day to keep up his share on the farm. He longed for an answer from Matilda. He dreamed about her often and daydreamed as he worked. Week after week, he waited. He asked Emery, but all he would say was, "It's in the Lord's hands."

One day, Adam walked into the Brandon General Store to do his trading. "Got a letter for ya, Adam," the storekeeper announced. "Looks like some nice handwritin' to me."

"Ja," Adam mumbled and went on looking about the store. "Here's a list Carolina sent. I brought in a case of eggs and a flat of cheese. Let me know the difference when you're done. I'm goin' down to Emery's shop." Adam started for the door.

"Don't forget your letter," the storekeeper reminded.

"Oh, ja," Adam said, "thanks for remindin' me." Adam stuck the letter in his pocket and waved to the sheriff across the street as he jumped up on his wagon. On the way to Emery's shop, Adam retrieved the letter. His heart sank when he realized it was from Matilda. *It must be a rejection if she responded by letter,* he thought. He drove on past the corner and out to the edge of town. Unfolding the page, Adam read,

Dear Mr. Utzinger,

I want you to know that I have given much prayer and thought to your question. I asked the advice of both Mr. and Mrs. Muller. I spent last weekend in Princeton and talked to my dear friends, Mr. and Mrs. Lang. My vater was in town visiting Mrs. Hartmann, so I asked their advice. Everyone speaks highly of your Christian character. So much so that I find myself wondering if I would be worthy.

My answer is yes, please make the request of my vater. He is looking forward to meeting you. You will find him at our claim six miles south of Princeton.

I should tell you that I enjoyed our conversation on the Muller's porch.

Cordially,
Matilda Mannweiler

Adam held the letter close to his heart. He put the team to a fast trot back to Emery's shop. By the smile on his face, Emery knew he had received an answer from Matilda. "What's the big grin this mornin', my friend?" the blacksmith chided. "Did you strike gold out there on the Halgrave place?"

"No, better than gold! I'll be making a trip to Princeton soon to have a talk with Matilda's vati. You might pray the Lord brings a favorable answer."

"You can count on my prayers, my friend." Emery slapped Adam on the back. "Adam, I told Matilda she'd never find a better husband than Adam Utzinger. She feels a lot of responsibility for her vati. She takes everything we pay her home to help with the claim. He spends some time with Olinda Hartmann. Matilda wishes they'd marry, but Olinda thinks she's too young for Johann. Johann gets discouraged and neglects the place."

"Do you think he'd accept some help? I could give him a hand when Matilda is home for a day or two." Adam thought about Matilda's father all the way home.

Peter offered to take care of the stock the next weekend. Adam saddled up and headed for Princeton. At the café, Helga greeted him at the counter, "Hallo, Mr. Utzinger." Her impish grin revealed that she knew full well what brought Adam to town.

"Any of those cinnamon rolls left to go with a hot cup of coffee?" Adam asked.

As Helga set the roll and coffee on the counter, she looked straight at Adam. "Matilda is a dear friend of mine. She's been through a lot. She deserves the best." Helga's eyes drilled into Adam's mind as she waited for a response.

Adam decided to accept the challenge with a strong response. "Matilda not only deserves the best, but she is the best. With her vater's permission, we will find out if God has a future for us."

A tear slipped down Helga's cheek. Her head lowered as she continued, "We've been good friends for almost three years. I guess

I'm afraid I'm losin' a friend." She gathered some dishes along the counter and turned toward the kitchen door.

"Maybe we all could be friends, Helga. We'll still be around." Adam took a bite of the roll and a draft of coffee. Helga slipped through the kitchen door.

Adam rehearsed his speech as he rode out the south road. He was surprised how his nerves played tunes on his spine. When he saw the little log cabin by the creek, he thought, *Must be lonesome out here all alone.* But for the path leading to the door, grass and weeds had taken over. Nervousness turned to sympathy.

Adam swung down from the saddle and flipped the reins around a fence post. As he approached the cabin door, he noticed that the garden had gone to weeds. Just as he lifted his hand to knock, the door opened. "Hallo, young man, I assume you're Utzinger. My daughter said you'd be comin' this way. Let's sit on that log over there by the river."

The two men walked slowly down a narrow path. The older man extended a hand and said, "The name's Johann Mannweiler. Not much of a place here. One more year and it'll be paid for. It was tough losin' the missus. Guess it was my fault, not taking good care of her. Never would have made it without the girl to keep me goin'."

"Can't imagine what that must have been like," Adam nearly whispered.

Adam's rehearsed words escaped him. Finally, he turned toward Johann and said, "I suppose you know why I've come to see you." As he paused, he saw sadness come over the face of his companion. He forced the next words out, "I would request your permission to court your daughter, Matilda." He saw Johann's body slump. A cardinal broke the silence, sounding a call from the top of a cottonwood. Adam wanted to put an arm of comfort around the old man.

At long last, the bushy head started to nod. "Ja, my little girl has become a woman. Don't know what I'll do without her. I've been told you're a good Christian man, a farmer, I take it."

"Wait a minute, Mr. Mannweiler, you're not losin' your daughter. She'll still be around. I'll be here with her and with you. I left my vater in Germany when I was eighteen years old. I need the wisdom of an older man." Adam stood up. Their eyes met. "Do we have your blessing?"

"Ja, I want what's best for Matilda. You be good to her, you hear me? She's a good girl." Johann's voice cracked. He stood and said, "The coffee's on, let's have a cup."

"Sounds good to me," Adam responded as he reached out his hand in a gesture of agreement. "Thank you, Mr. Mannweiler."

Inside, Johann took two cups from a narrow shelf. The coffeepot had been simmering on the stove. Dirty dishes were stacked on the washstand. An old chair with a cushion in the back stood by the fireplace. Adam wondered if that was where the old man slept. A horse harness in need of repair was draped over a log next to the chair. A board with the letters C-A-R-O-L-I and part of an N carved in it lay in the dust by the wall.

They sipped coffee in silence. When finished, Adam took his hat and turned toward the door. "I better get started for home, got a long ride ahead." After allowing Rowdy a long drink at the creek, he tipped his hat to the older man and rode away.

The loneliness Adam had experienced for so long was translated into sincere compassion for an old man. He tried to imagine what it was like for Johann Mannweiler to keep on working to firm his claim without his wife's help and companionship.

The next Sunday, Adam attended worship at the Evangelical Association at the Gahringer home. Preacher Krause was ready to deliver the message from the Word of God. Adam leaned against a doorframe in the back. Matilda was across the room, sitting on a low stool with Erika on her lap. She wore a lavender dress with lace at the neckline. A surge of admiration swelled through him as Erika fondled the gold cross in her hand.

As Michael shared some announcements regarding the upcoming Fox Lake Camp Meeting, Adam glanced toward Matilda. Their eyes met. He nodded, and she returned the nod. Her neck flushed.

After the service, as Matilda was guiding the Muller children to their wagon, Adam said softly, "Miss Mannweiler, may I stop for a visit this afternoon?"

"Yes, Mr. Utzinger, about 2:00 would be fine." Her smile imprinted on Adam's memory.

Adam found Matilda sitting on the porch. She stood and greeted, "Good afternoon, Mr. Utzinger, what a beautiful day. Come have a seat."

Adam wished he had a buggy so he could offer a ride in the country. He removed his hat and sat down. The quiet was comfortable. Adam leaned forward and began, "Miss Mannweiler, I visited your vater last Saturday. He has given his permission for me to court you, but he feels he's losin' his daughter."

"I know. I tried to tell him that I would still be here to help. It was very hard on Vati when my mutti died. He wanted to quit, but I kept urging him to keep on with the claim."

"That must have been hard for you as a young girl. How old were you when she died?" Adam wondered if he had touched her pain.

"Thirteen," she responded. "The hard part was that she died all alone. Vati and I had gone to town. We wanted her to go with us, but she insisted she had things to do at home. While we were in Princeton, a severe blizzard came up. Vati borrowed a big gelding and rode home through the storm. When he arrived, she had died in her bed."

"I'm so sorry, Miss Mannweiler," Adam comforted. "It's sad that she died all alone. Your vater feels he neglected her."

"I know he does." Matilda swallowed and looked up at Adam. "She really didn't die alone. She left me a note tucked in the page of my diary. It is printed on my memory. She wrote, 'Dearest Matilda, I love you. I knew my time had come. I saw Jesus! He smiled at me. I smiled back at Him. Please keep smiling!' I saw her in the coffin, and she was smiling. When I got saved at the camp meeting, Jesus let me know that Mutti is with him. It brought comfort." Her hand gently lifted the gold cross and allowed it to swing on the chain.

Adam shifted the conversation to excitement about the coming camp meeting. He shared briefly his conversion experience. "Miss Mannweiler," he said, "thank you for this time together. My brother, Peter, will be expecting me home for chores."

"I'm so glad you came today, Mr. Utzinger. When you nodded during the service, I knew you had talked to Vati." Matilda stood and put her hand on Adam's arm. "Thank you, Mr. Utzinger."

"Would you please call me Adam? I feel kind of stiff with the Mr. Utzinger."

She lifted her hand and smiled up at him. "Only if you call me Matilda."

"I'll be in town again next Sunday. Would you like to go for a ride out by the lake? I'll rent a buggy."

"I would like to do that. I could bring a picnic lunch," she offered. After a thoughtful pause, she continued, "We could ride to the lake instead of renting a buggy. I have the use of Star, the black mare. I love to ride, and it would give her a chance to run."

"That sounds good to me." He added, "Oh, and I'll bring some of Carolina's famous wheat bread and a jar of her chokecherry jelly." Adam offered his hand and said with a smile, "*Tschuss*, Matilda."

"*Tschuss*, Adam," she responded with a girlish grin. Once inside, she leaned against the door and breathed a deep sigh.

Adam swung into the saddle and put Rowdy to a full gallop out of town. *I'm sure glad the little girl grew up*, he thought.

"I know this is premature," Adam said to Peter and Carolina over coffee, "but I think I've found the woman I'll marry. This farm will not support two families. We need to give Barrett some notice if we decide to make a change."

Peter smiled and chided, "Why am I not surprised? I've seen stars in your eyes ever since you've been goin' to meetings in Brandon."

"I didn't hide it well, huh, *bruder*? Matilda is a sweet girl and she's mature for her age."

Carolina looked back at Adam as she took little Jane to her bed. "Why don't you bring Matilda out to the farm sometime? We'd love to meet her."

"We'll find a time for that. Matilda and I are goin' for a ride next Sunday. She's bringin' a picnic lunch. I offered some of your wheat bread and chokecherry jelly. What'll it take for me to keep my promise?"

"Just make sure she comes to visit," Carolina said, putting Jane down for the night.

The following Sunday, Matilda answered his knock dressed in a plain denim riding skirt and blouse. Her hair was pulled up in a bun, the sides curling out from under her bonnet. The picnic lunch was packed in saddlebags. After a few minutes of talk with Emery and Berta, Matilda handed Adam the lunch.

Adam was surprised at the brisk pace as she led the way to the stable. Star, a mare with a shiny black coat, came running at her call. Before Adam could reach for the saddle, Matilda smoothly swung it in place and drew the cinch tight. She slipped the bridle on and flipped the reins over Star's neck.

Matilda closed the stable door and said with a smile, "Ready to go?" Adam stepped up to assist her, but with her left foot in the stirrup, one hand on the horn, and the other holding her skirt, she smoothly lifted herself into the saddle. Adam felt a little unnecessary but admired the strength and skill of this woman.

At the edge of town, Adam let Rowdy out to a slow gallop. Star seemed challenged and came alongside. Rowdy snorted at the competition and stretched out the pace. Matilda and Star were ready for action. Adam looked over and drank in the beauty of her carefree smile. He pulled Rowdy to a walk and shouted, "These two don't know it's the Lord's Day. Guess we won't work 'em so hard."

They followed a narrow trail to a small lake surrounded by trees and grassy slopes. An old bullfrog was croaking by the lily pads. Adam dismounted and moved toward Matilda. She took his hand and slipped down from the saddle in a ladylike move. They allowed the horses to graze while they walked by the lake.

In the shade of a burly oak, Matilda spread a cloth and laid out fried chicken and potato salad to go with Carolina's bread and jelly. "What a feast," Adam said, looking across the spread at Matilda. He bowed his head and prayed. She smiled and handed him a plate.

Aware that the sun had moved to the western sky, Adam drew his watch from his pocket. Suddenly, his countenance fell.

"What is it, Adam?" Matilda asked, putting her hand on his arm.

"The watch," he breathed, "my vati gave it to me when I was twelve. It reminds me of home. I must write them and tell them of my new friend." He smiled and went on, "I need to get home for chores. I'll tell you more another time."

This was the first of many times together for this budding romance. On several occasions, Matilda came to the Halgrave farm. Whenever possible they went to visit Matilda's father. Adam helped the older man bring in prairie hay for his stock. They cut wood together, and a group from the Brandon church helped bring in the harvest.

Tired from a long day, Johann sat down in his chair. Adam and Matilda walked down by the creek. Matilda shivered from the cool fall breeze and pulled her shawl around her shoulders. Adam instinctively brought his arm around her. She leaned toward him and felt his warm strength. He stopped and drew her close. Her face was aglow in the light of the harvest moon. He bent down and touched his lips to hers in a soft kiss. She looked up with a bright smile and quiet laugh of acceptance. "Matilda, I've fallen in love with you." He waited.

"Adam," she said, "it means everything to me to see you working with my vati. He is much happier and relaxed. Thank you for including him in your life." Adam held her in his strong arms as she brought her arms around his neck. Their lips touched.

In the cabin, Matilda found her father sound asleep in his old chair. She curled up on her old bed feeling a sense of peace in her heart. Adam made it a practice to sleep in the loft in the barn when he was at the Mannweiler claim.

The next day, Johann and Adam were working both ends of the crosscut saw, cutting a large log to length. Adam pulled the saw his way and held tight, not allowing the saw to return toward Johann. The older man looked up and pulled still harder. Then he saw the smile on Adam's face. "Mr. Mannweiler," Adam shouted, "I'm not letting go of this saw until I get an answer to my question."

"What question?" Johann returned, still tugging on the saw.

"I want to marry your daughter; do we have your blessing?" Adam shouted back.

"Ja, you do, now let go of that saw and let's get this log cut up," Johann shouted.

Adam broke out laughing and let go of the saw. Johann fell over backward when the saw came loose. The two men bent over laughing. Adam put his arm around his future father-in-law and slapped him on the back. Johann said, "Now, no more of this Mr. Mannweiler stuff. From now on, it's Vati."

In the midst of the laughter, Matilda arrived with their afternoon lunch. "What's so funny?" She put her basket on a stump and started filling a cup with hot coffee. Adam stepped up to her and said, "I just asked your vati for his blessing on our marriage. Matilda, will you marry me?"

Matilda dropped the cup of coffee, splattering both her dress and Adam's boots. She threw her arms around Adam and said, "Yes, I'll marry you!" She turned and hugged her father. "Thank you, Vati, thank you!"

The three of them sat on the log they had been sawing and celebrated with slices of bread and honey along with hot coffee. Matilda put her mug down on a stump, looked at her husband-to-be, and questioned, "Adam, did you know that today is August 9?"

"I guess it is, why do you ask?" He lifted his hat and scratched his head.

She waited a moment and then responded, "It's August 9, 1859, and that means I am now eighteen years old. For a woman, that must mean I'm all grown-up."

Johann lifted his coffee cup and said, "To my grown-up daughter soon to be a wife." They laughed.

Earlier that summer, Adam and Peter had rented a quarter section of good crop land four miles west of Brandon. Best of all, it had a house separated into homes for two families. On October 1, 1859, Peter and Carolina moved into the larger of the two homes and Adam into the other.

During October, Matilda helped her vati with fall work, and the Utzinger boys got started on their new farm. They purchased a yoke of oxen and kept the plow going from dawn to dark.

November 29, 1859, was a cold blustery day in Brandon, Wisconsin. Adam, Peter, Carolina, and Jane, dressed in their Sunday best, climbed into the sledge for the trip to town. They were invited to the Muller home for Thanksgiving dinner which would be followed at 3:00 in the afternoon by the wedding of Adam and Matilda.

Adam and Peter took Zelig and Zelda to the stable out back, while Carolina, with Jane in her arms, went to the house. When the brothers arrived at the door, Emery welcomed them with a broad smile. "Happy Thanksgiving, come in, come in out of the cold. My, doesn't the groom look handsome today. Hang your coats there in the hall and find a warm place by the fire."

Moments later, a soft knock sounded on the door. Matilda shouted, "That will be Vati. Let me go to the door." She swung the door open and invited, "Come in, Vati, come in. I'm so excited that you are here for my wedding." She hardly knew her father with a well-trimmed beard and a new coat and hat.

Johann stepped back on the porch, reached off to his right, and drew Olinda to his side. "Matilda," he announced, "I want you to meet Olinda since last Saturday, Olinda Mannweiler."

Matilda screeched and threw her arms around her father. "Vati, and, Olinda, I am so happy for you." Tears flowed down Matilda's face. "I thought this would be the happiest day of my life, but I never knew how happy it could be." She gave Olinda a hug and said, "Mutti, I love you."

While everyone spoke words of congratulations to Johann and Olinda, Helga, who had arrived the day before to help with the preparations, put her arm around Matilda and said, "I guess we're *schwestern* now."

Matilda looked at her new sister and questioned, "Helga, did you know all this time? We talked half the night and you never told me about your mutti and my vati."

"I wanted you to have a surprise on your wedding day," Helga said with a loving smile.

Olinda finally got a chance to speak. "Matilda, you and Helga are grown-up now. You're getting married, and Helga has a beau. Your vati and I are going to firm up his claim and make a life for ourselves. I'm ready to go back on a claim, and Helga has the café with Barrett's help. We're happy."

Emery spoke up. "Bring on the turkey, let's have Thanksgiving. The preacher'll be here at three o'clock for another weddin' and we want to be ready."

Berta served a delicious Thanksgiving dinner. After dinner, Helga helped Matilda dress for the special occasion. Elder Krause arrived with a small black book in his hand. People from the association came for the celebration. The reverend invited Adam and Matilda to stand in front of him by the hearth and led them through promises to love, honor, and obey in sickness and in health, richer or poorer. He pronounced them husband and wife. "Adam," he said, "ain't ya gonna kiss her?" Adam did, and everyone clapped. Adam and Matilda made a commitment to each other until death do them part.

With Peter as driver, the bride and groom huddled down under warm blankets in the back of the sleigh on the way home. When they arrived at the door of their duplex, Adam swooped down and lifted Matilda into his arms. He held her for a moment, kissed her gently, and stepped over the threshold. "Matilda," he said, "I love you, and I want our home to be a place committed to God."

Matilda put her arms around her husband's neck and looked into his eyes. "Adam, I am honored to be your wife."

27

War

Brandon, Wisconsin
1859-1862

FOLLOWING THE WEDDING, MATILDA BUSIED herself making the Adam Utzinger half of the duplex attractive and homey. Adam spent the winter evenings fashioning furniture and making needed repairs. Working together deepened their love for each other. Adam became a class leader in the Brandon Evangelical Association, and meetings were held in their home.

Adam and Peter gradually expanded their farming operation. They purchased three milk cows and two brood sows. Winter cold gave way to the sunny days of late March. Adam said, "I'm gonna yoke the oxen and get started with spring's work." Every daylight moment, the brothers tilled the fields and scattered seed a handful at a time until, along with the wheat they planted the previous fall, they had 120 acres sown.

Spring rains and warmer days caused the seeds to germinate, sending forth blades that turned to flowing fields of grain. The heads of oats and wheat filled and turned golden as they ripened. One late summer morning, Adam observed, "It's all ripe at once, how will we get it set in shocks before it's past prime?"

The two brothers started cutting with the scythe and cradle. They hired two young men to tie it in bundles. In about a week, working dawn to dark, they finally finished the harvest. The bundles were set in shocks made up of eight bundles each.

One night, Matilda was awakened when Adam pulled her pillow out from under her head. In the moonlight, she saw her husband standing the pillows against each other in the middle of the room. "Adam, give me my pillow and come back to bed." When he didn't respond, Matilda realized he was dreaming about shocking grain, so she gently guided him back to bed. The next morning, she asked, "Adam, were you dreamin' about shocking grain last night?"

"Ja, how did you know?

"You took my pillow away from me and stood our pillows in a shock in the middle of the room. I had to get you back in bed." Matilda gave him one of her impish grins.

The warm winds and bright sun dried the shocks of grain. With flail and shovel, they separated the kernels from the straw and chaff. Some of the wheat was ground into fine flour and some was taken to market. The oats was ground into feed at the gristmill for the livestock. The best was saved for seed for the next year.

While the men worked to bring in the harvest, Matilda and Carolina stocked the root cellar with potatoes, carrots, onions, and beets from their gardens. They worked for hours over the hot stove, canning all kinds of fruit and vegetables. Matilda started laughing as they were peeling apples for a large batch of applesauce. "What's so funny?" Carolina probed.

"What do you think Adam would do if I got up at night and started peeling apples in my sleep?" The two women laughed and hugged each other. A tear slipped down Matilda's cheek. "Carolina, I am happy to be Adam's wife. I love being your friend and Jane's auntie. But here, it is our first anniversary, and I keep wondering when I will have a baby. Adam loves children so much. I want to give him a family."

Carolina wiped away the tear with her apron and assured, "God will give you children in his time. When Maria died, Peter and I had to learn that God gives and God takes away."

Whenever Adam went to Brandon, he would watch for things to read. Sometimes he bought a copy of the *Milwaukee Sentinel*. The *Sentinel* was supporting Abraham Lincoln for president in the upcoming election. The more he read, the more he sensed tension in the country. In fact, he saw one article that said some of the southern states were not allowing Lincoln's name on the ballot. Peter and Adam went to Brandon and cast their votes for Abraham Lincoln on November 6, 1860.

"Burrr! I guess winter is here to stay," Adam announced as he hung his jacket in the hall. "I'm sure glad we got the house banked for winter." He washed his hands and sat down at the table ready for supper. "Well," he said as he turned the page of the *Sentinel*, "Lincoln won the election. That'll make for trouble."

"What's that all about?" Matilda asked as she set a steaming bowl of gravy on the table. "Are you ready to pray so we can eat while the food's hot?"

Adam gave thanks for the food and prayed for the uniting of the states. He went on to say, "Lincoln won the election in a close race among the four candidates. The southern states are talking about seceding from the union. We could have a civil war on our hands if we're not careful."

Matilda's mind was not on the election. She was thinking about their first wedding anniversary with no signs of the arrival of a baby. "Adam," she said, "are you unhappy with me?"

"No," he answered, "I sure hope I don't get called up to serve in the army. My mutti would faint dead away."

"Adam! You're not listening to me!" Matilda slammed her fist on the table, pulled her apron off, and ran to the bedroom.

Adam pushed the *Sentinel* aside and shook his head wondering, *What's happening with her?* He walked slowly to the bedroom door. Matilda was lying facedown on the bed, sobbing. He sat down next to her. He put his hand on her shoulder and asked, "Matilda, what's wrong?"

"What's wrong?" she sobbed. "Here we are about to have our first anniversary and I've not given you a child." She could say no more.

Adam took her in his arms. "Matilda, I love you, and I'm not unhappy with you. You are my love and my joy. We'll have children when God is ready to give them to us. I was just thinking how hard it would be to leave you to serve in the army if we get into a war."

Adam and Matilda celebrated their anniversary on November 29, 1860. Before the new president could be inaugurated, states began to secede from the union. Lincoln was inaugurated on March 4, 1861. Adam saw trouble ahead when he read about the signing of the Constitution of the Confederate States of America in Montgomery, Alabama, on March 11. Civil war seemed unavoidable. Then Confederate forces bombarded Union soldiers at Fort Sumter and the civil war began.

April 10, 1861, started out like any other day. Adam went to the house for midmorning coffee. Matilda seemed a bit distant, and Adam noticed she only nibbled at the sweet roll by her cup. They were startled by a strong pounding on the door. "Who could that be?" Adam remarked as he opened the door. Standing at attention was a man dressed in a blue uniform.

The soldier spoke. "I am Sergeant Young of Regiment Wisconsin. I am looking for one named"—he looked at a clipboard—"Johann Adam Utzinger, a farmer, I believe, arrived in America from Germany in 1852."

Adam took a deep breath and nodded. "Ja, I'm Adam Utzinger."

"It is my duty to deliver this order to you." He handed Adam a sealed envelope. "You are to report to our temporary barracks on the west side of the town of Fond du Lac, Wisconsin, on April 20, 1861. The original First Regiment Wisconsin will be established in Milwaukee on April 27, 1861, to be mustered into federal service on May 17, 1861. After five days in Fond du Lac, you will be transported by train to Milwaukee to join the First Regiment. Do you have any questions?"

Adam was speechless. Matilda broke into tears. The sergeant saluted, turned about-face, and marched down the path to his horse.

With arms around each other, they walked around the house looking for Peter and Carolina. Adam called, "Peter, Carolina, we need to talk." The two couples gathered on the porch. Jane, sensing something was wrong, clung to her mother's skirt.

Adam held the envelope up. "Just got my call to serve in the Union Army, leavin' in ten days."

"I wondered what was happening when that soldier rode off in a cloud of dust," Peter responded. "We knew this might come, but not so soon."

Matilda was still crying. She looked at Carolina with a questioning look. Carolina nodded. Matilda dried her eyes. "Adam, Carolina and I talked yesterday, and we decided it was time to tell you that I'm with child. We're going to have a baby."

Adam knelt down by his wife. "Oh, Matilda, are you well? What can I do for you? When will this happen?"

Carolina stepped in, "Adam, this all takes time. It will be at least six months from now. Have you forgotten, you are going to be in the army? Peter and I will be here to help Matilda."

Suddenly, reality soaked in. Adam, though thrilled at the news, realized his son or daughter would be born while he was away serving his country.

The next ten days were a whirlwind. They arranged for most of Adam's $13 a month to be sent home to hire a man to work with Peter. Carolina assured Adam that she would help Matilda through this time and the birth of the child.

On April 19, Adam joined two other men on the trip to Fond du Lac. Adam's heart was heavy as he was assigned to a tent with three other men. He was given a blanket, a mess kit, and a towel. April showers turned into downpours every night. They waded through mud to get to the mess tent and the latrine. One of the men in his tent began to cough. He retched until he vomited. Adam began to run a fever, along with severe headaches and chills. The officer in charge ordered the four men from Adam's tent to return home. "We can't run the risk of that disease spreading through the whole Regiment Wisconsin when we get to Milwaukee."

While Adam felt some disloyalty to his country, he was elated to be able to return to Matilda.

Back home, Matilda saddled Rowdy with plans to spend some time with her father and Olinda. Upon arrival, Matilda startled her vati as he was stacking wood by the cabin. "*Gutten morgen*, Grandpa Mannweiler, a fine day it is."

"What's this grandpa stuff?" he huffed in surprise." Then understanding dawned, and he looked at his daughter with admiration. "Go tell Olinda and I'll be right in." By the time Johann stepped over the threshold, the two women had the birthing all planned.

One evening at supper, Matilda said, "I miss Adam so much. I'm worried about him being in battles in the war. It helps me to be here with you, Vati, seeing you and Olinda happy together. I still miss Mutti, but I love you too, Olinda. I took some flowers to Mutti's grave today. I still remember the smile on her face, and I know she's with Jesus. Thank you, Vati, for finishin' the cross marking her grave with her name."

Johann put his hand on his daughter's arm. "Matilda, it makes me proud to know that you are a good wife for Adam. We'll pray that he will be safe and that he returns to you and the baby soon."

Olinda straightened up, listened, and said, "Sounds like someone's in trouble. Do you hear that voice in the distance?" They rushed outside to see a man riding a horse at a swift gallop down the trail toward them. He was yelling something that sounded like, "Tilda! Tilda!"

Johann wondered if he should get his gun, but the rider was coming so fast he didn't want to leave the women.

The horse came to a skidding stop. The rider leaped to the ground and ran toward the three astonished viewers. They heard his words, "Matilda, they sent me back home. I don't have to go to the army. I'm home!" By now, Adam was lifting his wife in the air, swinging her around, and bringing her down into an embrace.

Johann was so surprised that he shouted, "That's my daughter, and you put her down cuz she's with child."

Olinda took her husband's arm, pulled him to herself, and said, "And that's the child's vati and he is home to stay."

Once things settled down, Adam told them the story of how the men in his tent were sick and all four were sent home.

Things returned to normal at the Utzinger farm. The closer she came to her time, the harder it was for Matilda to keep up with the work. In late August, Olinda came to help with harvesting and canning.

Adam secretly hoped for a boy, but he knew he would be thrilled with a daughter. In the early morning of September 2, 1861, Matilda reached across the bed to awaken her husband. "It's time, Adam, I'm going into labor. You better wake Olinda and go tell Carolina."

Adam bounded out of bed. "What shall I do? Matilda, are you all right?"

Matilda laughed and said, "Come on, Daddy, put your pants on and go get Olinda and tell Peter and Carolina."

About noontime, the baby let out his first cry. "You've got yourselves a son," Olinda announced. "A mighty good lookin' boy he is." She handed the little bundle to Adam who received him into his large hands.

"He's so tiny," Adam said. "Is he all right?" Adam held him awkwardly as if he were fragile. He placed the baby by his mother and kissed Matilda on the forehead. "We've got a son," he breathed. "What will we name him?"

Two weeks later, the Evangelical Association met in the Adam Utzinger home, and Albert Henry Utzinger was dedicated to the Lord.

The Minnesota Move
Wisconsin to Minnesota
1862

A MOOD OF DISCOURAGEMENT HUNG OVER the class meeting that gathered each week at the Adam Utzinger home. Word was out that the Union forces weren't doing well, and Lincoln was requesting an army of five hundred thousand men. With a cup of coffee in his hand, Jake Burkhardt said, "What's the future in working for a farm owner? It's frustrating to work hard and have little. I sure would like to have a farm of my own."

Adam chimed in, "I was talking to Emery the other day while he was shoeing Zelig. He says Minnesota has lots of good land available to conscript at $1.25 an acre. Old man Schulz, who farms out south of Brandon, has a son who left for Minnesota last spring and now has 160 acres of land. He's built a house. It sounds tempting to me."

The next day, during morning coffee, Adam asked, "Peter, what did you think last night when I shared about Minnesota? Matilda and I are givin' it serious thought. She's worried about the trip with Albert bein' so young."

Peter sipped his coffee through the sweetness of a cookie. "Jake was right. We are doin' a lot of work with little in return. It would mean living in covered wagons for several months. What do you think, Carolina?"

Carolina drew a deep breath. "Well, Peter, I've been waiting for the right moment to tell you. I'm almost certain that we'll be having an addition to our family come spring. That would make traveling harder."

"Oh, Carolina," Peter responded, "that's wonderful. Jane needs a brother or sister." His mind whirled with a heavy sense of responsibility.

At every class meeting, they prayed urgently for God's direction; and one after another, five families decided to make the move to take up land in Minnesota. Each family rigged a covered wagon for shelter and to haul their personal things. Adam and Matilda would drive the two Zs, and the other families each had a yoke of oxen. Two open wagons with ox teams were included for farm equipment, stoves, furniture, and supplies. They also took enough milk cows and calves to get herds started on their new claims.

Silas Utzinger was born to Peter and Carolina on April 30, 1862. During the course of the spring, baby girls were born to the Burkhardts, the Gahringers, and the Schroeders. Preparations went into full swing, anticipating a June 1, 1862, departure.

On the way home after saying good-bye to Johann and Olinda, Matilda looked up into Adam's eyes and confided, "I couldn't leave Vati if I didn't know he's happy with Olinda out on his claim." Adam put his arm around her to comfort her as she wept.

Adam was in Emery's shop having his wagon wheels repaired when the storekeeper's son came rushing in. "Mr. Utzinger, Pa sent me over to tell you that he has a post for you from Germany. He's sure you'll want to get it before leavin' town."

"Thanks a lot, son, I'll stop by when Emery finishes here."

"You'll have to sign here, and it'll be twenty-five cents please," the storekeeper said. Adam paid the price and put the letter in his pocket. That evening, the two couples sat at the table in Peter and Carolina's kitchen. Carolina poured the coffee, Matilda served apple pie, and Adam slit the envelope open. "It's from Helena and Mr. Woll," Adam said with surprise. As he unfolded the page, a smaller document fell to the table. Adam began to read:

My dear brothers, Peter and Adam,

It makes me sad to tell you that Vater died on January 21. He was buried in the church cemetery on the twenty-fifth. He died peacefully at home. Mutter is very frail and we are caring for her in our haus. Since none of Vater's sons is in Germany, Mr. Woll has purchased the Utzinger land on the Scharrhof and is distributing the inheritance to the sons.

Adam's share is with this letter. Peter's share has been held by the German government. There will be a search for Peter in Germany since he failed to report when called into the army.

Except for Mutter, we are all well here. The crops have been bountiful. The children are growing up rapidly. We wish we would get a letter from you.

Lovingly, your sister,
Helena Woll

The two brothers embraced and wept. Life had been so busy that they had written but few letters home. This was only the second word they had received from family in Germany. They put their thoughts down on paper, thanking the Wolls and telling them of their imminent move to Minnesota.

"Peter," Adam said, "we'll keep this money draft until we're ready to buy land in Minnesota. It'll make it possible for us to take more land than we had planned. We'll split your inheritance when it comes."

"No, Adam, that's your inheritance. It belongs to you. It was my doing that I didn't get out of Germany fast enough." Peter pushed his chair back from the table with finality.

On June 1, Adam and Matilda, with nine-month-old Albert, led out driving Zelig and Zelda. Peter and Carolina, with Jane, 3, and baby Silas, were next with their yoke of oxen followed by one of the supply wagons. Jake and Louisa Burkhardt were next with their three children: Louisa, 3; Charles, 1; and baby Caroline. Fred and Pauline Schroeder with their four children, Fredrick, 7; Henry, 5; Albert, 2; and baby Pauline, fell in line with the second supply wagon behind them. Mike and Mary Gahringer and their four kids, Eliza, 8; Mary, 5; Edward, 3; and baby Emily, brought up the rear.

A few miles down the trail, Adam handed the reins to Matilda and took his turn riding Rowdy to help with the stock. As he came around to follow the wagons, he shouted, "Hey, Mike, that's sure a good lookin' yoke of blue roans you got there."

"Yupp," Mike returned, "I'm proud of 'em. Been trainin' 'em for five years. Blue is the best nigh ox I've ever seen, and Buster, the off ox, can pull so hard I had to reinforce the yoke to keep him from breakin' it. They won me first prize at the ox pull in Brandon last year."

"Ja, oxen may be slower than horses, but they sure are durable and strong for heavy work."

Oxen are trained to obey voice commands. The driver walks on the left side of the team next to the nigh ox, the one most trained to respond to the driver's voice. The ox on the right side is called the off ox. The drivers are not abusive, but the crack of the whip is used to keep their attention.

As the days wore on, the babies napped on their mother's backs. The older children ran barefoot alongside, exploring as they went. Everyone found jobs to do to help. Prayers of thanksgiving were offered when they gathered for meals by the fire.

In the evening, as the sun lowered behind the clouds in the western sky, tired children found their beds in the wagons. The men took shifts guarding the camp and seeing that the animals were hobbled and tethered. The moon hovered over the camp as if to give the Father's protection over his children.

Adam rolled toward his wife and brought his arm across her warm body. "My dear," he whispered, "you're doin' a great job drivin' that team every day. Albert seems to be doin' just fine. He sure gets excited when I take him with me on Rowdy. He's a good kid. You're a great mutti. I love you."

"I love you too, Adam," she responded with a kiss. "I'm so tired. My arms feel like they could fall off from pulling on the reins all day. But it's getting better as the horses get used to the slow pace. Good night, Adam."

They set out at daylight each day to take advantage of the cooler morning hours. Adam said, "We'll bear to the right when we come to the Y and head toward Kilbourn City. That's where the *La Crosse and Milwaukee Railroad* crosses the Wisconsin River. Mr. Schulz says it's a good place to cross with the wagons."

They camped on the shore of Puckaway Lake. After supper, a commotion broke out near the lakeshore. Seven-year-old Frederick Schroeder shouted, "You're nothin' but a girl, and I worked harder today than you ever could."

Eight-year-old Eliza Gahringer's sharp voice penetrated the air, saying, "You're such a weakling that you can't even carry a pail of water to the cook table. You're nothin' but a weakling."

"You're a dumb girl, that's what," Frederick snarled as he grabbed a handful of Eliza's long blonde hair. "I'll show you how strong I am."

As quick as a wink, Eliza brought an arm around Frederick's neck and brought him down over her knee, sending him rolling in the dust. Sobbing, Frederick went running to the Schroeder wagon where he found little sympathy. The parents decided they needed to ease up on their expectations of the children.

Eliza loved to climb up and visit with Matilda while Albert took a nap. One day, Eliza said, "You really love Adam, don't you?"

"Why, of course I do, he's my husband. What makes you ask?"

"I don't know, it's just that I think I want a husband when I grow up, maybe like Adam." She waited and then went on, "I sure don't want one like Frederick. He makes me so mad sometimes."

When Eliza jumped down from the wagon, Matilda smiled. *That little girl is maturing very fast. She's almost the age I was when my mutti died.* Her hand went to the cross around her neck.

The travelers arrived at Kilbourn City with time to purchase supplies and prepare to cross the Wisconsin River the next morning. The sky was crystal clear with a gentle breeze out of the northwest as the wagon train wound its way down the trail toward the river. Matilda pulled her team to a stop just off the trail near the crossing. The ox teams stayed in line.

After checking the condition of the ford, Adam skillfully drove Zelig and Zelda across. Peter was ready to follow with his yoke of oxen.

Peter spoke to his nigh ox and guided the pair down to the river. He jumped up on the wagon. "Get up there," he called. "Gee a little, gee. Good, get up." He urged the animals across the river. Peter looked back to see Mike coming with the supply wagon. Jake and Fred followed. At lunchtime, Mike lifted his voice in praise for the safe crossing.

The trail followed along the river heading northwest. From a high vantage point, they looked across the valley. The dells along the river were bathed in bright sunlight. In awe of the beauty of God's creation, Matilda held her son close and offered praise to the God of her salvation. Adam read about the Israelites traveling for forty years with a goal to reach a land of promise.

Time passed with the steady step-by-step pace of the oxen. The babies cried. Eliza and Frederick were friends despite the occasional scrap. Jane and Louisa begged every day to sleep over in each other's wagons, and Edward felt left out. Mary and Henry, both going on six, begged Pauline to read with them and teach them new words. Albert Schroeder loved to brag about being bigger than "little Albert", and Charles would respond with, "I big boy too."

It had been a hot humid day on the trail. In the late afternoon, a dark cloud formed in the northwest. Heaviness hung over the camp. The animals were restless. Fred called the men aside and said, "It looks like we're in for a storm this evening. We need to have supper and get in our wagons early tonight. It feels like it did the night that windstorm came through Brandon in 1856."

A lull came over the camp. The children were not hungry. Gusts of wind whipped the canvas on the wagons. Sparky found a sheltered spot under the Gahringer's wagon and refused the bowl of food scraps. The cows and calves huddled together, switching away the pesky flies.

Darkness came early. The children went to their beds. The mothers held their babies to their breasts. Peter took the first watch. Suddenly, a flash of lightening split the sky, followed instantly by a crash of thunder. Sparky whined. A baby cried. Peter took shelter inside the tailgate of his wagon. Jane whispered, "Vati, I'm scared. I don't like that loud noise."

Adam and Matilda held each other with Albert between them. Bright flashes of lightening penetrated the canvas, making it as light as day. Thunder rumbled across the sky. The wind howled through the trees by the stream. "I'm glad we didn't park our wagon under those trees," Adam breathed.

Rain started to fall in torrents. Albert whimpered and looked at his mother with eyes full of fear. Matilda comforted him. The wagon swayed back and forth in the wind. A loud snap echoed through the camp, followed by a sudden thud.

"Adam, its Jake," came a whisper from the rear of the wagon. "That tree went down, and a branch hit our wagon. Our canvas is split, and everything is soaked."

Adam rushed toward the voice, saying, "Is your family all right? Bring them here. We'll make room for all of you."

Louisa was soaked to the skin, holding the baby close and towing a sobbing Charles by the hand. Jake returned with little Louisa over his shoulder.

Matilda found towels to help dry their drenched visitors. Adam dug out his wool horse blankets. "Here," he said, "they aren't fancy, but they'll keep you warm."

Finally, the storm passed. Peter continued his shift as watchman. When he checked on the animals, he found them huddled together, but unharmed by the storm. Next morning, the men unloaded Jake's wagon, setting everything out in the sun to dry. They repaired a broken hoop and mended the torn canvas.

Following the rain, the northwest breeze brought cooler days. Adam looked off in the distance and ventured, "Judging by the terrain and the western horizon beyond, I think we're close to the big river. I sure hope we can find a way to cross over to Minnesota."

They camped near the town of West Salem, Wisconsin. It was a stagecoach stop where drivers changed to fresh horses after the long climb from the river valley. Fred approached the livery man and inquired, "What's the trail like from here to La Crosse? Got any advice for first timers?"

"The stage drivers come in with tired horses. They drive 'em hard up that hill. The trail down is good if you watch your speed," the livery keeper offered. "Where're you headed?"

Peter answered, "We're on our way to take up claims in Minnesota. How's the crossing of the Mississippi? We have seven wagons, one team of horses and the rest oxen."

"The ferry goes when he's got a load. It'll take you about three trips. Best you get there in the mornin'."

The following day, they reached a vista. They stood in awe of the beauty of the river valley. "That's the mighty Mississippi," Adam affirmed. "You children will always be able to say you've seen the Mississippi River."

Adam led the way down the slope between the bluffs. Every curve in the trail brought another breathtaking view of the river. Adam said, "Matilda, look, that cluster of buildings must be La Crosse." He handed her the reins. "Keep 'em movin' and I'll ride out and find a place to camp."

Following a good night's rest, they set out for the ferry landing. The storekeeper in La Crosse said, "It'll take you a couple hours from here to the ferry." The sun was at quarter sky when the trail veered to the left, and Adam saw the landing. A partially loaded barge was ready to back away. He waved his hat and shouted to a deckhand. "We've got seven wagons needin' to get to Minnesota. What's our chances?"

The operator motioned for them to come aboard. Adam jumped up on the wagon and urged the team forward. Peter spoke to his nigh ox and guided his wagon in place. The operator put up his hand, indicating it was a load, and pulled away from the landing.

Peter and Adam returned on the ferry. Peter shouted, "Let's take the cattle and two wagons this time." The men herded the stock into a pen on board. Peter loaded the supply wagon, and Jake followed. The ferry pushed off once again.

The ferry returned and stood ready for the last three wagons. Fred guided his yoke of big black oxen on board. Adam took his whip and spoke to the oxen on the supply wagon. They followed along in order. Mike walked up to his blue roans and patted his nigh ox on the neck. "Okay, Blue and Buster," he said, "let's get this wagon on board."

Mike spoke firmly. "Get up, Blue, you too, Buster. Blue, haw now, get up there." They were moving up the ramp when suddenly, Buster went down on his front knees and then rolled to his side. "Whoa!" Mike commanded. "Whoa!" Blue stopped and put his head down toward Buster. Mike called out, "Get up, Buster, get up there." The ox didn't move. Mike came around, ready to urge Buster on with his whip, when he saw what had happened. He put his hands over his head and cried, "Oh! No! Buster, no!"

Buster's right front leg had stepped through a small space between the ramp and the ferry deck. His weight had come down so hard that the leg bone broke and opened a deep wound in the hide. Mike knew he had no choice but to put him down. He went to the rear of the wagon, lifted his rifle out, and checked for cartridges. Adam came up beside him and put his hand on his friend's shoulder. "Let me do it for ya, Mike," he offered.

"No, Adam, I have to do it myself. That animal gave his life for me. I'll save him any more pain." Mike walked around the wagon as he slipped a cartridge into the chamber. It was silent, and then the mournful report of the bullet.

A dockhand said to Mike, "I'll dispose of him for ya if you want." Mike nodded. The dockworker put a rope around Buster's neck and dragged him away with a team and wagon.

Adam brought the yoke of oxen from the supply wagon and pulled Mike's wagon on board. A sad group of pioneers gathered on the other side of the river. Mary knew she had to be strong to comfort the children and encourage Mike.

They camped by the river for the night. Peter spoke up. "I'm thinkin' that Adam and Mike should ride into La Crescent and see if they can find another ox. I think we should use some money from our common fund to help with the cost." It was agreed.

As they rode along, Adam could feel his friend's grief. "I don't know what to say, Mike, but I do understand what that yoke of oxen meant to you." It was silent.

"I was countin' on Blue and Buster to break the sod on our new claim. I trained those two big brutes to do whatever I asked of 'em."

It was obvious that Mike knew a lot about oxen. At the La Crescent sale barn, he found a Shorthorn-Holstein cross that he judged to weigh about two thousand pounds, about the size of Blue. When Mike had the animal's attention, he gave a command. The ox brought his head up and lifted his right front foot. Mike turned to the young man and said, "Give me a price on him, the red roan." They haggled, and Mike made the purchase. He put a leader in his nose and said, "Adam, you take the horses and head back to camp. I'm gonna get acquainted with this guy. I'll be there in an hour or so."

When Mike arrived, he took his new purchase to meet Blue. "Here, big boy," Mike said, "this is your new yoke mate. You better get acquainted because you'll be workin' together for a long time." Blue went on grazing, unimpressed. Mike continued, "Blue, this is Red, he'll be at your offside tomorrow, so be ready to go."

The wagons rolled out the next morning, with Blue and Red pulling together on the Gahringer wagon. Blue made sure Red knew who was boss.

Once in Minnesota, the five men expected to see wide open land waiting to be claimed by eager farmers. Instead, they found mile after mile of rolling hills covered with maple, oak, and walnut trees. Scouting ahead, Adam encountered a team and wagon standing in the shade alongside the trail. "Hallo," he called, assuming someone would be nearby. "Hallo, what a beautiful day."

An elderly man, startled out of a midmorning nap in the shade of an oak, grunted, "Ja, it's that all right."

"I didn't mean to disturb ya. We have seven wagons coming along, and I was checking out the trail. What's on ahead for us? We've heard there's good land in these parts up for claim." Adam waited.

The gentleman shook his head to clear his mind. He brushed some dust off of his hat and said, "Since they moved that Federal Land Office from Brownsville up here to Chatfield four years ago, we've had no end of farmers comin' this way. Not much good farmland left in these parts. Too many hills and trees here along the river. I've heard there's good land in Fillmore and Mower counties. You could inquire at the land office in Chatfield."

"How do we get to Chatfield?" Adam asked.

"Just keep on the trail west." He looked up and saw the seven wagons approaching. "With that train, it'll take you two or three days. It's a nice town down by the Root River."

"How far then to this place called Mower County?" Adam pursued. "We need to get claims for five families, build cabins, and break sod before winter."

Matilda brought the lead team to a stop. The gentleman continued, "I've never been there, but I hear 'bout a settlement called Hamilton maybe a couple days beyond Chatfield." He jumped on his wagon and tipped his hat. "Guess I better get my rig out of your way. Safe travelin' to ya. The Lord watch over ya!"

Adam responded, "Much obliged for the information. The Lord bless you too."

While eating lunch, Adam reported, "The man says there's a Federal Land Office in Chatfield a couple days on west. Let's spend the weekend in Chatfield and see what they have to offer." His words met with approval.

Blue had been doing a good job breaking Red in for the trail. Mike was satisfied with his choice but still missed Buster. Impatience laced with anticipation and excitement permeated the families. They were anxious to reach their destination, even though the covered wagons would be their homes for some time.

On Thursday evening, Matilda put Albert down for the night. She sat on her bed trying to pray. In vivid memory, she was thirteen years old arriving in Princeton, Wisconsin. Fear enveloped her, pressing in like a heavy weight at her father's determination to take his claim. She shivered at the cold in the log cabin. Pictures of her mother, sick and without food, moved through her mind. Tears filled her eyes as she fought for control.

Adam slipped in through the canvas flap. "Matilda," he whispered, "is Albert sleepin'?"

She choked as she answered, "I, I think, I think so." She tried to hide her feelings, but her husband knew her too well.

"Matilda, you're crying, what's wrong?" Moonlight penetrated through the canvas enough that he could see her face. He put his hand on her arm and waited. "Are you not feeling well, my dear?"

Suddenly, she threw her arms around her husband and sobbed. "I, I was just prayin' and thinkin'. I was rememberin' when my family came to Princeton and how Mutti died that winter. Talkin' about gettin' our claims brought back a flood of memories." She clung to him and shook with fear.

Adam held her and whispered, "I'm so sorry all that happened, Matilda. This time, it'll be different. We'll have plenty of time to build a house before winter. We have my inheritance. I'm gonna buy lumber and build a farmhouse. We have the stove in the supply wagon, and we can buy food. We'll be warm as toast all winter, I promise." He held her as the shaking gave way to peace.

"Oh, Adam, I'm sorry I got so frightened. I do trust you to take care of Albert and me." She pulled him close and breathed a deep sigh. Adam kicked his boots off and lay down by his wife. Sleep came.

Next morning, clouds and drizzle caused a slow start. Later, the sun broke through the overcast skies; and by midafternoon, they arrived at a settlement couched in the valley of the Root River. Mike said, pointing to a grassy area by the river, "This looks like a good spot to spend the weekend."

On Saturday, the five men walked into the Federal Land Office. "Welcome to Chatfield, Minnesota," the agent said. "My name's Baldwin Peters. What can I do for you men today?"

Peter spoke for the group. "We're five families camped out by the river. We left Brandon, Wisconsin, the first of June. We've heard there's good land available in Minnesota to claim on homestead rights. Can you help us?"

Baldwin rubbed his head. Peter smiled to himself, thinking, *No wonder he's so bald.* "Ever since they moved this office to Chatfield, we've had hundreds of people come from Wisconsin. Now most of the available land is over in Mower County on beyond Hamilton."

"What's land going for these days? What would a quarter section cost?" Fred asked.

Baldwin called attention to a table by a window. "This is a map of the survey that was completed about five years ago. The law says you can choose any unclaimed property, clear and fence a half acre, and live on it at least thirty days to qualify to file a claim here at this office. The government gets $1.25 an acre." He ran his finger over the survey. "The open claims are over in Mower County.

"The other thing we have is land for sale by owners who are giving up their claims. These have some improvements on them. Sometimes even a crop is growing. The price is set by the owner. The claims with a circle around the name are up for sale."

305

"For example," Baldwin continued, "the Southeast Quarter of Section 33 in Township 104 containing 160 acres is up for sale by Fred Greenslitt and his wife. They came here a few years ago and just got started when they had to return to Sauk County in Wisconsin. Fred's asking $500."

Adam's heart jumped when he heard of a quarter section for sale. He had more than $500 from his inheritance. He asked, "Mr. Peters, how would I find this Mr. Greenslitt if I were interested in that quarter of his?"

"He was in here just a day or so ago. He was goin' out to his claim to gather some things. Most likely, you'd find him there." Baldwin handed Adam a slip of paper. "Here's his offer and location. He would be glad to see you."

Peter had been studying the survey. "Mr. Peters, I see an eighty just south of the Greenslitt quarter that appears to be for sale. What do you know about that?"

Baldwin rubbed his head and thought for a long time. "Van Dusen, that's the name. George Van Dusen owns that eighty. He's from New York. I have his offer here too." The agent dug in a desk drawer and came out with a folded paper and handed it to Peter.

In the meantime, Jake, Mike, and Fred were looking at the survey map. They saw properties that raised their interest. Each of them made inquiries and received directions from Mr. Peters.

As the five men, satisfied with the information, moved toward the door, Baldwin remarked, "Jake McQuillan at the post office in Hamilton would be a good contact. He knows the area and could help you get acquainted with folks. Good luck to you. Stop back any time."

"Much obliged," Adam said. "I'm sure you'll be seein' us before long. Oh, by the way, is there a bank in town? I have a note from Germany that I'll need to cash."

"Yup, a bank opened here in Chatfield this year just for that purpose. It's down the street, there on the corner, the Root River Bank."

On the way out, Adam picked up a local newspaper. Skimming the front article, Adam said, "General Robert E. Lee took command of the Confederate Army of Northern Virginia on June 1. It also reports, that when Union General Ulysses Grant's army was surprised by Confederate forces in the Battle of Shiloh back in April, there were thirteen thousand Union and ten thousand Confederate casualties." Adam shook his head and breathed, "This war is getting more serious all the time."

Beyond the Root River, the landscape opened up to rolling hills. In the valleys, farmsteads could be seen with fields of wheat and oats, giving promise of harvest. Adam jumped up to ride alongside Matilda. "How do you like the looks of this? Would you like to live in that cabin over there on the hillside?" Adam put his arm around his wife. "I'm gettin' excited about finding our place, maybe not as hilly and wooded as it is here. When Baldwin pointed at a quarter section for sale about three miles west of Hamilton, my heart did a flip."

"Adam, I've been praying that God would bring us to the place he has for us. We need to trust him." She turned and smiled up at her husband.

Adam's attention was drawn to the movement ahead. "Looks like we've got company." A lone horseman was approaching slowly. Adam gave Matilda a little squeeze. "I'll go meet him." Mike joined him, and they rode out together.

The rider was hunched over in the saddle. His bay mare seemed tired. The gentleman was dressed in black trousers, a wrinkled white shirt, and a black vest. He had a pair of bulging saddlebags and a pack tied behind the saddle. His face was shaded by the brim of a black hat. At first, Adam thought he might be injured or sick.

"Hallo!" Adam called. Getting no response, he called again, "Hallo! Are you all right?" Again, he repeated, "Hallo, mister, a good day to you."

Startled, the rider straightened in the saddle. His hand went to his hat in greeting. "Good day to you," he responded tentatively.

"Sorry to startle you," Adam said. "I wondered if you were sick or wounded."

"No, not wounded, I read my Bible as I travel my circuit. The name's William Stegner, Rev. Stegner. I ride a circuit in these parts for the Evangelical Association. I held services in Hamilton on Sunday, and now I go to Chatfield. Where're you headed?"

Adam and Mike looked at each other in amazement. They dismounted, and Mike extended a hand of greeting and said, "We're five families movin' from Brandon, Wisconsin, lookin' for some of that great Minnesota farmland. We're from the Evangelical Association in Brandon. What a surprise to meet you out here."

"I guess I'm here to welcome you to the territory," Rev. Stegner said with a smile. The wagons had stopped, and the others gathered around. The preacher slipped his Bible into a saddlebag.

Adam said, "It's about time for a rest and some lunch. Rev. Stegner, would you join us once we find a spot out of this hot sun?"

The preacher offered, "Just up the road, you'll find some shade and a stream to water your stock. I'd be honored to fellowship with ya." He led the way.

Elder Stegner ate heartily. As he smacked his lips, Jake asked, "Elder, you ride this area often, can you tell us where to find good farmland that we can conscript? All five families are farmers. Where do you suggest we look?"

The preacher tugged on his beard. "Well, Hamilton's down the trail about fifteen miles. I meet with an evangelical group at the Jake McQuillan home just east of Hamilton. On west of there, it levels off to some good land. Phillip and Lucinda Eppard just moved onto a claim out there a couple of years ago. On beyond them would be my suggestion. Jake McQuillan at the post office could help you out."

The five men looked at one another with a knowing smile. Fred remarked, "That's the name the land office guy gave us in Chatfield."

Adam broke in, "Rev. Stegner, would you pray for us as we continue our search for our new homes?" The elder went to his knees. Everyone followed, and the preacher prayed fervently.

Standing to his feet, the preacher tipped his hat and said, "May God grant you the desire of your hearts." Rev. Stegner rode away, leaving the travelers amazed at God's hand at work among them.

Adam took up the reins and shouted, "Get up, Zelig and Zelda. Hamilton, here we come. Our Minnesota homes are just ahead." The trail continued through valleys, across streams, and finally down the slope into the town of Hamilton. Adam said, "Matilda, look at the signs. On the right side, it says, 'Mower County,' and on the left side, 'Fillmore County.' It looks like we'll be livin' in Mower County, Minnesota."

As they drove through Hamilton, Adam said, "The post office is over there, and Corey's Hotel."

"It looks like we'll be able to get all the supplies we need at Booth's and Randall's General Store," Matilda added.

"Look, Matilda"—he pointed—"there's a sawmill over there. We'll buy lumber there for our house." They moved on through town and camped by the river that night.

After breakfast, the women went to the general store, while the men checked on farm equipment. At the blacksmith shop, Mike asked the smithy, "What advice would you give a new farmer in Minnesota?"

"I'd tell him to get a Grasshopper," the smithy answered with a smile.

"A grasshopper?" Mike reacted.

"Yup, the most important piece of equipment for farmin' in Mower County." With a motion to follow, he went out the back door. Pointing, he said, "It's called a grasshopper plow made by a blacksmith in Illinois by the name of John Deere. Old man Jacob McQuillan brought one with him when he came here from Ohio back in '52. He was the first settler in these parts."

"McQuillan, is that the man at the post office?" Peter inquired.

"Nope, that's his son, Jake. Good people, the McQuillans. That's Jake's team by the post office now," the smithy observed.

The five men walked into the Hamilton Post Office. Behind the counter was a man of strong build, flashing blue eyes, and reddish-brown beard. "What can I do for you men this mornin'?" he offered. "I see you're camped down by the river."

Mike responded, "We're lookin' for Jake McQuillan."

"You found him. What's on your minds?" Jake extended a hand of welcome.

Adam spoke up. "We just pulled in from Brandon, Wisconsin, five families of us. Baldwin Peters at the Federal Land Office in Chatfield told us you might be willin' to help us find claims in the area." Adam waited as McQuillan gave some thought.

"Ya, I do that sometimes. It's not a business of mine, but I had a claim taken out from under me when I first came here, so I like to help people avoid problems."

Adam continued, "By the way, we met Elder Stegner on the trail. He said he holds meetin's in your house sometimes. We're from the Evangelical Association in Brandon. We'll be lookin' for some fellowship once we get settled."

Jake reached for his hat. "Preacher Stegner's a good man. We'll see you get an invitation next time he's in town. Let's step out to my wagon and I'll show you a map I've drawn up."

Jake pulled a pencil-drawn map out of a box behind the wagon seat. Adam immediately recognized the Greenslitt property marked For Sale by Owner. The other men looked at claims that were of interest to them.

Following some discussion, McQuillan said, "I suggest you move your wagons up the west road a couple of miles, just past Phillip and Lucinda Eppard's place. You'll find a little stream and some shade trees. I'll meet you there tomorrow morning and show you around the area."

The five families settled in their covered wagons next to a clear flowing stream west of Hamilton. Jake McQuillan arrived as the cool of morning gave way to a pleasant summer day. With five adventurous farmers in his wagon, Jake moved on west another mile. Turning in the seat, he pointed out, "This is Section 33 in Township 104. That's the quarter section owned by Greenslitt. They have offered to sell for $500. He has a small shelter for some stock, and he has a garden and some grain planted."

Jake motioned to the south. "Over there is the Van Dusen eighty. His price is $250. Again, he's not done much for improvements. Some sod has been broken, and there's a small cabin with a lean-to shelter."

After looking at several other properties, McQuillan returned his new friends to their camp. He touched the brim of his hat and said, "May the Lord lead you in your decisions." The five men waved, speaking words of gratitude, and each went to his family's wagon.

Adam said, "Matilda, I feel God is leading me to buy the Greenslitt quarter section. We have the money from my inheritance, and it looks like good land." They prayed together and decided that Adam should inform the others of his plan.

With his head bowed, Adam took a walk by the river. He leaned against the trunk of an oak tree. One by one, the other men joined him. It was quiet, but minds were whirling.

Mike broke the silence. "I'm gonna pick a quarter section, fence in a half acre, and build a cabin. After thirty days, I'll ride down to the Federal Land Office and have old Baldwin make out the papers. Gettin' it for $1.25 an acre sounds real good to me."

Adam followed, "Matilda and I agreed that we should look seriously at the Greenslitt quarter. If any of you have the same interest, we need to talk it over and seek the Lord's guidance."

Peter added, "That eighty of Van Dusen's looks good to me, unless either Jake or Fred is interested in it."

Both Fred and Jake shook their heads. Jake said, "No, I've got my eye on a quarter to conscript.

Fred simply said, "Me too."

Adam reminded the group of the importance of being open and honest in these decisions. He said, "We're brothers in Christ, and we're one in him."

Fred took a deep breath and said, "Adam, what you said about bein' honest is true. I need to say that I'm a little jealous of your inheritance. I know God will provide for me and my family, but to be honest, I envy what others have." He hung his head. It was still.

Mike waited and then admitted, "I confess that I have some of the same feelings. I want to be glad for you, Adam, and, Peter, for what you have, but sometimes my sinful self gets in the way. I respect both of you as friends."

Adam responded, "It's hard for me too. My inheritance came just before we left Brandon. It's hard to have what others don't have. I keep remindin' myself of what the Bible says about those who have, that much will be required."

Peter brought the conversation to a close by saying, "Let's all sleep on this overnight and talk in the mornin' to make sure we have an agreement among the five of us."

Adam spent the afternoon riding around the Greenslitt property. The more he saw it, the more he knew this would be home for his family. Excitement robbed all five men of sleep that night, but in the morning, they all were at peace with the choices they had made.

On June 21, 1862, Adam and Peter made the trip to Chatfield to meet with the Greenslitts and the Van Dusens. With the help of Baldwin Peters and the Root River Bank, the papers were signed and titles transferred.

Adam and Matilda rearranged their belongings, making the covered wagon their home while a house could be built. After supper, Adam took his Bible and read about the people of Israel crossing the Jordan River on dry ground to enter the Promised Land. He prayed, "God, you've been with us crossing rivers, weathering storms, climbing hills, all the way. Thank you for bringing us to our new home. Please give us strength to build a house, break the sod, and find food to eat." Matilda wiped a tear from her cheek when Adam said, "Amen."

"What is it, Matilda? Are you sad? I want you to be happy that we are finally home on our own land." He reached out and touched Matilda's arm.

"I just get so frightened when I think of that first winter on Vati's claim by Princeton. I miss Mutti and Vati so much. I pray Vati will be happy with Olinda." She broke into sobs. Albert whimpered and put his little hand on his mother's face and touched the gold cross at her neck. Adam wrapped his arms around his family, more determined than ever to build a safe and secure future for them.

Getting Ready for Winter
Minnesota
1862

MATILDA AWOKE ABRUPTLY, HER BODY covered with an itchy rash. In a moment, she realized she was dreaming about measles in Liverpool. She rolled close to her husband for comfort, only to find that he was gone. Through the canvas, she could see a narrow strip of daylight along the eastern sky. Then she heard the swishing sound of Adam's scythe cutting prairie grass. She thought, *Adam, are you out working at this early hour?*

Albert was sound asleep in his bed. Matilda breathed a prayer, "Thank you, God, for my husband and a beautiful little boy. Please, God, take care of Vati." She resolved, *I'll make some coffee and pancakes for Adam.*

"Good morning, my dear wife," Adam said as he slipped up behind Matilda and cuddled her in his arms. "I've got all the grass cut over there where we'll build our house. Tell me, what do you want in your house?"

"Oh, Adam," she responded, "I just want to make a good home for you and Albert."

"And for more kids yet to come," he said with a smile. "I love children. We'll have more children. Seriously, what do you want in your house?" Adam spun her around and kissed her gently.

"Could we have a pantry to store food and a stove with an oven so I can make good wheat bread? And a separate bedroom so Albert can nap while I work in the kitchen. Is that too much to ask?" She smiled up at her husband.

"That you'll have, and we start today." Adam gave thanks to God for the food and filled his plate with hotcakes and venison sausage. "After breakfast, I'm goin' over to see if Peter will go 50/50 with me on a grasshopper plow. I'll never dig through this sod without one."

With Zelig and Zelda hitched to the supply wagon, Adam waved to his son and threw a kiss to his wife as he headed across the trail to his brother's claim. Adam found Peter and Jane pulling weeds in the garden the Van Dusen's left behind. *"Gutten morgen, bruder,* looks like you're gettin' settled around here."

"Ja, I've got a good helper." Peter took Jane's hand and moved out of the garden. "What brings you over this mornin'?"

"I've been thinkin' about that grasshopper plow we saw in Hamilton. The sod is so thick on my house site that I can't get my spade through it. We're gonna need somethin' to get these fields broken up for the crops, and I'd like to use it to clear the sod for my house. Would you be interested in a 50/50 ownership?"

Jane whimpered when her pa took her to the cabin and announced to Carolina, "I'm goin' with Adam to buy a plow in Hamilton."

*   *   *

"Well, young man," Matilda said to her toddler son, "what'll we do today while Vati's gone to town?" She wondered, *Is this how Vati felt when he was alone after Mutti died?* She shook off the blues and breathed a prayer of thanksgiving. "Albert," she said, "how would you like to go exploring down along that stream? I bet we could find some berries or plums." She packed a lunch and a jar of water in her bag, and they started on an adventure.

*   *   *

In Hamilton, Adam said to his brother, "Let's go to the sawmill and see about purchasing lumber for my house. I could use some timbers and dimension lumber to get started."

The mill operator greeted the brothers as they jumped down from the wagon. "The name's Sherwood. What can I do for the Utzinger boys today?"

Stunned by the question, Peter responded, "How'd ya know our name? We've only been here a few days."

"You better get used to it. Word travels fast around here. Do you need some timbers to get started out there on the Greenslitt place?"

"Ja, you got that right," Adam responded. "Give me a good price and I'll buy lumber for the whole job from you. I see you have some competition down the river."

"This is Sherwood's 'sure wood,' the best in the county." They made a deal, and soon the wagon was loaded with timbers.

Next, they bought a grasshopper plow at the blacksmith shop and picked up their newly printed deeds at Randall's Print Shop.

As they left town, Jake McQuillan stepped out of the post office. Adam reined the team to a stop. "*Gutten tag*, Jake," he shouted.

"*Gutten tag*, how are the Utzinger brothers today? Looks like you're gettin' started out there on your farms. I see you bought a Grasshopper. You'll never be sorry. That sod is tough in these parts."

Peter nodded. "I'm ready to break some sod and see if I can get somethin' to grow yet this summer. Worth a try even if it just gets the sod worked down."

"That's right, it seems like it takes a year for the sod to rot down. By the way, we're havin' church at our house on Sunday. You'd be welcome. It's the first place east of town and around the corner to the left, the farmhouse and log barn. We start about 11:00 and dinner after. You don't have to bring anything. Just come and worship the Lord with us."

Adam tipped his hat. "Much obliged, Jake, we'd like that." Adam clucked at the team, and they pulled out of town.

Back home, Peter said, "Let's see what this plow'll do over there where you're diggin'." They yoked Peter's oxen to the plow, set it in the ground, and rolled over a whole row of sod the full length of Adam's building site. "Wow," Peter said with amazement, "that'll save hours when we get out in the field."

Feeling a bit hungry, Adam walked over to the cook site. He found Albert sound asleep and Matilda cooking plum sauce over the fire. A large pan of gooseberries sat on the tailgate.

"Looks like you were a busy lady while I was gone," Adam remarked. He made a sour face after pouring a handful of gooseberries in his mouth. "Uff, sour," he sneered.

"Serves ya right, bein' so greedy." Matilda smiled. "I found a tree with a honeybee's nest in it. That would sweeten the berries if we could get it."

"I'll get it tomorrow. I learned how to do that when I worked in the woods in New York. You just need some smoke to calm those honeybees down."

Adam diligently made use of every daylight hour, digging the hole and laying up rocks for cellar walls. He was anxious for the day that Matilda would have her kitchen. She never complained, but he could see the weariness in her eyes each evening at suppertime.

At breakfast one morning, Adam announced, "It's a nice day for a ride. I'm goin' over to Austin to have the deed to our land recorded at the county office." It was a long day, but he returned that evening with the deed stamped, "Recorded, July 9, 1862, County Recorder."

A week later, the cellar was completed, and the perimeter timbers were secure. Adam had supplies on site to build the walls and lay the floor. On July 18, Adam finished driving the pegs to hold the crossbeam in place. Matilda brought lunch in midafternoon. Adam rubbed his sweaty face on his sleeve and said, "I'm ready to build the walls. Sure could use some help. I hate to ask Peter to stop plowin' to help me out." A brisk summer breeze picked up dust and dry grass, spinning it across the prairie. "I wish that wind would blow up a shower. We could use the moisture and some relief from this July heat."

That evening, having finished the chores, Adam remarked, "Looks like I might get my wish. See that thunderhead formin' in the northwest?"

Matilda had just thrown the dishwater out when a flash of lightening crossed the sky, followed suddenly by a clash of thunder. "Adam," she cried, "get Albert in the wagon and grab those dried strips of venison and put them in the chest under the wagon. I'll get the washing off the line."

Adam knew from experience that hot summer days could trigger dangerous storms. The family quickly secured the campsite and climbed into the covered wagon. The canvas shuddered as the wind beat the driving rain against the wagon. Thick clouds covered the sun, enveloping the homestead in darkness. Cracking sounds echoed as hailstones slammed against the wagon. Lightning flashed, and thunder resounded. Albert whimpered and clung to his father. Wind gusts increased like huge crescendos against the vibrating cloth. Matilda prayed.

Sensing the wagon could blow over, Adam dragged everything that wasn't nailed down to the west side of the wagon floor. He pressed his own weight hard against the driving wind. Though it seemed like an eternity, calm came as suddenly as the storm had arrived. The darkened sky returned to brightness, and God announced his sovereignty with a rainbow in the east. They gave thanks for safety through the storm.

On Sunday morning, the two Utzinger families arrived at the Jake McQuillan home looking forward to hearing the Word of God. Preacher Stegner didn't let them down. He preached on the parable about a man who was left half dead along the road while a priest and a Levite tried to slip by unnoticed. A man called a Samaritan stopped, treated his wounds, and took him to an inn for care. He ended by encouraging his flock, as followers of Jesus, to help each other. "We have a new community here," the preacher said. "People are arrivin' almost every day. As Christians, we need to be reachin' out and helpin' each other."

During dinner, the men learned about Adam's house project and set Friday as the day to help him raise the walls. Adam responded, "I'm mighty thankful. It's good to help each other do the things we can't do alone. I'll be ready to help others when our house is built."

A spectacular sunrise greeted them on Friday morning. Wagons arrived as Adam wolfed down the last pancake. Word had spread through the grapevine, and families unknown to the Utzingers, came to be part of the community event. Food was plentiful. The children played games, and the women talked like they were starved for conversation. Once Adam shared his plan, the men seemed to know what job each neighbor could do best. By noon, the outside walls were up, most of the floor was nailed down, and a crew was ready to cut and set the rafters.

Tears rolled down Adam's face as he prayed over the noontime meal. Men ate as if famished, licking their lips with satisfaction. Some soft snoring was heard under an oak tree, but like clockwork, each man returned to his labor. By evening, the house stood ready for shingles and finishing touches. One by one, the men gathered their families each to his own wagon. As they moved out, Adam and Matilda could hear the soft strains of, "Amazing grace, how sweet the sound . . ."

Adam spent the days of early August splitting and installing clapboard shingles, building furniture, and setting windows and doors, bringing the house to completion. It was an exciting day when they moved from the covered wagon to their new house.

Matilda put curtains on the windows. She stocked her new pantry with supplies for the coming winter. The cellar provided a cool place for fruits and vegetables and a place for cheese to "ripen." Her heart was filled with gratitude, and her fears from the past turned to thanksgiving to the God who provides.

30

Life in Racine Township
Minnesota
1862-1865

NEW RESIDENTS CONTINUED TO FLOW into Mower County, Minnesota, as people learned of good farmland available at little cost. It was often said, "The dust never settled on the trail to Winona," as wagonloads of wheat were taken to market.

Adam Utzinger was winnowing wheat when Rev. Stegner rode into his yard. "*Gutten morgen*, Elder," Adam called as he lifted a shovelful of wheat into the wind. "I was just thinkin' about a cup of coffee. Let's go see what Matilda has on hand."

Albert tottered across the room with open arms to welcome their guest. Matilda checked the coffeepot and found enough to go with the cinnamon bread. After some small talk about the weather and the new neighbors on the section to the north, Elder Stegner leaned back and remarked, "It's sure been good attendance at meetings at the McQuillan house lately."

"Ja," Adam responded, "we got there a little late last Sunday and hardly got in the door."

The elder continued, "I've been wonderin' if we should get a group started west of Hamilton. In fact, I came here today to ask if you'd consider leadin' a class meeting in your home. We'd have preachin' meetings on Sundays, and you could have class meetings on

Wednesday nights. We'd be one church meetin' in two homes. I have the books you could use to become a class leader and an exhorter."

Adam smiled as he took a sip of coffee. "Truth is, Preacher, I was a class leader in Wisconsin for a year before movin' to Minnesota. I did the study under Elder Krause. I've got the books around here somewhere."

"Ain't that the way with our God? He has it planned before we ask. What do ya say, would you give it a try? We could announce it next Sunday and get started right away."

"I guess we better ask Matilda. It'd be more work for her than anyone. What do ya think?" Adam asked, giving her a wink.

"Sure, the ladies all help out with food. Maybe Carolina would take the children over to her cabin for a Sunday school lesson. I'm sure Lucinda would love to help her. We have lots of children needin' to learn about Jesus."

The meeting at the Jake McQuillan home the next Sunday was overflowing. To make room, Lucinda and Mary M took the children outside for a Bible story. Elder Stegner said as he started his sermon, "Today, we have some very good news." His voice cracked as he continued, "And we have some very sad news. The sad news is that your former pastor, Elder Seder, was killed in the Sioux Indian rebellion over northwest of Fort Ridgley on August 18. As a missionary out of New Ulm, he preached at an evangelical society of about seventy members by Fort Ridgley that Sunday. The next day, Seder and nearly all of the members were killed in a sudden attack by the Sioux. We must pray for his widow and three children." A pall of grief and tears moved over the gathering. Prayers were offered.

"The good news is," the preacher went on, "beginning next Sunday, our congregation will have two worship places. Adam and Matilda have agreed to hold services in their home three miles west of Hamilton. Adam served as a class leader in Wisconsin and is willing to hold meetings on Sundays and Wednesday evenings in his home. I'll preach at 11:00 here at the McQuillans' and at 1:30 at the Utzingers'."

Stagecoach drivers often left copies of newspapers at Booth's store. News of the civil war became the topic of conversation in every community gathering. At a class meeting in late September, Adam urged, "We must pray fervently for our nation and for our president. A recent report indicated that on September 17, in the Battle of Antietam, twenty-three thousand men were killed, wounded, or missing. Each one leaves a family in mourning."

Phillip Eppard requested, "Please pray for my friend David Felch who joined the Ninth Minnesota Infantry Regiment last month."

The group went to their knees in prayer, and Adam closed with an urgent prayer. Matilda poured steaming cups of coffee for their guests. One by one, the families left for home. Phillip lifted sleeping Mary to his shoulder and offered an arm to Lucinda, who was large with child, as they made their way to their wagon. Adam and Matilda walked with them in the moonlit autumn evening. Matilda broke the quiet. "Lucinda, Adam's leavin' for Winona early tomorrow with a load of wheat. Would you like me to come over and help you with some housework? I know it's hard when your time's so close."

"Oh, Matilda, that would be wonderful. I have three cheeses curin', and they're heavy for me to handle. Thank you, my friend, for offering." The Eppards drove away as Adam slipped his arm around his wife and walked slowly to the house.

Matilda fixed breakfast for Adam while he prepared to leave for Winona. He was thankful for a good wheat crop, and he expected to get a good price. He looked in on his sleeping son, gave his wife a kiss, and said, "I'm gonna check on buyin' a better harrow than that old homemade one I have. I want to break sod on the back forty this fall and plant some corn next year."

Rowdy whinnied a welcome when Matilda stepped into his stall to saddle up for her ride to visit Lucinda. With Albert in front of her and some cinnamon rolls and a jar of jam in the saddlebags, she praised God for the beautiful autumn morning. As she crossed the little stream along the way, she said to Albert, knowing he was too young to understand, "Over by those oaks would be a good place for a school."

"Thank you, Matilda, for coming," Lucinda welcomed. She soon sat down by the kitchen table and drew a deep breath. "I'm getting tired. I pray that this baby would come soon."

Matilda poured coffee, put out some rolls, and sat with her friend. Lucinda sipped from the cup and took a small bite. She was quiet, and sweat beaded up on her forehead. Matilda asked, "Are you all right, Lucinda? Can I get something for you?"

"Remembering how it was with Mary, I think my time is close. Mutti is coming to stay with me tomorrow, but I'm not sure that'll be soon enough." Matilda washed the dishes and tidied the house. At Lucinda's directions, she went down in the cellar and turned the cheeses and coated the ripe one with wax.

Mary and Albert played while Lucinda took a rest in the rocking chair. The children grew tired, so Matilda gave them some lunch and put them down for naps. Lucinda suddenly straightened up in the chair and winced, "Oooh," and settled back.

"Lucinda"—Matilda put her hand on her friend's shoulder— "what was that?"

"I'm not sure, but I would feel better if Mutti were here. She has delivered so many babies that I just feel safe with her."

Matilda reached for her coat and shawl. "The children are sleeping. I'll go tell your mutti that you need her. Rowdy needs a good run. I'll be back soon. Will you be all right?"

"Yes, Matilda, but do be careful. Tell Mutti to come ready to stay a few days."

Rowdy liked to run, and Matilda let him go. She waved at some women by the store as she sped through Hamilton. She thought, *Word'll be out that Lucinda had her baby before it ever happens.*

"Lucinda needs you. We think she's starting pains," Matilda shouted as she darted into Polly's kitchen.

Polly was canning crabapples at the stove. She pushed the pot to the back of the range, tossed her apron on a chair, and called over her shoulder as she headed for the bedroom, "Go over and tell Mary M I'm leavin' so she can watch the children. Jacob's down by the barn. Tell him to get the team ready."

Matilda delivered the messages and saw that Jacob was ready with his driving team and buggy. She called over her shoulder as she set Rowdy to a gallop, "I'll find Phillip in Hamilton."

Jake McQuillan came out of the post office just as Matilda rode up. She shouted, "Jake, find Phillip and tell him Lucinda's in labor." Jake waved his response, and Matilda urged Rowdy up the west road.

Luisa Burkhardt sensed the excitement from her home across the trail and came to be with Lucinda. Jacob and Polly arrived soon after Matilda, and the nervous father was not far behind.

With Lucinda in good hands, Matilda went home to do her chores. The next day, she learned that Phillip and Lucinda now had a little boy named George.

Babies were not the only new births in Racine Township that fall. On October 12, 1862, Preacher Stegner announced, "Rev. Kuter, presiding elder of the Minnesota District, will be here next Sunday to help us organize as an Evangelical Association society. We'll all meet at the Jake McQuillan home at 2:00 in the afternoon." The next Sunday, a new church was born and given the name *Salem Evangelical Association*. Officers were elected, and the families of Jake McQuillan, P. M. Eppard, Peter Utzinger, Adam Utzinger, J. Burkhardt, C. Werner, and G. Martin signed the charter. Worship and prayer meetings continued to be held in homes. New members were added to the congregation as neighbors invited neighbors.

Adam brought in two Canadian geese that he shot out of a flock that lingered on the way south. Days shortened as snow covered the countryside in December. The most exciting event at Christmastime was Matilda's announcement. "Adam, I'm now certain that I'm with child, and you'll be Vati again in midsummer." Adam was delighted and worked even harder in the woods each day to keep the fires burning with winter warmth.

Judge Felch began his first term representing Mower and Dodge counties in the Minnesota state senate in 1863. Phillip kept in touch with the senator regularly, receiving news regarding the war. The class meetings urgently prayed for the country as President Lincoln had issued a preliminary proclamation that all slaves in the territory captured by the Union Army would be free. In March of 1863, the congress enacted the first draft in American history. Adam led his class meeting in fervent prayer for the nation and the president.

"Good morning, Adam," Jake McQuillan greeted from behind the post office window. "How are you this beautiful spring day?"

"A fine day it is," Adam responded. "Any mail for the Utzingers?"

"Yup, in fact you have a registered letter. You'll have to sign for it. It's had me wonderin'; you know, with the draft and all."

Adam's hand shook as he signed his name and accepted the letter. "I guess I'll wait and open it with Matilda. She's doin' well, expectin' the baby and all." With his wagon loaded with lumber for an extension on the barn, Adam headed for home.

He was unhitching the team when Matilda, with Albert at her side, came to welcome him home. "Did Dan Booth take my cheeses in trade?" she asked. "I tried to make them like Lucinda's, and he always takes hers."

"Ja, he was glad to get 'em. He's got more customers than Lucinda can supply." Adam watered the horses and put them in their stall. Down on his knee, he gave Albert a hug and lifted him up to his shoulders. On the way to the house, Adam spoke slowly. "I'm a little worried, Matilda." Reaching for the letter, he continued, "This came in the mail today, a letter from Fort Snelling. You know, with the draft and all, and you with child."

Matilda took a deep breath and pulled close to her husband's side. "What does it say?" she hesitantly asked.

"I don't know, I wanted to open it with you." With Albert on his lap, they took mugs of coffee at the table. Adam opened the seal and read silently. "It's the new draft. I report in Rochester on August 3."

Matilda slumped over the table, too stunned to weep. Albert whimpered. Adam read on. "It says, draftees will be taken by number. My number is 198. Selection will take place in Rochester on August 3 through August 28."

Gaining composure, Matilda said, "At least the baby will be born by then." She fell into her husband's arms. "Oh, Adam, what will I do without you? The land, the chores, I can't do it all."

Adam comforted, "We'll make plans. Peter'll help. We need to trust the Lord. He promised to provide our every need, and he will."

In faith, Adam planted more acres of wheat than the year before. He cut and split an abundant supply of firewood and stacked all the prairie hay time permitted. Peter agreed to manage his brother's farm, and Adam's army pay would be used to hire young Harvey McQuillan as a farmhand.

With Polly McQuillan as midwife and Carolina assisting, Matilda gave birth to John Adam Utzinger on July 4, 1863. Adam held his little son in his arms with tears running down his face. "What a marvel it is to receive one God has created. How can I leave a month from now to go to war?"

The month of July went past swiftly. Little John made his presence known with healthy lungs and a demanding appetite. Peter arrived with his team and wagon early on August 3 to take Adam to Rochester. Following a four-way huddle with mother and father in tears and two little boys between them, Adam broke away and joined two other draftees on their way to war.

Family and neighbors surrounded Matilda with support as she adjusted to life without Adam. Her pillow was damp in the morning from nighttime tears. Harvest was in full swing, and the wheat crop was abundant. Peter and Harvey worked together on the two farms to bring in the crop. Harvey brought along his younger brother, Franklin, to turn the crank on the fanning mill to separate the wheat from the chaff.

"Time for a rest and a glass of lemonade," Matilda said to Harvey and Franklin who were fanning wheat on a hot mid-August day.

"Thanks, that would taste good," Harvey said. "We've filled a dozen grain sacks today all ready for market." Albert was exploring the fanning mill and John was snoozing in his mother's arms when Franklin asked, "Who's that walking on the trail? It looks like he's in a hurry."

Matilda looked. She stood up and looked more closely. "Could that be Adam?" she asked. "It looks like his walk." She remembered the day back in Wisconsin when he came home after being in the army for only a few days. *Could it happen again?* she wondered. The man started to run. Matilda caught her breath. "Come, Albert," she coaxed, moving toward the lane as fast as the child's legs could carry him.

"Matilda! Matilda!" she heard him call. She knew her husband's voice. They met and fell into an embrace. Baby John awakened and cried. Adam took his son in his arms to comfort him. Finally, he could speak. "I don't have to go. They reached the quota needed before they got to my number. I may have to go later, but not now."

Life returned to normal for the Utzinger family. At supper one evening, Adam said, "Zelig and Zelda are getting old. Raswell Stewart offered to trade me two yoke of oxen and two little colts for the team. The two Zs have been in the family a long time, but I need the oxen to keep the plow goin' all fall." By freeze-up, Adam had another forty acres ready for seeding.

Lucinda and Matilda became close friends. They often shared morning coffee, giving the children time to play together. Lucinda set her cup down abruptly. "These kids are going to be old enough for school first thing we know. We need a school building and a teacher."

With a slight smile, Matilda responded, "I've been thinkin' the same thing. Down in the oak grove by the creek would be my choice."

The entire community was saddened by the news that David Felch had died of a disease on October 1, 1864, and was buried in the National Cemetery in Memphis, Tennessee. The Evangelical Association held a memorial service and prayed more urgently for the end of the terrible war.

Winter of 1864 was cold and blustery. The men spent long hours cutting wood to keep their homes warm. Adam spent his evenings by the cookstove cutting holes in the fence posts to hold the rails in place. In the spring, he fenced in a pasture to keep the stock out of the grain fields.

By July, the whole countryside looked like a sea of gold as the breeze swept through the flowing wheat fields. Harvest required the hands of everyone, and the men set up caravans of wagons to haul their produce to market in Winona. One day, Phillip said to Adam, "For the first time in my life, I feel financially secure. My place is paid for, I have some stock, and the land is producing. We have two children, and Lucinda is expecting again this fall. God has been good to us."

Adam nodded in agreement. "Ja, I'm feelin' that way too. I only wish this war would end. There's still the chance I'll get called. Some of the reports are not very promising the way the battles are goin'."

That night, Adam snuffed out the candle, drew Matilda close, and said, "Phillip and I were talkin' today about how God has blessed our families so richly. I love you, Matilda, and you are such a good mutti to our boys. If it weren't for that draft hangin' over my head, I would be the most blessed man in the world." He kissed her tenderly.

Matilda responded with a smile, "And, Adam, I think God is gonna bless us again come spring."

"You mean . . . you mean another baby? Is that what you mean?"

"That's what I mean, Vati. Maybe we'll have a girl this time."

It was a chilly fall day when Harvey was born to Phillip and Lucinda on November 14, 1864. The next-day reports came that Union General Sherman had started a march across Georgia toward the Atlantic. "All war is hell," the general exclaimed. The residents of Racine Township were chilled by the news, but in spite of the falling temperatures and discouraging war news, they celebrated the birth of the Savior and looked forward with hope to the new year.

The Fire
Minnesota
1865

"OLD BESS IS SURE GIVIN' the milk this winter," Phillip boasted as he pushed the door shut against the wintery cold and set the foamy full milk pail by the sink. "She surprises me as cold as it's been the last couple weeks." He gave Lucinda a little snuggle. "You'll have to start another batch of cheese tomorrow."

"That's good," Lucinda responded. "Dan Booth says everyone in Hamilton wants my cheese. My cheese and butter pay the bill every time I do our trading."

Four-year-old Mary with two-year-old George tagging behind came running with arms outstretched, yelling, "Vati! Vati!" Phillip swooped his daughter to his shoulder as George hugged his knees. "Vati, your ears are cold," Mary said with a shiver.

George mimicked, "Co'd, Vati, Co'd." His father tussled his son's hair.

"Ja, I'm cold, it's forty below zero outside."

Lucinda served a supper of fried elk steak, potatoes, gravy and wheat bread. Phillip added wood to the fire and took an evening snooze in his favorite chair. Mary and George played, while Lucinda washed the dishes. After nursing little Harvey, she prayed with the children and tucked them in their beds.

Phillip stood up, stretched, and reached for his cap and coat. "It's a mighty cold night. I'm gonna check the stock."

By candlelight, Lucinda read from her Bible as she waited for her husband to return.

"All's well," Phillip assured as he hung his coat on a hook. "I'll tend the fire."

The candles were blown out, and the Eppard family was snug in bed for the night. At about midnight, Lucinda heard Harvey whimper from his cradle. She pulled her wool socks on her cold feet and lifted Harvey from his bed. The kitchen seemed hot and smoky as she prepared to nurse her baby. Shadows formed on the wall as she noticed the stovepipe was red hot. Panic hit when she saw flames bursting up from the timbers in the ceiling. "Phillip," she screamed, "the house is on fire!"

Phillip, on first reaction, grabbed the water bucket and threw the water at the blaze. He quickly knew it was too late. "Get the children in the sleigh," he ordered. "I'll yoke the oxen. Bring quilts and blankets."

Lucinda scurried to get George and Harvey to the door. "Mary," she shouted, "the house is on fire. Grab your coat. Bring your quilt with you. We must get to the sleigh. Vati is gettin' the oxen. We'll go to the neighbors."

Harvey and George were crying. Lucinda lifted George to her hip and held Harvey under one arm. "Come quick, Mary," she ordered, "we're goin' to the sleigh."

Lucinda made beds with the quilts and bundled the two boys together. "Stay here, Mary, I'm goin' back to the house."

The kitchen was burning hot when Lucy entered. She grabbed some deerskin robes, her Bible, some clothing, and her husband's hunting rifle and fled to the sleigh. Mary was comforting her brothers when she arrived. Mother and children huddled together under the quilts and robes in the sleigh.

Phillip brought the oxen from the barn. While he was yoking them, a beam near the chimney gave way, sending sparks flying into the cold winter night. Bo, Phillip's off ox, spooked and vaulted toward the open field. Phillip quickly tied Ben, his nigh ox, to the fence and ran after Bo. Finally, he captured the frightened animal and guided him back to the sleigh. Once they were moving, Phillip jumped into the sleigh. Shouting commands to the beasts, he brought his family across the fields to the neighbor's house. The startled neighbors invited them into their warm kitchen.

After the children were comforted and settled for the rest of the night, Phillip began to feel a severe pain in his feet. Looking down, he realized he wasn't wearing boots. His wool socks were caked with ice. He soaked his feet in warm water and clenched his teeth in pain.

Next morning, word spread quickly. Jacob arrived with his team and sled to take Phillip, Lucinda, and the children to his home where they would stay until a new house could be built. Neighbors pitched in to do the chores and help clean up the charred remains of the house.

Phillip was in severe pain. Polly cautioned, "Your toes are turning black, we need to get a doctor." She gave him some laudanum to relieve the pain.

Jake McQuillan responded, "They have a doctor in Grand Meadow. I'll saddle up and go fetch him."

Jake had some difficulty persuading the doctor to come with him, but finally, they arrived. Still under the influence of too much alcohol the night before, the doctor fumbled about attempting to amputate the blackened toes. Jacob finally stepped in and took the doctor by the arm. "Stop, that's enough!" he ordered. "Get ready, Phil, I'm takin' you to Rochester to find Dr. Mayo."

Jacob's spirited driving team was ready to run, and they made the eighteen-mile trip to Rochester in record time. In the little shanty that served as W. W. Mayo's office, the doctor exclaimed, "Those toes must come off!" Turning to his wife, he ordered, "Louise, get the chloroform ready." With Phillip spread out on the floor, a big book for a pillow, the little surgeon skillfully amputated the toes and bandaged his patient's feet. After Dr. Mayo carefully explained how to care for Phillip's feet as they healed, Jacob drove his son-in-law back home.

Discouraged by the pain in his feet and being stuck in his in-law's house, Phillip became agitated and restless. "I'm nothing but a failure. Can't even do my own chores," he spouted.

"The most important thing right now is for you to take care of your feet," Lucinda encouraged. "You'll be back out workin' before you know it. It's good for those nephews of ours to help out a little."

"Just leave me alone!" he shouted. "I never did amount to anything. No wonder my vati kicked me out of the house. And you," he snapped at Mary, "quit lookin' at my feet like I'm some kind'a cripple."

Discouraged, Lucida went to visit her friend Matilda. "I don't know what to do. Phillip is so angry. He gets cross with the children. Sometimes he refuses to come to the table for supper. He calls himself a worthless cripple."

Matilda drew a deep breath. "Men are that way, Lucinda. They feel responsible for their families, and when they hit hard times, they put the blame on themselves. That's what my vati did when Mutti died in Wisconsin. His anger scared me. He threatened to quit the claim. I didn't know what was gonna happen to us."

The two friends prayed. As Lucinda was leaving, Matilda offered, "How'd it be if Adam and I came over to have a visit with Phillip? The two of them are good friends."

"That would be kind of you," Lucinda responded as she stepped up on the wagon to leave.

The bitter cold of winter gave way to warmer days as February unfolded. At breakfast, Adam remarked, "What a sunny morning. Makes me feel like goin' somewhere."

"Me too," Matilda responded, "why don't we pay the Eppards a visit? I've been feelin' a little confined with the baby's arrival only a couple months away."

"I'm not sure it'd be the friendliest visit, but I could assure him the neighbors are takin' good care of things. Ja, let's pack the boys in the sleigh and take a ride."

After a proper welcome, Polly said, "Plenty of coffee on the stove and muffins just out of the oven. I'm gonna run over to Mary M's. She wants some help with a dress she's makin' for the little Ellenberg girl."

Phillip was friendly, but quiet. Conversation was strained. Lucinda put out the coffee and muffins. The two women helped the children get started playing. At the table, Adam ventured, "Well, Phil, your neighbors are doing a good job with your stock. The place looks pretty well cleaned up."

"I could care less. I'm such a cripple. I'll never get the place goin' again. Can't get a crop in this spring the way I am. I'm thinkin' I'll let the claim go."

Adam was taken back. He hesitated, and then he spoke. "That disappoints me, Phil. I thought you would have more confidence in your Christian friends than that. You know how the Bible says we're the body of Christ, and when one member hurts, we all hurt and that we are to help each other."

"Right now, I don't really care what the Bible says," Phillip hissed.

Adam backed off. Matilda leaned forward and said, "Phillip, you remind me of my vati after Mutti died. Sometimes he acted like a big baby. He wallowed around in his tears, talkin' about quittin'. Ja, it was tough havin' your house burn down and your feet hurtin' like they do, but are you gonna be a quitter? It's time you show a little appreciation for your family and friends who are willin' to help you. If another neighbor were in your place, you'd be the first one there to help 'em, wouldn't ya?"

Phillip straightened up and glared across the table at Matilda. "You have no idea what it's like to be crippled and not able to get out and work. I put years of work in that place, and now the house is gone, and it feels like everything is lost."

"You're right, I don't know how that feels. But I do know what it's like to have Mutti die in a cold cabin all alone, knowin' that I should've been there to help her. Vati and I wanted to quit, but we kept goin'. Now he has the claim paid for, and he's married again. I have Adam and our boys. It's worth keeping on, Phillip. We all want to help."

Adam reached a hand to Phillip. "We know it must be discouraging, but remember, we're all in this together. Otherwise, what is faith in the Lord all about? We'll all get our crops planted, and we'll help get a new house built. Everybody helped us with our house, we'll all help you."

After prayer, Adam and Matilda headed for home. As the team trotted along, Adam turned to his wife. "I wondered if Phillip would kick us out of the house when you implied he's a big baby."

"I was gettin' tired of his complainin' as if no one else ever had a problem. He'll get over it, but my knees were shaking the whole time."

Phillip did get over it. Soon he was out doing chores and even cutting wood and splitting fence rails. The winter was cold, but spring came early. With some help from neighbors, he planted even more acres of oats and had ground ready for wheat planting in early fall.

"Lucinda," Phillip started slowly, "I've been thinkin' about our new house. We have three children now, and I'm sure we'll have more. Let's build a two-story house with five bedrooms."

"How many kids do you think we're gonna have?" Lucinda reacted with a smile.

"The first three came pretty fast. We could have a dozen or so."

"Okay," Lucinda agreed, "but I want a big kitchen and a cookstove with a warmin' oven and a reservoir for hot water."

The warm March sunshine penetrated the earth, making an early start on the new house possible. Neighbors worked together to enlarge the cellar and lay up the rock walls. Adam was bringing in a wagonload of field stones for the cellar when he noticed Jake McQuillan riding up the lane. "*Gutten tag*," he called as he jumped down from his load, "you don't look dressed for diggin' a cellar."

"I didn't come for diggin'. I'm bringin' a post for ya. I thought you were so busy you wouldn't be comin' to town anytime soon. It looks pretty important."

The two men shook hands, and Jake handed Adam a letter. "You can pay me the two bits next time you're in town. You need to sign here." Adam's heart was pounding. *Here it is, spring plantin' time and Matilda's time is close. This is no time to be goin' off to war.* With a shaky hand, he signed and slit the envelope open with his jackknife. The message, "Your number is up for conscription. Report to Rochester Post on April 7, 1865." His eyes moistened as he looked up into the eyes of his friend.

Jake nodded his support. "If it's what I think it is, remember, we'll all be here for Matilda until you get back."

After unloading the load of stones, Adam urged his team to a steady trot toward home.

"You're home early. Did you get the foundation finished?" Matilda greeted as Adam jumped over the wagon wheel. He surprised Matilda with a long embrace, followed by a concerned look into her eyes. "I'm so worried about you and the coming baby and all." Her puzzled look changed when she saw the letter in her husband's hand.

"Oh, Adam," Matilda breathed, "it couldn't be a worse time. Can't you ask them to wait a month or two? I need you when the baby comes." Tears filled her eyes as she slumped in Adam's arms.

Adam answered, "Wars don't wait for babies to be born. We'll trust God and our neighbors. We only have a few days to get ready. Let's get started."

Adam left on April 7. Once again, the neighbors rallied around Matilda. They arranged to get Adam's crop planted. Eliza Gahringer, now twelve years old, came to stay with Matilda while waiting for the birthing. *O God,* Matilda prayed, *keep my man safe. I don't know what I'd do without him.*

32

A Heritage Not Forgotten
Minnesota
1865-1877

P HILLIP WALKED ACROSS THE BARNYARD with only a slight limp
to open the pasture gate, letting his milk cows in for morning
milking. A killdeer's distracting call announced the spring nesting
season. He thought, *My feet are healing, spring is here, and on Monday, my
neighbors will start framing up the house.*

Matt Engel and Phillip worked all day Saturday preparing for the
house raising. Even in Adam's absence, Matilda insisted that Sunday
worship be held at her house. By starting time, the house was packed,
including neighbors who had never attended worship before. Rev.
Kleinsorge announced, "Word reached us yesterday that the battle
in Virginia continues. Casualties are huge. Replacement soldiers are
being rushed to the front. We must spend our day in prayer for our
troops." The people went to their knees.

Matilda, now large with child, slumped to the floor in tears.
Lucinda held her friend and wept with her. Men prayed with fervor.
Preacher Kleinsorge closed the meeting with an urgent prayer for
God's victory over sin and war. As people left, families reminded each
other of the house raising at Phillip's the next morning.

Matt Engel had the cellar finished, ready for the men to frame
the walls and set the joists in place. Chimneys were formed brick
by brick. There was a quiet urgency as they worked. At dinnertime,

Phillip offered a prayer of thanks to the Lord for the kindness of his neighbors. The men devoured heaping plates of food, followed with large cuts of pie. Matilda looked up after refilling Phillip's coffee cup. Their eyes met. He stammered, "Thanks, thanks for puttin' me straight. I was bein' pretty childish. We're prayin' for Adam."

The Eppard house built in 1865
(replaced the house that burned)

Following a brief rest, the men resumed their labors. A short while later, Peter shouted over the sound of hammers and saws, "Look, that's Kleinsorge on his bay mare at full gallop." The men moved toward the trail. The preacher drew his horse to a skidding stop, jumped to the ground, and shouted, "It's over, it's all over, the war, it's all over." He caught his breath. "The stage came in about noon. The driver had news from Fort Snelling." He read from a flier:

> *General Robert E. Lee of the Confederate Army surrendered to General Ulysses S. Grant in a farmhouse at Appomattox, Virginia, on Sunday, April 9, 1865. Guns are quiet. The men are returning to their homes. The war is over.*

Matilda whispered, "Where's my husband? Where's Adam?"

The preacher smiled warmly and touched Matilda's shoulder. "Word is that the Minnesota Regiment was gathered at Fort Snelling ready to leave for the east when they got the news. Adam should be home in a few days."

Matt Engel asked, "Do you want to celebrate, or should we raise this house?"

It was quiet for a moment. Jake motioned with his hand. "Let's celebrate by raisin' this house!" A few hours later, when the men left to do their chores, the house was framed and ready for siding and roof. Phillip slipped his arm around Lucinda. "What do ya think, Mutti, will it hold all the kids we'll have?"

Lucinda grinned and nudged Phillip toward the barn. "You better go get the milkin' done."

The Utzinger house was quiet that evening. All Matilda could think about was, *When will my husband come home?* Eliza played with Albert and John, while Matilda fixed bread and milk for supper. After prayers, the boys were tucked in their beds.

"Mrs. Utzinger," Eliza said, "the kitchen's cleaned up. Is there anything else you need before I get ready for bed?"

"No, thank you, Eliza. Rest well."

Matilda sat in the rocker with her knitting needles at a steady click. Sparky barked as if a bear were invading the place. He stopped suddenly. Matilda thought, *That seems strange.*

The door squeaked open. Matilda sucked in a frightened breath. "Anyone home?" came a familiar voice.

"Adam!" Matilda shrieked. "Adam, you're home!" She struggled to her feet, dropping her knitting to the floor. They met in a tearful embrace and a kiss. Aware of Eliza's mouth-open surprise, Adam backed away.

"Ja, I'm home and home to stay. The war's over."

On Sunday, the church gathered for worship in the Adam Utzinger home. News had swept the country that President Lincoln had been shot while attending the Ford Theater the night of April

15. The congregation sat in stunned quietness. Preacher Kleinsorge waited in silence, and then he prayed.

Life went on in Racine Township. On April 28, 1865, Matilda awakened early. She nudged Adam. "You better get Carolina. My time is here." Adam dashed across the road in his nightshirt and chore jacket with the news. Later that morning, Adam introduced Albert and John to their little sister, Sarah.

That fall, the wagons rolled to Winona with a bumper wheat crop. Phillip and Lucinda moved into their new house. Under the leadership of Elder Long, the Salem Evangelical Association grew, with the Gahringer, Zimmerman, Henslin, Krause, Eichorn, and Schroeder families adding their names to the roster.

By the following summer, Matilda was with child once again. Lucinda gave birth to "Little Lucinda" on December 14, 1866. Adam and Matilda welcomed baby Emma on February 27, 1867. The neighbor ladies jokingly accused Matilda and Lucinda of being in a race.

Preacher Von Wald, a spirited leader, was appointed to Salem Evangelical in 1868. The church continued to grow, meeting in several homes across the area. To bring all of the home groups together as one congregation, Preacher Von Wald announced a camp meeting to be held near the grove of oaks by the stream just west of the Eppard claim. Preacher Warner was called to be the evangelist.

Adam rigged up the old covered wagon and took his family to the camp meeting. On their way, Matilda looked up at her husband. "I remember the day Helga and I gave our hearts to the Lord at the Brandon Camp Meeting. I'm prayin' for people to come to faith at the Salem meetings."

Preacher Warner's voice resounded with power. One by one, the neighbors responded to the invitation. Adam spent most of the night praying with the new believers. God was at work in Racine Township.

The next day, Matilda was washing the dishes with a group of ladies. She remarked, "Every time I pass this place on my way to town, I visualize a schoolhouse under these oaks. My boys need more teachin' than I can give 'em."

"Ja," Pauline Schroeder agreed, "I've got four of 'em that should be in school. I say we need to talk to our men and get somethin' goin'."

Inspired by the camp meeting, Salem Evangelical built a building that would serve as both a school and a church. With a coatroom entrance, a large hall, a woodshed attached to the back, and two outhouses at a distance to the rear, a school was ready to open at freeze-up 1869. County School District 66 was organized with Mrs. Gove as the first teacher. The families scraped together enough to pay her a meager salary.

On Sundays, the schoolroom became a church. As the Sunday school superintendent, Adam led the opening exercises. The children laughed when he told stories about sailing on board the *Robert Harding*. Children's classes were held in each corner of the room. Worship followed, with hearty singing, and powerful preaching of God's Word. The people were exhorted to keep the Sabbath Day and to flee from the use of liquor and tobacco. But most of all, the preacher, in keeping with their evangelical traditions, gave the call to a heart warmed by the Spirit of God and to enter into a living relationship with Jesus as Savior.

Mrs. Gove wrote the script for the first Christmas program at the schoolhouse. The little building bulged with an overflow crowd. Lucinda, with baby Phillip on her lap and "Little Lucinda" at her side, had goose bumps when eight-year-old Mary, in her angel costume, proclaimed in a loud voice, "Fear not: for, behold, I bring you good tidings of great joy, which shall be to all people. For unto you is born this day in the city of David a Saviour, which is Christ the Lord." Her son George was a shepherd, and Harvey made it through his piece with a bit of prompting from Mrs. Gove.

Matilda, with baby Amelia asleep in her arms and Emma at her side, smiled to herself when she saw Eliza Gahringer as Mary and Fredrick Schroeder as Joseph. She couldn't help remembering how they fought with each other on that trek across Wisconsin. Albert and John were shepherds, and Sarah said her piece while shyly twisting the hem of her dress.

To everyone's surprise, Dan Booth showed up for the program and proudly handed a bag of hard candy and peanuts to each child as they left for home. Dan smiled with pride when old Jacob McQuillan said, "Thanks, Dan, for givin' the boys and girls a Christmas treat."

Next day, Lucinda was on her way up the cellar steps when she heard the door from the woodshed open. "Who's there?" she called.

"It's me, your pa, got any coffee around here? I need to have a talk with my beautiful daughter." Jacob pulled a chair up to the kitchen table. "Your ma and I are havin' a disagreement, and I need some advice."

"Far be it from me to give my pa advice," Lucinda said with a smile as she poured two cups of coffee. "I don't see how anyone could have a disagreement with Ma."

"Lucinda, you know I've not been feelin' the best. I'm gettin' up in age, and I keep thinkin' about the family I left back in Delta. Things weren't good between me and John when we left. I need to mend things with him before I die. My brothers are there, and they have families I've not met." He took a deep breath. "I'm wantin' to go back to Ohio."

"Why don't you go? It'd be a good summer trip for you and Ma."

"That's the problem, I really wanna go back to stay. Elizabeth's grave is there and . . ." His voice trailed off.

"What does Ma think about this?"

"She says she can't leave her children and grandchildren here in Minnesota. Harvey's takin' over the farm, and the others are scattered." He took a sip of coffee. "Lucy, I hate leavin' you and your children. But ever since Dan Booth took our land, I've not really been at home here. Then your sister, Little Matilda, disappeared—some say the Indians took her—and little Walter died. I've got an empty hole in my heart." He dabbed a tear on his sleeve.

The next summer, Jacob and Polly boarded the stagecoach and headed back to Ohio. In September, Polly returned to Minnesota. Sitting at the table in Lucinda's kitchen, a tear slipped down Polly's cheek as she confided, "Lucy, a load lifted from your pa's shoulders when he made peace with his son, John. Now his health is failing, and he's made plans to be buried next to Elizabeth in the Delta cemetery. He's a good man, Lucy, a good man." Her shoulders shook as she put her head down in her arms.

Lucinda knelt by her mother and waited. Finally, she ventured, "Ma, you must feel abandoned. We all love you so much. What will you do?"

"No, Lucinda, not abandoned. I know his heart. He loves me, and he loves all of you. He just had to go back. The loss of the land broke something in him. He's forgiven Mr. Booth, but the loss has lingered. He's at peace, and he's lookin' forward to his heavenly home. My heart is here with my family."

The mother and daughter fell into a tearful embrace. Polly choked, "Lucy, you've been my faithful one. Your children are my joy. Let's keep our faces to the wind and not look back."

The 1870s brought good days to the farmers in Racine Township. Each fall, they planted larger fields of winter wheat. Winona came to be known as one of the largest wheat-shipping ports in the country. Adam worked day and night to provide for his growing family. Albert and John worked alongside their father all summer and were good students at District 66 during the winter months.

New birth was common among the settlers. The milk cows produced a calf each year, and springtime was the season for colts to be born. Adam built an addition on his house with the arrival of baby Jane on August 10, 1872, and then George not much later on December 6, 1874. Phillip and Lucinda were filling the rooms in their new house with the birth of baby John on April 19, 1871, and Sadie followed on September 5, 1875.

But far more important births were happening in the township. One occurred in the Utzinger home as Adam led his family in devotions. He pushed the Bible across the table to Albert and said, "Find John 3 and read verses 1-7."

Albert read the story about Nicodemus coming to Jesus at night and how Jesus told Nicodemus that you can't see the kingdom of God unless you're born again. And Jesus said you have to be born of water and of Spirit.

Ten-year-old Sarah screwed up her face in wonder. "Vati, when Birdie had her colt, a lot of watery stuff came out. Was that born of water?"

Adam answered, "I guess it was. That would be born once, wouldn't it? What do you think Jesus meant when he said you must be born again?"

"Vati, it sounds like you need to be born twice."

"That's a good answer, Sarah. Have you been born twice?"

"I don't know. I know I was born from Mutti like the little colt came out of Birdie."

The conversation went on to talk about spiritual birth through the forgiveness of sin. That evening at bedtime, Sarah said to her mother, "Mutti, I know I've sinned and need to be born over."

"Yes, Sarah, all of us are sinners. We all need to be born again by our Savior, Jesus. Are you sorry about your sin?" Matilda helped her daughter to repent of her sin and enter into a relationship with Jesus that would mature through the rest of her life.

The next morning, Sarah said, "Vati, last night, I got born over. I repented my sin and Jesus came in and forgave me."

Adam hugged his daughter and affirmed, "All the angels in heaven are happy that you now have a new life with Jesus forever."

The schoolhouse was packed with worshipers every Sunday morning. Lucinda loved to teach the little ones who were still too young to go to school. She told Bible stories about how much Jesus loved them, and she taught them to sing songs about the Savior.

Rev. Walch came as the new preacher at the Evangelical Association. One early spring Sunday, the women were preparing for the after-church dinner while the men gathered by the hitchin' rail.

Mike Gahringer ventured, "Mary and I were talkin' the other night, and we think it's gettin' too crowded at the school and we need to build a church."

"I've been wonderin' about that too," Preacher Walch shared. "It sure was crowded in there this mornin'. My wife says it's hard to teach all the children in such a small room."

The men of the congregation met to consider the need for a church building. Seeing that the decision looked favorable, Jacob Burkhart spoke up. "I ain't got much money to give, but if the location would suit ya, I'd give a piece of ground from my claim by the trail." The offer was accepted, and Matt Engel was hired to supervise the building on the slope just to the west and across the trail from Phillip Eppard's farm.

Spring rains and the warming sun in 1876 awakened the dormant winter wheat fields the farmers had planted the previous fall. By mid-June, Racine Township was a sea of flowing green wheat fields showing a touch of gold and the promise of a bumper crop. The church families knew a good wheat crop would provide for their needs as well as tithes, which would be given to complete the church building. Each Sunday, the church gathered at the school with anticipation of the new building.

It happened on a hot July morning. Something in the west rose up in the sky like a winter snowstorm. Phillip stood in the middle of his barnyard, peering to the west. With hands on his hips, he moaned, "Not here, Lord. Oh, God, don't let it happen here." He went down on his knees, appealing to God. First one, then another, then a huge swarm of grasshoppers covered the ground. The sun went nearly dark. Phillip ran to the house.

The children came dashing in, waving their hands, brushing the grasshoppers away. Lucinda grabbed the washing from the line and ran for the woodshed door. "What is that, Vati?" George cried. "I don't like those sticky things."

Phillip sat with his elbows on the table, disgust written on his face. "Grasshoppers," Phillip lamented, "thousands of grasshoppers.

They'll strip our fields in a day. We'll have no crop this year. They've been comin' every year west of us. The farmers have been fightin' 'em, but each year, they lay their eggs in the ground and move on in larger numbers the next year."

Discouraged farm families arrived quietly for worship the next Sunday at the schoolhouse. Preacher Walch led out in a hymn but found little enthusiasm in the gathering. Adam stepped forward with a request. "Reverend, I'd like to address the church." Receiving a nod of approval, Adam continued, "I've written a letter to Governor Pillsbury, appealing to him to set a day of urgent prayer in the state, asking our God to rid the land of grasshoppers. The governor has been reluctant, but I invite all of you to sign this letter, and we'll ask Judge Felch to deliver it to the statehouse."

Following the initial shock of the loss of the wheat crop in 1876, the Racine Township farmers found ways to work together to save their livestock. Summer rains brought back the prairie grass, providing feed for the winter. Adam cut loads of wood from his wood lot and sold it for enough money for food. Miraculously, enough money came in to keep the church building project going.

Having received considerable urging from the people, Governor Pillsbury proclaimed April 26, 1877, as a day of prayer. People gathered in cities and towns across the state to pray for relief from the grasshopper plague. The next day, it started to sleet. The temperature dropped, and within hours, the fields were covered with a deep layer of snow. The grasshopper eggs, in the process of hatching, were totally destroyed. Any remaining grasshoppers left as suddenly as they had arrived.

The church held a special day of thanksgiving. Adam shared, "I stand to tell you that I was going through a dry time in my faith. God's answer to the grasshopper prayers has revived me. I would like to urge us to hold a revival in our church. Let's invite an evangelist to hold meetings every night for a week or so."

"Yea! Yea!" came the responses of agreement.

Elder Walch added, "I suggest we invite Rev. Von Wald, your former preacher and a well-known evangelist, to return for these meetings."

During a lull in farmwork while the wheat was ripening, Elder Von Wald arrived ready to preach God's Word. Prayer had prepared the way, and the church was overflowing on opening night. The gospel hymn sing was joyous, and the male quartet received ovations for encores. The music slowed to a quiet reverence. Von Wald stepped to the pulpit. A Holy Spirit hush fell over the congregation.

He spoke softly. "Tonight, we will look at Romans 3:22-24. This is one of the most important passages ever written. In it, we find three words that I want you to understand. Receiving the meaning of these words by faith will change your life.

"The first word is *righteousness*. Righteousness is the gracious gift of God received by faith in Jesus Christ that brings you into a right relationship with God. It is the Holy Spirit working within you, giving you the desire to please and honor God in everything you do." The preacher backed away from the pulpit and put his hand up for attention. "Remember that now. Hold on to it, we're goin' on to the next word.

"The next word is *sin*. Sin is the power ruling in all people to separate us from God's righteousness. Sin ultimately leads to death. Sin is the desire and the will to please ourselves. Verse 23 says, 'For all have sinned and come short of the glory of God.'" With that, Von Wald stepped to the side of the podium. "Do you get the picture? There's a war going on inside of us. Jesus wants us for righteousness, and we want everything for ourselves. Sin is at work in us to take us to death. Hold on now, we're goin' to the next word." He returned to the pulpit.

"The third word is *justification*. Justification is God's declaration that you have not sinned. Verse 24 says we are 'being justified freely by his grace through the redemption that is in Christ Jesus.' This means that God has a free gift for us that declares that we have not sinned and can be in right relationship with our Heavenly Father."

The preacher walked down to floor level and walked across the room. "Now you have the three words. Hold on to them," he urged. Holding the attention of every person, he took a firm position in the middle of the platform.

"Now let's get this in real words that all can understand. First of all, I am a sinner. I know I'm a sinner, and I was your preacher long enough that you know I'm a sinner. I also know that you are sinners, every one of you. The Bible says, 'If we say we are without sin, the truth is not in us.'" He took a deep breath, "Are you with me now? Since I'm a sinner, I ask you, what would it take to remove my sin so I can have a right relationship with God?

"The Bible says, 'The wages of sin is death.' It would cost my death to have a right relationship with God. That's pretty expensive, don't you think? Okay, I'm willing to give up my life if that's the price. But God says, if you die in your sin, you will be under God's judgment, separated from him forever. That doesn't sound too good." The reverend paced to one side and back again, holding the attention of everyone in the room.

"What then will it cost me to get free from the grip that sin has on my life? The answer is—are you ready for this?" He held the people in suspense. "The answer is, *nothing!*" His voice echoed through the church.

"The truth is, Jesus Christ paid your sin debt for you so you are justified and have no sin. Where then is my sin? What sin? You have no sin, the debt is paid." The preacher stood tall in the middle of the stage.

"Look at it this way." He held out his right hand, palm up. "Imagine with me that all of my sin is here in my hand. Every nasty thought or act I ever committed, all of my selfishness. All of it is here in my hand." Preacher Von Wald fixed his eyes upon his right hand and shouted, "Every damnable bit of it, every one of my sins is right here!" He shuddered as he looked with disdain at his hand.

He turned to the congregation and held out his left hand and continued, "Here in this hand is all of the righteousness of the sinless

Son of God, Jesus Christ. Have you got the picture? Here in one hand is all of my sin. In the other hand is all of Jesus's righteousness. At the cross, Jesus took my sin on himself and put his righteousness on me. He took my sin to the cross and died his death for my sin and the sin of the entire world. I stand here now without sin because Jesus has died for my sin in my place. My justification cost me nothing, but it cost Jesus everything." Von Wald moved back to the pulpit, allowing what he just said to soak in.

"Don't say it!" he shouted. "I know what you're thinkin'. No, you can't go out and sin all you want because Jesus has paid the price. No, once you know he has paid the price and you are free from sin, you'll want to obey him. You'll want to please and honor him with all your heart. And even more, he has given us his Holy Spirit to empower us to live our lives for him.

"How many of you want this relationship with God through Jesus? Come to Jesus, ask him to forgive your sin. I invite you to receive this most valuable gift right now. Come, let me pray for you to receive this marvelous gift."

A hush came over the people like a gentle breeze. The preacher waited, allowing the Holy Spirit to work in the gathering. "I do," came a voice from near the back. "I do," another voice was heard.

Von Wald stepped to floor level. "Please stand, all of you. Come forward, commit your life to Jesus. Come, recommit your life to the Lord." First, a few steps were taken, and then a surge of people, church members and visitors alike, moved toward the front.

Adam, as a class leader, was on the platform. He went to his knees. People turned to their neighbors, asking forgiveness for disagreements they had with each other. They prayed with each other. Small groups formed to pray with those desiring to receive forgiveness and to know the saving grace of Jesus.

Gradually, the people moved to their wagons to head for home. Adam and Matilda tucked the little ones into their beds. With a fresh cup of coffee, Adam sat at the kitchen table with his head in his hands. Matilda put her hands on his shoulders. "Are you troubled, my husband?" she asked.

"No, not troubled, overwhelmed!" he responded. "I never knew that Jesus has taken my sin to the point that I have no sin. And not only me, but every person who would trust him as Savior. I know I still sin, but God's Word teaches me that even the sin I have not yet committed is already forgiven through Jesus's death on the cross." He turned, pulled Matilda to his lap, and gently kissed her. "Matilda," he whispered, "we must pass this on to our children and to our children's children. We must pray for the generations yet to come. We must see that this heritage is not forgotten."

A Note from the Author

PHILLIP AND LUCINDA'S SON, GEORGE Eppard, was my grandfather. In 1890, George married Adam and Matilda's daughter, Sarah. Their daughter, my aunt Ruth Eppard Wolfgram, was in her nineties when she told me that Grandma Sarah often prayed that one of her grandsons would become a pastor. I'm that grandson. Because of my grandmother's prayers, this heritage of faith has been passed through the generations. When I was forty-two years old, I recommitted my life to Jesus in a heartwarming experience in the pietistic evangelical tradition. Along with my wife, Janice, God led me to make some major adjustments in my life and ministry. I know that the prayers of these godly ancestors made an eternal impact on my life. It is now my privilege to make sure this heritage is not forgotten.

If this book has awakened in you a desire to grow in your relationship with God, here is a prayer that may help you get started:

> Holy God, I know that you love me and that you want me to be in right relationship with you. I am avoiding you and living for myself. I realize that my selfishness is keeping me from that relationship. I thank you, Jesus, for taking my sin to the cross where you died in my place so I may live a new life. I surrender my life of sin to you and receive your forgiveness. Thank you for this inexpressible gift. Amen.

If you sincerely prayed this prayer, you will begin to see change in your life. It is important that you read the Bible regularly and reach out to find Christian friends who can help you grow. You would be welcome to contact me through my website:

www.marvineppard.com

Afterword

THESE FOUR STALWART PIONEERS, PHILLIP, Lucinda, Adam, and Matilda, my great-grandparents, were men and women who lived their faith following the traditions of their pietistic evangelical heritage based on Christ's example for godly behavior. They had still more children. Lydia and Ella were born to Phillip and Lucinda, making a total of nine. Adam and Matilda welcomed Clara, Ella, and Amanda to their family, a total of eleven. They prayed that their children would come to know Jesus as Savior. Phillip and Lucinda's son, George, and Adam and Matilda's daughter, Sarah, were married on May 15, 1890. They had four children: Mae, Lela, Ruth, and Theodore (Ted). They grew up in the Evangelical Church that was founded by their grandparents. My father, Ted Eppard, told me that he went forward in an evangelistic meeting in that church when he was about fifteen years old and accepted Jesus as his Savior. That is my heritage, a heritage not forgotten.

Top row: Emma, John, Herman, Millie, Janie
Middle row: Sarah, Adam Utzinger, Matilda Mannweiler Utzinger, Albert
Front row: Clara, Amanda

Top row: Lydia, Sadie, John, Martin, Harve, Lucinda
Middle row: Mary, Phillip Eppard, Lucinda McQuillan Eppard, George
Front: Ella

When Phillip was ninety-five years old, his pastor wrote about him. "His philosophy is to see the bright side of what God puts into life. What is the use of becoming ugly even if everything does not go 100 percent, for then those round about us might become ugly too and we would have a real time." The pastor continued, "We attribute much of this fine spirit, toward life, to the sturdy Christian character." When he died on November 13, 1928, at the age of ninety-six, his obituary called him "a great spirit housed in a friendly soul."

In Lucinda's obituary, we find these words, "At age of ten, she was happily converted to God and soon afterward joined the church in which she proved to be a faithful and sincere member until the end. She was an earnest Christian praying much in secret . . . One of her former pastors just recently said of her, 'She was one of the noblest Christian women I ever knew.'" She died on September 9, 1913, at age seventy-one.

Obituary for Lucinda McQuillan Eppard

357

Adam's oldest son, Albert, wrote about his father in 1936. "He was a very religious man. He was converted in Wisconsin in a Methodist meeting. He joined the Evangelical Church in Wisconsin . . . He reconsecrated himself in a meeting held by Rev. Von Wald, which led nearly all the members of the church to do the same . . . He prayed effectively with the seekers and helped many to press into the kingdom of God. He surely has stars in his crown . . . He dwelt much in secret prayer. He was faithful to the end. He died July 7, 1912, at age seventy-nine."

Matilda was a godly woman about whom her son Albert wrote, "Mother was converted at a camp meeting at Fox Lake, Wisconsin, at the age of fifteen, and joined the Evangelical Church. She was the last surviving charter member of the local Evangelical Church. In early years, the services were often held in her home. The early ministers often enjoyed her hospitality, and so did many other people." She died March 2, 1930, at age eighty-eight.

And the story goes on. Phillip and Lucinda's oldest daughter, Mary, married Frank Plantikow, a seminary graduate who served as a circuit rider in southwestern Minnesota. They lived in a "slant-roofed upper floor of a frame building, possibly a barn or shed." She cared for their family and fought prairie fires and the grasshopper plague while her husband was off on the circuit.

Albert, Adam and Matilda's oldest son, taught school in several places before graduating from Naperville College in Illinois. He was licensed to preach in 1889 and served Evangelical churches until his health failed.

There was a double wedding on May 15, 1890, in which George Eppard married Sarah Utzinger and John Utzinger married Lucinda Eppard (Little Lucinda). George farmed with his father, Phillip, and he and Sarah later lived in the house on the Eppard homestead. John farmed with his father, Adam, taking a place just to the west. These families served and grew in Christ in the Racine Evangelical Church.

In 1936, Albert Utzinger closed his tribute to his parents, Adam and Matilda, by writing, "There are 32 great-grandchildren now, with more to follow. Twenty-five persons married into the family and form part of it. Seven are added by adoption, making a total of 105 at the present time. Of these nearly all who are old enough profess to be Christians and are members of the Evangelical Church. This is a remarkable record of one family owing in large measure to the piety and fidelity of Adam Utzinger and his good wife, Matilda."

Yes, the story does go on, generation to generation. What a heritage! May it be a heritage not forgotten.

George Eppard and Sarah Utzinger Eppard
(The author's grandparents)

Theodore Eppard and Janet Chamberlain Eppard
(The author's parents)

Historical Sources

Compiled by the Inter-state Publishing Company, *History of Mower County* (Mankato, MN: The Free Press Publishing House, 1884)

Franklyn Curtiss-Wedge, Editor, *The History of Mower County, Minnesota* (Chicago: H. C. Cooper, Jr., & Company, 1911)

History of Fillmore County, Minnesota (Minneapolis: Minnesota Historical Company, 1882)

Franklyn Curtiss-Wedge, Compiler, *History of Fillmore County, Minnesota* (Chicago, H. C. Cooper, Jr. & Company, 1912)

May Benson, *A Letter to My Daughters, The Story of Lucinda McQuillan Eppard and Her Family* (A term paper for a University of Minnesota history class, 1978)

Obituary of Lucinda McQuillan Eppard

Albert H. Utzinger, *Mrs. Adam Utzinger* (A two-page typewritten obituary, a sketch of the life of his mother, by Albert, the oldest of her eleven children, March 1930)

Albert H. Utzinger, *Life Sketch of Adam Utzinger* (A five-page typewritten story of the life of his father, by Albert, the oldest of his eleven children, September 9, 1936)

Mae Zeller, Eight handwritten pages from her scrapbook under the headings of "First Settlers," "Philip Martin Eppard," and "Matilda and Adam Utzinger," recorded April 4, 1967

Centennial Anniversary, 1862-1962 (Church Bulletin for Salem Church, Evangelical United Brethren, Racine, Minnesota, August 1962)

Racine Recorder (Centennial Edition, 1890-1990, published July 20-22, 1990)

Rev. A. Stapleton, *Annals of the Evangelical Association of North America and History of the United Evangelical Church* (Publishing House of the United Evangelical Church, 1896)

Rev. Albert Utzman, *Old Resident of Racine Visited,* (A newspaper interview with Phillip Martin Eppard on his ninety-fifth birthday, October 1927)

New York Passenger List of the *Robert Harding,* record of Adam Utzinger's passage (Ancestry.com)

Salem Evangelical Cemetery, information recorded from tombstones, completed May 22, 1976

Lila Ellenberg, Notes regarding early pioneers in Mower County

Mower County Civil War Soldiers Part 1 (Copyright 2008 MnGenWeb—Webization by Kermit Kittleson, posted May 17, 2008)

Daniel L. Booth, *Plat map of Hamilton,* (Recorded in Territory of Minnesota, Fillmore County, on July 29, 1857. Booth also recorded a plat of Section 6, 103-13, on July 4, 1856)

Mower County Recorder, Austin, Minnesota (Filing dates of land purchase on record in this office: Adam Utzinger, July 9, 1862, and Peter Utzinger, July 3, 1862)